Eça de Queiroz

The Crime of Father Amaro

Scenes from the Religious Life

Translated and with an introduction
by Margaret Jull Costa

Dedalus

Funded by THE ARTS COUNCIL OF ENGLAND

Dedalus would like to thank The Arts Council of England in London, The Portuguese Book Institute and The Camões Institute in Lisbon and The Calouste Gulbenkian Foundation for their assistance in producing this book.

Published in the UK by Dedalus Ltd,
Langford Lodge, St Judith's Lane, Sawtry, Cambs, PE28 5XE
email: DedalusLimited@compuserve.com
website: www.dedalusbooks.com

ISBN 1 873982 89 5

Dedalus is distributed in the United States by SCB Distributors,
15608 South New Century Drive, Gardena, California 90248
email: info@scbdistributors.com web site: www.scbdistributors.com

Dedalus is distributed in Australia & New Zealand by Peribo Pty Ltd,
58 Beaumont Road, Mount Kuring-gai, N.S.W. 2080
email: peribo@bigpond.com

Dedalus is distributed in Canada by Marginal Distribution,
Unit 102, 277 George Street North, Peterborough, Ontario, KJ9 3G9
email: marginal@marginalbook.com web site: www.marginal.com

Dedalus is distributed in Italy by Apeiron Editoria & Distribuzione,
Località Pantano, 00060 Sant'Oreste (Roma)
email: grt@apeironbookservice.com web site: www.apeironbookservice.com

First published in Portugal in 1880
First published by Dedalus in 2002

Typeset by RefineCatch Limited, Bungay, Suffolk
Printed in Finland by WS Bookwell

A C.I.P. listing for this book is available on request.

Portuguese Literature from Dedalus

Dedalus, as part of its Europe 1992–2002 programme, with the assistance of The Portuguese Book Institute, The Camões Institute in Lisbon and The Calouste Gulbenkian Foundation, has embarked on a series of new translations by Margaret Jull Costa of some of the major classics of Portuguese literature.

Titles so far published:

The Mandarin (and other stories) – Eça de Queiroz

The Relic – Eça de Queiroz

The Tragedy of the Street of Flowers – Eça de Queiroz

The Crime of Father Amaro – Eça de Queiroz

Lúcio's Confession – Mário de Sá-Carneiro

The Great Shadow (and other stories) – Mário de Sá-Carneiro

The Dedalus Book of Portuguese Fantasy – editors Eugénio Lisboa and Helder Macedo

Forthcoming titles include:

Cousin Basílio – Eça de Queiroz

The City and the Mountains – Eça de Queiroz

The Maias – Eça de Queiroz

The Illustrious House of Ramires – Eça de Queiroz

THE TRANSLATOR

Margaret Jull Costa has translated the works of many Spanish and Portuguese writers. She won the 1992 Portuguese Translation Prize for *The Book of Disquiet* by Fernando Pessoa, and her translation of Eça de Queiroz's *The Relic* was shortlisted for the 1996 prize; with Javier Marías, she won the 1997 International IMPAC Dublin Literary Award for *A Heart So White* and, in 2000, she won the Weidenfeld Translation Prize for José Saramago's *All the Names*.

She has translated the following books for Dedalus: *The Adventures of the Ingenious Alfanhuí* by Rafael Sánchez Ferlosio, *Lúcio's Confession* and *The Great Shadow* by Mário de Sá-Carneiro, *The Dedalus Book of Spanish Fantasy* (with Annella McDermott), *The Dedalus Book of Portuguese Fantasy* (eds. Eugénio Lisboa and Helder Macedo), *Spring and Summer Sonatas* and *Autumn and Winter Sonatas* by Ramón del Valle-Inclán, and, by Eça de Queiroz: *The Mandarin*, *The Relic*, *The Tragedy of the Street of Flowers* and *The Crime of Father Amaro*.

ACKNOWLEDGEMENTS

The translator would like to thank Maria Manuel Lisboa, Dan McEwan and Ben Sherriff for all their help and advice. I would also like to acknowledge the generous financial assistance of East Midlands Arts Board.

Introduction

Leiria, the setting for *The Crime of Father Amaro*, is a small town about 60 miles north of Lisbon. The street that now bears Eça de Queiroz's name is little more than a back alley. Given the portrait that he paints of the town's inhabitants, this is, perhaps, hardly surprising. According to Eça, the population of nineteenth-century Leiria were narrow-minded, credulous bigots. What was offensive to the good people of Leiria, however, remains a joy to both reader and translator. For the power of the novel lies not just in its unflinching exploration of small-town hypocrisy, but in the sheer verve of the writing and in the strength of characterisation. Eça's description of what he believed to be a stagnant society is bursting with life and humour. From the first page, on which we meet José Migueis, the 'exploding boa constrictor' of a parish priest, to our encounter on the final pages with the smug and pompous Conde de Ribamar and his vision of a Portugal which is 'the envy of the world', we are treated to a gallery of riveting minor characters: Father Natário is a man with a talent for hatred; the parish priest of Cortegaça is so in love with food that he even spices his sermons with cookery tips; Dona Maria da Assunção with her room full of religious images is agog for any hint of sex; Libaninho, who never misses a mass and flirts with all the girls, in fact has a penchant for army sergeants; the administrator of the municipal council spends from eleven o'clock to three each day ogling a neighbour's wife through a pair of binoculars; Canon Dias cares only for belly and bed. Between them, the clerics and their devout followers commit every one of the seven capital sins.

As with Dickens, whom Eça greatly admired (though he disliked his sentimentality), the secret of his humour lies in the dialogue and in the detail. Eça has as keen an ear for the way ordinary people speak as he does for the puffed-up excesses of politicians and political radicals. And he can give us the character of a person in one telling detail, for example, the whole of Canon Dias' saytr nature is revealed in the large, hairy hand with which he pats Amélia's cheek; the vanity of the lawyer and 'wit' Pinheiro is there in the way he 'smoothes his poet's hair'; Father Amaro's cowardice is embodied in his undignified flight – 'teeth chattering in terror' – from the barking dogs barring his way to Amélia's bedroom; the fastidious nature of a clerk is summed up in one sentence: 'Pires took off his oversleeves and put away his air cushion.' And Eça can puncture pomposity with one well-judged phrase. This is how he describes a section of Lisbon's petite bourgeoisie, incensed by the events of the Paris Commune: 'Men, wielding toothpicks, urged vengeance.' It is not often that one finds the words 'toothpick' and 'vengeance' in the same sentence.

He is the master, too, of the bathetic juxtaposition of events. When Amaro and Amélia exchange their first kiss, Amélia's aunt is dying in the next room; when they first have sex, Dionísia, Amaro's maid, goes downstairs and hides in the coal cellar until they have finished; the lovers' trysting place is the Cathedral sexton's filthy bedroom, and every sound they make, every creak of the bed, is heard by the sexton's neurotic, paralysed daughter in her room immediately below.

Equally striking is Eça's eye for the physical world – when Amaro realises that Amélia loves him, he is described as being like 'a plump sparrow in a warm shaft of sunlight'; when Amaro and Amélia are lying together in bed looking up at the roof beams, they hear 'a cat padding across, occasionally catching a loose tile' or the rustle of a bird's wings as it alights; and Eça notices how cows drink 'delicately, noiselessly' and how fields fill up with mist.

All these qualities give Eça's writing a rare density and vitality that lend further substance to his vision of 1870s Portugal.

The Crime of Father Amaro is an attack on provincialism, on the power of a Church that allies itself with the rich and powerful, tolerates superstition and supports a deeply unfair and un-Christian society, and, more particularly, it is an attack on the absurdity of imposing celibacy on young men with no real priestly vocation. It is also, I think, like many of his novels, a critique of the position of both men and women in Portuguese society of the time. São Joaneira is kindly and well-meaning, but with a daughter to support after the death of her husband, she becomes the mistress of, first, the precentor and, then, the Canon. The old maids in the book are all mean-spirited, vain, petty and tyrannical, but utterly cowed by men's authority. Amélia is a simple, essentially good-natured girl, but her whole view of life has been skewed by the overwhelming presence in her life of priests. On the one hand, women's lives are so narrow that a walk alone to the shops seems daring; on the other, the foundling hospitals cannot cope with the number of abandoned babies, and women who 'slip' end up on the street or struggling to bring up illegitimate children on their own. The only woman who appears to have any influence over men in the novel is Teresa, the Countess' friend (whom we meet in chapter III), but hers is, in a way, the influence of a charming, precocious child and depends entirely on that most ephemeral quality – beauty. The men apparently have the power, but are, in a sense, little more than large, spoiled children. Dr Godinho, for all his booming rhetoric, is afraid of upsetting his lovely, devout wife; when the Canon's ghastly but devoted sister, Dona Josefa, is stricken with pneumonia, he is lost and bereft; and every priest's and every petit bourgeois' household depends for its smooth running on loyal, hard-pushed maidservants, who, unsurprisingly, often seem to fall ill. The men both despise women and need them. The women live in constant fear of offending God, priest, husband, protector or society.

* * * * *

Although *The Crime of Father Amaro* is usually described as Eça's first novel, it is also, in a sense, his fourth. Plagued by his friends for something to publish in their magazine, Eça sent them the unedited draft of a novel – the first version of *Father Amaro* – on the understanding that they would send him proofs, which he would then edit and return. For some still unexplained reason, his friends, in 1875, began serialising the unedited draft. Eça was incandescent with rage: 'May Satan devour you, you murderers!' He eventually forgave them and submitted a longer, revised version of the novel to a publisher. This second version appeared in 1876 and was greeted by almost total silence. Eça even had to beg one of his friends to write a review. However, despite disappointment at this lack of response, Eça had already begun work on a new novel, *Cousin Basílio*. This dealt with the adulterous affair between the ne'er-do-well Basílio and Luísa, a bored middle-class wife. The novel was an instant popular and critical success and was immediately translated into several languages. Its success – it has to be said – was due in large part to what was perceived as its racy nature. However, when the great Brazilian novelist, Machado de Assis, accused Eça of squandering his talents and of pandering to the worst excesses of realism and Zolaesque naturalism in the 1876 version of *Father Amaro*, and to a salacious public in *Cousin Basílio*, Eça was stung. He acknowledged the influence of Balzac and Zola, but denied that his work was a mere imitation of such novels as *La Faute de l'Abbé Mouret*. It was possibly in response to this criticism, though, that Eça went back to *Father Amaro* and almost completely rewrote it. That third and final version (on which this translation is based) was published in 1880, and the title page bore the words: 'Corrected, rewritten and entirely different in form and plot from the original edition.' In a letter to his friend, Ramalho de Ortigão, Eça wrote: '*The Crime of Father Amaro* is an entirely new novel; all that remains of the book you originally read is the title.'

So how does this last, much longer version differ from the first and, in particular, the second version? Eça removed the more obviously sensationalist elements – Amaro seducing Amélia in the confessional; Amaro hearing Amélia in labour; Amaro drowning his new-born son; João Eduardo seeing Amélia's corpse being prepared for the coffin. He gave both Amaro and Amélia more of an inner life, so that Amélia, in particular, becomes a far more interesting and more complex person. He also added two new characters – Father Ferrão and

Totó – and fleshed out two already existing characters, Dr Gouveia and the goodhearted but virulently anticlerical Morgado. Father Ferrão – the kindly priest who brings spiritual comfort to Amélia later in the novel – provides a necessary contrast to the corrupt and venal clergy who otherwise populate the novel. He also offers a version of Christianity with which Eça had no quarrel, the gospel of equality and tolerance preached by Jesus, rather than the corrupt version which Eça and, in the novel, Dr Gouveia detest. Indeed, Dr Gouveia – the rationalist doctor – becomes the moral voice of the book, expressing many of Eça's own views on morality and on Church and State. Totó, the sexton's hysterical, paralysed daughter, is perhaps the boldest addition to the book, providing as she does a grotesque counterpoint to the lovers' sexual encounters. Her cries of 'There go the dogs!' underline the animal lust that Amaro and Amélia try to dress up as romantic love.

It becomes clear in this version that, as Father Ferrão says of João Eduardo's article in *The District Voice*, Eça is not writing against the priests, but against the Pharisees, be they religious or lay, for the priests are not the only hypocrites. In the expanded 1880 version Eça gives the likes of Father Natário, Canon Dias, Dona Josefa, Bibi – the secretary general, Dr Godinho and Carlos the pharmacist ample opportunity to condemn themselves out of their own mouths. We are presented with a whole society which – with a few rare exceptions – would not know the truth if it was bitten by it. The 1876 version ends with Amaro's flippant comment that now he is careful only to confess married women. Both versions place the novel in a specific historical context, the period before and after the 1871 Paris Commune, thus contrasting the smug stagnancy and backwardness of nineteenth-century Portugal – city and country – with the social and political upheavals occurring elsewhere in Europe. The 1880 version goes further and has the unbearably self-satisfied Conde de Ribamar – Father Amaro's protector – pontificate about Portugal as an ideal of peace, prosperity and stability. Father Amaro, Canon Dias and the Count are standing, at the time, beneath the statue of Luís de Camões, Portugal's national poet, whose masterpiece, *The Lusiads*, celebrates Portugal's bold, heroic past. As Eça comments: 'a country for ever past, a memory almost forgotten'.

* * * * *

José Maria de Eça de Queiroz was born on 25th November 1845 in the small town of Povoa de Varzim in the north of Portugal. His mother was nineteen and unmarried. Only the name of his father – a magistrate – appears on the birth certificate. His mother returned immediately to her respectable family in Viana do Castelo, and Eça was left with his wetnurse, who looked after him for six years until her death. Although his parents did marry – when Eça was four – and had six more children, Eça did not live with them until he was twenty-one, living instead either with his grandparents or at boarding school in Oporto, where he spent the holidays with an aunt. His father only officially acknowledged Eça when Eça himself was forty. His father did, however, pay for his son's studies at boarding school and at Coimbra University, where Eça studied Law. After working as the editor and sole contributor on a provincial newspaper in Évora, he made a trip to the Middle East. Then, in order to launch himself on a diplomatic career, he worked for six months in Leiria as a municipal administrator, before being appointed consul in Havana (1872–74), Newcastle-upon-Tyne (1874–79) and Bristol (1879–88). In 1886, he married Emília de Castro with whom he had four children. His last consular posting was to Paris, where he served until his death in 1900.

He began writing stories and essays as a young man and became involved with a group of intellectuals known as the Generation of '70, who were committed to reforms in society and in the arts. He published only five novels during his lifetime: *The Crime of Father Amaro* (3 versions: 1875, 1876, 1880), *Cousin Basílio* (1878), *The Mandarin* (1880), *The Relic* (1887) and *The Maias* (1888). His other novels were published posthumously: *The City and the Mountains, The Illustrious House of Ramires, To the Capital, Alves & Co., The Letters of Fradique Mendes, The Count of Abranhos* and *The Tragedy of the Street of Flowers.*

I

It was Easter Sunday when the people of Leiria learned that the parish priest, José Miguéis, had died of apoplexy in the early hours of the morning. The priest was a large, red-faced man, known amongst the other clergy of the diocese as 'the glutton of all gluttons'. Remarkable tales were told of his voracious appetite. Carlos, the apothecary, loathed him, and whenever he saw the priest leaving the house after a post-prandial nap, face all flushed and body replete, he would say:

'There goes the boa constrictor, off to digest his lunch. One day he'll explode!'

And explode he did, after a fish supper, just when Senhor Godinho, who lived opposite, was celebrating his birthday, and his guests were wildly dancing a polka. No one regretted his death, and there were few people at his funeral. Generally speaking, he was not greatly respected. He was basically a peasant with the manners and thick wrists of a farm labourer; he had hairs sprouting from his ears and was brusque, gravel-voiced and coarsely spoken.

The devout ladies had never taken to him: he used to belch while hearing confession and, having always lived in village parishes or in the mountains, was oblivious to certain finer points of religious devotion. He thus immediately lost nearly all his female confessants, who went instead to the unctuous Father Gusmão, who always knew the right thing to say.

And when the pious ladies who did remain faithful came to José Miguéis with talk of scruples and visions, he would scandalise them by grunting:

'Nonsense, Senhora! Pray to God for some common sense and a bit more grey matter.'

He found their keenness on fasting particularly irritating.

'Why there's nothing wrong with eating and drinking, woman,' he would roar, 'nothing wrong at all!'

He was a staunch supporter of Prince Miguel, and thus the

views of the liberal parties and of their newspapers filled him with irrational choler.

'Damn them!' he would exclaim, brandishing his vast red umbrella.

Latterly, he had grown more sedentary and lived entirely alone apart from an old maidservant and a dog called Joli. His only friend was the precentor, Valadares, who was in charge of running the diocese at the time because, for the last two years, the Bishop, Dom Joaquim, had been resting at his estate in Alto Minho, a martyr to his rheumatism. The priest had a great deal of respect for the precentor, an austere man with a large nose and poor eyesight, who was a great admirer of Ovid and who pursed his lips when he talked and liked to pepper his conversation with mythological allusions.

The precentor was fond of the priest. He used to call him Friar Hercules.

'"Hercules" because he's strong,' he explained, smiling, 'and "Friar" because he's a glutton.'

At the priest's funeral, the precentor himself sprinkled holy water over the grave and, since he had been in the habit of offering the priest a daily pinch of snuff from his gold snuff-box, he muttered to the other canons as he threw the first ritual handful of earth onto the coffin:

'That's the last pinch he's getting from me!'

The whole chapter of canons laughed uproariously at the diocesan governor's joke; Canon Campos repeated it that same night while taking tea at the house of Novais, the local deputy, where it was greeted with delighted laughter, and everyone praised the precentor's many virtues and remarked respectfully that 'the precentor really was most terribly witty'.

Days after the funeral, the priest's dog Joli turned up, wandering across the square. The maid had been taken to hospital with a fever, the house was all shut up, and the dog, abandoned, trailed its hunger from door to door. It was a small, very fat mongrel, that bore a faint resemblance to the priest. Accustomed to being around cassocks and desperate for a master, as soon as it saw a priest it would go whimpering after him. But no one wanted poor Joli; they would drive him away with the tips of their umbrellas, and the dog, like a spurned suitor, would howl all night in the streets. One morning, the dog was found dead outside the poorhouse; the dung wagon carried it off and, when the dog was no longer to be seen in the square, the priest José Miguéis was finally forgotten.

Two months later, the people of Leiria learned that a new parish priest had been appointed. Apparently, he was a very young man, just out of the seminary. His name was Amaro Vieira. His appointment was put down to political influence, and the local newspaper, *The District Voice*, which supported the opposition, wrote bitterly of Golgotha, of 'favouritism at court' and of 'the reactionary clergy'. Some priests were quite shocked by the article and it was spoken of in resentful terms in the presence of the precentor.

'Oh, there's certainly been some favouritism, and he does have sponsors,' said the precentor. 'The person who wrote to me confirming the appointment was Brito Correia.' (Brito Correia was then Minister of Justice.) 'He even says in the letter that the priest is a handsome, strapping lad. So it would seem,' he added with a smug smile, 'that "Friar Hercules" will perhaps be succeeded by "Friar Apollo".'

Only one person in Leiria, Canon Dias, had actually met the new priest, for the Canon had taught him Ethics in his first years at the seminary. At that time, said the Canon, the priest had been a shy, spindly, pimply youth.

'I can see him now in his threadbare cassock and looking for all the world as if he were suffering from worms! But he was good lad and bright too.'

Canon Dias was a well-known figure in Leiria. He had grown fat of late, his prominent belly filling his cassock; and his grizzled hair, heavy eye bags and thick lips brought to mind tales of lascivious, gluttonous friars.

Old Patrício, who had a shop in the square, was an arch liberal and would growl like a guard dog whenever he walked past a priest, and sometimes, when he saw the plump Canon crossing the square after lunch, leaning his weight on his umbrella, he would snarl:

'The old rogue's the image of João VI!'

The Canon lived alone with his older sister, Senhora Josefa Dias, and a maid, who was an equally familiar sight in the streets of Leiria, shuffling along in her carpet slippers, with her dyed black shawl drawn tight around her. Canon Dias was said to be rich; he owned rented properties near Leiria, gave turkey suppers and had some fine wine in his cellar. However, the main fact about him – much commented on and gossiped over – was his longstanding friendship with Senhora Augusta Caminha, whom everyone called São Joaneira, because she came from São João da Foz. São Joaneira lived in Rua da Misericórdia and took in lodgers. She had a daughter, Amélia, a girl of twenty-three, pretty, healthy and much sought-after.

Canon Dias had shown himself to be extremely pleased with the appointment of Amaro Vieira. In the apothecary's shop, in the square and in the cathedral sacristy, he praised Amaro's application as a seminarian, as well as his prudence, his obedience and even his voice: 'It's a joy to listen to! Exactly what one needs for putting a bit of feeling into Holy Week sermons.'

He confidently predicted a golden future, doubtless a canonry, possibly even the glory of a bishopric!

And one day, with great satisfaction, he showed the coadjutor of the cathedral – a silent, servile creature – a letter he had received from Amaro Vieira in Lisbon.

It was on an evening in August, and they were strolling together over the bridge. The new road to Figueira was under construction at the time; the old wooden bridge over the Lis had been destroyed and now everyone crossed by the much-vaunted new bridge, Ponte Nova, with its two broad stone arches, strong and stout. Work, however, had been suspended – something to do with the illegal expropriation of land. One could still see the muddy parish road which the new road was supposed to improve upon and incorporate; the ground was covered in layers of ballast, and the heavy stone rollers used to compact and smooth the macadam surface lay half-buried in the black, rain-drenched earth.

The new bridge was surrounded by tranquil open country-side. The river rose amongst low, rounded hills clothed in the dark green of new pine trees; further off, amongst the thick woods, were the small farms that lend these melancholy places a touch of lively humanity, with their bright whitewashed walls shining in the sun, with the smoke from their chimneys growing blue in the clear, clean air. Downstream, where the river flowed through low-lying fields and between banks lined with pale willows, the broad, fertile plain of Leiria, sunlit and well-watered, extended as far as the sandy beaches of the coast. From the bridge, one could see little of the city – part of the cathedral with its heavy, Jesuitical stonework, a corner of the cemetery wall overgrown with nettles, and the sharp, black tips of the cypress trees; the rest was concealed by the rugged hill bristling with rough vegetation on which stood the crumbling castle ruins, redolent of the past and surrounded at evening by the circling flight of owls.

At the foot of the bridge, the ground slopes down to an avenue that runs alongside the river for a short way. It is a secluded place, full of ancient trees. It is called the Alameda Velha. There, strolling slowly along, talking quietly, the Canon was discussing Amaro Vieira's letter with the coadjutor and telling him about an idea that the letter had given him, an idea which struck him as 'brilliant, absolutely brilliant'. Amaro had asked him, with some urgency, to arrange a rented house for him to live in, cheap, well-situated and, if possible, furnished; he spoke, more to the point, of renting rooms in a respectable guesthouse. 'As you can see, dear teacher,' Amaro wrote, 'that is what would suit me best; I do not, of course, require anything luxurious, a bedroom and a small sitting room would be perfectly adequate. What matters is that the house should be respectable, quiet and central, with a kind landlady who does not charge the earth; I leave all this to your discretion and good sense, and I assure you that these favours will not fall on barren ground. The landlady must, above all, be quiet and well-bred.'

'Now my idea, friend Mendes, is this: to put him up at São Joaneira's house!' said the Canon gleefully. 'Isn't that a wonderful idea?'

'Splendid!' said the coadjutor in his servile tones.

'She's got the bedroom downstairs, with a sitting room right next door and another bedroom which he could use as a study. It's nicely furnished, with good bedlinen . . .'

'Oh, excellent linen,' said the coadjutor respectfully.

The Canon went on:

'It would be a good opportunity for São Joaneira; she could easily charge six *tostões* a day for rooms, bedlinen, meals and a maid. And she will have the honour of having the parish priest right there in her house.'

'It's Amélia I'm not sure about,' remarked the coadjutor timidly. 'People might talk. She's still a very young woman . . . and they say the new priest is also very young. You know how tongues around here wag . . .'

The Canon stopped walking.

'Nonsense! Father Joaquim lives under the same roof as his mother's goddaughter, doesn't he? And Canon Pedroso lives with his sister-in-law and one of his sister-in-law's sisters, a girl of nineteen. Now really . . .'

'All I meant was . . .' began the coadjutor.

'No, I see no problem whatsoever. São Joaneira occasionally rents out rooms anyway, so it's almost like a guesthouse already. Even the secretary-general stayed there for a few months!'

'But a clergyman . . .' suggested the coadjutor.

'What further guarantee could one need, Senhor Mendes!' exclaimed the Canon. Then, stopping again and speaking in a confidential tone: 'And you see it suits me very well, Mendes. It suits me down to the ground, my friend.'

There was a brief silence. Lowering his voice, the coadjutor said:

'Yes, you are very good to São Joaneira.'

'I do what I can, my dear friend, I do what I can,' said the Canon. And in a tender, warmly paternal voice, he added: 'And she deserves it too. She's kindness itself, my friend.' He stopped and rolled his eyes. 'You know, if I'm not at her house at nine o'clock in the morning sharp, she starts to get quite agitated. "My dear child," I say to her, "there's no reason to get so upset." But that's the way she is. When I was ill with the colic last year, she actually lost weight, Senhor Mendes! And she's so considerate. When it's time to kill the pig, the best cuts are always for the "holy father", that's what she calls me.'

His eyes shone and he spoke with almost drooling contentment.

'Ah, Mendes,' he added, 'she's a wonderful woman!'

'And very pretty too,' said the coadjutor respectfully.

'Oh, yes,' exclaimed the Canon, stopping again. 'She's certainly well-preserved, because she's no spring chicken, you know, but she hasn't got a single grey hair on her head, not a one! And her complexion . . .' Then more quietly and with a greedy smile: 'And this part here, Mendes,' indicating the area of the throat beneath the chin by slowly stroking it with his plump hand: 'Perfection itself! And she keeps everything in the house spotless! And so thoughtful! Not a day passes without her sending me some present, a little jar of jam, a bowl of creamed rice or some delicious black pudding from Arouca! Yesterday she sent me an apple tart. You should have seen it! The apples were so smooth and creamy! Even my sister Josefa said: "It's so delicious you would think she'd cooked the apples in holy water!"' Then placing one hand on his heart: 'It's that kind of thing that touches you right here, Mendes. I know I shouldn't talk like that, but it's true.'

The coadjutor listened in envious silence.

'I'm perfectly well aware,' said the Canon, stopping again and weighing each word. 'I'm perfectly well aware of the rumours flying around . . . But it's a complete and utter calumny! I just happen to be very fond of the family. I was when her husband was alive. You know that, Mendes.'

The coadjutor nodded.

'São Joaneira is a respectable woman, Mendes!' exclaimed the Canon, striking the ground with the point of his umbrella. 'A respectable woman!'

'The work of poisonous tongues, sir,' said the coadjutor mournfully. And after a silence, he added softly: 'But it must all work out very expensive for you.'

'Exactly, my friend. Since the secretary-general left, the poor woman has had her house empty, and I've had to help her out.'

'She has got that small farm,' commented the coadjutor.

'A mere strip of land, my dear fellow, a mere strip. And then there are taxes to be paid and labourers' wages. That's why the new priest is such a godsend. With the six *tostões* that he gives her, plus a little bit of help from me and with what she gets selling vegetables from the farm, she can get by quite nicely. And that would be a great relief to me, Mendes.'

'A great relief!' echoed the coadjutor.

They fell silent. Evening was coming on; the cloudless sky was pale blue, and the limpid air utterly still. The river was very low at that time of year; small sandbanks glittered here and there and the shallow water murmured softly as it rippled over the pebbles.

On the opposite bank, two cows, watched over by a young girl, came down the muddy path that ran alongside a bramble patch; they waded slowly into the river and, stretching out necks worn bare by the yoke, they drank delicately, noiselessly; now and then they would raise their kindly heads and look about them with the passive serenity of contented beings, and threads of water, glinting in the sun, hung down from the corners of their mouths. As the sun sank, the water lost its mirror-like clarity, and the shadows cast by the arches of the bridge grew longer. A crepuscular mist rose from the hills, and, adorning the horizon, towards the sea, were blood-red and orange-tinged clouds warning of more hot weather to come.

'Lovely evening!' said the coadjutor.

The Canon yawned, made the sign of the cross over his gaping mouth, and said:

'We'd better get back in time for the Angelus.'

Shortly afterwards, as they were climbing the steps up to the cathedral, the Canon paused and, turning to the coadjutor, remarked:

'So it's decided then, friend Mendes, I'll install Amaro at São Joaneira's house! I'm sure it will prove to be a godsend to us all.'

'A real godsend,' agreed the coadjutor respectfully.

And they went into the church, making the sign of the cross.

II

A week later, the new priest was due to arrive on the coach from Chão de Maçãs that brought the post in the evening, and so from six o'clock onwards, Canon Dias and the coadjutor were strolling up and down the Largo do Chafariz, waiting for Amaro.

It was late August. Along the avenue by the river, between two lines of old poplars, one could see the ladies in their pale dresses as they walked to and fro. Beyond an archway, outside a row of lowly hovels, old women sat spinning at the door; grubby children played on the ground, revealing bare distended bellies; and chickens pecked ravenously amongst the filth and detritus. From around the bustling fountain came the scrape of water jugs on stone; bickering maidservants were ogled at by cane-wielding soldiers wearing dirty fatigues and huge misshapen boots; girls, each with a plump water jug balanced on her head, went about in pairs, swaying their hips; and two idle officers, their uniforms unbuttoned over their stomachs, stood chatting, waiting to see 'who might turn up'. The mail coach was late. As evening fell, a small light could be seen shining in the niche of a saint above the arch and, immediately opposite, the dim lights in the hospital came on one by one.

It was dark by the time the coach, lanterns glowing, appeared on the bridge, proceeding at the sedate pace dictated by the team of scrawny white horses drawing it, and coming to a halt by the fountain, outside the inn; the assistant from Patrício's shop immediately set off back across the square carrying a bundle of newspapers; Baptista, the innkeeper, a black pipe clamped in his mouth, was unhitching the horses, swearing softly to himself; and a man in a tall hat and a long ecclesiastical cloak, who had been sitting next to the driver, climbed gingerly down, clutching the iron guards on the seat, then stamped his feet on the ground to get the blood flowing again and looked around him.

'Amaro!' cried the Canon, who had gone over to him. 'How are you, you rascal!'

'Master!' said the other joyfully. And they embraced, while the coadjutor stood with head bowed and biretta in hand.

Shortly afterwards, the people still in the shops saw a slightly stooped man, wearing a priest's cape, walking across the square, flanked by the slow bulk of Canon Dias and the lanky form of the coadjutor. Everyone was aware that this was the new priest, and it was said in the pharmacy that he was 'a fine figure of a man'. Ahead of them, carrying a trunk and a cloth bag, went João Bicha, who was drunk already and kept muttering the Benedictus to himself as he went.

It was nearly nine o'clock, and night was closing in. Around the square the houses were already sleeping; the shops in the arcade glowed with the sad light of oil lamps, and one could make out indolent figures at the counters talking and arguing. The dark, twisting streets leading down into the square, lit by one moribund streetlamp, seemed uninhabited. And in the silence the cathedral bell was slowly tolling for the souls of the dead.

Canon Dias was patiently explaining the 'arrangements' to the new priest. He had not looked for a house for him because that would have involved buying furniture, finding a maid and endless other expenses. He had thought it best to take rooms for him in a respectable, comfortable boarding house, and (as the coadjutor could confirm) São Joaneira's house was without equal in that respect. It was clean and airy, with no unpleasant kitchen smells; the secretary-general had stayed there and the schools inspector; and São Joaneira (Mendes knew her well) was a thrifty, God-fearing woman, always ready to oblige.

'It will be a home from home. You'll have two courses at mealtimes and coffee . . .'

'And what about the price, Master?' said the priest.

'Six *tostões*. Why, she's almost giving it away! You'll have a bedroom and a sitting room . . .'

'A lovely sitting room,' remarked the coadjutor respectfully.

'And is it far from the cathedral?' asked Amaro.

'Two steps away. You could go and say mass in your slippers. Oh, and there is a young woman living there too,' continued the Canon in his slow way. 'She's São Joaneira's daughter. A very pretty girl of twenty-three. She has her moods, but she's got a good heart . . . This is your street.'

It was a narrow street of low, shabby houses cowering beneath the high walls of the old poorhouse, with one dim streetlamp at the far end.

'And this is your palace!' said the Canon, knocking on a narrow door.

On the first floor, overhanging the street, were two old-fashioned wrought-iron balconies adorned with rosemary bushes in wooden tubs; the upper windows were tiny and the wall so uneven that it looked like a piece of battered tin.

São Joaneira was waiting at the top of the stairs, accompanied by a skinny, freckled maidservant holding up an oil lamp to light the way. The figure of São Joaneira stood out sharply against the whitewashed wall. She was tall, stout and somewhat sluggish-looking, but with very white skin. She already had lines around her dark eyes, and her tangled hair, with a scarlet comb in it, was growing thin around the temples and near her parting; but she was also endowed with plump arms, an ample bosom and clean clothes.

'Here's your new lodger,' said the Canon, as he climbed the stairs.

'It's a great honour to have you here, a great honour. But you must be worn out. Come this way, and mind the step.'

She led him into a small room decorated in yellow, with a vast wickerwork sofa against one wall and, opposite, a table covered in green baize.

'This is your sitting room, Father,' said São Joaneira, 'where you can receive visitors and relax . . . Here,' she said opening a door, 'is your bedroom. And there's a chest of drawers and a wardrobe . . .' She pulled out the drawers and praised the bed, prodding the mattress. 'Oh and a bell you can ring should you need anything . . . The keys to the chest of drawers are here . . . And if you want a higher pillow . . . Now there's only one blanket at the moment, but you just have to ask . . .'

'That's fine, Senhora, excellent,' said the priest in his soft, low voice.

'And if there's anything else you require . . .'

'Dear lady,' cried the Canon cheerily, 'what he wants now is some supper!'

'Supper is ready too. The soup's been on since six o'clock . . .'

And she went off to chivvy the maid along, saying from the bottom of the stairs:

'Come on, Ruça, get a move on!'

The Canon sat down heavily on the sofa and took a pinch of snuff.

'You'll have to make do, my lad. This is the best we could get.'

'Oh, I'm quite happy anywhere, Master,' said Amaro, putting on his slippers. 'Remember what the seminary was like, and in Feirão, my bed used to get soaked every time it rained.'

From the square came the sound of bugles.

'What's that?' asked Amaro, going over to the window.

'It's the half-past nine call to quarters.'

Amaro opened the window. At the end of the street, the lamp was growing dim. The night was very dark, and the city was enclosed in a hollow silence, as if covered by a vault.

After the bugles came the slow roll of drums moving away towards the barracks; a soldier, who had been tarrying in one of the alleyways near the castle, hurried past beneath the window; and from the walls of the poorhouse came the constant shriek of owls.

'It's a bit gloomy,' said Amaro.

But São Joaneira was calling down to them:

'You can come up now, Father. The soup's on the table!'

'Go along now, you must be positively faint with hunger, Amaro!' said the Canon, heaving himself to his feet.

Then, seizing Amaro by the sleeve, he said:

'Now you'll find out what chicken soup is like cooked by São Joaneira. Absolutely mouthwatering!'

In the middle of the dining room, which was lined with dark paper, the table with its bright white cloth was a cheering sight, as were the china plates and the glasses glinting beneath the strong light of a green-shaded oil lamp. Delicious smells emerged from the soup tureen, and the plump chicken served on a platter with succulent white rice and pork sausages looked like a dish fit for a king. Slightly in the shadows, one could see the delicate colours of porcelain in a china cabinet; in one corner, by the window, was a piano, covered with a faded satin cloth. Sounds of frying came from the kitchen and these, combined with the fresh smell of laundered linen, made Amaro rub his hands in glee.

'This way, Father, this way,' said São Joaneira. 'You might be in a draught over there.' She closed the shutters on the windows and brought him a small box of sand in which to place his cigarette butts. 'And you'll have a little jelly, won't you, Canon?'

'Well, just to be companionable,' said the Canon jovially, sitting down and unfolding his napkin.

São Joaneira, meanwhile, as she bustled about the room, was admiring the new priest, who had his head bent over his plate, drinking his soup, blowing on each spoonful. He was a good-looking man with very dark, slightly curly hair. He had an oval face, smooth olive skin, large, dark eyes and long eyelashes.

The Canon, who had not seen him since the seminary, thought him much stronger and more manly-looking.

'You were such a skinny little lad . . .'

'It's the mountain air,' said Amaro, 'it did me good!'

Then he described his sad existence in Feirão, in Alta Beira, and the harsh winters spent alone with shepherds. The Canon held the wine bottle high above Amaro's glass and poured it in, making the wine bubble.

'Well, drink up, man, drink up! You never had wine like this at the seminary.'

They talked about the seminary.

'I wonder what happened to Rabicho, the bursar,' said the Canon.

'And Carocho, the one who used to steal potatoes.'

They laughed and drank, caught up in the pleasure of remembering, recalling old times: the rector's chronic catarrh, the teacher of plainsong who one day accidentally dropped the copy of Bocage's erotic poetry that he had been carrying in his pocket.

'How time flies!' they said.

São Joaneira then set down on the table a deep dish of baked apples.

'Well, I'll have to have some of that!' exclaimed the Canon. 'A baked apple is a thing of beauty, and I never turn down the chance to eat one. She's a wonderful housekeeper, our São Joaneira, oh yes, a wonderful housekeeper!'

She laughed, revealing the fillings in her two large front teeth. She went to fetch the port, then placed on the Canon's plate, with a great show of devotion, one crumbling baked apple dusted with sugar; and clapping the Canon on the back with her soft, plump hand, she said:

'He's a saint, Father, an absolute saint! I owe him so much!'

'Now, now, that's quite enough of that,' said the Canon, but a look of adoring contentment spread over his face. 'Lovely drop of port!' he added, sipping his wine. 'Lovely!'

'It's the same bottle we had for Amélia's birthday, Canon.'

'Where is Amélia?'

'She went over to Morenal with Dona Maria. Then, of course, they went to spend the evening with the Gansosos.'

'São Joaneira's a landowner too, you know,' explained the Canon, referring to Morenal. 'It's almost an estate!' And he roared with laughter, his shining eyes tenderly caressing São Joaneira's ample body.

'Don't listen to him, Father, it's just a little scrap of land,' she said.

Then, seeing the maid leaning against the wall, racked with coughing, she said:

'Go and cough in the other room, will you. Honestly!'

The girl left, pressing her apron to her mouth.

'She doesn't seem at all well,' remarked Amaro.

Yes, the girl was very sickly. The 'poor lamb' was her

goddaughter, an orphan, and possibly tubercular. She had taken her in out of pity . . .

'And because the maid who was here before was carried off to the hospital, the shameless hussy . . . She got involved with a soldier you know . . .'

Father Amaro slowly lowered his eyes and, nibbling on a few crumbs, asked if there had been much illness that summer.

'Just a bit of colic from eating too much unripe fruit,' snorted the Canon. 'People stuff themselves with water-melons and then get bloated with all that water . . . And fevers of course . . .'

They talked then about the intermittent fever common in the country and about the air in Leiria.

'I'm much stronger these days,' said Father Amaro. 'Yes, thank God, my health is good now.'

'And may God keep you in good health too, because you don't know how precious it is until you lose it,' exclaimed São Joaneira. And she launched into an account of the household's one great misfortune: a sister, not quite right in the head, who had been paralysed for the last ten years. She was nearly sixty now and last winter she'd caught a very nasty cold and ever since then, poor dear, she'd been on the decline . . . 'Earlier this evening, she had a coughing fit, and I really thought her time had come. But she's quieter now.'

Sitting with the cat on her lap and monotonously rolling bread balls between her fingers, she spoke further about that 'misfortune', then about her Amélia, about the Gansosos, about the former precentor and about how expensive everything was . . . The Canon, replete, was finding it hard to keep his eyes open; everything in the room was gradually falling asleep, even the oil lamp was burning down.

'Well, my friends,' said the Canon, bestirring himself at last, 'it's getting late.'

Father Amaro got up and, eyes lowered, said grace.

'Do you need a nightlight, Father?' asked São Joaneira solicitously.

'No, Senhora, I never use one. Goodnight!'

And he went slowly down stairs, toothpick in mouth.

São Joaneira lit the way for him with the oil lamp. On the first stair, however, Father Amaro turned and said pleasantly:

'Of course, tomorrow is Friday and a fast day.'

'Oh, no,' said the Canon, who was pulling on his cloak, yawning, 'tomorrow you'll be having lunch with me. I'll call for you here, then we'll visit the precentor, go to the cathedral and take a turn about the town . . . We'll be having squid, you know, which is a near miracle here, because we almost never get fish.'

São Joaneira reassured Father Amaro:

Don't you worry, Father, I always keep the fast days.'

'I only mention it,' said Father Amaro, 'because nowadays, alas, no one bothers.'

'Oh, you're absolutely right,' she broke in, 'but I put the salvation of my soul above all else.'

Downstairs the bell rang loudly.

'That'll be my daughter,' said São Joaneira. 'Go and open it, will you, Ruça!'

The door slammed and they heard voices and laughter.

'Is that you, Amélia?'

A voice called out 'Bye, then!' And almost running up the stairs, her clothes slightly caught up at the front, came a lovely young woman, strong, tall and sturdy, a white shawl over her head and clutching a sprig of rosemary in her hand.

'Come along, dear. The new parish priest is here. He arrived tonight. Come along.'

Amélia had stopped, slightly embarrassed, looking up at the stairs where Father Amaro was standing leaning on the banister. She was breathing hard from running; her face was flushed, and her dark, lively eyes were shining; she exuded an air of freshness and of brisk country walks.

Father Amaro continued on down, keeping close to the banister to allow her to pass, and murmured 'Good evening', his eyes downcast. The Canon stumped down the stairs towards her saying:

'And what time do you call this, you scamp?'

She giggled shyly.

'Now off to bed with you,' he said, patting her cheek with his large, hairy hand.

She ran past him, and the Canon left, having fetched his umbrella from the downstairs living room, and having told the maid not to bother lighting the stairs for him:

'It's all right, I can see. Now don't you catch cold, young lady. I'll see you at eight then, Amaro. Be up and ready! Off you go, young lady, goodnight, and pray to Our Lady of Charity to get rid of that cough of yours.'

Father Amaro closed his bedroom door. The bed had been turned down, and the clean white sheets gave off the good smell of freshly laundered linen. Above the bed hung an old engraving of Christ crucified. Amaro opened his breviary, knelt down by the bed and made the sign of the cross; but he was tired and kept yawning; above him, too, through the ritual prayers he was mechanically reading, he began to hear the tick-tack of Amélia's shoes and the rustle of her starched petticoats as she undressed.

III

Amaro Vieira was born in Lisbon in the house of the Marquesa de Alegros. His father was the Marquis' servant; his mother was the personal maid and almost a friend of the Marchioness. Amaro still owned a book, *Child of the Jungle*, complete with crude, coloured illustrations, on the first blank page of which was written: 'To my esteemed maid and ever-faithful friend, Joana Vieira – from the Marquesa de Alegros.' He also owned a daguerrotype of his mother: a stout woman with thick eyebrows, a large mouth with sensually parted lips and a high colour. Amaro's father had died of apoplexy, and his mother, who had always been so healthy, succumbed a year later to an inflammation of the larynx. Amaro was six years old at the time. He had an older sister who had lived with their grandmother in Coimbra since she was small, and an uncle, a wealthy grocer in the Estrela district of Lisbon. However, the Marchioness had grown fond of Amaro; she kept him at home with her, in a kind of tacit adoption, and she began, with great scrupulousness, to watch over his upbringing.

The Marquesa de Alegros was widowed when she was forty-three and spent most of the year living quietly on her estate in Carcavelos. She was by nature a passive, languidly benevolent person; she had her own chapel, was devoted to the priests at São Luís, and always had the interests of the Church at heart. Her two daughters, having been brought up both to fear Heaven and to care deeply about Fashion, were at once excessively devout and terribly chic, speaking with equal fervour about Christian humility and the latest clothes from Brussels. A journalist of the time said of them: 'Every day they worry about what dress they should wear when it comes to their turn to enter Paradise.'

Adrift in Carcavelos, on that estate criss-crossed by aristocratic avenues full of the cries of peacocks, the two girls grew bored. They plunged into the occupations afforded them by Religion and Charity: they made clothes for the parish poor and embroidered antependia for the church altars. From May to October they were entirely absorbed in the work of 'saving their souls'; they read benign devotional literature. With no theatre, no visitors and no dress shops, they welcomed the priests' visits and gossiped about the virtues of the various saints. God was their summer extravagance.

The Marchioness had decided from the very beginning that Amaro should enter the ecclesiastical life. His thinness and his pallor seemed to cry out for a life of seclusion; he was already fond of the chapel, but what he liked most was to be amongst women, snuggled up in the warmth of their skirts, listening to them talk about saints. The Marchioness did not want to send him to school because she feared the impiety of the times and that he might get into bad company. Her own chaplain taught him Latin, and her eldest daughter, Dona Luísa, who had a hooked nose and read Chateaubriand, gave him lessons in French and geography.

Amaro was, as the servants put it, a 'bit of a namby-pamby'. He never played games and never ran about in the sun. When he accompanied the Marchioness on an afternoon stroll along the avenues of the estate, and she took the arm of Father Liset or of Freitas, her respectful administrator, he would walk by her side, silent and shy, fiddling clammily with the linings of his trouser pockets and feeling slightly afraid of the thick groves of trees and the lush, tall grasses.

He became increasingly fearful. He could only sleep with a nightlight burning and with his bed drawn up near that of an old nursemaid. The maids feminized him; they thought him pretty and would encourage him to nestle amongst them; they would tickle him and smother him in kisses, and he would roll in their skirts, brushing against their bodies, uttering little contented shrieks. Sometimes, when the Marchioness went out, they would dress him up as a woman, all the while hooting with laughter; and he, with his languid manner and voluptuous eyes, would abandon himself to them, half-naked, his face flushed. The maids also made use of him in their intrigues with each other: Amaro became their bearer of tales. He became a tittletattler and a liar.

By the time he was eleven, he was helping with Mass, and on Saturdays, he would clean the chapel. That was his favourite day; he would shut himself up inside, place the saints on a table in the sunlight and kiss each one of them in turn with a mixture of devout tenderness and greedy delight; and he would work away all morning, humming the *Santissimo*, getting rid of any moths in the Virgins' dresses and polishing the Martyrs' haloes.

Meanwhile, he was growing up; his pale, diminutive appearance remained unchanged; he never laughed out loud and he always had his hands in his pockets. He was constantly in and out of the maids' rooms, rummaging about in drawers; he would finger their dirty petticoats and sniff the padding they wore in their clothes. He was also extremely lazy, and in the mornings, it was hard to wrench him from the unhealthy, lethargic somnolence in which he lay, swathed in blankets and with his arms around the pillow. He was already slightly hunched, and the servants used to call him 'the little Father'.

One Sunday before Ash Wednesday, as she walked out onto the terrace after morning mass, the Marchioness suddenly dropped dead of an apoplexy. In her will, she left a legacy that would pay for Amaro, the son of her maidservant Joana, to enter the seminary at fifteen and become ordained. Father Liset was charged with carrying out this pious duty. Amaro was, by then, thirteen.

The Marchioness' daughters immediately left Carcavelos and went to live in Lisbon, in the house of their paternal aunt, Dona Bárbara de Noronha. Amaro was sent to his uncle's house, also in Lisbon. His uncle, the grocer, was a very fat man, married to the daughter of an impoverished civil servant; she had only accepted his proposal in order to escape her father's house, where the meals were frugal, where she had to make the beds and where she was never allowed to go to the theatre. But she loathed her husband, his hairy hands, the shop, the area they lived in, as well as her very commonplace married name, Senhora Gonçalves. Her husband, though, adored her as the delight of his life, his one luxury; he loaded her with jewels and called her 'his duchess'.

Amaro did not find in his uncle's house the affectionate, feminine atmosphere in which he had been so warmly wrapped in Carcavelos. His aunt barely noticed him; dressed in silks, her face heavily powdered, her hair in ringlets, she spent all day reading novels and newspaper reviews of plays, waiting for the moment when Cardoso, the Teatro da Trindade's leading man, would pass by beneath her windows, tugging at his shirt cuffs. The grocer, however, seized on Amaro as an unexpected extra pair of hands and set him to work in the shop. He made Amaro get up at five o'clock every morning, and the boy would sit at one corner of the kitchen table, trembling in his blue cloth jacket, hurriedly dipping his bread in his coffee. Both aunt and uncle hated him; his aunt called him 'the slowcoach' and his uncle called him 'the donkey'. They begrudged him even the sliver of beef that he ate for his supper. Amaro grew even thinner and cried himself to sleep every night.

He knew that when he was fifteen, he would enter the seminary. His uncle reminded him of this every day:

'Don't think you're going to spend the rest of your life here, idling your time away! As soon as you're fifteen, it's off to the seminary with you. I'm under no obligation to support you, you know. I don't believe in keeping a dog and barking myself.'

And the boy began to think of the seminary as a liberation.

No one ever consulted him about his inclinations or his vocation. They simply thrust a surplice on him; his passive, easily-led nature accepted it, as he would a uniform. Indeed, he did not dislike the idea of becoming a priest. Since leaving the perpetual prayers of Carcavelos, he had retained his fear of Hell, but had lost his fervour for the saints; however, he remembered the priests who used to visit the Marchioness' house, sleek men with very white skin, who dined with the nobility and took snuff from golden snuff boxes; and he liked the idea of a profession in which one spoke softly to women –

living amongst them, gossiping, conscious of their penetrating warmth – and received gifts from them on silver trays. He remembered Father Liset and the ruby ring he wore on his little finger; and Monsignor Savedra with his fine gold-rimmed spectacles, sipping his glass of Madeira. The Marchioness' daughters used to embroider slippers for them. One day, he had seen a bishop, a jovial, well-travelled man, who had been a priest in Bahia and had visited Rome; and there in the living room, surrounded by adoring women, all smiling beatifically, with his priestly hands that smelled of eau-de-cologne resting on the gold handle of his walking stick, he had sung for them in his beautiful voice:

Mulatto girl from Bahia
Born in Capujá . . .

A year before entering the seminary, his uncle sent him to a teacher to give him a better grounding in Latin, and thus excused him from serving behind the counter. For the first time in his life, Amaro was free. He went to school alone and wandered the streets. He saw the city, watched the infantry performing military drill, peered in at the doors of cafés, read posters advertising plays at the theatres. Above all, he began to notice women – and everything he saw filled him with deep melancholy. The saddest time was at dusk, on his way back from school, or on Sundays after he had been for a walk in the Jardim da Estrela with his uncle's assistant. He had been given a garret room, with a tiny window looking out over the rooftops. He would lean there watching as points of light gradually lit up the city below: rising up from there, he seemed to hear a dull murmur: it was the sound of the life he did not know and which he decided must be wonderful, with cafés ablaze with light and women in silk dresses rustling along the colonnades outside the theatres; he lost himself in vague imaginings, and fragmented female forms would suddenly loom out of the black depths of night: a foot shod in a serge ankle boot and a leg encased in a very white stocking, or a plump arm with the sleeve pushed up to the shoulder . . .

Down below, in the kitchen, the maid would begin singing as she washed the dishes: she was a fat girl with a lot of freckles; and then he felt like going downstairs and brushing past her, or sitting in a corner and watching her plunge the dishes into the scalding water; he remembered other women he had seen in the narrow streets, bareheaded, wearing noisy, starched skirts and down-at-heel shoes: and a kind of languor rose up from the depths of his being, a desire to embrace someone, a desire not to feel alone. He judged himself to be most unfortunate and even considered killing himself. But then his uncle would call up to him from downstairs:

'I hope you're studying, you good-for-nothing.'

And sitting there rubbing his knees together, feeling utterly wretched, his head dropping with sleep as he sat hunched over Titus Livius, Amaro would grind away at the dictionary.

It was around that time that he began to feel a certain dislike for the life of a priest, *because he would not be able to marry*. The friends he had made at school had already introduced certain curiosities and corruptions to his feminized nature. He smoked cigarettes on the sly and grew still thinner and paler.

He entered the seminary. During the first few days, the long, rather damp stone corridors, the dim oil-lamps, the narrow rooms with their barred windows, the black cassocks, the regimented silence, the tolling of the bells, all filled him with a gloomy, terrified sadness. But he soon made friends; his pretty face found favour. The other boys began to address him as *tu*, to include him, during break times and on Sunday walks, in their conversations full of tales about the teachers, calumnies about the rector and endless complaints about the melancholy nature of the cloistered life; for almost everyone spoke with longing of the freedom they had left behind: the boys from villages could not forget the bright, sunlit threshing floor, the maize harvests when people sang and embraced, the lines of oxen heading homewards as the fields filled up with mist; those who came from small towns missed the quiet, winding streets where you could flirt with girls, the bustling market days, the great adventures they had instead of studying Latin. The paved courtyard set aside for recreation, with its spindly trees, high, somnolent walls and monotonous ball games, was simply not enough: they felt oppressed by the narrowness of the corridors, by the room dedicated to St Ignatius where they had their morning meditations and where they studied at night; and they envied all those whose future, however humble, at least belonged to them – the muleteer whom they saw leading his animals down the street, the carter singing tunelessly to the shrill squeaking of wheels, and even the wandering beggars, leaning on a stick, a dark saddlebag slung over one shoulder.

From the window in one corridor, one could see a bend in the road: at dusk, amidst much cracking of whips, a luggage-laden carriage drawn by three mares used to pass by, throwing up a cloud of dust; the happy passengers, with rugs over their knees, would blow out smoke from their cigars. How many eyes followed them! How many desires journeyed with them to lively towns and cities, through cool dawns and beneath bright stars!

And in the refectory, sitting before the meagre bowl of vegetable broth, while the gruff-voiced regent of studies would launch into a dreary reading of letters from some missionary in China or the bishop's pastorals, how they longed for suppers at home with their families! A good slice of fish! The freshly slaughtered pig! Hot crackling sizzling on the plate! The delicious smell of stewed pork!

Amaro had nothing very dear to miss; he had left behind him only his brutal uncle and his aunt's bored, powdered face, and yet, gradually, he began to long for his Sunday walks, for the bright light from the gas lamps and the return from school, with his books bound together with a leather strap, when he would press his nose to the windows of shops in order to study the nakedness of mannequins. Slowly, though, like an indolent sheep, his dull nature fell in with the rules of the seminary. He dutifully learned what was in the textbooks; he was prudent and exact in his ecclesiastical duties; and, as a

silent, hunched, figure, bowing low to the teache
managed to get good marks.

He never understood those who seemed bliss
with life in the seminary and who bruised their knees
meditated, with bowed heads, upon extracts from the *Imitation of Christ* or from St Ignatius; in the chapel, they would grow pale and their eyes would roll back in ecstasy; even at break time or on walks, they could be found reading some slender volume entitled *In Praise of Our Lady*; and they took delight in obeying the slightest of rules – even going up stairs only one step at a time as St Bonaventura recommends. For these boys, the seminary was a foretaste of Heaven; for him, it merely combined the humiliations of prison with the tedium of school.

He could not understand the ambitious students either: those who wanted to be the bishop's trainbearers, or, in the high-ceilinged rooms of a bishop's palace, to be the ones to draw aside the old damask portières; or those who wanted to live in a great city once they were ordained, to serve in some aristocratic church and sing in a sonorous voice before the wealthy devotees who, with a rustle of silk, would gather on the carpet before the high altar. Others even dreamed of careers outside the Church: they hoped to become soldiers and to walk the paved streets with sword clinking, or else take up the good life of the farmer, out and about by dawn, wearing a wide-brimmed hat and mounted on a good horse, trotting along the roads, giving orders to those working on threshing-floors piled high with grain, or dismounting at the door of wine cellars. And apart from a few very devout students, every one of them, whether aspiring to the priesthood or to some secular career, wanted to escape the narrowness of the seminary in order to eat well, earn some money and meet women.

Amaro did not want anything.

'I'm not sure really . . .' he would say dully.

Meanwhile, he would listen politely to those for whom studying at the seminary was the equivalent of being a galley slave, and was much troubled by their conversations which were full of an impatient longing to live life freely. Sometimes

,oys would talk about running away. They would make plans, calculate the height of windows, the adventures that might befall them in the black night on the black roads; they anticipated the bars of inns where one could drink, the billiard halls, the warm bedrooms of women. Amaro would become very agitated; in his bed, late at night, he would toss and turn, unable to sleep, and in his deepest imaginings and dreams, he would burn with desire for Woman, like a silent, red-hot coal.

In his cell there was an image of the Virgin crowned with stars and standing on a sphere, gazing up at the immortal light, while trampling a serpent underfoot. Amaro would turn to her, as if to a refuge, and would say a Hail Mary; but when he lay looking at the lithograph, he would forget all about the holiness of the Virgin and would see before him merely a pretty blonde girl; he would sigh adoringly; he would cast lubricious glances at her as he undressed; in his curiosity he would even imagine himself lifting the chaste folds of the image's blue tunic to reveal shapely forms, white flesh . . . Then it seemed to him that he could see the eyes of the Tempter glinting in the darkness of the room, and he would carefully sprinkle his bed with holy water, but he never dared reveal these ecstasies in the confessional on Sundays.

How often had he heard the teacher of Moral Theology preaching in his nasal voice on the subject of Sin, comparing it to the serpent, and exhorting the seminarians, with unctuous words and large gestures, and with the slow, mellifluous pomp of his sentences, to follow the Virgin's example and trample the 'vile serpent' under foot! And then there was the teacher of Mystical Theology who, after taking a pinch of snuff, would speak to them of their duty to 'conquer Nature'! And quoting from St John Chrysostom and St Chrysologus, St Cyprian and St Jerome, he would explain the saints' curses against Woman, whom he called, in the language of the Church, Serpent, Sting, Daughter of Lies, Gateway to Hell, Fount of Crime, Scorpion . . .

'And as our father St Jerome called her,' and at this point, he would always loudly blow his nose, 'the Path to Iniquity, *iniquitas via*!'

Even his textbooks were obsessed with Woman! What kind of creature was this, then, who, in theology, was either placed on the altar as the Queen of Grace or had barbarous curses heaped upon her? What power did she have, that this legion of saints should one minute rush to meet her, passionate and ecstatic, unanimously handing over to her the Kingdom of Heaven, and at the next, uttering terrified sobs and cries of loathing, flee from her as if she were the Universal Enemy, hiding themselves in wildernesses and in cloisters so as not to see her and to die there from the disease of having loved her? Unable precisely to define these troubling feelings, he nevertheless experienced them. They would constantly resurface, demoralizing him, so that before he had even made his vows, he was already longing to break them.

And he felt similar rebellions of nature all around him: the studying, the fasting, the penances might cow the body, give it mechanical habits, but, inside, desire stirred silently, like a nest of impassive snakes. Those of sanguine temperament suffered most, as painfully constrained by the Rule as their thick, plebeian wrists were by their shirt cuffs. As soon as they were alone, their true temperament would erupt: they would fight, squabble, provoke arguments. Amongst the more phlegmatic, nature, constrained, produced great sadnesses and languid silences; they would find an outlet then in minor vices: gambling with an old pack of cards, reading a novel, or, after much intrigue, getting hold of a packet of cigarettes – ah, the charms of sin!

In the end, Amaro almost envied the studious ones; at least they were happy, perpetually studying, scribbling notes in the silence of the high-ceilinged library, they were respected, they wore glasses, they took snuff. He himself even had sudden ambitions in that direction, but confronted by those vast tomes, he would be overcome by unbearable tedium. He was, however, devout: he would pray, he had limitless faith in certain saints and a terrible fear of God. But he hated the cloistered life of the seminary. The chapel, the weeping willows in the courtyard, the monotonous meals in the long, flagstoned refectory, the smells in the corridors, all this made him feel sad and irritable: it seemed to him that he could only be a good, pure believer if he were allowed to enjoy the freedom of the street or the peace of a garden, away from those black walls. He lost weight, he broke out in sweats, and in his last year, after the prolonged Holy Week services, when the weather began to grow hot, he was admitted to the infirmary with a nervous fever.

He was finally ordained around the Ember Days prior to St Matthew's feast day, and shortly afterwards, while he was still at the seminary, he received this letter from Father Liset:

'My dear child and new colleague,

Now that you have been ordained, I feel it is my duty to give you a full account of the state of your financial affairs, for I wish to carry out to the end the responsibility placed upon my weak shoulders by our much-lamented Marchioness, who bestowed on me the honour of administering the legacy she left to you. For, although worldly goods should matter little to a soul devoted to the priesthood, good accounts always make for good friends. I must tell you, my dear child, that the legacy left to you by our dear Marchioness – to whom you should lift up your soul in eternal gratitude – has now been entirely used up. I also take this opportunity to tell you that, after your uncle's death, your aunt, having sold the shop, plunged into a life on which I would prefer not to venture an opinion: she fell victim to the passions and, having formed an illegitimate union, lost her money along with her virtue and now runs a boarding house in 53 Rua dos Calafates. The only reason I mention this sordid business, a matter from which a tender young priest like yourself should be shielded, is in order to give you a true account of your respected family. Your sister, as you doubtless know, married a wealthy man in Coimbra, and although money should not be a primary consideration in a marriage, it is nevertheless important for your future circumstances that you should be in possession of this fact. Regarding our dear rector's plans to send you to the parish of Feirão in Gralheira, I will speak with a few important people who are kind enough to heed a poor priest who asks only for God's mercy. I hope I will prove successful. My dear child, persevere in the paths of virtue, of which I am sure your good soul is full, and be assured that you will find happiness in this our holy ministry when you come to understand the many balms and consolations that are poured upon your heart merely by serving God! Farewell, my dear child and colleague. You can be sure that my thoughts will be with you, the ward of our late, lamented Marchioness, who is doubtless in Heaven, to which her many virtues will have taken her, praying all the while to the Virgin, whom she so loved and served, for the happiness of her dear ward.

Liset.

PS The name of your sister's husband is Trigoso.

Two months later, Amaro was appointed parish priest to Feirão, in Gralheira, in the mountain region of Beira Alta. He remained there from October until the snows melted.

Feirão is a poor parish of shepherds and, at that time of year, almost entirely uninhabited. Amaro spent most of his time in idleness, pondering his own boredom by the fireside, listening to the winter howling in the mountains. In spring, several well-populated parishes fell vacant in the districts of Santarém and Leiria, parishes with good livings. Amaro wrote at once to his sister, telling her of his wretched life in Feirão. Urging him to be frugal, she sent him twelve *moedas* so that he could travel to Lisbon and find another parish. Amaro left at once. The clean, sharp mountain air had strengthened his blood, and he was now a strong, upright, pleasant young man, with a healthy glow to his dark skin.

As soon as he arrived in Lisbon, he went straight to his aunt's house in Rua dos Calafates: he found her greatly aged, overly powdered and wearing a large false chignon adorned with bright red ribbons. She had grown very devout, and it was with pious joy that she opened her skinny arms to Amaro.

'But you're so handsome! Just look at you! Who would have thought it! Goodness, what a change!'

She admired his cassock and his tonsure, and, pouring out to him her many misfortunes, exclaiming all the while about the salvation of her soul and the various food shortages, she led him up to a room on the third floor overlooking a narrow courtyard.

'You can live as well as an abbot here, and it's very cheap,' she said. 'I would love to let you stay for free, but . . . Oh, I've been so unhappy, Joãozinho . . . I mean, Amaro. I just can't seem to get Joãozinho out of my head . . .'

The next day, Amaro went to São Luís in search of Father Liset. He had gone to France. Then he remembered the Marchioness' youngest daughter, Dona Joana, who was married to the Conde de Ribamar, a Councillor of State, a man of influence and a loyal member of the Regeneration party since 1851, who had twice been a minister.

As soon as he had put in his request for a new parish, Amaro, acting on his aunt's advice, went one morning to the house of the Condessa de Ribamar, in Rua Buenos Aires. A coupé was waiting at the door.

'The Countess is just about to go out,' said a servant in a white tie and light alpaca jacket, who was lolling, cigarette in mouth, in the doorway that led into the courtyard.

At that moment, a lady in a pale dress emerged from a baize-lined door and came down the stone steps at the far end of the paved courtyard. She was tall, thin and blonde, with a mass of tiny curls over her forehead, a pair of gold-rimmed spectacles perched on her long, sharp nose, and, on her chin, a small mole from which sprouted a few fair hairs.

'Don't you recognise me, Countess?' said Amaro, stepping forward and bowing, his hat in his hand. 'It's me, Amaro.'

'Amaro?' she said, as if she did not know the name. 'Good heavens, it's you! It can't be! Why, you're a grown man! Who'd have thought it!'

Amaro smiled.

'Well, I would certainly never have expected it!' she went on, still astonished. 'And are you living in Lisbon now?'

Amaro explained about his appointment to the parish of Feirão and how poor the parish was . . .

'So I've come to ask for your help in finding another appointment, Countess.'

She listened to him with her hands resting on a tall, pale silk parasol, and Amaro was aware of the smell of face powder and fresh cotton chambray emanating from her.

'Leave it with me,' she said. 'Don't worry about it. My husband will have a word. I'll make sure of that. Look, come and visit.' And with one finger on her lips, she said: 'Now wait, tomorrow I'm going to Sintra. Sunday's impossible. The best thing would be if you came back in a fortnight. In a fortnight's time, in the morning, I'll be here.' And laughing, showing her long, healthy teeth. 'I can just see you now translating Chateaubriand with my sister Luísa! How time passes!'

'And how is your sister?' asked Amaro.

'Very well. She lives on an estate in Santarém.'

She offered him a suede-gloved hand, and when he shook it, her gold bracelets tinkled; then, slim and lithe, she jumped into the coupé, with a movement that revealed a flash of white petticoat.

Amaro began to wait and hope. It was July, the hottest time of the year. He said morning mass at São Domingos, and spent the day, in slippers and cotton jacket, idling at home. Sometimes he would go and chat to his aunt in the dining room; the windows would be closed, and in the half-darkness, one could hear the monotonous buzz of flies; his aunt sat crocheting at one end of an old wickerwork sofa, her spectacles poised on the end of her nose; Amaro, yawning, leafed through an old copy of some edifying magazine.

When evening fell, he would go out and take a few turns around the Rossio square. The still, heavy air was suffocating: from every corner came the repetitive cry of 'Water! Cool water!' On the benches, beneath the trees, tramps in patched clothes lay dozing; empty carriages for hire trotted slowly round and round the square; the lights in the café windows glowed; and overheated people drifted about, yawning, dragging their idleness with them along the pavements.

Amaro would then withdraw to his room, leaving the window open to the heat of the night, and in his shirtsleeves, with his boots off, he would stretch out on his bed and ponder his hopes for the future. He kept remembering, with a little rush of pleasure, what the Countess had said: 'Don't worry about it. My husband will have a word.' And he could already picture himself, tranquil and important, in a parish in some pretty town, in a house with a garden full of cabbages and lettuces, receiving trays of sweetmeats from devout, wealthy ladies.

His spirit was at rest. The exalted moods provoked by the imposed continence of the seminary had been soothed by the satisfactions given him by a sturdy shepherdess, whom he used to watch as she rang the bell for mass on Sundays, her woollen skirt swaying and her cheeks flushed as she pulled on the bell rope. In his present serene mood, he punctually gave Heaven the prayers demanded by ritual, his flesh was contented and quiet, and he was doing his best to get himself well set up.

At the end of the fortnight, he went back to the Countess' house.

'She's not in,' the stable boy told him.

The next day, he returned, somewhat worried. The green baize doors stood open, and Amaro went slowly and timidly up the broad, red carpet, fixed in place by metal stair rods. A soft light came in through the skylight; at the top of the stairs, on the landing, seated on a scarlet morocco leather bench, a servant was dozing, leaning back against the glossy white wall, head drooping, mouth open. It was terribly hot and that profound, aristocratic silence frightened Amaro; he stood there hesitantly for a moment, his parasol dangling on his little finger; he discreetly cleared his throat to wake the servant, who seemed terrifying to him with his fine black sideboards and his thick gold watch-chain; and he was just about to go back down the stairs when, from behind a portière, he heard a man's loud laughter. He wiped the whitish dust off his shoes with his handkerchief, straightened his cuffs, and, face ablaze, entered a large room with walls lined with yellow damask; the sunlight was pouring in through the open balcony doors, and he could see groves of trees in the garden. In the middle of the room three men stood talking. Amaro stepped forward and stammered:

'F-forgive me for intruding . . .'

A tall man, with a grizzled moustache and gold-rimmed spectacles, turned round, surprised, a cigar in one corner of his mouth and his hands in his pockets. It was the Count.

'I'm Amaro . . .'

'Ah,' said the Count, 'Father Amaro! I've heard all about you! Please, come in . . . My wife spoke to me about you. Please . . .'

And addressing a short, stout, almost bald man wearing white trousers that were too short for him, he said:

'This is the gentleman I was telling you about.' He turned to Amaro. 'This is the minister.'

Amaro bowed humbly.

'Father Amaro,' the Count went on, 'grew up in my mother-in-law's house. Indeed, I believe he was born there . . .'

'That is so, Count,' said Amaro, who remained at a distance, his parasol in his hand.

'My mother-in-law, who was very devout and a great lady – of a sort one simply doesn't find nowadays – made a priest of him. There was even a legacy, I believe . . . Anyway, here he is a parish priest . . . Where exactly, Father Amaro?'

'In Feirão, sir.'

'Feirão?!' said the minister, to whom the name was unfamiliar.

'In the Gralheira mountains,' the man beside him explained. He was a thin man, squeezed into a blue frock coat, and he had very white skin, superb, ink-black sideboards and an admirable head of lustrous, pomaded hair immaculately parted.

'In a word,' concluded the Count, 'ghastly! Up in the mountains, with only the poorest of parishioners, no distractions, terrible weather . . .'

'I've already put in a request for a different parish, sir,' said Amaro timidly.

'Fine, fine,' said the minister. 'We'll sort something out.' And he chewed on his cigar.

'It's only fair,' said the Count, 'indeed, necessary. Young, active men should be assigned to the difficult parishes in the cities. It's obvious. But that's not what happens; for example, near my estate in Alcobaça, there's a gout-ridden old priest, a former seminary teacher, who's a complete imbecile! That's how the people come to lose their faith.'

'Yes, you're right,' said the minister, 'but being placed in a decent parish should, of course, be a reward for good service. There has to be some incentive . . .'

'Absolutely,' replied the Count, 'but professional service to the Church, not service to the government.'

The man with the superb black sideboards seemed about to object.

'Don't you agree?' the Count asked him.

'I have the greatest respect for your opinion, of course, but if I may . . . I believe that the priests in the city are of great service to us in electoral crises. Of great service!'

'Well, yes, but . . .'

'Look, sir,' the man went on, the bit between his teeth now. 'You just have to look at Tomar. Why did we lose there? Purely and simply because of the attitude of the priests.'

The Count responded:

'Forgive me, but it shouldn't be like that. Religion and the clergy are not electoral agents.'

'Forgive me . . .' the other man began.

The Count stopped him with a firm gesture; then speaking slowly and gravely, using words imbued with an authority backed up by vast knowledge, he said:

'Religion can and should help established governments, operating, shall we say, as a brake . . .'

'Exactly, exactly,' drawled the minister, spitting out bits of chewed cigar end.

'But to descend into intrigue,' continued the Count in measured tones, 'into imbroglios . . . Forgive me, my dear friend, but that is not the act of a Christian.'

'But I'm a Christian, Count!' exclaimed the man with the superb sideboards. 'A real Christian, but I am also a liberal.

And, as I understand it, the representative government . . . yes . . . given the most solid guarantees of . . .'

'Ah,' broke in the Count, 'but do you know the effect of that? It discredits the clergy and it discredits politics.'

'But surely the majority vote is a sacred principle,' bellowed the man with the sideboards, his face scarlet, emphasising the word 'sacred'.

'It's a perfectly respectable one.'

'Now really, sir, really!

Father Amaro was listening, frozen to the spot.

'My wife probably wants to see you,' said the Count. And going over to a portière, which he lifted, he said: 'Please, go in. Joana, it's Father Amaro!'

Amaro went into another room, this time lined with satiny white paper, with furniture upholstered in a pale fabric. In the window bays, between long, milk-white damask curtains, caught back almost at floor-level by silk ties, stood white pots containing slender bushes with delicate, flowerless foliage. The cool, subdued lighting lent a cloud-like tone to all these various whites. A parrot was perched on one black foot on the back of a chair, its body contorted as, with the other foot, it scratched its green head in leisurely fashion. Embarrassed, Amaro bowed in the direction of the sofa where he could make out the blonde froth of curls crowning the Countess' head and the glint of her gold-rimmed spectacles. A plump young man with chubby cheeks was sitting before her on a low chair, resting his elbows on his spread knees, and absorbed in swinging a tortoise-shell pince-nez back and forth like a pendulum. The Countess had a small dog on her lap and was smoothing the dog's cotton-white coat with one thin, fine, veined hand.

'How are you, Father Amaro?' The dog growled. 'Stop it, Jewel . . . As you see, I've already spoken on your behalf. Stop it, Jewel . . . The minister is next door.'

'Yes, Senhora,' said Amaro, still standing.

'Sit down here, Father Amaro.'

Amaro sat on the edge of an armchair, his parasol still in his hand, and only then did he notice a tall woman standing by the piano, talking to a blond young man.

'And what have you been up to, Father Amaro?' asked the Countess. 'Tell me, how is your sister?'

'She lives in Coimbra now; she's married.'

'Ah, married!' said the Countess, fiddling with the rings on her fingers.

There was a silence. Amaro, eyes downcast, feeling awkward and nervous, kept stroking his lips with his fingers.

'Has Father Liset gone abroad?' he asked.

'Yes, he's in Nantes. His sister is dying,' said the Countess. 'But he's the same as always, so kind and gentle, the very soul of virtue!'

'I prefer Father Félix,' said the fat young man, stretching his legs.

'Don't say such things, cousin! Heavens! And Father Liset is so worthy of respect. Besides there are other, kinder ways of putting these things. And he's so tender-hearted . . .'

'Yes, but Father Félix . . .'

'Now, stop it! Father Félix is a man of great virtue, granted, but Father Liset's sense of religion is somehow . . . ,' with a delicate gesture she sought the right word, 'finer, more distinguished. And he mixes with very different people.' Then, smiling at Amaro: 'Don't you agree?'

Amaro did not know Father Félix and could not remember Father Liset.

'Father Liset must be getting on a bit now,' he said in order to say something.

'Do you think so?' asked the Countess. 'But he's so well-preserved. And such vivacity and enthusiasm! He's really quite special.' And turning to the woman standing by the piano, she said: 'Don't you think so, Teresa?'

'Just a moment,' replied Teresa, absorbed in what she was doing.

Amaro looked at her properly for the first time. She seemed to him like a queen or a goddess, so tall and strong, with magnificent shoulders and bosom; her slightly wavy, dark hair was in stark contrast to her pale, aquiline face, reminiscent of Marie Antoinette's imposing profile; her black, short-sleeved dress with its square neckline, and the long train decorated with black lace broke up the monotonous whiteness of the room; her neck and arms were covered by black gauze through which one could glimpse the whiteness of her flesh; her figure had the firmness of ancient marble statues, but was alive with the warmth of rich blood.

She was smiling and talking softly in a harsh-sounding language that Amaro could not understand, all the time opening and closing her black fan, and the handsome, blond young man wearing a monocle was listening to her, twirling one end of his slender moustache.

'Were your parishioners terribly devout, Father Amaro?' the Countess asked.

'Oh, yes, excellent people.'

'Of course, nowadays, it's only in the villages that one finds real faith,' she said piously. She complained about having to live in the city, a slave to luxury; she wished she could spend all her time on her estate in Carcavelos, praying in the old chapel and chatting to the good people of the village. Her voice grew tender.

The chubby young man laughed:

'Oh, come off it, cousin!' If he was obliged to hear mass in a little village chapel, he would probably lose his faith altogether. He simply couldn't understand the point of religion without music. Was it possible to have a religious celebration without someone with a really good contralto voice?

'Well, it's certainly more enjoyable,' said Amaro.

'Of course it is. It's entirely different. It has *cachet*! Cousin, do you remember that tenor . . . what was his name? Vidalti. Do you remember Vidalti on Maunday Thursday, in the chapel at the English College, singing the *Tantum ergo*?'

'I preferred him in *The Masked Ball*,' said the Countess.

'Oh, really, cousin!'

The blond young man came over and shook the Countess' hand, speaking in a low voice and smiling. Amaro admired his noble mien and his gentle blue eyes; he noticed that he had dropped a glove and humbly picked it up for him. When the young man left, Teresa, having first walked unhurriedly over to the window to gaze out at the street, sat down on a love seat with an abandon that only emphasised the magnificent sculptural forms of her body; then, turning languidly to the plump young man, she said:

'Shall we go, João?'

The Countess said:

'Father Amaro was brought up with me in Benfica, you know.'

Amaro blushed; he felt Teresa turn on him her beautiful, dark, glittering eyes, like black satin covered with water.

'And are you living outside Lisbon now?' she asked, yawning slightly.

'Yes, Senhora, I arrived a few days ago.'

'In a village?' she asked, slowly opening and closing her fan.

Amaro saw precious stones glinting on her slender fingers; stroking the handle of his parasol, he said:

'In the mountains, Senhora.'

'Can you imagine anything more dreadful,' said the Countess. 'Constant snow, no roof on the church apparently, with only shepherds as parishioners. Awful! I've asked the minister if we can get him moved. You ask him too . . .'

'Ask him what?' said Teresa.

The Countess explained that Amaro had applied for a better parish. She spoke about her mother and how fond she had been of Amaro . . .

'She just adored him. Now what was it she used to call you . . . can you remember?'

'I don't know, Senhora.'

'Brother Malaria! Isn't that funny? Because Senhor Amaro was always so pale and spent all his time in the chapel . . .'

But Teresa, addressing the Countess, said:

'Do you know who this gentleman looks like?'

The Countess studied him; the plump young man held the pince-nez to his eyes.

'Doesn't he look like that pianist we saw last year?' Teresa went on. 'I can't quite remember his name . . .'

'Oh, I know, Jalette,' said the Countess. 'Yes, he does slightly. Not his hair though.'

'Of course not his hair, the pianist didn't have a tonsure!'

Amaro blushed scarlet. Teresa got to her feet and, dragging her magnificent train behind her, went over and sat down at the piano.

'Do you read music?' she asked, turning to Amaro.

'We learn music in the seminary, Senhora.'

She ran her hand over the low notes and then played the phrase from *Rigoletto*, reminiscent of a Mozart minuet, sung by Francis I, who is saying goodbye to Madame de Crécy after the party in the first act, and whose desolate rhythms express the limitless sadness of dying love and of arms disentwining in a final, supreme farewell.

Amaro was captivated. That luxurious, cloud-white room, the passionate piano music, Teresa's neck and throat which he could see beneath the black transparency of the gauze, the thick, goddess-like plaits of her hair, the peaceful groves of trees in the noble garden all vaguely suggested to him the kind of superior existence led by characters in novels, a life of exquisite carpets, upholstered carriages, operatic arias, tasteful melancholy and love affairs full of rare pleasures. Sinking back into the softness of the armchair, listening to the aristocratically plangent music, he thought of his aunt's dining room and its pervasive smell of fried onions; and he felt like a beggar who, given some delicious soup, is too frightened to taste and enjoy it, thinking that soon he will have to return to his usual harsh diet of stale crusts of bread and the dust of the roads.

Meanwhile, Teresa, abruptly changing tunes, began singing that old English aria of Haydn's that speaks so eloquently of the sadness of separation:

> The village seems asleep or dead
> Now Lubin is away! . . .

'Bravo! Bravo!' exclaimed the Minister of Justice, who appeared at the door, gently clapping his hands. 'Excellent! Absolutely delightful!'

'I have a favour to ask of you, Senhor Correia,' said Teresa, standing up.

The Minister hurried gallantly to her side.

'What is it, what is it?'

The Count and the man with the magnificent sideboards had also come into the room still arguing.

'Joana and I have a favour to ask,' said Teresa to the Minister.

'I've already asked him, twice in fact!' said the Countess.

'But, my dear ladies,' said the Minister, making himself comfortable in a chair, legs outstretched, a satisfied look on his face, 'what is all this about? Is it some very serious matter? I promise most solemnly to . . .'

'Good,' said Teresa, tapping him on the arm with her fan. 'Now where is there a good vacancy for a parish priest?'

'Ah,' said the Minister, realising what she meant and looking at Amaro, who bowed his shoulders and blushed.

The man with the sideboards, who was still standing up, gravely twirling the pendants on his watch chain, stepped forward, bursting with information.

'The best current vacancy, Senhora, is in Leiria, district capital and bishop's see.'

'Leiria?' said Teresa. 'Oh, I know, aren't there some ruins there?'

'A castle, Senhora, built by Dom Dinis.'

'Leiria would be excellent.'

'Forgive me, Senhora,' said the Minister, 'but Leiria is a bishop's see, a city . . . and Father Amaro is still a very young cleric . . .'

'But you're very young too, Senhor Correia,' exclaimed Teresa.

The Minister smiled and bowed.

'Say something,' said the Countess to her husband, who was tenderly scratching the parrot's head.

'What's the point, poor Correia has been routed! Cousin Teresa called him "young"'.

'I say,' said the Minister. 'It's not such an exaggeration, I'm not exactly ancient.'

'You liar!' cried the Count. 'You were already plotting with the best of them in 1820!'

'That was my father, you wretch!'

Everyone laughed

'Right, Senhor Correia,' said Teresa, 'it's all settled then. Father Amaro will go to Leiria.'

'All right, all right, I give in,' sighed the Minister wearily. 'But this is an abuse of power.'

'Thank you,' said Teresa, holding out her hand to him.

'You seem different today,' said the Minister, looking at her hard.

'I'm just happy,' she replied. She looked at the floor for a moment, distracted, lightly tapping her silk dress, then she got suddenly to her feet, went over to the piano and began singing the same sweet English aria:

> The village seems asleep or dead
> Now Lubin is away . . .

Meanwhile, the Count had gone over to Amaro, who stood up.

'That's settled then,' the Count said. 'Correia will sort things out with the Bishop. You'll receive your appointment as parish priest in a week's time. So you needn't worry about it any more.'

Amaro bowed and went humbly over to the Minister, who was standing by the piano.

'Minister, I would just like to thank you . . .'

'Oh don't thank me, thank the Countess,' said the Minister, smiling.

'Senhora, thank you,' he said to the Countess, bowing low.

'Oh, it's Teresa you should thank. She's obviously trying to buy indulgences.'

'Senhora . . .' he started saying to Teresa.

'Remember me in your prayers, Father Amaro,' she said and continued singing in her mournful voice of how sad the village was when Lubin was away.

A week later, Amaro received confirmation of his nomination to the post. But he never forgot that morning in the house of the Condessa de Ribamar – the Minister with his too-short trousers, comfortably ensconced in the armchair, promising him the job; the bright, calm light of the garden glimpsed through the window; the tall, blond young man who kept saying 'Yes' . . . He could not get that sad aria from *Rigoletto* out of his head and he was pursued by the image of Teresa's white arms beneath the black gauze. Instinctively he imagined those arms slowly, slowly encircling the blond man's elegant neck; he hated him then, as well as the barbarous tongue he spoke and the heretical land he came from, and his temples throbbed with the idea that one day he might have to confess that divine woman and, in the dark intimacy of the confessional, feel her black silk dress brush against his old lustrine cassock.

One day, at dawn, after his aunt had repeatedly embraced him, he left for Santa Apolónia station, with a Galician porter to carry his trunk. Dawn was breaking. The city was silent, and the streetlamps were going out. Sometimes a cart would rattle by over the cobbles; the streets seemed to him interminable; villagers from outside Lisbon were beginning to arrive, muddy-booted legs joggling on either side of their donkey mounts; here and there shrill voices selling newspapers rang out; and the young lads employed by theatres were rushing around with their pots of glue, sticking up posters on street corners.

When he reached the station, the bright sun was tinging with orange the sky behind the mountains on the far side of the river; the river lay unmoving, veined with dull, steel-grey currents, and, on it, the occasional sailing barge drifted by, slow and white.

IV

The following day, the whole town was talking about the arrival of the new parish priest, and everyone knew that he had brought with him a tin trunk, that he was tall and thin, and that he addressed Canon Dias as 'Master'.

São Joaneira's closest friends, Dona Maria da Assunção and the Gansoso sisters, had all gone to her house first thing in the morning 'to get all the details . . .' It was nine o'clock; Amaro had already gone out with Canon Dias. São Joaneira, looking radiant and full of self-importance, received them at the top of the stairs, still in her morning garb, with her sleeves rolled up, and she immediately launched into an animated account of the priest's arrival, his exquisite manners, what he had said . . .

'Just come downstairs with me and you can see for yourselves.'

She showed them Amaro's room, the tin trunk, the shelf she had put up for his books.

'Oh, very nice,' said the old ladies, 'very nice indeed,' as they walked slowly about the room as respectfully as if they were in church.

'Lovely overcoat!' remarked Dona Joaquina Gansoso, stroking the edging of the coat where it hung on the stand. 'I bet that cost a pretty penny.'

'And he's got very good quality underwear!' said São Joaneira, lifting the lid of the trunk.

The group of old ladies peered in admiringly.

'I'm so pleased that he's a young man,' said Dona Maria da Assunção piously.

'Oh, yes, so am I,' said Dona Joaquina Gansoso authoritatively. 'Being in the middle of your confession and seeing the dewdrop on the priest's nose after he's taken a pinch of snuff, the way you did with Raposo, was just awful! It's enough to make an unbeliever of you! And as for that brute José Miguéis . . . No, give me a young man every time!'

São Joaneira went on to show them Amaro's other marvels – a crucifix still wrapped up in a sheet of old newspaper and an album of photographs, the first of which showed the Pope blessing the Christian world. They all went into ecstasies over this.

'Oh, isn't he a love,' they said.

As they left, they all kissed São Joaneira fervently and congratulated her because, by having the new parish priest as lodger, she had taken on an almost ecclesiastical authority.

'Come back tonight,' she called down from the top of the stairs.

'Oh, we will!' called back Dona Maria da Assunção, who was already at the street door, doing up her cape. 'Then we can have a good look at him!'

Libaninho, the most active male devotee of the church in Leiria, arrived at midday. He ran up the stairs, calling out in his high voice:

'São Joaneira!'

'Come up, Libaninho, come up,' she said from her seat by the window, where she was sitting sewing.

'So the new parish priest has come, has he?' asked Libaninho as his fat, lemon-yellow face and gleaming bald pate appeared round the dining-room door; then he minced over to her, swaying his hips.

'So what's he like, then? Does he seem nice?'

São Joaneira launched again into her glorification of Amaro: his youth, his pious air, the whiteness of his teeth . . .

'Bless him!' Libaninho said, almost drooling with devout tenderness. But he couldn't stay, he had to get back to the office. 'Goodbye, my dear, goodbye!' And he patted São Joaneira's shoulder with one plump hand. 'You're looking lovelier each day, you know. And I said that Hail Mary for you yesterday, just as you asked me to, so don't say I never think of you.'

The maid had come into the room.

'Hello, Ruça! Oh, dear, you are thin. Try praying to Our Lady Mother of Mankind!' And glimpsing Amélia through the half-open door of her room: 'Don't you look a picture,

Amélia! You're the girl to show me the path to salvation all right!'

Then off he bustled, loudly clearing his throat, and scuttled down the stairs, trilling:

'Bye now, girls! Bye!'

'Libaninho, are you coming tonight?'

'Oh, I can't, my dear, I can't!' And his voice almost broke with sadness. 'Tomorrow is St Barbara's day. I have six Our Fathers to say.'

Amaro had gone to visit the precentor with Canon Dias and had given him a letter of recommendation from the Conde de Ribamar.

'Oh, I knew the Count well,' said the precentor. 'We met in '46, in Oporto. We're old friends. I was the priest at Santo Ildefonso, oh, years ago now.'

And leaning back in his old damask armchair, he spoke with satisfaction of his life: he told anecdotes about the Junta, discussed the men of the time, imitated their voices (this was one of his specialities), their tics, their eccentricities, especially Manuel Passos, whom he described strolling in the Praça Nova, in a long, grey overcoat and a broad-brimmed hat, declaring: 'Courage, fellow patriots! Xavier won't give in!'

The ecclesiastical gentlemen of the cathedral chapter roared with laughter. There was an atmosphere of great cordiality. Amaro left feeling very pleased.

Afterwards, he dined at Canon Dias' house, and they went for a stroll together along the road to Marrazes. A soft, tenuous light spread over the countryside; on the hills, in the blue air, there was a sense of repose, of sweet tranquillity; whitish smoke rose up from the hamlets, and one could hear the melancholy sound of bells as the animals wended their way back to the farms. Amaro paused by the bridge and, looking around at the pleasant landscape, he said:

'I think I'll get on very well here!'

'Superbly I should say,' said the Canon, taking a pinch of snuff.

It was eight o'clock by the time they reached São Joaneira's house.

All her old friends were gathered in the dining room. Amélia was sitting sewing beside the oil lamp.

Dona Maria da Assunção had dressed in her Sunday black silk; she was wearing a reddish-blonde wig covered in ornamental black lace; her bony, mittened hands, which lay solemnly on her lap, glittered with rings; a thick gold chain made of filigree hung from the brooch at her neck down to her waist. She was sitting very stiff and erect, her head slightly tilted, her gold-rimmed spectacles perched on her rather equine nose; she had a large, hairy mole on her chin, and whenever she spoke of religious feelings or of miracles she would make an odd movement with her neck and then open her mouth in a silent smile that revealed enormous, greenish teeth, like wedges hammered into her gums. She was a wealthy widow and suffered from chronic catarrh.

'This is our new parish priest, Dona Maria,' São Joaneira said.

Dona Maria rose to her feet and, much moved, performed a shallow curtsey with just a slight movement of her hips.

'And these are the Misses Gansoso of whom I'm sure you've heard,' said São Joaneira to Amaro.

Amaro bowed shyly. There were two Gansoso sisters. They were thought to be wealthy, but often took in lodgers. The older sister, Dona Joaquina Gansoso, was a scrawny woman with a very large, elongated head, lively eyes, turned-up nose and thin lips. Wrapped in her shawl, sitting very upright, her arms folded, she talked incessantly in a shrill, domineering voice and was always full of opinions. She spoke disparagingly of men and devoted herself entirely to the Church.

Her sister, Dona Ana, was extremely deaf. She never spoke and would sit with eyes downcast, her hands in her lap, calmly twiddling her thumbs. She was a stout woman and always wore the same black dress with yellow stripes, edged at the neck with ermine; she dozed all evening and only occasionally made her presence felt with a sudden heavy sigh. It was said that she nursed a fatal passion for the post master. Everyone pitied her, but admired her skill in cutting up paper to make boxes for sweets.

Dona Josefa, Canon Dias' sister, was also there. Her nickname was 'the dried chestnut'. She was a shrivelled, hunched creature, with a sibilant voice and wrinkled skin the colour of cider; twitching with nervous rage, her little eyes ever ablaze with anger, she lived in a perpetual state of irritation, full to the brim with bile. She was much feared. Dr Godinho referred to her mischievously as Leiria's Central Station of gossip.

'Did you go for a long walk, Father?' she immediately asked, drawing herself up very straight.

'We went almost to the end of the Marrazes road,' said Canon Dias, sitting down heavily behind São Joaneira.

'It's so pretty there, don't you think, Father?' said Dona Joaquina Gansoso.

'Oh, very.'

They spoke of the lovely countryside around Leiria, of the excellent views; Dona Josefa particularly enjoyed the riverside walk; she had even heard tell that there was nothing to compare with it in Lisbon itself. Dona Joaquina Gansoso preferred the Church of the Incarnation up the hill.

'You get a wonderful view from there.'

Amélia said, smiling:

'I really love that part near the bridge, under the willows.' And biting through the thread with which she was sewing, she added: 'It's so sad.'

Amaro looked at her then for the first time. She was wearing a blue dress that fitted closely over her lovely bosom; her plump, white throat emerged from a turn-down collar; her white teeth gleamed between fresh, red lips; and it seemed to Amaro that a fine down created a soft, subtle shadow at the corners of her mouth.

There was a brief silence. Canon Dias' eyelids were already growing heavy, his mouth beginning to gape.

'What can have happened to Father Brito?' asked Dona Joaquina Gansoso.

'The poor man's probably got a migraine,' remarked Dona Maria da Assunção pityingly.

A young man standing by the sideboard said:

'I saw him out riding today, heading for Barrosa.'

'Well, frankly,' said the Canon's sister, Dona Josefa Dias, sourly, 'it's a miracle you noticed.'

'Why do you say that, Senhora?' he said, getting up and going over to the old ladies.

He was tall and dressed all in black; standing out against the white skin of his regular, rather weary features was a short, very dark moustache, whose drooping ends he was in the habit of chewing.

'"Why?" he asks!' exclaimed Dona Josefa Dias. 'You never even take off your hat to him!'

'Me?'

'He told me so himself,' she said in a cutting voice, then added: 'Father, Senhor João Eduardo here needs setting on the right path.' And she gave a malicious laugh.

'I don't happen to think I'm on the wrong path,' João Eduardo said, laughing, his hands in his pockets. And he kept glancing over at Amélia.

'Oh, very funny!' said Dona Joaquina Gansoso. 'Well, you're certainly not going to get into Heaven after what you said this evening about the Holy Woman of Arregaça!'

'Really!' roared the Canon's sister, turning on João Eduardo. 'And what did you have to say about her, pray? You don't perhaps think she's an impostor, do you?'

'Oh, good heavens!' said Dona Maria da Assunção, clutching her hands and staring at João Eduardo in pious horror. 'Did he say that? Good heavens!'

'No,' said the Canon gravely; he had woken up and was unfurling his red handkerchief. 'João Eduardo would never say such a thing.'

Amaro asked:

'Who is the Holy Woman of Arregaça?'

'You mean you haven't heard of her, Father?' exclaimed an astonished Dona Maria da Assunção.

'You must have,' declared Dona Josefa Dias firmly. 'They say the newspapers in Lisbon are full of it.'

'It certainly is a pretty extraordinary case,' said the Canon in a low voice.

São Joaneira interrupted her knitting, took off her spectacles and said:

'Oh, Father, you just can't imagine! It's the miracle of miracles!'

'Oh, it is, it is!' they all agreed.

There was a moment of devout silence.

'But what is it?' asked Amaro, filled with curiosity.

'You see, Father,' began Dona Joaquina Gansoso, straightening her shawl and speaking in solemn tones, 'the Holy Woman lives in a neighbouring parish and has spent the last twenty years in bed . . .'

'Twenty-five,' Dona Maria da Assunção corrected her quietly, tapping her on the arm with her fan.

'Twenty-five? I heard the precentor say it was twenty.'

'No, it's twenty-five,' affirmed São Joaneira, 'twenty-five.'

And the Canon agreed, nodding gravely.

'She's completely paralysed, Father,' the Canon's sister said, eager to join in. 'And she looks like a ghost! Her arms are this thin,' and she held up her little finger, 'and to hear her speak you have to put your ear right up against her mouth.'

'It's only by the grace of God that she's still here,' said Dona Maria da Assunção mournfully. 'Poor woman! It makes you think . . .'

Amongst the old women an emotion-filled silence fell. João Eduardo, who was standing behind them, hands in pockets, was smiling and chewing his moustache. He said:

'According to the doctors, Father, she suffers from some sort of nervous disease.'

The irreverence of this remark caused a scandal amongst the devotees, and Dona Maria da Assunção took the precautionary measure of making the sign of the cross.

'Merciful God!' boomed Dona Josefa Dias, 'You may say that in front of anyone else, but not in front of me. I consider it an insult.'

'He might be struck down by a thunderbolt,' muttered a terrified Dona Maria da Assunção.

'Absolutely' exclaimed Dona Josefa Dias, ' you are a man without religion and with no respect for holy things.' Then turning to Amélia, she said sourly: 'I certainly wouldn't want him to marry a daughter of mine!'

Amélia reddened, and João Eduardo, who also turned red, bowed sarcastically and said:

'I am merely repeating what the doctors say. As for the rest, believe me, I have absolutely no ambitions to marry anyone in your family. Not even you, Dona Josefa!'

The Canon gave an embarrassed laugh.

'How dare you!' she spluttered.

'But what does the Holy Woman do?' asked Father Amaro, trying to restore peace.

'Everything, Father,' said Dona Joaquina Gansoso. 'She never leaves her bed and she has prayers for every occasion; anyone she prays for receives the grace of Our Lord; people only have to touch her and they are cured. And when she takes communion, she starts to rise up until she's floating in the air, with her eyes lifted up to heaven; it's quite alarming really.'

But at that moment, a voice at the door called out:

'Hello, everybody! What's all this then?'

The voice belonged to an extremely tall, sallow youth with sunken cheeks, a brush of tangled hair and a Quixotic moustache; when he laughed, he looked as if he had a shadow in his mouth because he had lost nearly all his front teeth; and there was a lingering look of sentimentality in his sunken eyes, which were surrounded by dark circles. He was carrying a guitar.

'So how are you?' everyone asked.

'Pretty bad,' he said glumly, sitting down. 'I've still got pains in my chest and a slight cough.'

'The cod liver oil didn't help then?'

'No,' he said disconsolately.

'A trip to Madeira, that's what you need,' said Dona Joaquina Gansoso authoritatively.

He laughed with sudden hilarity.

'A trip to Madeira? That's a good one! You're a real card, Dona Joaquina! A poor clerk earning eighteen *vinténs* a day, with a wife and four children to keep, going on a trip to Madeira!'

'And how is Joanita?'

'Not too bad, poor thing. She's got her health, thank God! She's nice and plump and always has a good appetite. It's my two youngest who are ill, and to make matters worse, the maid just took to her bed too. All one can do is have patience!' He shrugged.

Then turning to São Joaneira and patting her knee, he said:

'And how's our Mother Abbess today?'

Everyone laughed, and Dona Joaquina Gansoso explained to Amaro that the young man, Artur Couceiro, was most amusing and had a beautiful singing voice. He was the best singer of popular songs in Leiria.

At that point, Ruça came in with the tea, and São Joaneira, holding the teapot high above the cups to pour, was saying:

'Come along, ladies, come along. This is really excellent tea. I bought it in Sousa's shop . . .'

And Artur offered around the sugar with his usual joke:

'Salt anyone?'

The old ladies took small sips from their saucers, carefully selected a slice of buttered toast and sat down, chewing thoughtfully; and because of the risk of staining from dripping butter and tea, they prudently placed their handkerchiefs on their laps.

'Would you like a cake, Father?' asked Amélia, holding out the plate to him. 'They're fresh today from Encarnação.'

'Thank you.'

'Have a piece of angel cake.'

'Well, if it's angel cake, I will,' he said, beaming. And as he picked up the slice with the tips of his fingers, he looked up at her.

Artur usually sang for them after tea. On the piano, a candle illuminated the sheet music, and as soon as Ruça had cleared away the tea things, Amélia sat down and ran her fingers over the yellow keys.

'So what is it to be today?' asked Artur.

Everyone shouted out their requests:

"The Warrior", "The Wedding at the Graveside", "The Unbeliever", "Never more"!

From his corner, Canon Dias said dully:

'Couceiro, give us "Naughty Uncle Cosme"!

The women all cried out reprovingly:

'Honestly! Really, Canon! What an idea!'

And Dona Joaquina Gansoso declared:

'Certainly not! Give us something with real feeling so that Father Amaro can get an idea of your singing.'

'Yes, yes,' they all cried, 'something with real feeling, Artur!'

Artur cleared his throat, adopted a look of great sorrow and sang dolefully:

Farewell, my angel, I leave without you!

It was 'The Farewell', a song from the romantic days of 1851. It spoke of a final goodbye, in a wood, on a pale autumn afternoon; then, the solitary reprobate, who had inspired a fateful love, wandered, with windswept hair, by the sea; there was a forgotten grave in a distant valley, over which pale virgins wept in the moonlight.

'Lovely, absolutely lovely,' they all murmured.

Artur was singing tenderly, his gaze abstracted; however, in the intervals, while the piano played on, he would smile at those around him and in his shadowy mouth one could see the remains of rotten teeth. Carried away by that morbid, sentimental melody, Father Amaro was standing by the window, smoking and studying Amélia: the light traced a luminous line around her delicate profile; he could see the harmonious curve of her breast; and he watched the gentle rise and fall of her long-lashed lids as her eyes went back and forth from the music to the keyboard. João Eduardo, standing beside her, was turning the pages for her.

But Artur, one hand on his chest, the other raised in the air, in a gesture of utter desolation, was singing the final verse:

> And from this wretched life I will one day
> Find rest in the darkness of the grave!

'Bravo! Bravo!' they all exclaimed.

And Canon Dias said quietly to Amaro:

'No one can touch him when it comes to love songs.' Then he yawned loudly. 'You know, that squid we had for lunch has been repeating on me all evening.'

But it was time for a game of lotto. Everyone chose their usual cards, and Dona Josefa Dias, her greedy eyes glinting, was already rattling the big bag of numbers.

'Sit down here, Father,' said Amélia.

It was a seat next to her. He hesitated, but the others had all moved up to make room, and so he sat down, blushing slightly and shyly adjusting his clerical collar.

A heavy silence fell; then, in a calm voice, the Canon began drawing the numbers. Dona Ana Gansoso was dozing in her corner, snoring quietly.

The light from the lamp fell directly on the table, so that all their heads were in darkness; and the bright light falling on the dark cloth emphasised the cards blackened with use and the bony, claw-like hands of the old ladies, fiddling with their glass counters. On the open piano the candle was burning down with a tall, straight flame.

The Canon growled out the numbers, using the venerable, traditional calls:

'Number one, all alone, thirty-three, all the threes . . .'

'I need twenty-one,' said a voice.

'I've got thirty-three,' gloated someone else.

And the Canon's sister said urgently:

'Mix the numbers up, brother, go on!'

'And bring me that forty-seven, even if you have to drag it out of there,' said Artur Couceiro, his head resting on his hands.

In the end, the Canon won. And Amélia, looking round the room, said:

'Aren't you playing, João Eduardo? Where are you?'

João Eduardo emerged from behind the curtain at the window.

'Have a card, go on, play.'

'And you might as well collect everyone's money while you're on your feet,' said São Joaneira. 'You can be the banker!'

João Eduardo went round with a saucer. There were ten *réis* missing when he had finished.

'I've put my money in!' everyone exclaimed excitedly.

It turned out to be the Canon's sister who had not touched her little pile of coins. Bowing, João Eduardo said:

'I don't believe Dona Josefa has put her money in yet.'

'Me?' she shouted, furious. 'Well, really! I was the first. Honestly! I put in two five-*réis* coins. The cheek of the man!'

'I see,' he said. 'Oh, well, it must have been me then. There we are.' And he muttered to himself: 'Hypocritical old thief!'

And the Canon's sister was meanwhile whispering to Dona Maria da Assunção:

'He wanted to see if he could get away with it, the rascal. No fear of God, that's his problem.'

'The only person who isn't happy is Father Amaro,' they observed.

Amaro smiled. He was tired and distracted; sometimes he even forgot to mark his card, and Amélia would say to him, touching his elbow:

'You haven't marked your card, Father.'

They had both had a three, and she had beaten him; now they both needed a thirty-six in order to win.

Everyone in the group noticed.

'Now let's see if they both win together,' said Dona Maria da Assunção, gazing at them adoringly.

But thirty-six was not called; other people had other blanks to fill; Amélia was afraid that the winner would be Dona Joaquina Gansoso, who kept fidgeting on her chair, demanding a forty-eight. Amaro was laughing, drawn in despite himself.

The Canon drew out the numbers with mischievous slowness.

'Oh come on, Canon, faster!' they kept telling him.

Amélia, leaning over her card, her eyes shining, murmured:

'I'd give anything for the thirty-six to be called.'

'Really? Well, there it is . . . number thirty-six!' said the Canon.

'We won!' she cried triumphantly, and picking up Amaro's card and hers, she showed them to the others, proud and very flushed, so that they could check the cards.

'God bless you both,' said the Canon jovially, emptying out the saucerful of coins in front of them.

'It's like a miracle,' said Dona Maria da Assunção piously.

But it had struck eleven o'clock, and after that final triumph, the old ladies began putting on their shawls again. Amélia sat down at the piano, quietly playing a polka. João Eduardo went over to her and said in a low voice:

'Well, congratulations on winning at lotto with the parish priest. *Such* excitement!' And before she could reply, he said an abrupt 'goodnight', haughtily wrapping his cloak around him.

Ruça lit the way. The old ladies, well wrapped up, went down the stairs, bleating out their 'goodnights'. Artur was strumming his guitar and softly singing 'The Unbeliever'.

Amaro went to his room and began reading his breviary, but he grew distracted, thinking about the old ladies, Artur's rotten teeth and, above all, Amélia's profile. As he sat on the edge of the bed, his breviary open, staring at the lamp, he could see her hair, her small hands with their rather dark fingers bearing the marks of needle-pricks, the charming down on her upper lip . . .

His head felt heavy after lunch at the Canon's and after the monotonous game of lotto, and he felt thirsty too after the squid they had eaten and the port they had drunk. He wanted some water, but there was none in his room. He remembered then that in the dining room there was a jug containing good, cool water from the Morenal spring. He put on his slippers, picked up the candlestick and went slowly up the stairs. There was a light on in the room, but the door curtain was drawn: he lifted it, but immediately stepped back with a sharp intake of breath. He had caught a glimpse of Amélia in a white petticoat, unfastening her corset; she was standing by the lamp, and the short sleeves and low neckline of her blouse revealed her white arms and her delicious bosom. She uttered a cry and ran into her room.

Amaro stood stock still, beads of sweat on his forehead. They might think he had done this on purpose. Indignant words would doubtless emerge from behind the curtain, which was still swaying angrily.

But Amélia's voice asked calmly from within:

'What did you want, Father?'

'I just came up to get some water . . .' he stammered.

'That Ruça, honestly! She's so forgetful. I'm sorry, Father, really I am. There's a water jug just by the table. Have you found it?'

'Yes, yes, I have.'

He went back down the stairs carrying a full glass of water; his hand was shaking and water overflowed onto his fingers.

He went to bed without praying. Later that night, Amélia could hear nervous footsteps walking back and forth: it was Amaro, still in his slippers and with his cape around his shoulders, smoking and pacing excitedly up and down the room.

V

Upstairs, she could not sleep either. On the chest of drawers, in a bowl, the night light was burning down, giving off the foul smell of scorched oil; the whiteness of her discarded petticoats stood out starkly on the floor; and the eyes of the cat, who was equally restless, glinted phosphorescent and green in the darkness of the room.

In the house next door, a child was crying. Amélia could hear the mother rocking the cradle, singing softly:

> Go to sleep, go to sleep, my little man,
> Your mother has gone to the fountain.

It was poor Catarina, who took in ironing, and whom Lieutenant Sousa had left with a babe in arms and pregnant with another in order to go off to Estremoz and get married to someone else. She used to be so pretty, so blonde, and now she was all shrivelled up, nothing but skin and bone.

> Go to sleep, go to sleep, my little man,
> Your mother has gone to the fountain.

Amélia knew that lullaby. When she was seven years old, her mother used to sing it on long winter nights to her little brother, who had died.

She remembered it well. They were living in a different house then, near the Lisbon road; there was a lemon tree outside her window and her mother used to spread little João's nappies on its glossy leaves to dry in the sun. Amélia had never known her father. He had been a soldier and had died young, and her mother still sighed when she spoke of the handsome figure he used to cut in his cavalry uniform. When she was eight years old, she was sent to a teacher. She remembered her so clearly. Her teacher was a plump, white-skinned old lady who had been a cook for the nuns in the Santa Joana convent in Aveiro; she would put on her round glasses and sit by the window sewing, and she was full of stories about convent life: the bad-tempered scribe who was always poking around in her rotten teeth; the lazy, easy-going nun with the strong Minho accent, who was in charge of taking in foundlings; the teacher of plainsong who was a great admirer of the irreverent poet Bocage and who claimed to be descended from the rebellious Távoras; and a nun who had died of love, and whose ghost, on certain nights, would walk the corridors moaning plaintively and calling out: Augusto! Augusto!

Amélia would listen to these stories, enraptured. She was so keen on church ceremonies and saints that her ambition at the time was to be 'a pretty little nun with a very white veil'. Her mother was much visited by priests. The precentor Carvalhosa, a sturdy old man with a nasal voice, who wheezed asthmatically as he climbed the stairs, was a daily visitor, a friend of the family. Amélia referred to him as her godfather. When she returned from her teacher's house, she would always find him there, chatting to her mother in the living room, with his cassock unbuttoned to reveal a long black velvet waistcoat embroidered with yellow flowers. The precentor would ask what she had learned and have her repeat her times table.

There were social gatherings in the evening: Father Valente would come and Canon Cruz, and a little old man with a bald head, a bird-like profile and blue-tinted glasses, who had been a Franciscan friar and whom everyone called Brother André. Her mother's female friends came too and brought their knitting; another visitor was Captain Couceiro, of the infantry, whose fingers were stained black with tobacco and who always brought his guitar with him. At the stroke of nine, however, she was sent to bed, but through a crack in the wall she could see the light and hear the voices; later, a silence would fall, and the Captain, strumming his guitar, would sing a lively Brazilian song, the 'Lundum da Figueira.'

Thus she grew up amongst priests. Some she did not like at all, for example, fat, sweaty Father Valente, with his soft, fleshy hands and small fingernails. He liked her to sit on his lap, where he would stroke her ear, and she could smell his breath which reeked of onions and cigarettes. Her great friend was Canon Cruz, very thin and white-haired, whose collar was always pristine white and whose buckles gleamed. He used to enter the room very slowly, press one hand to his chest and bow, and he spoke in a soft, sibilant voice. By then, she knew the catechism and the doctrine, and for the slightest misdemeanour her teacher would warn her of the punishments meted out by Heaven, so that she came to think of God as a being who dealt out only suffering and death and whom it was necessary to placate by praying and fasting and making novenas and by ingratiating oneself with priests. That is why, if ever she went to bed without saying a Hail Mary, she would perform a penance the following day, fearful lest God should make her ill with a fever or cause her to fall down the stairs.

But the best time of her life was when she began taking music lessons. Her mother had an old piano in one corner of the dining room, which was kept covered up with a green cloth and which was so out of tune that it served instead as a sideboard. Amélia liked to sing as she went about the house, and the precentor appreciated her light, clear voice, and her mother's friends used to say to her:

'You've got a piano, why don't you have someone teach the girl to play? It's always good to have a skill like that. It could prove very useful!'

The precentor knew a good teacher, the former organist at Évora Cathedral, a most unfortunate man whose only daughter, a very pretty girl, had run away to Lisbon with a second lieutenant; two years later, Silvestre da Praça, who often went to Lisbon, had seen her walking down Rua do Norte, wearing a scarlet blouse and with her eyes all made up, arm in arm with an English sailor. The old man had fallen into a great melancholy and into equally great poverty; out of charity, he had been given a post in the archives of the diocesan tribunal. He looked like a sad figure out of some picaresque novel. He was a great beanpole of a man and let his fine, white hair grow down to his shoulders; he had weary, watery eyes, yet there was something very touching about his kindly, resigned smile, and about the skimpy, waist-length, wine-red cape with its astrakhan collar that he wore and in which he always looked so cold. People called him Mr Stork because he was so tall and thin and seemed so solitary. One day, Amélia had called him that to his face, but had immediately bitten her lip, embarrassed.

The old man smiled.

'Go on, call me Mr Stork if you like! What's wrong with the name? After all, I do look like a stork!'

It was winter then. The heavy rains and the southwesterly winds blew ceaselessly, and the harsh weather was an affliction to the poor. Starving families went to the Town Hall to beg for bread. Mr Stork came every day at midday to give her a piano lesson; his blue umbrella left a rivulet of rain down the stairs; he would be shivering with cold, but with his old man's pride, he did his best, when he sat down, to hide his sodden shoes and their flapping soles. What he complained about most was having cold hands, which prevented him from playing properly and, in the office, from writing.

'My fingers go all stiff,' he would say sadly.

But after São Joaneira had paid him for the first month of lessons, the old man turned up looking very pleased and wearing a pair of thick, woollen gloves.

'They look nice and warm, Mr Stork!' said Amélia.

'I bought them with your money, my dear young lady. Now I'm saving up for some woollen socks. God bless you, my dear, God bless you!'

And his eyes filled with tears. Amélia became 'his dear little friend'. He confided in her: he would tell her about his financial problems, about how much he missed his daughter, about his glorious career at Évora Cathedral, when he would accompany the Benediction before the Archbishop himself, resplendent in a scarlet surplice.

Amélia did not forget Mr Stork's woollen socks. She asked the precentor to give him a pair.

'And why should I? Just for your sake?' he said with his loud laugh.

'Yes, for my sake.'

'She doesn't mean it, Precentor!' said São Joaneira. 'The very idea!'

'I do mean it! You will give him a pair, won't you?'

She threw her arms about his neck and smiled sweetly at him.

'You siren!' said the Precentor, laughing. 'The cheek of the girl. She's the very devil. Oh well, there you are.' And he gave her some money to buy the socks.

The following day, she wrapped them up and wrote on the paper in large letters: 'To my dear friend Mr Stork, from his pupil.'

One morning, seeing him looking even paler and gaunter than usual, she said suddenly:

'Mr Stork, how much do they pay you at the office?'

The old man smiled:

'Well, my dear girl, how much do you think? A pittance. Four *vinténs* a day. But Senhor Neto helps me out . . .'

'But is that enough, four *vinténs*?'

'Of course not.'

They heard her mother approaching, and Amélia gravely resumed the air of a student and began practising her scales, looking very serious.

But after that, she so pestered and pleaded with her mother to give Mr Stork lunch and supper on the days that he taught her, that her mother finally gave in. Thus the two of them became close friends. And poor Mr Stork, emerging from cold isolation, took refuge in that unexpected friendship as if in a warm shelter. He found in her the feminine element that all old men love, the soft, caressing timbre of voice and the thoughtfulness of a nurse; he found in her the sole admirer of his music; and she was always interested in his stories of the old days, in his memories of the ancient Cathedral in Évora that he loved so much, and which made him exclaim, whenever he spoke of processions or church celebrations:

'Ah, Évora's the place for that!'

Amélia worked very hard at her playing; it was the best and most precious thing in her life: she could play quadrilles and ancient arias by old composers. Dona Maria da Assunção was surprised that he did not teach her *Il Trovatore*.

'So lovely!' she used to say.

But Mr Stork only knew classical music: Lully's lovely, ingenuous arias, motifs from minuets, and elegant, pious motets from sweet monastery days.

One morning, Mr Stork found Amélia looking very pale and sad. She had been complaining of feeling unwell since the previous evening. It was a very cold, cloudy day. The old man thought it would be best if he left.

'No, no, Mr Stork,' she said, 'play something nice for me.'

He took off his cape, sat down and played a simple, but very sad tune.

'That's beautiful!' said Amélia, standing next to the piano.

And when the old man played the final notes, she asked:

'What is it?'

Mr Stork told her that it was the beginning of a *Meditation* composed by a friend of his who was a friar.

'Poor man,' he said. 'He certainly had his cross to bear.'

Amélia immediately wanted to hear his story, and sitting down on the piano stool, with her shawl wrapped about her, she said:

'Tell me, Mr Stork, tell me!'

As a young man, his friend had fallen passionately in love with a nun; she had died in the convent as a consequence of that unfortunate love affair; and he, out of pain and longing, had become a Franciscan friar . . .

'I can see him now . . .'

'Was he handsome?'

'Indeed he was. A handsome young man in the prime of life . . . One day, he came to see me while I was playing the organ: "What do you think of this?" he said. It was a piece of sheet music. It opened in the key of D minor. He started playing and playing . . . Oh, my dear, what music! But I can't remember the rest!'

And much moved, the old man once again played the plangent notes of that *Meditation* in D minor.

Amélia thought about the story all day. That night she had

a high fever and her sleep was filled with obscure dreams, all dominated by the figure of the Franciscan friar, standing in the shadow of the organ in Évora cathedral. She saw his deep-set eyes shining in his gaunt face, and in the distance, the pale nun, in her white habit, clinging to the black bars of the monastery, her body racked by the sorrows of love. Then, through the cloister came a line of Franciscan friars on their way to the choir. He came last of all, his shoulders stooped, his hood over his face, his sandals scuffing the stone floor, while a great bell sent the death knell ringing out in the cloudy air. Then the scene changed to a vast black sky into which a mystical wind swept up two lovingly entwined souls in monastic garb, and emanating from them, as they turned and turned, was the ineffable sound of insatiable kisses; but they dissolved like mist and, out of the vast darkness, she watched the emergence of a huge blood-red heart, pierced by swords, and the drops of blood falling from the heart filled the sky with scarlet rain.

The next day, her fever had abated. Dr Gouveia reassured São Joaneira:

'It's nothing to worry about, Senhora. She is fifteen, after all. Tomorrow she'll feel a bit sick and dizzy and then that will be that. She'll be a young woman.'

São Joaneira understood what he meant.

'She's a hot-blooded young thing and she'll be a woman of strong passions!' added the old doctor, smiling and taking a pinch of snuff.

Around this time, the precentor, having had his lunchtime bowl of soup, dropped dead of apoplexy. This was a terrible shock for São Joaneira. She spent the next two days weeping and moaning and wandering from room to room in her petticoats, her hair all dishevelled. Dona Maria da Assunção and the Gansoso sisters came to try and calm her down, to ease her pain, and Dona Josefa Dias summed up the feelings of everyone present, saying:

'Don't worry, my dear, you'll soon find another protector.'

The precentor died at the beginning of September. Dona Maria da Assunção, who had a house on the beach at Vieira, suggested that São Joaneira and Amélia go with her to take the waters in order to give São Joaneira a change of scene and a change of air, good, healthy air, and thus dissipate her grief.

'It would be a great kindness on your part,' São Joaneira had said. 'I keep remembering that it was here he used to put his umbrella, and that over there he used to sit watching me sew . . .'

'Now, now, enough of that. Eat and drink, take some sea-water baths, and see how you feel. He was in his sixties, you know.'

'Ah, my dear, it's in times of trouble that one knows who one's friends are.'

Amélia was only fifteen, but she was already tall and shapely. She loved Vieira! She had never seen the sea before and she never tired of sitting on the beach, fascinated by that vast expanse of gentle, blue, sunlit water. Sometimes, the slender thread of smoke from a steamship would cross the horizon; the monotonous, sighing rhythm of the waves lulled her to sleep; and all around her, as far as the eye could see, the sands glittered beneath the navy blue sky.

How well she remembered it! She would get up early in the morning. That was the time for bathing: the canvas tents were lined up along the beach; the ladies sat on deck chairs chatting, their sunshades open; the men, in white shoes, were stretched out on mats, smoking and tracing lines in the sand, while the poet Carlos Alcoforado, terribly tragic and much stared at, would walk gloomily along the seashore, all alone apart from his Newfoundland dog. Amélia would emerge from her tent, wearing her blue flannel bathing suit, a towel over her arm, and shivering with fear and cold; she furtively made the sign of the cross and then, holding the hand of the bathing assistant and slithering on the sand, she would enter the water, wading with difficulty through the greenish waves boiling about her. A wave would rush, foaming, towards her, and she would dive in, only to bob up again, breathless and excited, spitting salt water. But when she came out of the sea, she felt so pleased with herself. With a towel coiled about her head, she would drag herself back to the changing tent, panting and struggling with the weight of her sodden bathing suit, but smiling and exhilarated; and all around her friendly voices would ask:

'What's it like today? A bit chilly, eh?'

Then, in the afternoon, they would go for walks along the beach, collecting shells; they would watch the nets being hauled in and the sardines, seething in their thousands, gleaming on the wet sand; they would gaze on long vistas of sumptuous golden sunsets above the vast expanse of sad sea which sighed and grew dark.

Soon after she arrived, Dona Maria da Assunção had been visited by a young man, the son of a relative of hers, Senhor Brito de Alcobaça. The young man's name was Agostinho, and he was about to start his fifth year at university as a law student. He was a slender youth, who affected a monocle, had a brown moustache and a goatee beard, and wore his long hair combed back. He could recite poetry, play the guitar, recount anecdotes about first-year students and tell jokes, and he was well-known amongst the men in Vieira because 'he knew how to talk to women'.

'He's a rogue that Agostinho,' they would say. 'Always joking with the ladies. He's the life and soul of every party.'

Amélia noticed right from the start that Agostinho's eyes were always fixed on her, like the eyes of a lover. Amélia would blush scarlet and feel her breast swell beneath her dress; she admired him and found him 'very charming'.

One day in Dona Maria da Assunção's house, Agostinho was called upon to recite a poem.

'But, dear ladies, I can't do it to order, you know!' he exclaimed jovially.

'Now, don't play hard to get,' they insisted.

'All right, then, let's not fall out over it.'

'What about "The Jewess",' suggested the tax-collector from Alcobaça.

'"The Jewess?', Agostinho said, 'No, it has to be "The Dark-haired Girl"!' And he looked straight at Amélia. 'It's a poem I wrote yesterday.'

'Fine, agreed!'

'And I'll accompany you,' said a sergeant from the 6th Infantry, picking up a guitar.

A silence fell. Agostinho pushed back his hair, adjusted his monocle, rested both his hands on the back of a chair and, fixing his gaze on Amélia, he began:

> 'To *The Dark-haired Girl* from Leiria.
> Born amongst the green fields
> For which Leiria is so famous,
> Your face, my dear, is fresh as a rose,
> And your name sounds like a mel . . .'

'Excuse me,' exclaimed the tax-collector, 'but Dona Juliana seems to be unwell . . .'

This was the daughter of the clerk of the court from Alcobaça; she had grown suddenly very pale and was slowly sliding off her chair in a swoon, arms hanging loose, chin on her chest. They splashed her face with water and helped her into Amélia's room. When they had loosened her clothing and given her some vinegar to sniff, she raised herself up on one elbow and looked around; her lips began to tremble and she burst into tears. Outside, the men in the group were saying:

'It must be the heat.'

'I know what kind of heat she's suffering from,' snorted the sergeant from the 6th Infantry.

Greatly put out, Agostinho fiddled with his moustache. Some of the ladies took Dona Juliana home. Dona Maria da Assunção and São Joaneira, well wrapped up in their shawls, went too. It was windy, a maid lit the way with a lantern, and they walked along the sand in silence.

'This is all to your advantage, you know,' Dona Maria da Assunção said to São Joaneira in a low voice, hanging back slightly.

'Mine?'

'Yes, yours. Didn't you realise what was going on? Back in Alcobaça, Juliana was being courted by Agostinho, but here the lad only has eyes for Amélia. Juliana realised when she saw him reciting that poem to Amélia, and, of course, she fainted!'

'Oh, really!' said São Joaneira.

'Don't pooh-pooh the idea. Agostinho inherited a nice bit of money from his aunts. He's a real catch!'

The following day, at the bathing hour, São Joaneira was getting changed in the tent and Amélia was sitting on the sand, waiting and staring out to sea.

'Hello there. All alone?' a voice behind her said.

It was Agostinho. Amélia said nothing and began tracing patterns in the sand with her sunshade. Agostinho sighed, smoothed out another area of sand with his foot and wrote AMÉLIA. Her face scarlet, she made as if to rub it out.

'Now, now!' he said. And bending down, he whispered: 'That's the name of "The Dark-haired Girl" you see. "Her name sounds like a melody"!'

She smiled and said:

'Well, you made poor Juliana faint yesterday.'

'What do I care about her? I'm sick of the silly nincumpoop. What does she expect? That's the way I am. I can as easily say that I no longer care about her as I can that there's a person for whom I would do anything . . . I know . . .'

'Who is it? Is it Dona Bernarda?'

She was a hideous old woman, the widow of a colonel.

'That's right,' he said, laughing. 'That's who I'm in love with, Dona Bernarda.'

'Ah, so you're in love!' she said slowly, concentrating on drawing in the sand.

'Tell me something, are you making fun of me?' exclaimed Agostinho, pulling up a chair and sitting next to her.

Amélia immediately stood up.

'Don't you want me to sit next to you?' he asked, offended.

'No, I was just tired of sitting down.'

They both fell silent for a moment.

'Have you been into the sea yet?' she asked.

'I have.'

'Is it cold today?'

'It is.'

Agostinho had grown extremely monosyllabic.

'Are you annoyed with me?' she asked sweetly, placing her hand on his shoulder.

Agostinho looked up and seeing her lovely, golden face all smiles, he said fiercely:

'I'm mad about you!'

'Sh!' she said.

Amélia's mother emerged breathlessly from inside the tent, a scarf around her head.

'Cooler today, don't you think?' Agostinho remarked, removing his straw hat.

'Oh, I didn't know you were here.'

'Just out for a stroll. About time for lunch, don't you think?'

'Won't you join us?' said São Joaneira.

Agostinho gallantly offered his arm.

And from then on he was always by Amélia's side, bathing with her in the morning and walking by the sea in the afternoon; he would collect shells for her and had written her another poem – 'The Dream'. One verse was terribly passionate:

> I held you against my breast
> And felt you tremble, flutter, surrender . . .

She murmured these lines excitedly to herself at night, sighing and hugging the pillow.

October was coming to an end, the holidays were over. One night, Dona Maria da Assunção's happy band and their friends went for a moonlight walk. On the way back, however, the wind got up, heavy clouds filled the sky and a few drops of rain fell. At the time, they were in a small pine forest, and the ladies ran, shrieking, for cover. Agostinho grabbed Amélia by the arm and, laughing loudly, plunged into the trees, far from the others. Then, amidst the monotonous, moaning murmur of the branches, he said to her in a low voice, his teeth clenched:

'I'm mad about you!'

'I know you are,' she muttered.

But Agostinho suddenly adopted a grave tone.

'I may have to leave tomorrow.'

'You're leaving?'

'Possibly. It isn't certain yet. I have to register at university the day after tomorrow.'

'You're leaving . . .' sighed Amélia.

Then he seized her hand and squeezed it hard.

'Write to me!' he said.

'And will you write to me?' she asked.

Agostinho grasped her by the shoulders and covered her mouth with bruising, voracious kisses.

'Stop it, stop it!' she gasped.

Then with a soft moan, like a bird cooing, she abandoned herself to him. Suddenly Dona Joaquina Gansoso's shrill voice called:

'The rain's letting up. Come on, come on!'

And Amélia, flustered, broke free and ran to huddle beneath her mother's umbrella.

The following day, Agostinho did, in fact, leave. The first rains had arrived, and soon Amélia, her mother and Dona Maria da Assunção would also have to go back to Leiria.

The winter passed.

One evening, in São Joaneira's house, Dona Maria da Assunção reported that, according to a letter she had received from Alcobaça, Agostinho Brito was about to marry a young woman from Vimeiro.

'Good heavens!' exclaimed Dona Joaquina Gansoso, 'The lucky little madam will get his thirty *contos*!'

And in front of everyone, Amélia burst into tears.

She had loved Agostinho, and she could not forget those kisses that night in the dense pine forest. It seemed to her then that she would never be happy again. Recalling the young man in the story that Mr Stork had told her, who, out of love, had sought the solitude of a monastery, she even began considering becoming a nun; she became intensely devout – an exaggerated expression of the tendencies slowly bred into her sensitive nature by her long association with priests ever since she was a little girl; she sat all day reading prayer books; she covered her bedroom walls with colour lithographs of saints;

she spent long hours at church, praying to Our Lady of the Incarnation. She heard mass every day and wanted to take communion every week, and her mother's women friends thought her 'an exemplary young woman who could bring virtue even to the unbelieving'.

It was at around this time that Canon Dias and his sister, Dona Josefa Dias, began to frequent São Joaneira's house. The Canon quickly became 'a friend of the family'. He and his dog became as regular a fixture after lunch as the precentor and his umbrella had been before.

'He's such a good friend and so very kind to me,' São Joaneira would say. 'But not a day goes by that I don't remember the dear precentor!'

The Canon's sister had by then organised, with São Joaneira, the Association of the Servants of Our Lady of Compassion. Dona Maria da Assunção and the Gansoso sisters also joined, and São Joaneira's house became an ecclesiastical centre. This was the high point of São Joaneira's life; as Carlos the pharmacist said with a yawn: 'The Cathedral has moved to Rua da Misericórdia.' As well as the canons, the new precentor came every Friday. There were images of saints in the dining room and in the kitchen. Maids were routinely questioned on doctrine before they were employed. For a long time, it was the place where reputations were made and unmade: if it was said of a man, 'he does not fear God', it was one's sacred duty to discredit him. Nominations for the posts of sexton, gravedigger and sacristan were arranged there through subtle intrigues and pious words. The members took to wearing a kind of dark purple habit, the whole house smelled of candle wax and incense, and São Joaneira even monopolized the sale of hosts.

And so the years passed. Gradually, however, the devout group dispersed; the relationship between Canon Dias and São Joaneira was the subject of much gossip and this drove away the other Cathedral canons; as had become traditional in that diocese, fatal to all precentors, the new precentor had also died of apoplexy; the Friday games of lotto were no longer any fun. Amélia had changed greatly; she had grown; she had become a lovely twenty-two-year-old woman with velvety eyes and dewy lips, and she now found her former passion for Agostinho 'childish nonsense'. She was still devout, but her devotion had changed; what she loved now about religion and the Church was the pomp and ceremony – the beautiful sung masses accompanied by organ music; the gold-embroidered copes that gleamed in the torchlight, the high altar resplendent with fragrant flowers, the clink of the chains bearing the silver censers, the fiery unison of hallelujahs that would burst forth from the choir. The Cathedral became her Opera House; God was her luxury. She liked to dress up for Sunday mass, to perfume herself with eau-de-cologne and kneel confidently on the carpet before the high altar, smiling up at Father Brito or at Canon Saldanha. But on certain days, as her mother put it, she would 'shrivel up': then her old despondency would return, making her skin grow sallow and tracing two deep lines at the corners of her mouth; at such times, she was filled by foolish, morbid longings, and her only consolation then was to stay at home and sing the *Santíssimo* or the gloomiest parts of the *Agonia*. When her mood lifted, her taste for the more cheerful rites returned, and then she regretted that the Cathedral was such a large stone structure built in a cold, Jesuitical style; she would have preferred a cosy little church, all gilded and carpeted and lined with paper and lit by gas; and with handsome priests officiating at an altar adorned like an *étagère*.

She was twenty-three when she met João Eduardo, on the day of the Corpus Christi procession, in the house of the notary, Nunes Ferral, where João Eduardo worked as a clerk. Amélia, her mother and Dona Josefa Dias had gone to watch the procession from the notary's splendid balcony that was draped with yellow damask hangings. João Eduardo was there, looking modest and serious and all dressed in black. Amélia had known him for some time, but on that afternoon, seeing the whiteness of his skin and the solemnity with which he knelt down, he seemed to her 'an excellent young man'.

That night, after tea, plump Nunes, in his white waistcoat, strode about the room, exclaiming enthusiastically in his high voice: 'Take your partners! Take your partners!' while his eldest daughter, with great brio, pounded out a French mazurka. João Eduardo went over to Amélia.

'Oh, I never dance!' she said rather abruptly.

João Eduardo did not dance either, but went and leaned against a door, his hand in his waistcoat, his eyes fixed on Amélia. She noticed and looked away, but she felt glad; and when João Eduardo, spotting an empty chair, came and sat beside her, Amélia, flattered, immediately made room for him, drawing in the silk frills on her dress. The clerk was greatly embarrassed and fiddled nervously with his moustache. At last, Amélia turned to him:

'So do you not dance either?'

'Why don't *you*?' he said softly.

She leaned back and, smoothing the folds of her dress, said:

'Oh, I'm too old for such things, too serious.'

'And do you never laugh?' he asked with an insinuating edge to his voice.

'Only if there's something to laugh about,' she replied, looking at him out of the corner of her eye.

'Me, for example?'

'You? Now you're making fun of me. Why would I laugh at you? Really! What is there about you that would make me laugh?' And she fluttered her black silk fan.

He fell silent, trying to think of clever, flattering things to say.

'So you really, really never dance?'

'I told you "No". You do ask a lot of questions!'

'That's because I'm interested in you.'

'Oh, really!' she said, indolently shaking her head.

'Honestly I am!'

But Dona Josefa Dias, who had been watching them, frowning, came over at that point, and João Eduardo stood up, feeling intimidated.

At the end of the evening, when Amélia was out in the corridor putting on her cloak, João Eduardo went over to her, hat in hand, in order to say:

'Make sure you wrap up warm. You don't want to catch cold.'

'So you're still interested in me, then?' she said, drawing her woollen shawl around her neck.

'Oh, very interested, believe me.'

Two weeks later, a travelling company performing *zarzuelas* came to Leiria. There was much talk about the contralto, La Gamacho. Dona Maria da Assunção had a box and she invited São Joaneira and Amélia to join her; two nights before, Amélia was still frantically making a flowery cotton dress decorated with blue silk ribbons. While La Gamacho, with her powdered face and her Valencian mantilla, rather wearily wielded a sequinned fan and sang a shrill, heartfelt *malagueña*, João Eduardo, in the stalls, could not take his besotted eyes off Amélia. He went up to her afterwards and offered to accompany her back to Rua da Misericórdia; São Joaneira and Dona Maria da Assunção followed behind with the notary, Nunes.

'So did you like La Gamacho, Senhor João Eduardo?'

'To be honest, I didn't even notice her.'

'What were you doing then?'

'I was looking at you,' he replied resolutely.

She immediately stopped walking and said in a slightly shaken voice:

'Where's Mama got to?'

'Forget about your Mama.'

And then, João Eduardo, his face close to hers, spoke to her of his 'great passion'. He took her hand and kept frenziedly repeating:

'I love you so much. I love you so much.'

Amélia was still much excited by the music at the theatre; the hot summer night and its vast vault glittering with stars filled her with languor. She let him hold her hand and she sighed softly.

'Do you love me too?' he asked.

'Yes,' she said and passionately squeezed João Eduardo's fingers.

But it was, as she put it later, 'probably just infatuation', for, days later, when she had got to know João Eduardo better and when she could talk freely with him, she realised that she was 'not at all drawn to him'. She respected and liked him, and thought him a nice young man; he would make a good husband, but inside her, her heart still slept.

The clerk, however, began visiting the house in Rua da Misericórdia almost every night. São Joaneira admired his 'determination' and his honesty, but Amélia grew 'cold'. She would wait for him to pass by her window in the mornings on his way to work, and would make eyes at him in the evening, but that was merely so as to keep him happy, in order to have in her empty existence some small amorous interest.

One day, João Eduardo spoke to her mother about marriage.

'It's up to Amélia,' said São Joaneira, 'but as far as I'm concerned . . .'

And when her mother consulted her, Amélia replied ambiguously:

'Perhaps later, but not just yet, we'll see.'

It was tacitly agreed that they would wait until he had obtained the post of amanuensis in the district government offices, a post generously promised to him by Dr Godinho, the fearsome Dr Godinho!

And this had been Amélia's life until Amaro arrived, and during the night, these memories came to her in fragments, like scraps of cloud blown along and scattered by the wind. It was late by the time she fell asleep, and when she woke, the sun was already high, and she was still yawning and stretching when she heard Ruça say in the dining room:

'Father Amaro is just on his way out with the Canon; they're going to the Cathedral.'

Amélia leaped out of bed, ran to the window in her nightdress, raised one corner of the curtain and peeped out. It was a splendid morning, and Father Amaro was standing talking to the Canon in the middle of the road, blowing his nose on a white handkerchief and looking very elegant in his fine cloth cassock.

VI

Right from those first few days, Amaro felt happy, swathed as he was in comfort. São Joaneira took almost maternal care over his underwear, she made him little treats to eat, and his room was always 'bright as a new pin!' Amélia treated him with the piquant familiarity of a pretty relative: 'They really hit it off,' as Dona Maria da Assunção said delightedly. The days slipped by easily for Amaro, with good food, a soft mattress and the sweet company of women. The weather was so mild that the lime trees in the garden of the bishop's palace had flowered already: 'Almost a miracle!' people said. The precentor, who stood in his nightshirt looking out at them every morning from his bedroom window, recited verses from Virgil's *Eclogues*. For Amaro, after the prolonged gloom of his uncle's house in Lisbon, the discomforts of the seminary and the harsh winter in Gralheira, life in Leiria was like entering a warm, dry house after having spent all night tramping the mountains amidst thunder and rain and finding a cheerful, crackling fire and a bowl of delicious, steaming soup.

Well wrapped up in a big cloak, thick gloves and woollen socks beneath his tall, red-shanked boots, he would set out early to say morning mass at the Cathedral. The mornings were cold, and at that hour, only a few devout women, dark shawls over their heads, would be knelt in prayer here and there near the gleaming white altar.

He would go straight to the sacristy and hurriedly pull on his vestments, stamping his feet on the flagstones, while the sluggardly sacristan told him the news of the day.

Then, with the chalice in his hands and eyes lowered, he went into the church; there, having cursorily genuflected before the Holy Sacrament, he walked slowly up to the altar, where the two wax candles burned palely in the bright light of morning, then he put his hands together and, head bowed, murmured:

'*Introibo ad altare Dei.*'

'*Ad Deum qui laetificat juventutem meam,*' the sacristan would respond, carefully pronouncing each syllable of the Latin.

Amaro was no longer filled by the tender devotion he had felt when he first celebrated mass. 'I'm used to it now,' he said. And since he took supper early and, at that hour, had still had no breakfast, he was beginning to feel hungry and would deliver the holy readings of the Epistle and of the Gospel in a rapid, monotone mumble. The sacristan stood behind him, arms folded, slowly stroking his thick, neatly trimmed beard and casting sideways glances at Casimira França, the cathedral carpenter's devout wife, whom he had had his eye on since Easter. Broad swathes of sunlight poured in through the side windows. The vague sickly smell of dried rushes filled the air.

Having gabbled his way through the Offertory, Amaro cleansed the chalice with the purificator; the sacristan, slightly bowed, fetched the hosts and presented them to him, and Amaro could smell the rancid hair oil that gleamed on the sacristan's head. At that point in the mass, Amaro, out of mystical habit, was always filled by genuine emotion. Arms outstretched, he would turn to the congregation and loudly utter the universal exhortation to prayer: *Orate, fratres*! And the old women leaning against the stone pillars, with their idiotic faces and drooling mouths, would clasp their long, black rosaries more tightly to their chests. Then the sacristan would kneel behind him, lightly grasping the hem of Amaro's chasuble in one hand and holding up the bell in the other. Amaro would consecrate the wine and would take the Host in his hands – *Hoc est enim corpus meum*! – lifting up his arms to Christ and his blood-red wounds where He hung on the dark rosewood cross; the bell would toll slowly; cupped hands would beat breasts; and in the silence, they could hear the ox carts jolting by over the broad flagstones outside the Cathedral, on their way back from market.

'*Ite missa est*!' Amaro would say at last.

'*Deo gratias*!' the sacristan would answer with a loud sigh, relieved that his duties were over.

And when, having kissed the altar, Amaro came down the

steps to give the blessing, he was already thinking gleefully of breakfast in São Joaneira's bright dining room, with some of her excellent toast. At that hour, Amélia would be waiting for him with her hair loose over her dressing gown, and the good smell of almond soap on her fresh skin.

Half-way through the day, Amaro would go up to the dining room where São Joaneira and Amélia would be sewing. He was bored downstairs, he would say, and had just come up for a chat. São Joaneira would be sitting on a small chair by the window, her spectacles perched on the end of her nose while she sewed and with the cat snuggled up amongst the folds of her woollen skirt. Amélia would be working at the table, with the sewing basket beside her. When she had her head bent over her work, he could see the straight, clean parting in her hair, almost drowned by her abundant locks; her large gold earrings, in the form of droplets of wax, trembled and cast a tiny, flickering, tremulous shadow on her fine throat; the faint bistre shadows beneath her eyes shaded smoothly into the delicate golden brown of her skin, beneath which beat her strong blood; and her full breast slowly rose and fell. Sometimes, she would stick her needle in the cloth, stretch languidly and smile wearily. Then Amaro would say jokingly:

'Come on, lazybones! A fine housewife you'd make!'

She would laugh then and they would talk. São Joaneira knew all the interesting news of the day: the major had dismissed his maid; someone had offered Carlos the postman ten *moedas* for his pig . . . Ruça would occasionally go to the cupboard for a plate or a spoon: then they would talk about the price of food and about what there was for supper. São Joaneira would remove her spectacles, cross her legs and, bouncing one slipper-shod foot up and down, would tell him the menu:

'We've got chickpeas today. I don't know if you like chickpeas, but I thought just for a change . . .'

Amaro liked everything and even discovered that he and Amélia shared certain tastes in food.

Then, growing bolder, he would rummage in the

workbasket. One day, he had found a letter; he asked her who her lover was, but she replied emphatically as she continued her backstitching:

'Oh, no one loves me, Father . . .'

'Well, I wouldn't say that,' he said, but then stopped, his face flushed, and he gave an embarrassed cough.

Sometimes Amélia would treat him with extreme familiarity; one day, she even asked him to hold a skein of silk thread for her to wind.

'Honestly, Father!' exclaimed São Joaneira. 'What cheek! Give some people an inch . . .'

But Amaro made himself ready, laughing contentedly: he was at their disposal, even as a holder of skeins! They just had to tell him what to do. And the two women laughed out loud, charmed by his manners, which they found 'almost touching'. Sometimes Amélia would put down her sewing and take the cat on her lap, and Amaro would go over to her and run his hand down the cat's spine, so that the cat arched its back and purred with pleasure.

'Do you like that?' she would say to the cat, her face all flushed and a tender light in her eyes.

And Amaro would murmur in a slightly troubled voice:

'There kitty, kitty, kitty!'

Then São Joaneira would get up to give her idiot sister her medicine or to go into the kitchen. And they would be left alone; they did not speak, but their eyes held a long, silent dialogue that filled them both with the same sleepy languor. Amélia would softly sing 'The Farewell!' or 'The Unbeliever'. Amaro would light a cigarette and listen, tapping his foot.

'That's really lovely,' he would say.

Amélia would sing more loudly, sewing furiously; and at intervals, she would draw herself up and study her tacking or her backstitching, smoothing it out with one long, polished fingernail.

Amaro thought she had beautiful nails, because everything about her seemed to him perfection: he liked the colours of her dresses, he liked her walk, the way she ran her fingers through her hair, and he even gazed tenderly at the white petticoats that she hung out to dry at her bedroom window, suspended from a cane. He had never lived in such intimacy with a woman before. When he noticed her bedroom door ajar, he would cast greedy glances inside, as if trying to catch glimpses of paradise: a skirt hanging up, a discarded stocking or a garter left on top of the trunk were all like revelations of nakedness that made him turn pale and clench his teeth. And he could never get enough of seeing her talk or laugh or walk along in her starched skirts that brushed against the narrow door frames. By her side, feeling weak and languid, he forgot he was a priest: the Priesthood, God, the Cathedral, Sins were left far down below somewhere; he could see them very faintly from the height of his rapture, as from the top of a hill one can see the houses disappearing into the valley mists; and he thought only how infinitely sweet it would be to kiss her white throat or to nibble the lobe of her ear.

Occasionally, he would rebel against this weakness and stamp his foot.

'For heaven's sake, I must be sensible! I must show some self-control!'

He would go downstairs then and leaf through his breviary; but as soon as he heard Amélia's voice upstairs or the tick-tack of her boots on the floorboards . . . that would be it! His devotion was snuffed out like a candle; his good resolutions fled, and his mind was once more filled by a flock of vehement, insinuating temptations, rubbing up against each other like doves in a dovecote. He was utterly enslaved, and how he suffered! He would bemoan his lost liberty then: how he longed not to see her, to be far from Leiria, in some remote village, amongst placid people and with only an old housekeeper for company, full of proverbs and ideas for saving money, and where he could stroll in his garden when the lettuces were growing green and where the cockerels crowed as the sun came up. But Amélia was calling to him from above, and the enchantment would begin again, ever more insidious.

Supper time was the best part of the day, at once the happiest and the most dangerous of times. São Joaneira would carve, while Amaro talked and spat olive stones into the palm of his hand before lining them up on the table cloth. Ruça, whose consumption grew worse with each day that passed, served the food clumsily, constantly coughing. Amélia would sometimes spring up to look for a knife or a plate in the sideboard, and Amaro would immediately get up too, eager to help.

'No, you stay where you are, Father,' she would say. And she would place a hand on his shoulder, and their eyes would meet.

Amaro, legs outstretched and napkin on stomach, felt utter contentment, savouring the warmth of the room; after his second glass of red Bairrada wine, he would grow expansive and make little jokes; sometimes, with a tender gleam in his eyes, he would even fleetingly touch Amélia's foot under the table; or else, adopting a look of sincerity, he would say how he wished he had a little sister like her.

Amélia enjoyed dipping her bread in the juices of the stew, and her mother always said to her:

'I really wish you wouldn't do that in front of Father Amaro.'

And he would say, laughing:

'But I like doing it too. You see we're in sympathy! In tune!'

And they both dipped their bread in the juices and, for no good reason, burst out laughing. When dusk fell, Ruça would bring in the lamp. The gleaming glasses and plates made Amaro feel even happier and even more tender; he would call São Joaneira 'Mama'; Amélia would smile, eyes downcast, biting into the peel of her tangerine. Then coffee would be served, and Father Amaro would spend ages cracking open nuts with the back of his knife and tipping the ash from his cigarette into his saucer.

Canon Dias always arrived around then; they would hear him lumbering up the stairs, calling out:

'Permission for two to enter!'

It was him and his dog, Trigueira.

'God bless, and a very good evening to one and all!' he would say, peering round the door.

'Would you like a drop of coffee, Canon?' São Joaneira would immediately ask.

He would sit down, with a loud 'Uf!' and say: 'Yes, why not!' Then clapping Amaro on the shoulder and looking at São Joaneira, he would ask:

'How's our boy, then?'

They all laughed and discussed the stories of the day. The Canon usually had a copy of the newspaper, *The Popular Daily*, in his pocket; Amélia was interested in the latest serial and São Joaneira in the amorous messages in the personal column.

'Honestly, some people just have no shame!' she said gleefully.

Amaro talked about Lisbon, about the scandals of which his aunt had told him, about the noblemen he had met in the house of the Conde de Ribamar. Amélia listened with rapt attention, her elbows on the table, absentmindedly chewing on a toothpick.

After supper, they all visited São Joaneira's crippled sister. The nightlight would be sputtering out on the bedside table, and the poor old woman, barely visible beneath the bedclothes, and wearing a ghastly black lace cap on her head, which only made her pale face, wrinkled as a rennet apple, seem even paler, would stare at them all fearfully with her small, sad, sunken eyes.

'It's Father Amaro, Aunt Gertrudes!' Amélia bawled in her ear. 'He's come to see how you are.'

The old lady made a supreme effort and said in a plaintive voice:

'Ah, it's the boy.'

'Yes, that's right, it's the boy,' they all said, laughing.

And the old lady kept murmuring in amazement:

'It's the boy, it's the boy.'

'Poor soul!' Amaro would say, 'Poor soul! May God give you a good death!'

And with that, they went back into the dining room where Canon Dias was sitting slumped in the old armchair upholstered in green cotton, his hands folded on his belly. He would say:

'How about a bit of music, Amélia?'

She would sit down at the piano.

'Play "The Farewell", Amélia,' São Joaneira would say, taking up her knitting.

And Amélia, lightly touching the keys, would begin to sing:

> Ah, farewell, farewell!
> Gone now are the days
> When I lived happy by your side . . .

Her voice was filled with melancholy, and Amaro, blowing out his cigarette smoke, found himself plunged into a mood of pleasant sentimentality

When he went downstairs to his room at night, he was always in a state of high excitement. He sat down to read *The Canticles to Jesus*, a translation from the French published by the Society of the Slaves of Christ. It is a devout work, written in a clumsy, would-be lyrical style, which couches prayers in the language of lust. Jesus's presence is invoked and demanded with the stammering impatience of wild concupiscence: 'Oh, come, beloved of my heart, adorèd body, my impatient soul desires you! I love you with a desperate passion. Burn me! Scorch me! Come! Crush me! Possess me!' And a divine love, grotesque in its intentions, obscene in its physicality, moans and roars and declaims its way through a hundred inflamed pages in which the words 'pleasure', 'delight', 'delirium' and 'ecstasy' are repeated over and over with hysterical insistence. These frenetic monologues, breathing mystical lust, are followed by imbecilic advice from sacristans, devout notes answering tricky questions about fasting, as well as prayers for women in labour! A bishop gave his approval to this excellently produced little book, and students read it in convent schools. It is both devout and titillating; it has all the eloquence of eroticism and all the sentimentality of religious devotion; it is bound in morocco leather and is given to confessants to read: it is the canonical Spanish fly!

Amaro would read until late, slightly troubled by those

sonorous lines, each one tumescent with desire; and sometimes, in the silence, he would hear Amélia's bed creaking upstairs: the book would slip from his hands, he would lean his head back in his armchair, close his eyes and imagine her in her corset sitting at the dressing table, loosening her plaits; or bent over, undoing her garters, so that the half-open neck of her chemise revealed her two white breasts. He stood up, clenching his teeth, feeling a brutal longing to possess her.

He suggested that she too should read *The Canticles to Jesus*.

'It's a really lovely book and so devout!' he said one evening, placing the book in her work basket.

The following day, at breakfast, Amélia looked terribly pale and had dark circles under her eyes. She complained of insomnia and palpitations.

'Did you enjoy the *Canticles*?'

'Oh, yes, the prayers are really beautiful!' she replied.

She did not look at Amaro all day. She seemed sad and, sometimes, for no reason, her face would flame with blood.

The worst times for Amaro were Mondays and Wednesdays, when João Eduardo came to spend the evenings *en famille*. Then Amaro did not emerge from his room until nine o'clock, and when he went up for tea, it filled him with despair to see the clerk with his cloak wrapped about him, sitting next to Amélia.

'Those two have been chattering away as usual, Father!' São Joaneira would say.

Amaro smiled wanly, slowly cutting up his toast, his eyes fixed on his cup.

When João Eduardo was there, Amélia was not as cheerfully familiar with Amaro, indeed, she barely raised her eyes from her sewing; the clerk said little, but sat smoking a cigarette, and there were long silences during which one could hear the wind moaning as it blew down the street.

'I pity anyone out at sea tonight!' São Joaneira would say as she slowly knitted a sock.

'Too right!' João Eduardo would say.

His words and manners irritated Father Amaro; he detested

his lack of religious feeling and his neat, black moustache. When he was there he felt trammelled by his own priestly shyness.

'Play something, Amélia,' São Joaneira would say.

'I'm too tired!' Amélia would reply, leaning back in her chair with a weary sigh.

São Joaneira, who did not like to see 'glum faces', would suggest a game of three-handed brag, and Father Amaro would then take up his brass candlestick and go down to his room, feeling most unhappy.

On such nights, he almost hated Amélia; he found her stubborn. The clerk's inclusion in the household seemed to him scandalous: he even resolved to speak to São Joaneira and tell her that allowing her daughter's young man into the house like that could not possibly be pleasing in the eyes of God. Then, when he was feeling more reasonable, he decided to forget all about it, he even considered leaving the house and the parish. He would imagine Amélia wearing a crown of orange blossom and João Eduardo in tails, his face all flushed, returning from the Cathedral, married . . . He saw the bridal bed with its lace-trimmed sheets . . . And all the evidence, the certainty that she loved that 'fool of a clerk' pierced his chest like daggers . . .

'Well, let them get married, and the Devil take them . . .'

He hated her then. He would ostentatiously lock the door as if to keep the sound of her voice and the rustle of her skirts out of the room. But shortly afterwards, he would sit as he did every night, motionless and anxious, listening with pounding heart to the noises she made upstairs as she undressed, still chattering to her mother.

One day, Amaro had lunched at the house of Dona Maria da Assunção and then gone for a stroll along the road to Marrazes; on his return later that afternoon, he had found the street door in Rua da Misericórdia open; on the mat on the landing were Ruça's cotton slippers.

'Silly girl!' thought Amaro. 'She must have gone to the well and forgotten to close the door.'

He remembered that Amélia had gone to spend the afternoon with Dona Joaquina Gansoso, on a farm near Piedade, and that São Joaneira had mentioned going to visit the Canon's sister. He slowly closed the door and went up to the kitchen to light his lamp; the streets were wet from the morning rain and he was still wearing his rubber galoshes, so his feet made no noise on the floor; as he went past the dining room, he heard a loud cough from behind the cotton portière at the door of São Joaneira's bedroom; surprised, he cautiously lifted one edge of the curtain and peered through the half-open door. Merciful God! São Joaneira, wearing only a white petticoat, was lacing up her corset; and there, on the edge of the bed, in his shirtsleeves, sat Canon Dias, huffing and puffing!

Amaro went downstairs, gripping the banister; very slowly he closed the front door behind him and wandered about near the Cathedral. The sky had clouded over and small drops of rain were falling.

'Good heavens,' he kept saying in astonishment.

He had never for a moment suspected such a thing. São Joaneira, slow, lazy São Joaneira! The Canon, his former teacher of Moral Theology! An old man, untroubled by the sexual impulses of young blood, who should be enjoying the peace that came with age, good food and ecclesiastical honours. What was a strong young man supposed do then, one whose veins burned with the demands of abundant life? So it was true what people had whispered in the seminary, what old Father Sequeira, for fifty years the parish priest in Gralheira, used to say: 'They're all made of the same clay.' They were all made of the same clay all right – they rise in the ranks, they are admitted to chapters, they run seminaries, they guide minds, they are all the while wrapped up in God as if in a state of permanent absolution, and yet meanwhile, in some back alley, there is a quiet, plump woman in whose house they can smoke cigarettes and pinch chubby arms, finding some respite from devout poses and from the austerity of their office.

Other thoughts followed: what kind of people are they, São Joaneira and her daughter, to live off the late-blooming lubricity of an old Canon? São Joaneira had certainly been pretty, trim, desirable – once! In how many other arms had she lain before ending up, in her declining years, with that stingy, ageing lover? The two women were simply not honest! They took in guests, they lived as concubines. Amélia went alone to church, to the shops, to the farm, and who knows, with those dark eyes of hers, perhaps she had already had a lover! He mulled over particular memories, making connections: one day, she had been standing by the kitchen window, showing him a pot of columbines; they had been alone and suddenly, blushing furiously, she had placed one hand on his shoulder and looked up at him with shining, pleading eyes; on another occasion, she had brushed her breast against his arm!

Night had fallen and with it came a fine rain. Amaro hardly felt it as he walked briskly along, obsessed by a single delicious idea that made him tremble: to become the girl's lover, just as the Canon was the mother's lover! He could already picture that easy life of shame: while, upstairs, plump São Joaneira showered kisses on her asthmatic Canon, Amélia would creep down to his room, clutching her white petticoats to her, a shawl about her bare shoulders . . . He would wait for her in a state of frenzy. He no longer felt for her a sentimental, almost painful love; now the wicked idea of two priests and their two concubines living cosily together filled that man bound by his vows with depraved pleasure. He almost skipped down the street. What a find that house had turned out to be!

The rain was falling heavily now. When he entered, a light was on in the dining room. He went up.

'Goodness, you're frozen!' Amélia said, when she shook his hand and noticed that it was cold and damp from the mist outside.

She was sitting at the table, sewing, a cloak about her shoulders; nearby, João Eduardo was playing a game of brag with São Joaneira.

Amaro sat down, feeling rather awkward; for some reason, the presence of the clerk brought him abruptly back to harsh reality; seeing him, her fiancé, so close to Amélia, as she sat beside the familiar oil lamp, bent over a piece of honest sewing, in her dark, high-necked dress, all the hopes that had been dancing wildly about in his imagination gradually shrank and shrivelled, one by one.

And everything around him seemed somehow more modest: the wallpaper with its pattern of green sprigs, the cupboard full of gleaming Vista Alegre china, the charming, pot-bellied water jar, the old piano balanced precariously on its three well-turned legs, the toothpick holder they were all so fond of – a chubby Cupid holding an open umbrella bristling with toothpicks – and that quiet game of brag accompanied by the time-honoured jokes. It was all so proper!

Then he fixed on the rolls of fat on São Joaneira's neck as if expecting to find there traces of the Canon's wet kisses: 'You are definitely a cleric's concubine.' But Amélia? With those long, lowered eyelashes, those fresh young lips! She probably knew nothing of her mother's licentious behaviour, or else, she knew about it and was determined to establish herself firmly in the security of a legal marriage. Amaro scrutinised her from the shadows as if to find proof of her virginal past in her placid face.

'Are you a bit tired tonight, Father?' São Joaneira asked. And to João Eduardo: 'A trump please, Mr Head-in-the-Clouds.'

The lovesick clerk was not concentrating.

'It's your turn,' São Joaneira kept telling him.

Then he forgot to 'buy cards'.

'Really, my boy,' she said languidly, 'I'll box your ears in a minute.'

Amélia continued sewing, head bowed; she was wearing a small black jacket with glass buttons that disguised the shape of her bust.

And Amaro grew angry with those eyes fixed on their sewing, with that loose-fitting jacket hiding her greatest beauty. And he could not even hope! Not one bit of her would ever belong to him, not even the light in her eyes or the whiteness of those breasts. She wanted to get married and was keeping *everything* for the other man, for that simpering idiot, playing cards! He hated him then, with a hatred that was mingled with envy for his black moustache and his right to love . . .

'Are you feeling unwell, Father?' asked Amélia, seeing him fidgeting in his chair.

'No, I'm fine,' he said sharply.

'Oh,' she responded with a slight sigh, resuming her rapid tacking.

The clerk, as he shuffled the cards, had begun talking about a house he wanted to rent, and the conversation turned to domestic arrangements.

'Bring me a light!' shouted Amaro to Ruça.

He went down to his room, feeling desperate. He placed the candle on the sideboard; the mirror was there before him, and he saw himself in it; he felt ugly and ridiculous with his shaven face, his stiff clerical collar and, at the back, that hideous tonsure. He instinctively compared himself with the other man who had a moustache and all his hair as well as his freedom! Why am I tormenting myself? The other man could be a husband; he could give her his name, a house, motherhood; he could only give her feelings of guilt and the terror of sin! Maybe she did like him, despite his being a priest, but she wanted above all to marry; what could be more natural? She could imagine herself, poor, pretty, alone, and she longed for a legitimate, lasting arrangement that would ensure the respect of her neighbours, the consideration of shopkeepers, and all the advantages of honour.

He hated her then, he hated her prim dress and her honesty. The stupid girl did not realise that right beside her, beneath a black cassock, a devoted lover watched her, followed her, trembling and impatient. He wished she was like her mother or, worse, entirely free, wearing elegant clothes and an impudent topknot, that she showed her legs and stared brazenly at men, a woman as easy as an open door . . .

'Good God, I'm wishing that the girl was a shameless hussy!' he thought, slightly shocked at himself. 'But of course, we can't think of decent women, so we have to go to prostitutes. A fine dogma.'

He was suffocating. He opened the window. The sky was

dark; the rain had stopped; only the owls nesting in the poorhouse wall broke the silence.

The taciturn darkness of the sleeping town touched him. And he felt once again, rising up from the depths of his being, the love he had felt for her initially, which was pure and devoutly sentimental: he saw her pretty head, her beauty transfigured and luminous against the thick blackness of the night; and his whole soul went out to her in a swoon of adoration, as if he were praying to the Virgin Mary or saying the Ave Maria; he eagerly begged her forgiveness, fearful lest he had offended her; he said out loud: You are a saint. Forgive me! It was a sweet moment of carnal renunciation.

Then, almost frightened by the delicate sensibilities he had just discovered in himself, he set to thinking nostalgically about what a good husband he would be were he free. Loving, devoted, cheerful, always on his knees in adoration before her. How he would love their little baby son, tugging at his beard. The idea of that unobtainable bliss filled his eyes with tears. He rained down desperate curses on the stupid marchioness who had made him a priest and the bishop who had confirmed him!

'They ruined me, ruined me!' he said, slightly crazed.

Then he heard João Eduardo coming down the stairs and the rustle of Amélia's skirts. He ran over to peer through the keyhole, biting his lips enviously. The door banged shut. Amélia went up the stairs, singing softly to herself. The feeling of mystical love that had pierced him for a moment, as he gazed out at the night, had passed; and he lay down seething with desire for her and for her kisses.

VII

Some days later, Father Amaro and Canon Dias had gone to lunch with the local priest in Cortegaça. He was a jolly, charitable old man who had lived in that parish for thirty years and was said to be the best cook in the diocese. All the neighbouring clergy knew about his famous game stew. It was his birthday and other guests were there too – Father Natário and Father Brito. The former was a brusque, irascible fellow, with deep-set, malicious eyes and pockmarked skin. He was known as the Ferret. He was bright and argumentative; he had a reputation as a great Latin scholar and was alleged to possess an iron logic; people said of him: 'He's a viper!' He lived with two orphaned nieces to whom he claimed to be devoted; he was constantly praising their virtue and referred to them as 'my two little roses'. Father Brito was the strongest and most stupid priest in the diocese; he had the appearance, manners and rude health of a sturdy peasant from the Beira who handles a crook well, drinks a skin of wine, happily ploughs his fields or plies the trowel when there's any building to be done and, during hot June siestas, has his brutal way with the girls on the maize ricks. The precentor – always so apt in his mythological comparisons – used to call him 'the Nemean Lion'.

He had an enormous head covered in woolly hair that came down as far as his eyebrows; his tanned skin had a bluish tinge to it from daily contact with the cut-throat razor; and when he gave one of his bestial laughs, he revealed very small teeth kept very white by a diet of corn bread.

When they were just about to sit down at the table, Libaninho arrived in a state of great agitation, arms flapping, beads of sweat standing out on his bald head, and exclaiming in shrill tones:

'Oh, my dears, you must forgive me, I got held up. I dropped in at the Church of Our Lady of the Hermitage where Father Nunes was saying a votive mass. It was just what I needed and I feel so much better for it!'

Gertrudes, the priest's tough old housekeeper, came in at that point bearing a vast tureen of chicken soup, and Libaninho skipped around her and began his usual jokes.

'You know, Gertrudes, I know who could make you happy!'

The old woman gave a ponderous, kindly laugh that made her bosom quake.

'Well, you've left it a bit late in the day . . .'

'Ah, women are like pears – best when they're big and ripe. That's when they're good and juicy!'

The priests cackled with laughter and happily settled down to eat.

The entire lunch had been cooked by the priest, and as soon as they began their soup, the compliments began to fly.

'Wonderful. Absolute heaven. Gorgeous.'

The excellent man was scarlet with pleasure. He was, as the precentor used to say, 'a divine artist'. He had read every cookbook and knew innumerable recipes, and he was very inventive. As he himself said, tapping his skull, a lot of his best ideas had come out of his own head! He was so absorbed in his 'art' that, sometimes, in his Sunday sermons, he would give to the faithful kneeling before him not God's word but advice on ways of cooking salt cod or what spices to use in stews. And he was perfectly contented there with his vegetable patch and with old Gertrudes – who also had superb taste in food – and he had but one ambition in life: to have the bishop to lunch one day.

'Now, Father Amaro, please, have a bit more stew! Dip a bit of bread in the sauce. That's it! What do you think, eh?' Then, modestly: 'I know I shouldn't say so, but the stew has turned out really well today.'

As Canon Dias remarked, it was good enough to tempt St Anthony in the desert! They had all removed their capes and were sitting in their cassocks, collars loosened, eating slowly, barely talking. The following day was the festival of Our Lady of Joy, so the bells in the neighbouring chapel were ringing out; and the good midday sun glittered brightly on the china, on the fat blue jugs brimming with Bairrada wine, on the saucers full of red peppers, on the cool bowls of black olives, while the good priest himself, eyes wide, bit his lip as he carefully carved white slices from the breast of the stuffed capon.

The windows opened onto the garden outside. Two large red camellia bushes grew by the window, and above the tops of the apple trees was a bright patch of intensely blue sky. A water wheel creaked in the distance, and washerwomen could be heard pounding clothes.

On the sideboard, amongst various books, a figure of Christ, with yellow skin and scarlet wounds, stood sadly on a pedestal against the wall; and beside him, cheerful saints beneath glass domes recalled the gentler side of religion: the kindly giant St Christopher crossing the river with, on his shoulder, the divine child, smiling and bouncing the world in his hand like a ball; the gentle shepherd St John dressed in the fleece of a sheep and wielding not a crook but a cross; the good gatekeeper St Peter, carrying in his clay hand the two holy keys that open the locks to Heaven! On the walls, in garish lithographs, the patriarch St Joseph was leaning on a crook from which white lilies bloomed; St George's rearing horse trampled the belly of a startled dragon; and good St Anthony was standing by the side of a stream, smiling and talking to a shark. The clink of glasses and the clatter of knives filled the room and its smoke-blackened oak ceiling with unaccustomed jollity. And Libaninho, as he demolished his food, joked:

'Gertrudes, my flower, pass me the green beans, will you? And don't look at me like that, you minx, you make my heart pound.'

'You old devil!' said Gertrudes. 'Mind what you're saying. You should have spoken up thirty years ago, you rascal . . .'

'Oh, Gertrudes,' Libaninho exclaimed, rolling his eyes, 'don't say things like that, you send shivers down my spine!'

The priests were all choking with laughter. They had drunk two jugs of wine already, and Father Brito had unbuttoned his cassock, revealing a thick woollen vest on which the maker's label, in blue stitching, was a cross superimposed on a heart.

A poor man came to the door mournfully repeating the *pater noster*, and while Gertrudes was placing half a loaf of corn bread in his bag, the priests discussed the bands of beggars currently roaming the parishes.

'There's such a lot of poverty!' said the good priest. 'Canon Dias, do have a bit of wing!'

'A lot of poverty and a good deal of idleness too,' said Father Natário harshly. He knew a lot of farms that were short of labourers, and yet you get these great hulks, strong as oaks, bleating out their *pater nosters* at people's doors. 'They're nothing but a bunch of scroungers!'

'Now, now, Father Natário,' said the priest. 'There is genuine poverty out there. There are families around here, a man, his wife and their five children, who sleep on the ground like pigs and eat nothing but weeds.'

'Well, what do you expect them to eat?' exclaimed Canon Dias, licking his fingers after having gnawed all the flesh off the capon wing. 'Do you expect them to eat turkey? To each his own.'

The good priest settled back in his chair, smoothed his napkin over his stomach and said unctuously:

'Poverty is, of course, pleasing to Our Lord.'

'Exactly,' put in Libaninho in simpering tones, 'if there were only poor people in the world, this would be the Kingdom of Heaven right here.'

Father Amaro commented gravely:

'And it's a good thing that the rich have something to leave their money to, for building chapels, for example . . .'

'Property should be in the hands of the Church,' broke in Natário authoritatively.

Canon Dias belched loudly and added:

'For the glory of religious worship and the propagation of the faith.'

The main cause of poverty, Natário declared pedantically, was immorality.

'Now, don't let's get into that,' said the priest, pulling a face. 'At this very moment, in this parish alone, there are more than twelve single women all pregnant. And, gentlemen, if I speak to them, if I reprehend them, they just laugh in my face.'

'Where I come from,' said Father Brito, 'around the time of the olive harvest, there was always a shortage of workers, and so migrant workers would be called in. And the shameless behaviour that went on . . .' He told them about the migrant workers, men and women, who travelled around offering their services at various farms, about their promiscuous lives and wretched deaths. 'You had to rule them with a rod of iron!'

'Oh, dear, oh dear,' said Libaninho to no one in particular, but clutching his head in his hands. 'It is such a sinful world. It's enough to make your hair stand on end.'

But the parish of Santa Catarina was the worst. The married women there had lost all morals.

'They were like bitches on heat,' said Father Natário, loosening his belt buckle.

And Father Brito told them about a case in the parish of Amor: girls of sixteen or eighteen who used to meet together in a hayloft – Silvério's hayloft – and spend the night there with a bunch of ne'er-do-wells.

Then Father Natário, whose eyes were already glinting, his tongue sharpened, leaned back in his chair and, speaking very clearly, said:

'Well, I don't know what goes on in your parish, Brito, but it's the person at the top who sets the tone . . . And I've heard tell that you and the adminstrator's wife . . .'

'That's a lie!' shouted Brito, turning scarlet.

'Oh, Brito!' everyone said, in gentle admonishment.

'It's a lie!' he yelled.

'And just between ourselves, my friends,' said Canon Dias, lowering his voice, a mischievous, confiding light in his beady eyes, 'she's quite a woman too.'

'It's a lie!' boomed Brito. Then, in a torrent of words: 'I know who's been spreading this around, it's the owner of the Cumeada estate, and all because his administrator didn't vote for him in the election. But sure as I'm standing here, I'll break every bone in his body!' His eyes were bloodshot and he was shaking his fist: 'Every bone!'

'It's really not that important,' said Natário.

'I'll break every bone, every one!'

'Calm down, old chap!' said Libaninho tenderly. 'Get a grip on yourself.'

But reminded of the influence wielded by the estate owner, who was, at the time, the opposition candidate and had won two hundred votes, talk turned to elections. Everyone there, apart from Father Amaro, knew, as Natário put it, how 'to stitch up votes for a deputy'. The anecdotes flowed; each of them had some triumph to recount.

At the last election, Father Natário had bought eighty votes.

'Good heavens!' they all said.

'And do you know how? By a miracle!'

'A miracle?' they repeated, shocked.

'Yes, gentlemen.'

He had come to an arrangement with a missionary, and on the eve of the election, people in the parish had received letters from Heaven, all signed by the Virgin Mary, in which they were asked, with promises of salvation and threats of eternal damnation, to vote for the government candidate. Clever, eh?

'Brilliant!' they all said.

Only Amaro seemed surprised.

'Well,' said their host ingenuously, 'I wish I'd thought of that. I have to slog round from door to door.' Then he smiled sweetly and added. 'It's always worth telling them that you'll let them off the tithe, of course.'

'And then there's the confessional,' said Father Natário. 'It all goes through the women, but you can rely on them. You can get a lot of votes in the confessional.'

Father Amaro, who had been silent until then, said gravely:

'But confession is a very serious act, and using it like that in an election . . .'

Father Natário, who, by then, had two scarlet roses in his

cheeks, and whose gestures were grower ever wilder, said rather rashly:

'You don't mean you take confession seriously, do you?'

There was general amazement.

'Take confession seriously?' shouted Father Amaro, pushing back his chair, his eyes staring.

'Now really Natário!' they all exclaimed.

'Listen, dear creatures! I don't mean that confession is to be taken lightly. I'm no freemason, you know that. All I'm saying is that it's a means of persuasion, of finding out what's going on, of directing the flock this way or that . . . And when it's used in the service of God, it's a real weapon, yes, that's what it is – absolution is a weapon!'

'A weapon!' they all exclaimed.

Their host protested, saying:

'Natário, really, that's going too far!'

Libaninho had crossed himself and was saying that his legs were positively trembling with fear.

Natário got annoyed.

'Are you telling me,' he thundered, 'that each of us, just because we're priests and because the bishop placed his hands on us three times and said the *Accipe*, that we each have a direct mission from God – that, when it comes to absolution, we are God!'

'Of course!' they all cried. 'Of course!'

And Canon Dias, brandishing a forkful of beans said:

'*Quorum remiseris peccata, remittuntur eis*. That's the formula, and the formula is everything, my boy . . .'

'Confession is the very essence of the priesthood,' said Father Amaro in scholarly fashion, fixing Natário with his gaze. 'Read St Ignatius! Read St Thomas!'

'Leave him to me,' yelled Libaninho, leaping from his chair, in support of Amaro. 'Leave him to me, my friend. Just let me at the impious swine!'

'Gentlemen,' bawled Natário, enraged at the opposition he had aroused, 'just answer me this.' And turning to Amaro, he said: 'You, sir, for example, when you've had your breakfast, eaten your toast, drunk your coffee and smoked your cigarette, you then go into the confessional, perhaps worrying about some family business or lack of money or suffering from a headache or a stomach ache, do you really think that you are there, like a God, to absolve people of their sins?'

The argument took them by surprise.

Canon Dias, put down his knife and fork, raised both arms, and with comic solemnity exclaimed:

'*Hereticus est*! You're a heretic!'

'*Hereticus est* indeed!' grumbled Father Amaro.

But Gertrudes came in at that point with a large dish of rice pudding.

'Let's talk no more about these things,' said their host sagely. 'Let's just eat our rice pudding. Gertrudes, get the bottle of port out!'

Natário, leaning on the table, was still hurling arguments at Amaro.

'To absolve is to exorcise grace. Grace is an attribute of God alone: no writer speaks of grace as being transmissible. Therefore . . .'

'I have two objections,' cried Amaro, in polemical pose, wagging a finger.

'My dears,' said their good host, greatly upset. 'Stop arguing, you won't enjoy your pudding.'

He poured out the port in order to calm them down, filling the glasses slowly and carefully.

'1815!' he said. 'It's not every day you drink a port like this!'

In order to savour it, having first held it up to the light, they all leaned back in their leather chairs, and the toasts began. The first was to their host, who murmured: 'My pleasure, my pleasure . . .' his eyes full of tears of satisfaction.

'To His Holiness Pius IX!' cried Libaninho, raising his glass. 'To the martyr!'

Much moved, they all drank. Libaninho then intoned Pius IX's hymn in a falsetto voice. The priest prudently told him to stop because the gardener was outside trimming the box hedge.

They lingered over dessert, savouring every mouthful.

Natário had grown sentimental and spoke of his two nieces, his two little roses, and quoted from Virgil, meanwhile dipping chestnuts in his port wine. Amaro, slumped in his chair, his hands in his pockets, was staring mechanically out at the trees in the garden, thinking vaguely about Amélia, about her body: he even sighed with desire for her as Father Brito, red-faced, was talking about beating some sense into the Republicans.

'Long live Father Brito's walking stick!' shouted Libaninho enthusiastically.

But Natário had started discussing ecclesiastical history with the Canon and, back in argumentative mode, returned to his vague theories about the doctrine of Grace: he said that a murderer or a patricide could be canonized if God's grace had been revealed to them. He rambled on, stumbling over his words, mouthing phrases learned at school. He cited saints who had led scandalous lives, others who, through their work, must have known, practised and loved vice. Hands on hips, he declared:

'St Ignatius was a soldier.'

'A soldier!?' bawled Libaninho. Getting up, he ran over to him and put one arm about his neck in a gesture of childish, drunken affection. 'A soldier, eh? And what rank did he hold? What rank did he hold, my dear St Ignatius?'

Natário pushed him away.

'Get off me, man! He was a sergeant in the infantry.'

Everyone roared with laughter.

Libaninho was ecstatic.

'Ooh, a sergeant in the infantry!' he said, raising his hands beatifically. 'My dear St Ignatius! Blessed and honoured be he for all eternity!'

Then the priest proposed taking their coffee under the vine trellis outside.

It was three o'clock. Everyone got up, slightly unsteady on their feet, emitting thunderous belches and laughing drunkenly; only Amaro had kept a clear head and steady legs, but he was nevertheless in a rather maudlin mood.

'Right then, gentlemen,' said their host, finishing his

last sip of coffee, 'what we need now is a walk to the farm.'

'To help digest our lunch,' grunted the Canon, getting to his feet with some difficulty. 'Off we go to the farm, then.'

They took the short cut from Barroca, a narrow cart track. The sky was still very blue and the sun warm. There were ditches on either side of the path, which was thick with brambles; beyond, the flat fields were still full of stubble; here and there the slender leaves of the olive trees stood out in silhouette; the round hills on the horizon were covered ith dark green pines; there was utter silence, broken only occasionally by a cart creaking down some distant lane. In the midst of the light and of that serene landscape, the priests walked along slowly, stumbling slightly, their eyes shining, their bellies full, joking with each other and feeling that life was good.

Canon Dias and the country priest were strolling arm in arm, arguing. Brito, next to Amaro, was vowing to drink the blood of the owner of the Cumeada estate.

'Be sensible, Brito, be sensible,' Amaro said, taking a puff of his cigarette.

And Brito, striding along beside him, snarled:

'I'll eat his liver!'

Libaninho, behind them, on his own, was singing in a high voice:

Little brown bird
Come out here . . .

Ahead of them all went Father Natário: he was carrying his cape over one arm, dragging it in the dust; his cassock was unbuttoned behind to reveal the filthy lining of his waistcoat; and his bony legs, in their laddered black woollen socks, unable to keep a straight line, kept sending him bumbling into the brambles.

And meanwhile, Brito, his breath stinking of wine, was growling:

'I'd just like to get hold of a stick and beat the living

daylights out of them. All of them!' He made a sweeping gesture embracing the world.

His wings are broken
So he won't appear . . .

Libaninho droned on in the background.

They suddenly stopped: ahead of them Natário was saying furiously:

'You fool, watch where you're going! You idiot!'

He had reached a bend in the road. He had collided with an old man leading a sheep; he had fallen over and, in his vinous rage, was shaking his fist at him.

'God forgive me, Father,' the man was saying humbly.

'You idiot!' bawled Natário, eyes flashing. 'I'll have you for this!'

The man was stammering and had removed his hat, revealing his white hair; he looked like a former farmhand who had grown old in the job; he was possibly someone's grandfather, and bowed, scarlet with shame, he shrank back into the hedge to allow the priests – all jolly and flushed with wine – to pass him on the narrow cart track.

Amaro decided not to go with them to the farm. At the edge of the village, at the crossroads, he took the Sobros path back to Leiria.

'It's a whole league back into town,' said the priest. 'I'll have them saddle up the mare for you, Father.'

'Certainly not. I've got strong legs!' And throwing his cape over his shoulder, Amaro set off, singing 'The Farewell!'

Just by Cortegaça, the Sobros path broadens out and runs alongside an estate surrounded by a mossy wall the top of which bristles with glinting glass. When he reached the low red gate, he found a large spotted cow blocking the way; amused, he prodded it with his umbrella, and as the cow trotted off, udders swaying, Amaro turned to find Amélia standing at the door. She greeted him, smiling:

'Are you frightening away my cows, Father?'

'Oh, it's you! What miracle is this?'

She blushed slightly.

'I came to visit Dona Maria da Assunção's estate. I just came to have a look at the farm.'

Beside Amélia, a girl was arranging cabbages in a basket.

'So this is Dona Maria's estate.'

And Amaro stepped inside the door.

A broad driveway, lined with old cork oaks providing delicious shade, led up to the house which could be seen at the far end, gleaming white in the sunlight.

'That's right. Our farm is on the other side, but you can reach it through here as well. Come on, Joana, hurry up!'

The girl put the basket on her head, said goodbye and set off towards Sobros, swaying her hips.

'It certainly looks like a very fine property,' commented Amaro.

'Come and see our farm,' Amélia said. 'It's only a little plot of land, but just to get an idea. We can go this way . . . Look, let's go and see Dona Maria, would you like to?'

'Yes, I would.'

They walked up the tree-lined path in silence. The ground was covered with dry leaves and, between the widely spaced trunks, the flowers on the clumps of hydrangeas hung their heads, grown yellow in the rain; at the end of the drive squatted the old, one-storey house. Along the wall huge pumpkins were ripening in the sun, and doves fluttered on the roof blackened by the winter rains. Behind it the orange trees formed a mass of dark green foliage, and a water wheel creaked monotonously.

A little boy passed them, carrying a bucket.

'Where did your mistress go, João?' asked Amélia.

'To the olive grove,' said the boy in a soft, drawling voice.

The olive grove was some way off, at the far end of the estate; the ground was muddy and a person would have to wear clogs to get there.

'We'll get too dirty,' said Amélia. 'Let's forget about Dona Maria, shall we? Let's go and see the garden instead . . . This way, Father . . .'

They were standing opposite an old wall overgrown with clematis. Amélia opened a green door and they went down three crumbling stone steps into an area shaded by a broad vine trellis. Near the wall roses grew all year round; on the other side, amongst the stone pillars supporting the trellis and the twisted feet of the vines, one could see a large field of grass, yellow in the sun; the low, thatched roofs of the cattle sheds stood out darkly in the distance, and from there a thread of white smoke vanished up into the intensely blue air.

Amélia kept stopping to explain what was planted where. Barley was going to be sown there; and he must see the onions, they were so pretty . . .

'Dona Maria takes great care of everything!'

Casting sideways glances at her, his head bowed, Amaro listened to her talking; in the silence of the fields, her voice seemed sweeter and more mellifluous; the fresh air brought a more piquant colour to her cheeks, and her eyes shone. She hitched up her dress to avoid a puddle, and the glimpse that he had of her white stocking troubled him as much as if it were a foretaste of her naked skin.

At the far end of the vine trellis, they walked alongside a stream, and across a field. Amélia laughed at Amaro because he was afraid of toads, and he then pretended to be even more afraid. There aren't any snakes, are there, Miss Amélia? And he brushed against her, recoiling from the tall grasses.

'Do you see that ditch? Well, on the other side is our farm. You can get in through that gate, do you see? But you look tired. You're obviously not much of a walker. Look out, a toad!'

Amaro gave a start and bumped against her shoulder. She gave him a gentle push and said with a playful laugh:

'You really *are* scared!'

She was so happy, so alive. She spoke of 'her farm' with the satisfied pride of one who knows about farm work and about being a landowner.

'It looks like the gate is shut,' said Amaro.

'It's not, is it?' she said. She gathered up her skirts and ran over. It was indeed closed. What a shame. And she impatiently rattled the narrow bars of the gate which were set in two strong stone posts flanked by thick brambles.

'The tenant must have taken the key!'

She crouched down and called across the field, lengthening out the vowels as she did so:

'Antó-o-nio-o-o! Antó-o-nio-o-o!'

No one replied.

'He must be somewhere in the back,' she said. 'What a bore! But if you like, there's a place up ahead where we could climb over. There's an opening in the hedge that we call the goat-leap. We can jump down onto the other side.'

And contentedly walking along by the brambles, splashing through the mud, she went on:

'When I was a little girl, I never used the gate, I always jumped through there. I used to land with quite a thump when the ground was slippery! You might not think it, but I was a real tomboy! You'd never know it, would you, Father? Now, of course, I'm getting old!' And turning to him with a smile that showed her white teeth, she said: 'Don't you think so, Father, don't you think I'm getting old?'

He smiled. He found it hard to speak. The sun beating down on his back, after all the wine he had drunk at lunch, had a softening effect on him; the sight of her, of her shoulders, and the way he and she occasionally brushed against each other filled him with intense, unremitting desire.

'Here it is,' said Amélia, stopping.

There was a narrow opening in the hedge; the field on the other side was lower down and very muddy. From there São Joaneira's farm could be seen: the flat field extended as far as an olive grove, and the fine grass was starred with tiny white daisies; a black spotted cow was munching the grass and, beyond, you could see the pointed roofs of cottages and flocks of sparrows fluttering about them.

'What do we do now?' asked Amaro.

'We jump,' she said, laughing.

'Here goes!' he shouted.

He wrapped his cape about him and jumped, but he slipped

on the damp grass, and Amélia leaned towards him, laughing helplessly and waving her hands.

'Goodbye, then, Father, I'm off to find Dona Maria. You're a prisoner in the farm now. You can't jump over and you can't get through the gate! You're a prisoner . . .'

'But Miss Amélia, please!'

She sang mockingly:

> Here I sit all alone
> Now my lover is in prison!

Her flirtatious manner excited Amaro, and with arms outstretched, he said pleadingly:

'Jump! Jump!'

She said in a childish voice:

'I'm afraid, I'm afraid!'

'Jump, Miss Amélia!'

'Here I come!' she called.

She jumped and fell against his chest with a little shriek. Amaro slipped, then steadied himself. Feeling her body in his arms, he embraced her hard and kissed her passionately on the neck.

Amélia pulled away and stood before him, breathing hard, her face ablaze, tremulously adjusting the folds of her woollen shawl around her head and neck. Amaro said:

'Amélia!'

But she suddenly snatched up her dress and ran the whole length of the hedge. A dazed Amaro strode after her. When he reached the gate, Amélia was talking to the tenant, who had appeared with the key.

They crossed the field beside the stream and then the courtyard covered by the vine trellis. Amélia went ahead, chatting to the tenant, and behind came Amaro, deep in thought, his head bowed. By the house, Amélia stopped, and blushing, still drawing her shawl around her neck, said:

'António, show Father Amaro the way out, will you? Good afternoon, Father.'

And then she ran across the damp earth to the far end of the estate, to the olive grove.

Dona Maria da Assunção was still there, sitting on a stone, chattering away to old Patrício; a band of women, wielding large sticks, were beating the branches of the olive trees.

'What's this, you silly girl? Why all this running? Foolish creature!'

'I ran all the way,' Amélia said, panting, her face scarlet.

She sat down next to the old woman and remained there, motionless, still breathing hard, her hands in her lap, her mouth half-open, her eyes staring into space. Her whole being was absorbed by but one thought:

'He loves me! He loves me!'

She had been in love with Father Amaro for a long time, and sometimes, alone in her room, she had despaired to think that he did not see the love in her eyes. From the very first, as soon as she heard him call up from downstairs for his breakfast, she felt her whole being fill up with joy for no reason, and she would start singing as volubly as a bird. Then she noticed that he seemed sad. Why? She knew nothing of his past, but, remembering the friar from Évora, she wondered if perhaps he had become a priest because of some disappointment in love. She would idealise him then; she imagined he must have a very tender nature, and it seemed to her that his pale, elegant person exuded some special fascination. She wanted to have him as her confessor; how good it would be to kneel at his feet in the confessional, to be close to his dark eyes and to hear him talking in his low voice about Paradise. She loved his soft mouth; she turned pale at the idea of being able to embrace him in his long black cassock! When Amaro went out, she would go into his bedroom where she would kiss the pillowcase and take away with her the hairs in his comb. Her cheeks flamed with colour when she heard him ring the bell.

If Amaro was to dine with Canon Dias, she would be in a bad mood all day, she would quarrel with Ruça, and even speak ill of him, say that he was stubborn and far too young to inspire respect. Whenever he mentioned some new young female confessant, she would sulk, filled with childish jealousy.

Her old religious devotion was reborn, full of sentimental fervour; she felt an almost physical love for the Church; she would have liked to embrace and to plant lingering little kisses on the altar, the organ, the missal, the saints, on Heaven itself, because she made no real distinction between them and Amaro; they seemed to her mere appendages of his being. She read her missal, all the time thinking of him as if he were her personal God. And Amaro had no idea that when he was pacing agitatedly back and forth in his room, she was upstairs listening, fitting her heartbeats to his steps, hugging her pillow to her, weak with desire, blowing kisses into the air, where she imagined his lips to be.

It was growing dark as Dona Maria and Amélia returned to the town. Amélia walked ahead in silence, urging her donkey onwards, while Dona Maria da Assunção chatted to the boy labourer who had hold of the donkey's halter. As they passed the Cathedral, the Angelus was rung, and Amélia, as she prayed, could not take her eyes off the great stone walls of the Cathedral that had clearly been built solely so that he would celebrate mass there. She remembered the Sundays when, as the bells were tolling, she had seen him give the blessing from the steps of the high altar; and everyone bowed, even the ladies from the Carreiro estate, even the Baronesa de Via-Clara and the district governor's haughty wife with her prominent nose. They had bowed beneath his raised hands and they too probably thought what lovely dark eyes he had! And he had held her in his arms by the hedge! She could still feel on her neck the warm pressure of his lips: passion ran like a flame through her whole being; she let go of the donkey's halter, pressed her hands to her breast and, closing her eyes, put her whole soul into this one prayer:

'Our Lady of Sorrows, my protectress, please make him love me!'

Some of the canons were sauntering about outside the Cathedral, talking. The lamps were already lit in the pharmacy opposite, and behind the scales could be seen the majestic figure of Carlos the pharmacist, in his beaded cap.

VIII

Father Amaro returned home, terrified.

'Now what? Now what?' he kept saying as he leaned, with shrinking heart, at the window.

He would have to leave São Joaneira's house at once. He could not continue there in that state of easy familiarity, not now that he had behaved so boldly with Amélia.

She had not seemed particularly outraged, merely stunned; she had perhaps felt constrained by respect for the clergy, by politeness towards a guest, by consideration for Canon Dias' friend. But she might tell her mother or the clerk . . . And the scandal that would ensue! He could already see the precentor crossing his legs and looking at him hard – the pose he always adopted when he was about to reprimand someone – then telling him gravely: 'It is precisely this kind of irregularity that brings dishonour on the priesthood. I would expect no less from a satyr on Mount Olympus!' They might exile him once more to the mountains. What would the Condesa de Ribamar say?

And if he did continue living in the same house as her, the constant presence of those dark eyes, of the warm smile that dimpled her chin, the curve of her breasts . . . then his secretly growing passion, constantly provoked, driven deep inside him, would send him mad, and he might 'do something foolish'.

He decided then to speak to Canon Dias: his naturally weak character always required the sustenance of someone else's reasoning and experience, and the ecclesiastical discipline was so ingrained in him that he usually consulted the Canon, judging him more intelligent simply because he was his superior in the hierarchy, for Amaro still had the dependent nature of a seminarian. Besides, if he wanted to live somewhere alone, he would need Canon Dias' help to find a house and a maid, for the Canon knew Leiria as well as if he had built it himself.

He found the Canon in his dining room. The wick in the oil lamp glowed a dull red. In the brazier, the embers too glowed red amongst the ashes. The Canon sat dozing in an armchair, lulled by the heat of the fire, his cape over his shoulders, his feet wrapped in a blanket, his breviary on his knees. His dog Trigueira was dozing too, stretched out on one of the folds of the blanket.

When the Canon heard Amaro approaching, he very slowly opened his eyes and grunted:

'Hm, must have dropped off!'

'It's still early,' said Father Amaro. 'They haven't even sounded the retreat. Why so tired?'

'Ah, it's you,' said the Canon, giving an enormous yawn. 'I got back late from the priest's house, had a cup of tea, and tiredness got the better of me . . . So, has anything happened?'

'No, I was just passing.'

'Well, the priest at Cortegaça certainly did us proud. That stew was superb! I think I may have overindulged,' said the Canon, drumming his fingers on the cover of his breviary.

Amaro, sitting near him, was slowly stirring the embers.

'You know, Father,' he said suddenly. He was about to add: 'Something odd has happened,' but he stopped himself and muttered: 'I'm in a funny mood today; I've been feeling a bit out of sorts lately . . .'

'Yes, your colour's not good,' said the Canon, looking at him. 'You need a good purgative.'

Amaro said nothing for a moment, staring at the fire.

'I've been considering changing my lodgings.'

The Canon looked up, opening wide his sleepy eyes.

'But why?'

Father Amaro moved his chair closer and said in a low voice:

'You see . . . I've been thinking, it is a bit odd being in a house with two women, with a young girl . . .'

'Oh, that's just gossip! As I see it, you're the lodger, and that's that. Don't worry, man. It's just like staying at an inn.'

'No, Father, you don't quite understand . . .'

And he sighed; he wished the Canon would question him and make it easier for him to confide his problem.

'Is this something you've just thought of today, Amaro?'

'Yes, I have been thinking about it today. I have my reasons.' And he was about to say: 'I did something foolish,' but he lost his nerve.

The Canon looked at him for a moment:

'Be honest with me, man!'

'I am being honest.'

'Is it that it's too expensive?'

'Of course not!' said Amaro, shaking his head impatiently.

'So it must be something else then . . .'

'Well, what do you expect?' And in a jovial tone which he thought would please the Canon. 'After all, we priests like the good things of life too.'

'I see, I see,' said the Canon smiling, 'I understand. What with me being a friend of the family and all, you're trying to tell me in the nicest way possible that you can't stand living there!'

'No, no, that's not it at all!' said Amaro, getting to his feet, irritated by the Canon's obtuseness.

'Well,' said the Canon, opening his arms, 'if you want to move, you must have your reasons. It seems to me that it would be better . . .'

'I know, I know,' Amaro said, striding about the room, 'but I've decided. Can you see if you can find me a cheap house with a bit of furniture . . . You know more about that kind of thing than I do . . .'

The Canon said nothing, sunk in his armchair, slowly scratching his chin.

'Hm, a cheap house,' he muttered at last. 'I'll have a think . . . possibly . . .'

'You understand, don't you?' said Amaro urgently, approaching the Canon. 'São Joaneira's house . . .'

But at that point, the door creaked open, and Dona Josefa Dias came in. Having discussed the lunch, Dona Maria da Assunção's cold, the liver disease that was eating away at dear

Canon Sanches, Amaro left, almost glad now that he had not unburdened himself to the Canon.

The Canon remained by the fire, pondering. Amaro's decision to leave São Joaneira's house was actually most welcome; when he had brought him as a guest to Rua da Misericórdia, he had agreed with São Joaneira to reduce the allowance he had been giving her for years now on the 30th of every month. But he had regretted it immediately; when São Joaneira had no lodgers, she would sleep alone on the first floor; the Canon could then enjoy the affections of his lady freely, and Amélia, in her bedroom upstairs, was completely unaware of this cosy arrangement. When Father Amaro arrived, São Joaneira had given up her room and now slept in an iron bedstead next to her daughter; and the Canon realised then, as he himself mournfully admitted, that 'this had ruined everything'. In order to savour fully the joys of the siesta with his São Joaneira, they had to ensure that Amélia was having lunch somewhere else, that Ruça had gone to the well, and to make various other troublesome arrangements; and he, a Cathedral canon, in selfish old age, when he most needed to take good care of his health, found himself forced to wait and watch, having to take his regular, necessary pleasures when he could, as if he were a schoolboy in love with his teacher. Now if Amaro left, São Joaneira would go back to her bedroom on the first floor, and there would be a return to the old comforts, to those tranquil siestas. He would, it is true, have to increase her allowance again . . . But, yes, that's what he would do!

'Why not! The important thing is that a man should feel comfortable,' he said to himself.

'What are you mumbling to yourself about?' asked his sister, Dona Josefa, waking from the slumber into which she had fallen in her chair next to the fire.

'I was just racking my brains as to how best to mortify my flesh during Lent . . .' said the Canon with a crude laugh.

Ruça always called Father Amaro for tea at the same time, and that day he went slowly up the stairs with quavering heart, fearing that he would find an angry São Joaneira, already informed of the insult to her daughter. Instead he found only Amélia – who, when she heard his footsteps on the stair had snatched up her sewing and, with head bowed low, was stitching furiously away, her face as red as the handkerchief she was busily hemming for the Canon.

'Good evening, Miss Amélia.'

'Good evening, Father.'

Amélia usually greeted him with an amiable 'Hello!' or 'So there you are!'; her formality terrified him, and he immediately blurted out:

'Miss Amélia, please forgive me . . . It was wrong of me . . . I didn't know what I was doing, but please, believe me . . . I've decided to leave. I've even asked Canon Dias to find somewhere else for me live . . .'

He did not look up as he spoke and so did not see Amélia raise her eyes to him, surprised and utterly disconsolate.

Just then, São Joaneira came in and, standing in the doorway, opened her arms wide and said:

'There he is! Now, I've already heard from Father Natário what a wonderful lunch it was, so tell us all about it!'

Amaro had to describe the different courses, Libaninho's jokes, the theological discussion, and then they talked about the farm; and Amaro went back downstairs without having dared tell São Joaneira that he was going to leave, which to her, poor woman, meant a loss of six *tostões* a day!

The following morning, before going to prayers, the Canon went to Rua da Misericórdia. Amaro was standing at his window, shaving.

'Hello, Master! Any news?'

'I think I've found a new home for you. It happened by chance this morning. There's a little house near where I live, which is a real find. Major Nunes has been living there, but he's moving to number 5.'

The suddenness of this displeased Amaro; he continued glumly shaving and asked:

'Is it furnished?'

'Oh, yes, it's got furniture, china, bed linen, everything.'

'So . . .'

'So you just have to move in and start your new life. And between ourselves, Amaro, I believe you're right. I've been thinking about it, and it's best if you live alone. So hurry up and get dressed, and we'll go off and see the house.'

Amaro, dumbstruck, was still desolately shaving.

The house was in Rua das Sousas, a very old, one-storey building with worm-eaten timbers; the furniture, as the Canon admitted, 'had seen better days'; a few faded lithographs hung gloomily from large black nails; and the disgusting Major Nunes had left behind him broken windows, gobs of spit on the floor, the walls covered with marks where he had struck his matches, and, on a window sill, there was even a pair of faded black socks.

Amaro took the house. And that same morning, the Canon arranged a maid for him, Maria Vicência, a very devout person, tall and thin as a pine tree, and previously cook to Dr Godinho. And (as Canon Dias remarked) she was sister to the famous Dionísia.

Dionísia had once been Leiria's equivalent of *La Dame aux Camélias*, of Ninon de Lenclos or Manon; she had enjoyed the honour of being the mistress of two district governors and of the terrifying owner of the Sertejeira estate; and the frenzied passions she had aroused had been a cause of tears and fainting fits in nearly every wife and mother in Leiria. Now she took in other people's ironing and starching, acted as an intermediary with pawnbrokers and knew pretty much all there was to know about childbirth; she facilitated 'the odd little adultery', to use the words of old Dom Luís da Barrosa, known as 'Wicked Dom Luís', she procured young female farmhands for gentlemen civil servants, and knew everything about the love life of everyone in the district. Dionísia was always to be seen out and about, wearing a check shawl fastened over her immense bosom, which trembled beneath the grubby blouse she ordinarily wore, and she trotted discreetly along, with, as before, a smile for everybody except that now her two front teeth were missing.

The Canon told São Joaneira of Amaro's decision that very

afternoon. It was a great shock to the excellent lady. She complained bitterly of Amaro's ingratitude.

The Canon coughed significantly and said:

'Well, actually, I was the one who arranged it. And I'll tell you why; it's because this business of you sleeping upstairs is ruining my health.'

He gave other reasons of prudence and hygiene and added, tenderly stroking her neck:

'And don't you worry about losing any income! I'll make my usual contribution, and since the harvest was good this year, I'll chip in a bit more to pay for any of Amélia's little fancies. Now give me a big kiss, Augustinha, you naughty thing. You know, I think I'll dine here tonight.'

Amaro, meanwhile, was downstairs packing his clothes. But he kept stopping and sighing sadly, looking round the room at the soft bed, the clean white cloth on the table, the big upholstered chair where he would sit reading his breviary while he listened to Amélia singing to herself upstairs.

'Never more!' he thought. 'Never more!'

Farewell to those sweet mornings spent at her side, watching her sew. Farewell to those after-supper gatherings by the light of the oil lamp! Farewell to the cups of tea round the stove, when the wind howled outside and the rain dripped from the cold eaves. All that was over.

São Joaneira and the Canon appeared at the door of his room. The Canon looked radiant, but São Joaneira said in wounded tones:

'I know all about it, you ungrateful boy!'

'Yes, it's true, Senhora,' said Amaro with a sad shrug. 'But there are good reasons . . . I'm so sorry . . .'

'Look, Father,' said São Joaneira, 'please don't be offended by what I'm about to say, but, you see, I'd come to love you like a son . . .' And she dabbed at her eyes with her handkerchief.

'What nonsense!' exclaimed the Canon. 'Surely he can still visit, come and have a chat in the evenings, drink his coffee here. The man isn't going to Brazil!'

'I know, I know,' said the poor woman tearfully, 'but it's not the same thing as having him here with us.'

But she knew that people were better off in their own homes . . . She recommended a good washerwoman and told him that he only had to ask if he needed china or sheets . . .

'You just have to ask, Father!'

'Thank you, Senhora, thank you.'

And as he finished packing his clothes, Amaro bitterly regretted the decision he had taken. Amélia had clearly said nothing. Why then leave that cheap, comfortable, friendly house? He hated the Canon for his hasty zeal.

It was a sad supper. Amélia, doubtless to explain her pallor, complained of a headache. Over coffee, the Canon demanded his 'ration of music', and Amélia, either out of habit or intentionally, sang their favourite song:

Ah, farewell, farewell!
Gone now are the days
When I lived happy by your side!
The fateful moment now draws nigh
When we must go our separate ways!

The tearful melody transfused with the sadness of separation so moved Amaro that, afterwards, he had to get up, go over to the window and rest his face against the glass to conceal the tears running unstoppably down his cheeks. Amélia's fingers fumbled so over the keys that even São Joaneira said:

'Amélia, please, play something else.'

But the Canon got wearily to his feet and said:

'Well, ladies and gentlemen, it's time we were going. Come along, Amaro. I'll walk with you to Rua das Sousas . . .'

Amaro asked to say goodbye to São Joaneira's idiot sister, but she was very weak after a bad attack of coughing and was asleep.

'Leave her be then,' said Amaro. And squeezing São Joaneira's hand, he said: 'Thank you for everything, Senhora, and please believe . . .'

He stopped, a lump in his throat.

São Joaneira was dabbing at her eyes with one corner of her white apron.

'Come on, now,' said the Canon, laughing, 'as I said before, the man isn't setting sail for the Indies!'

'It's just that one gets so fond of people . . .' whimpered São Joaneira.

Amaro tried to make a joke. Amélia, deathly pale, was biting her lip.

Then Amaro went downstairs; and the same João Ruço who, very drunk and singing the Benedictus, had carried his trunk to Rua da Misericórdia when he first arrived in Leiria, now took him off to Rua das Sousas, equally drunk, but this time singing 'The King has come . . .'

That night, when Amaro found himself alone in that gloomy house, he was filled with such intense melancholy, such black despair that, in his weakness, he felt like crawling into a corner to die.

He stood in the middle of the room and looked around him at the narrow iron bedstead with its hard mattress and red bedspread, at the tarnished mirror gleaming on the table; there was no washstand, but on the window ledge stood a small basin and jug, with a tiny bit of soap; everything in the room smelled musty, and outside, in the black street, the sad rain fell ceaselessly. What a life! And that was how it would always be!

With clenched fists, he raged against Amélia: he blamed her for the comforts he had lost, for the lack of furniture, for the expense to which he would be put, for that icy solitude! Any woman with a heart would have come to his room and said: 'Why are you leaving, Father Amaro? I'm not angry with you.' She, after all, was the one who had provoked his desire with her flirtatious ways and her tender glances. But no, she had allowed him to pack his bags and go down the stairs, without so much as a friendly word, instead wildly pounding out that waltz entitled 'The Kiss!'

He swore then never to go back to São Joaneira's house. He strode up and down the room thinking of ways in which he could humiliate Amélia. What, for example? He could spurn her like a dog! He could become an influential figure amongst Leiria's devout society, a close colleague of the precentor; he could lure the Canon and the Gansoso sisters away from Rua da Misericórdia; he could conspire with the ladies in the best circles to snub her at the high altar during Sunday Mass; he could let it be known that her mother was a prostitute . . . He would discredit her, spatter her with mud! And as he left the Cathedral after Mass, he would relish the sight of her slinking by in her black cape, scorned by everyone, while he stood chatting to the wife of the district governor and being gallant to the Baronesa de Via-Clara! Then, at Lent, he would preach a brilliant sermon, and in the main square and in the shops, she would hear people say: He's a great man that Father Amaro!' He would become an ambitious intriguer and, protected by the Condesa de Ribamar, he would climb the ecclesiastical ranks: what would she think when one day he became Bishop of Leiria and, looking pale and interesting in his golden mitre, he walked down the Cathedral nave past a kneeling, penitent congregation, followed by the censer-bearers and accompanied by the strident music of the organ? What would have become of her by then? She would be a scrawny, wizened figure wrapped in a cheap shawl. And what of João Eduardo, her chosen one, her husband? He would sit hunched over his papers, a poorly paid clerk with nicotine-stained fingers and wearing a threadbare jacket, a barely perceptible figure always quick to flatter, but inwardly envious. And he, as Bishop, on the vast hierarchical stairway that reaches up into Heaven, would be far above mere men by then, in the zone of light cast by the face of the Lord our God! He would be a member of the Upper Chamber and the priests in his diocese would tremble when he frowned.

The church bell next door slowly struck ten o'clock.

What would she be doing at that hour, he wondered. She would probably be sitting in the dining room sewing; the clerk would be there; they would be playing cards and laughing; in the dark beneath the table, she might perhaps touch his foot with hers! He remembered her foot, the little flash of stocking he had seen when she jumped over the puddles at the farm; and his inflamed curiosity climbed all the way up the curve of her leg to her breasts, past beauties he could but imagine . . . God, how he loved the wretched girl! But he could not have her! And yet any other ugly, stupid fellow could go to Rua da Misericórdia and ask for her hand in marriage, could walk into the Cathedral and say to him: 'Father, marry us', and then, protected by Church and State, could kiss those arms and those breasts. But he could not! He was a priest! It was all the fault of that ghastly woman the Marquesa de Alegros!

He detested the whole secular world for having stripped him for ever of all his privileges, and since the priesthood excluded him from participation in human and social pleasures, he took refuge, instead, in the idea of the spiritual superiority his status gave him over other men. That miserable clerk might be able to marry and possess Amélia, but what was he in comparison with a priest on whom God had conferred the supreme power of deciding who should go to Heaven and who to Hell? And he gloated over this idea, gorging his spirit on priestly pride. However, a troubling thought soon surfaced: his dominion was valid only in the abstract region of souls; he would never be able to put his power into triumphant action in society. He was a God inside the Cathedral, but he had only to go out into the square and he was a mere obscure plebeian. An irreligious world had reduced the sphere of influence of all priestly action to the souls of a few overly devout ladies . . . And that was what he regretted, the social diminution of the Church, the mutilation of ecclesiastical power, which was limited now to the spiritual, with no rights over men's bodies, lives and wealth. He did not have the authority a priest had in the days when the Church was the nation, and the parish priest was temporal master of his flock. What did it matter to him that he had the right to open or close the doors of Heaven? What he wanted was the ancient right to open or close the doors of dungeons! He wanted clerks and Amélias to tremble at the mere shadow cast by his cassock. He would have liked to have been a priest in the old Church, when he would have enjoyed the advantages brought by the power of denunciation and by the kind of terror that an executioner inspires, and there, in that town, under the jurisdiction of his

Cathedral, he would have made all those who aspired to the joys that were forbidden to him tremble at the thought of excruciating punishments, and, thinking of João Eduardo and Amélia, he regretted not being able to bring back the bonfires of the Inquisition! In the grip of a fury provoked by thwarted passion, this inoffensive young man spent hours nursing grandiose ambitions of Catholic tyranny, for there is always a moment when even the most stupid priest is filled by the spirit of the Church in one of its two phases, that of mystical renunciation or that of world domination; every subdeacon at one time or another believes himself capable of being either a saint or a Pope; there is not a single seminarian who has not, albeit for an instant, aspired longingly to that cave in the desert in which St Jerome, looking up at the starry sky, felt Grace flow into his heart like an abundant river of milk; and even the potbellied parish priest who, at close of day, sits on his balcony probing the hole in his tooth with a toothpick or, with a paternal air, slowly sips his cup of coffee, even he carries within him the barely perceptible remnants of a Grand Inquisitor.

Amaro's life grew monotonous. March was coming to a damp, chilly end; and after the service in the Cathedral, Amaro would go home, take off his muddy boots and sit in his slippers feeling bored. He ate at three o'clock, and he never lifted the cracked lid of the tureen without remembering, with a feeling of intense nostalgia, the meals he had had in Rua da Misericórdia, when Amélia, wearing the whitest of collars, would pass him his bowl of chick pea soup, smiling and affectionate. Vicência, vast and erect, like a soldier in skirts, stood beside him to serve; she always seemed to be suffering from a heavy cold and would keep turning her head away to blow her nose noisily on her apron. She was not fussy about cleanliness either; all the knife handles were sticky with grease from the dirty washing-up water. Sad and indifferent, Amaro did not complain; he ate badly and in haste; he would ask for a cup of coffee and spend hour upon hour sitting at the table, plunged in silent tedium, now and then tipping the ash from his cigarette into the saucer, feeling his feet and his knees growing cold in the wind that blew in through the cracks of that bleak room.

Sometimes, the coadjutor, who had never once visited him in Rua da Misericórdia, would drop in after supper and sit a long way from the table, not saying a word, his umbrella between his knees. Then, in an attempt to please Amaro, he would invariably say:

'You're much better off here, you know; it's always best to have your own place.'

'Hm,' Amaro would grunt.

At first, to soothe his own hurt and anger, Amaro would speak slightingly of São Joaneira, attempting to provoke the coadjutor, who was a native of Leiria, into retailing the scandals of Rua da Misericórdia. The coadjutor, out of pure servility, would merely smile perfidiously and say nothing.

'There's something fishy going on there, don't you think?' Amaro would begin.

The coadjutor would shrug, holding his hands up, palms spread, with a mischievous look on his face, but he did not utter a sound, fearing that his words, if repeated, might offend the Canon. So they would sit on glumly, occasionally exchanging the odd, inconsequential remark: a baptism that had taken place; what Canon Campos had said; an altar cloth that needed washing. These conversations bored Amaro; he felt very little like a priest and very remote from the ecclesiastical clique: he was not interested in the canons' intrigues, the precentor's much-commented-upon favouritism, the thefts from the poorhouse, the diocesan tribunal's wranglings with the district government, and he felt indifferent to and ill-informed about the ecclesiastical gossip in which the priests took such feminine pleasure and which was as puerile as a child's tantrum and as convoluted as a conspiracy.

'Is the wind still blowing from the south?' he would ask at last, yawning.

'It is,' the coadjutor would reply.

Amaro would light the lamp; the coadjutor would get to his

feet, shake his umbrella and leave, with a sideways glance at Vicência.

That was the worst time, at night, when he was left alone. He tried to read, but books bored him; grown unused to reading, he kept losing the thread. He would go over to the window and look out; the night was dark and the streets gleamed dully. When would this life be over? He would light a cigarette and begin pacing up and down, his hands behind his back, from the basin to the window. Sometimes he went to bed without praying, and he had no scruples about it; he felt that having renounced Amélia was enough of a penance in itself, and there was no need for him to wear himself out reading prayers; he had made his 'sacrifice' and he felt more or less even with Heaven.

And so he continued to live alone: Canon Dias never came to see him in Rua das Sousas because, he said, just going into the house made his stomach churn. And Amaro, growing more sullen by the day, did not go back to São Joaneira's house. He was very shocked that she had not sent him an invitation to the Friday gatherings; he attributed that 'snub' to Amélia's hostility towards him, and in order not to see her, he swapped with Father Silveira, and so instead of saying the midday mass to which she used to come, he said the nine o'clock mass instead, furious at having to make yet another sacrifice.

Every night, when she heard the door bell ring, Amélia's heart beat so fast that, for a moment, she could barely breathe. Then she would hear João Eduardo's boots come creaking up the stairs or would recognise the soft tread of the Gansoso sisters' galoshes, and she would lean back in her chair, closing her eyes, as if wearied by an oft-repeated despair. She was waiting for Father Amaro, and sometimes, around ten o'clock, when she knew he would not come, her melancholy became so painful that her throat would grow tight with repressed sobs, and she would have to set aside her sewing and say:

'I'm going to lie down, I've got a really splitting headache!'

She would lie prone on the bed, desperately murmuring over and over:

'Dear Lady of Sorrows, my protectress, why does he not come, why does he not come?'

During the first few days, immediately after his departure, the whole house had seemed deserted and gloomy. When she had gone into his bedroom and seen the hooks empty of his clothes and the sideboard empty of his books, she had burst into tears. She went over and kissed the pillow on which he had slept, and clutched wildly to her breast the last towel on which he had dried his hands! His face was always there before her, he appeared in all her dreams. With separation, her love only burned more strongly, like a solitary bonfire, the flames growing ever higher.

One afternoon, she had gone to see a cousin of hers who worked as a nurse in the hospital, and when she reached the bridge, she saw a lot of people standing gawping at a young woman wearing a short, scarlet jacket and with her obviously false hair all dishevelled; she was shaking her fist and hoarsely cursing a soldier, a big country lad with a round, coarse, still beardless face; he had his back turned to her, and was shrugging his shoulders, his hands in his pockets, muttering:

'I didn't do anything to her, honest . . .'

Senhor Vasques, who ran a clothier's in the main square, had stopped to look, disapproving of such a 'lack of public order'.

'Has something happened?' Amélia asked him.

'Oh, hello, Miss Amélia! It's just some soldier's prank. He threw a dead rat in her face, and the woman is kicking up a terrible fuss. Slut!'

Then the woman in the red jacket turned round, and Amélia was horrified to see Joaninha Gomes, her friend from school, who had gone on to become Father Abílio's mistress. The priest had been suspended and had abandoned her; she had left for Pombal, then for Oporto, sinking ever lower, until she finally returned to Leiria, where she lived in an alley near the barracks, growing thinner and thinner, used by a whole regiment. Dear God, what an example!

And she too loved a priest! Just as Joaninha once had, she too wept over her sewing when Father Amaro did not arrive.

Where was that passion leading her? To Joaninha's fate? To being the parish priest's mistress? And she could already imagine herself being pointed at in the street, in the square, then later abandoned by him, with his child inside her, without so much as a crust of bread to eat! And like a gust of wind that instantly clears the sky of clouds, the sharp horror of that encounter with Joaninha swept from her mind the morbid, amorous mists in which she was losing her way. She decided to take advantage of their separation and to forget about Amaro; she even considered hastening her marriage to João Eduardo in order to take refuge in a more pressing duty; for some days, she tried hard to feel interested in him; she even began embroidering a pair of slippers for him . . .

But gradually the 'bad idea' which, when attacked, had shrunk away and played dead, began slowly to uncoil, to rise up and invade her again. Day and night, whether she was sewing or praying, the idea of Father Amaro, his eyes and his voice, would appear to her like stubborn, ever more alluring temptations. What was he doing? Why did he not come to see her? Did he like someone else? She suffered from vague, fierce, searing jealousies. And that passion wrapped about her like an atmosphere from which she could not escape, which followed her if she attempted to flee, and which gave her life! In the fire running through her, all her honest resolutions shrivelled and died like feeble flowers. Whenever the memory of Joaninha resurfaced, she would push it irritably away and would hastily go over all the nonsensical reasons she could think of for loving Father Amaro. She had only one idea now: to throw her arms around his neck and kiss him, oh, yes, kiss him! And then, if necessary, die.

She began to grow impatient with João Eduardo's love. She found it 'stupid'.

'Oh, no!' she would think when she heard his step on the stairs at night.

She could not stand him with his eyes always fixed on her, she could not stand his black jacket, his boring conversations about the district government.

And she idealised Amaro. Her nights were shaken by lewd

dreams and, during the day, she lived in a state of jealous agitation and suffered from fits of black melancholy which, as her mother said, 'made you feel like shaking her'.

She grew sullen.

'Good heavens, girl, whatever's wrong with you?' her mother would exclaim.

'I don't feel well. I think I might be sickening for something.'

She did, in fact, look very pale and had lost her appetite. And one morning, she was confined to bed with a fever. Her frightened mother called in Dr Gouveia. After seeing Amélia, the old practitioner came back into the dining room, contentedly taking a pinch of snuff.

'What do you think, Doctor?' São Joaneira asked.

'Marry the girl off, São Joaneira, marry her off now. I've told you so before.'

'But, Doctor . . .'

'Get her married off now, São Joaneira, now!' he kept saying as he went down the stairs, slightly dragging his rheumaticky right leg.

Amélia eventually got better, to the great joy of João Eduardo, who was in torment as long as she was ill, regretting not being able to nurse her himself and occasionally shedding a sad tear on the documents drawn up by his dour employer, Nunes Ferral.

The following Sunday, at the nine o'clock mass, as Amaro went up to the altar, he noticed Amélia amongst the distant congregation; she was sitting next to her mother and wearing her black silk dress with all the ruffles. He closed his eyes for a moment, barely able to hold the chalice steady in his trembling hands.

When, after mumbling his way through the Gospel, Amaro made the sign of the cross over the missal, then crossed himself and turned back to the congregation saying *Dominus vobiscum*, the wife of Carlos the pharmacist said to Amélia 'the priest looks so pale you'd think he was in pain'. Amélia did not reply, bent over her prayer book, her face scarlet. And during mass, sitting back on her heels, absorbed in thought, her face passionate and ecstatic, she drank in his presence, his thin hands holding up the host, his handsome head bowed in ritual adoration; her skin prickled with sweet excitement whenever he uttered some rapid Latin phrase out loud; and when Amaro, his left hand on his breast and his right hand outstretched, pronounced to the congregation the *Benedicat vos*, she, her eyes wide open, projected her whole soul towards the altar, as if he were the God beneath whose blessing heads bowed along the whole length of the Cathedral, right to the very back where the villagers with their heavy walking sticks stood gazing in astonishment at the golden monstrance.

As they were leaving, it started to rain, and Amélia and her mother were standing at the door with the other ladies, waiting for the rain to let up.

'Hello! Fancy seeing you here!' Amaro cried, coming over to them, his face stark white.

'We're waiting for the rain to stop, Father,' said São Joaneira, turning round, and adding reproachfully: 'And why have you not been to see us, Father? Was it something we did? It's enough to make people talk . . .'

'I-I've been very busy,' stammered Amaro.

'But you could have come over for a while in the evening. You know, it's quite upset me. And everyone has noticed. It's most ungrateful of you, Father!'

Blushing, Amaro said:

'Well, enough is enough. I'll come round tonight and may all be forgiven . . .'

Amélia, who was equally red-faced, was trying to conceal her agitation by gazing up at the heavy sky, as if frightened by the storm.

Amaro then offered them his umbrella. And while São Joaneira was opening it, carefully gathering up her silk dress, Amélia said to Amaro:

'Until tonight, then.' And in a quieter voice, looking fearfully around her: 'Please come. I've been so miserable! I've been quite mad. Please come, for my sake!'

On his way home, Amaro had to keep himself from

running along the streets in his cassock. He went into his room, sat down at the foot of the bed, and stayed there saturated with happiness, like a plump sparrow in a warm shaft of sunlight: he remembered Amélia's face, the curve of her shoulders, the sweetness of their meetings, the words she had spoken: 'I've been quite mad.' The certainty that the girl loved him blew through his soul like a powerful gust of wind and whispered in every corner of his being with the melodious murmur of unconfined joy. And he strode about the room, arms outstretched, wanting to possess her body that very instant; he felt prodigiously proud; he stood in front of the mirror puffing out his chest, as if the world were a pedestal built for him alone. He could scarcely eat. How he longed for the night. The weather cleared up in the evening, and he kept checking his silver fob watch and looking irritably out of the window at the bright day still lingering on the horizon. He polished his shoes himself and pomaded his hair. And before leaving, he carefully said his prayers because, in the presence of that newly acquired love, he was suddenly superstitiously afraid that God or the scandalised saints might spoil it for him, and he did not want to give them reason for complaint by neglecting his devotions.

As he walked down Amélia's street, his heart was beating so fast he had to stop, scarcely able to breathe; and the hooting of the owls roosting on the poorhouse wall, which he had not heard for weeks, sounded to him like sweet music.

And the expressions of surprise when he entered the dining room!

'How good to see you! We thought you'd died! A miracle! . . .'

Dona Maria da Assunção was there, as were the Gansoso sisters. They enthusiastically pushed back their chairs to make room for him and to admire him.

'So what have you been up to? You're looking thinner, you know.'

Libaninho was standing in the middle of the room imitating rockets shooting up into the sky. Artur Couceiro improvised a *fado* on the guitar:

The parish priest has come back home
To partake of São Joaneira's tea,
Let joy, let joy be unconfined,
And let's talk him to his knees!

There was applause, and São Joaneira, rocking with laughter, said:

'It was pure ingratitude on his part.'

'Ingratitude, you say,' snorted the Canon. 'Stubbornness more like.'

Amélia said nothing, her cheeks burning, her startled, shining eyes fixed on Father Amaro, to whom they had given the Canon's armchair, in which he leaned back, tumescent with pleasure, making the ladies laugh with his jokes about Vicência's ineptitude.

Alone in a corner, João Eduardo sat leafing through an old scrapbook.

IX

Thus Amaro resumed his close relations with Rua da Misericórdia. He dined early, read his breviary and, barely had the church clock struck seven than he would wrap his cloak about him, cross the main square and go past the pharmacy, where the regulars were standing around airing their usual views, their plump hands resting on the handles of their umbrellas. As soon as Amaro saw the light on in the dining-room window, all his desire would rise up in him again, but at the shrill sound of the door bell, he still sometimes felt a vague fear that he might encounter a distrustful São Joaneira or a cold Amélia. Out of superstition he always entered the house with his right foot.

He would find the Gansoso sisters already there, along with Dona Josefa Dias and the Canon; the latter often dined at São Joaneira's now and, at that hour, he would be slumped in his armchair, and, waking from his nap, would say with a yawn:

'Ah, there's my boy!'

Amaro would go and sit next to Amélia, who was sewing at the table; the penetrating look they exchanged each night was like a mutual, silent oath to each other that their love had grown since the previous evening, and sometimes, beneath the table, they would even passionately rub knees. Then the evening chatter would begin. Always the same topics, problems at the poorhouse, what the precentor had said, how Canon Campos had dismissed his maid, the latest gossip about Novais' wife . . .

'Remember, love thy neighbour!' the Canon would mutter, stirring briefly in his armchair before belching and once more closing his eyes.

Then João Eduardo's boots would creak on the stairs, and Amélia would immediately open up the table for a game of cards; the players were Dona Joaquina Gansoso, Dona Josefa and Father Amaro; since Amaro played badly, Amélia, his 'teacher', would sit behind him to 'guide' him. Arguments would break out as soon as the first cards were dealt. Then Amaro would turn to Amélia, their faces so close that their breath mingled.

'This one?' he would ask, indicating the card with a languid eye.

'No, no! Wait, let me see,' she would say, her face bright red.

Her arm would brush against Amaro's shoulder, and Amaro could smell the eau-de-cologne in which she always doused herself.

Opposite them, next to Joaquina Gansoso, sat João Eduardo, chewing his moustache and gazing at her passionately. In order to free herself from those two languorous eyes fixed on her, Amélia had finally told him that it was positively indecent to stare at her all night in full view of the parish priest, with whom you had to be on your best behaviour.

Sometimes she would even say to him, laughing:

'João Eduardo, go and talk to my mother, otherwise she might fall asleep.'

And João Eduardo would go and sit next to São Joaneira, who would be drowsily knitting, her spectacles perched on the end of her nose.

After tea, Amélia would sit down at the piano. An old Mexican song, 'La Chiquita', was all the rage in Leiria at the time. Amaro thought it 'delicious' and smiled with pleasure, showing his white teeth, as soon as Amélia began to sing in languorous, tropical tones:

When I sailed forth from Old Havana . . .

But it was the next verse that he loved best, when Amélia, leaning back, slightly rolling her eyes and gently moving her head, would voluptuously pronounce each syllable, as her fingers lightly brushed the keys:

If a little dove comes to your window
Treat him with love because that dove is me.

And how delightful, how Mexican she sounded as she trilled:

Ay chiquita que sí,
Ay chiquita que no-o-o-o!

But the old ladies would demand that he continue the game and so he would sit down again, humming the last notes of the song, with a cigarette in the corner of his mouth and his eyes shining with happiness.

Friday was the big night. Dona Maria da Assunção would always wear her beautiful black silk dress, and because she was rich and had aristocratic connections, everyone deferred to her and gave her the best place at the table, where she would sit down, affectedly swaying her hips and with much rustling of silk. Before tea was served, São Joaneira would always take her into her bedroom where she kept a bottle of fortified wine, and there the two friends would sit on low chairs and chat. Then Artur Couceiro, who looked gaunter and more tubercular with each day that passed, would sing the latest *fado* he had composed, called the 'Confession Fado', which he had written specially to please that pious gathering of skirts and cassocks:

In the chapel of love,
At the back of the church,
I opened my heart
To Father Cupid . . .

This was followed by a confession of tender little sins, an act of loving contrition and an equally loving penance:

Six kisses in the morning,
A single embrace before bed
And to calm the tender flames of love
Breakfast on unleavened bread.

That composition, which was at once gallant and devout,

was much appreciated by Leiria's ecclesiastical society. The precentor had requested a copy and had enquired as to the name of the composer, saying:

'And who is this witty Anacreon?'

When told that it was none other than the clerk in the municipal council offices, he spoke of him in such glowing terms to the wife of the district governor that Artur finally received the eight thousand *mil réis* increase for which he had been begging for years.

Libaninho was another constant presence at those gatherings. His latest prank was to steal kisses from Dona Maria da Assunção; the old lady would protest loudly and then, fanning herself furiously, shoot him greedy glances. Then Libaninho would disappear for a moment only to return wearing one of Amélia's petticoats and one of São Joaneira's bonnets; he would then feign a burning, lubricious passion for João Eduardo, who would retreat, red-faced, to loud shrieks of laughter from the old ladies. Brito and Natário sometimes came as well, and then they would all play lotto. Amaro and Amélia always sat next to each other, and they would spend all night, their knees pressed together, both of them scarlet-cheeked, as if somehow numbed by the same urgent desire.

Each night, Amaro left São Joaneira's house more in love with Amélia than ever. He would walk slowly down the street, pleasurably pondering the delicious feelings which that love provoked – certain looks she gave him, the passionate rise and fall of her breast, the lascivious way she touched his knee or squeezed his hand. At home, he would undress quickly because he liked to think about her as he lay snuggled up beneath the blankets in the dark; and then, like someone smelling one flower after another, he would go over in his mind, one by one, the many proofs she had given him of her love, until he was intoxicated by pride. She was the prettiest girl in the town! And she had chosen him, the priest, the man eternally excluded from feminine dreams, the neutral, melancholy creature who prowls the shores of sentiment like a suspicious intruder. Then his own passion would become mingled with concern for her, and, eyes closed, he would murmur:

'Bless her, poor love, bless her!'

But his passion was sometimes full of impatience too. Having spent three hours with her eyes upon him, three hours absorbing the voluptuousness that her every movement exuded, he would feel so heavy with desire that he would have to keep a tight rein on himself in order not to commit some folly, right there in the room, in front of her mother. Then later, at home, he would desperately twine his arms about himself: he wanted her there at that very moment, offering herself up to his desires; he would think up various schemes – he would write to her, they would find a little house where they could share their love, they would plan a walk to some farm. But all these ideas struck him as both flawed and dangerous when he recalled Dona Josefa's prying eyes and the gossipy Gansoso sisters. Confronted by these difficulties, which rose before him like the encircling walls of a citadel, the old complaints returned: Not being free! Not being able to walk straight into that house and say that he wanted to marry her and to enjoy her without sin, at his leisure! Why had they made a priest of him? It was all the fault of that silly old woman, the Marquesa de Alegros! He had not voluntarily given up his man's heart. They had driven him into the priesthood the way they might drive an ox into a corral.

Then, pacing excitedly up and down his room, he would take his accusations further and fulminate against Celibacy and against the Church: why did the Church forbid its priests, who were, after all, men living amongst men, that most natural of satisfactions, one that even the animals enjoy? Do they imagine that as soon as an old bishop says to a strong, young man 'Thou shalt be chaste' that his blood suddenly grows cold? And that a single Latin word – *accedo* – tremulously spoken by a frightened seminarian will be enough to contain for ever his formidably rebellious body? And who had come up with the idea in the first place? A council of decrepit bishops, withered as parchments, useless as eunuchs, emerging from the depths of their cloisters, from the peace of their colleges. What did they know about Nature and its temptations? Let them spend two or three hours next to Amélia and even they would see desire rise up beneath their cloak of sanctity. We can avoid and dodge everything except love. And if that is so, why then did they stop priests from feeling it and experiencing it with purity and dignity? Or is it better to seek it out in vile alleyways? Because the flesh is weak.

The flesh! He would ponder the three enemies of the soul – THE WORLD, THE DEVIL AND THE FLESH. And they appeared in his imagination as three very real figures: an extremely beautiful woman; a black creature with fiery eyes and cloven hooves; and the world, a vague, marvellous thing (wealth, horses, mansions) whose most perfect personification seemed to him to be the Conde de Ribamar. But what harm had they done to his soul? He had never seen the Devil; the beautiful woman loved him and was his only consolation; and from the world, the Count, he had received only protection, kindness and warm handclasps . . . And how could he avoid the influences of the Flesh and the World? Only by fleeing, as saints once used to do, to the sands of the desert and the company of wild beasts. Had his teachers in the seminary not told him, though, that he belonged to a militant Church? Asceticism was therefore wrong, since it was a dereliction of saintly duty. He did not understand, he simply did not understand!

Then he tried to justify his love with examples from divine literature. The Bible was full of weddings. Amorous queens advance in their jewel-encrusted robes; the bridegroom, leading a white lamb, comes to meet them, a turban of pure linen about his head; the Levites bang silver cymbals and call out God's name; the iron doors of the city swing open to admit the caravan that has come to carry off the bridal pair; and the sandalwood chests containing the treasures of the dowry creak as they are bound with purple cords onto the backs of camels. Beneath the lions' hot breath and to the acclaim of the plebeian crowd, the martyrs in the arena marry with a kiss. Even Jesus himself did not always maintain his inhuman saintliness; in the streets of Jerusalem and in the market places of the City of David, he was cold and absorbed, but he had a place of sweet ease in Bethany, beneath the sycamores of the Garden of Lazarus; there, while his lean Nazarene friends are drinking milk and plotting, he is gazing out at the golden roofs of the temple, at the Roman soldiers throwing the discus near the Golden Gate, at the loving couples walking beneath the trees in Gethsemane, and he places one hand on the golden hair of Martha, who loves him and sits at his feet, engrossed in her spinning.

His love, therefore, was an infraction of canon law, but not a sin of the soul; it might displease the precentor, but not God; it would be perfectly legitimate in a priesthood with more human rules. He thought of becoming a Protestant, but where, how? This seemed even more of an impossibility than transporting the Cathedral up to the Castle on the hill.

He would shrug then, scornful of all these muddled inner arguments. Mere philosophy and prattle! He was mad about Amélia – that much was clear. He wanted her love, her kisses, her soul . . . And if the bishop were not so old, he would want the same, as would the Pope!

Sometimes he was still pacing his room, talking to himself, at three o'clock in the morning.

João Eduardo, walking along Rua das Sousas late at night, had often seen a dim light burning in Father Amaro's window. For like all those thwarted in love, João Eduardo had recently got into the sad habit of wandering the streets into the early hours.

The clerk had noticed Amélia's liking for the parish priest right from the start. But knowing her upbringing and the devout habits of the house, he had attributed her almost humble attitude towards Amaro to her respect for him as a priest, for his status as confessor.

Instinctively, though, he began to hate Amaro. He had always detested priests. He thought them 'a danger to civilisation and to freedom'; he believed them to be intriguers with lustful habits, constantly conspiring to bring back the dark days of the Middle Ages; he loathed confession, which he judged to be a terrible weapon against domestic peace; and he had vague religious beliefs that rejected ritual, prayer and fasting, but admired the poetical, revolutionary Jesus, the friend of the poor, and 'the sublime spirit of God that fills the whole Universe'! He had been going to mass regularly since he had been in love with Amélia, but only in order to please São Joaneira.

And he wanted to get married quickly in order to remove Amélia from that world of religious fanatics and priests, afraid that he might later have a wife who was terrified of Hell, who spent hours praying the Stations of the Cross in the Cathedral and confessing to priests who 'drag from confessants the secrets of the bedroom'.

When Amaro had started visiting Rua da Misericórdia again, João Eduardo had been greatly annoyed. 'So the rascal's come back,' he thought. But annoyance had turned to distress when he saw that now Amélia treated Amaro with an even more tender familiarity, that in his presence she became unusually animated, that there seemed to be some kind of flirtation going on. She blushed scarlet whenever Amaro entered the room! She listened to him with ardent admiration. She always made sure to sit next to him when they played lotto.

One morning, he went to Rua da Misericórdia in a state of some agitation, and while São Joaneira was chatting in the kitchen, he said sharply to Amélia:

'Miss Amélia, I really don't like the way you behave with Father Amaro.'

She looked up, shocked:

'Whatever do you mean? How do you expect me to treat him? He's a friend of the family, he used to be a lodger here . . .'

'I know, I know . . .'

'But don't worry, if it annoys you, I won't go near the man again.'

Reassured, João Eduardo reasoned that 'there was nothing going on'. He put her behaviour down to an excess of religious devotion, to her enthusiasm for the priesthood.

Amélia decided then to disguise what she felt in her heart; she had always considered the clerk to be rather obtuse, but if he had noticed, how could the all-seeing Gansoso sisters possibly fail to notice, or the Canon's sister with her long training in malice. That is why, from then on, whenever she heard Amaro coming up the stairs, she would adopt a distracted, artificial air; but, alas, as soon as he spoke to her in his soft voice or turned on her those dark eyes that set her nerves trembling, then, like a thin layer of snow melting beneath a strong sun, her coldness would vanish and her whole person became one continuous expression of love. Sometimes, she was so absorbed in her private ecstasy that she even forgot João Eduardo was there, and was surprised when she heard his melancholy voice in some other corner of the room.

She felt too that her mother's friends treated her 'inclination' for the priest with silent, friendly approval. He was, as the Canon said, a very pretty boy; and the old ladies' flirtatious manners and glances exuded an admiration for him that created a favourable climate in which Amélia's passion could grow. Dona Maria da Assunção occasionally whispered in her ear:

'Just look at him! He inspires real fervour. He's the pride of the clergy. There's no one else quite like him!'

And they all thought João Eduardo to be 'a ne-er-do-well'! Amélia no longer concealed her indifference towards him; the slippers she had begun embroidering for him had long since vanished into her work basket, and she no longer waited at the window to watch for him on his way to work.

Certainty had taken root in João Eduardo's soul, a soul, as he put it, which was now blacker than the night.

'She's in love with the priest,' he had concluded. And to the pain of his ruined happiness was added concern for her threatened honour.

One afternoon, seeing her leaving the Cathedral, he waited for her outside the pharmacy, and with great resolve said:

'I want to talk to you, Miss Amélia . . . Things can't go on like this . . . I can't . . . You're in love with the priest.'

She bit her lip and turned pale.

'How dare you insult me like that!'

And, outraged, she tried to walk on.

He grabbed the sleeve of her jacket.

'Listen, Miss Amélia, I don't mean to insult you, but you don't understand . . . It's nearly breaking my heart . . .' And his voice faltered with emotion.

'You're wrong, you're wrong . . .' she stammered.

'Swear to me then that there's nothing between you and the priest!'

'I swear on my own salvation that there's nothing between us. But I'll tell you something else, if you ever mention this again, or insult me, I'll tell Mama everything, and you needn't ever come to our house again.'

'But, Miss Amélia . . .'

'Look, we can't stand here talking. Dona Micaela is over there watching . . .'

An old lady had lifted the muslin curtain at a low window and was peering out with gleaming, greedy eyes, her withered face pressed eagerly to the glass. They parted, and the old lady, disappointed, let the curtain fall again.

That night, while the ladies were noisily discussing the missionaries who were preaching in Barrosa, Amélia, swiftly plying her needle, said to Amaro in a low voice:

'We must be careful . . . Don't look at me so much and don't sit so close. Someone has already noticed.'

Amaro immediately pushed his chair back to be nearer Dona Maria da Assunção, but despite Amélia's advice, he could not take his eyes off her in silent, anxious interrogation, afraid that her mother's distrust or the old ladies' malice might already be 'creating a scandal'. After tea, amidst the noise of chairs being rearranged for lotto, he asked her quickly:

'Who was it who noticed?'

'No one. I'm just afraid. We must hide our feelings.'

From then on there were no more sweet, stolen glances, no more chairs drawn up close together at the table, no more secrets; and they took a kind of piquant pleasure in affecting cold manners, proud in their certainty of the passion inflaming them. While Amaro somewhere else in the room chatted to the ladies, it was delicious to Amélia to adore his presence, his voice, his jokes, with her eyes chastely fixed on João Eduardo's slippers which, very astutely, she had once again begun to embroider.

The clerk, however, was still troubled; it bothered him to find the priest there every night, looking so at home, with his prosperous face, enjoying the old ladies' veneration. Amélia, it was true, behaved herself and was faithful to him, but he knew that the priest wanted her, was watching her, and despite that oath on her own salvation, that assurance that 'there was nothing between them', he feared that the stubborn admiration of the old ladies, for whom the priest was 'an angel', was seeping into Amélia; he would only be happy once (having obtained a post with the district governor) he had removed Amélia from that fanatical household; but this happiness was a long time in coming, and every night, he left Rua da Misericórdia feeling more in love, but with his life devoured by jealousy and a hatred of all priests and yet lacking the courage to give Amélia up. That was when he started wandering the streets until late; sometimes he even retraced his steps in order to look up at her closed windows; then he would stroll along the avenue by the river, but the cold rustle of the branches over the black waters only made him feel even sadder; he would go then to the billiard hall, and for a while would watch the pairs of men playing, and the scorekeeper, his hair all dishevelled, leaning on the cue rest, yawning. The room would be filled by the choking smell of cheap oil. Then he would leave and walk slowly over to the office of the local newspaper, *The District Voice*.

X

The editor of *The District Voice*, Agostinho Pinheiro, was, in fact, a relative of João Eduardo's. He was popularly known as Rickets, because of the large hump on his back and because of his scrawny, consumptive body. He always looked rather grimy, and his sallow, effeminate face and debauched eyes spoke of ancient, infamous vices. He had (so it was said in Leiria) been up to all kinds of roguery. And he had so often heard people exclaim 'If it wasn't for that hump on your back, I'd break your bones' that, finding his hump sufficient protection, he had acquired an air of serene impudence. He was from Lisbon, which made him even more suspect in the eyes of Leiria's grave bourgeois inhabitants; he attributed his hoarse, grating voice to his lack of tonsils, and, since he played the guitar, he deliberately kept his nicotine-stained fingernails long.

The District Voice had been created by a group of men known in Leiria as the Maia Group, who were particularly hostile to the district governor. Dr Godinho, who was the group's leader and official candidate, had found in Agostinho, as he put it, 'just the man they needed', for what the group needed was an unscrupulous rogue who knew how to spell and who could redraft in sonorous terms the insults, calumnies and allusions that they brought to his office in the form of unedited jottings. Agostinho was a shaper of villainies. They paid him fifteen *mil réis* a month and allowed him to live above the office in a crumbling third-floor apartment in an alleyway off the main square.

Agostinho wrote the editorial, the local news, as well as the *Correspondence* from Lisbon, and Prudêncio, a graduate, wrote the literary pages under the heading *Cultural Notes from Leiria*. He was a very decent lad, who found Agostinho utterly repulsive; however, such was his appetite for publicity that he made himself sit down fraternally at the same desk every

Saturday to check the proofs of his prose – a prose so overflowing with imagery that the people who read it would mutter: 'Such opulence!'

João Eduardo was equally aware that Agostinho was a worthless individual, and he would never have dared to be seen in the street with him during the day, but he enjoyed going late at night to the newspaper office, where he would smoke cigarettes and listen to Agostinho talking about Lisbon, about the different jobs he had had – on the editorial staff of two newspapers, in a theatre in Rua dos Condes, in a pawnshop and in various other institutions. His visits to Agostinho were secret.

At that time of night, the typesetting room on the first floor was closed (the newspaper was printed on Saturdays), and João Eduardo would find Agostinho upstairs, hunched over his desk, wearing an old fur jacket whose silver fastenings had long since been pawned, poring over long sheets of paper by the ghastly light of an oil lamp; he was busy composing the newspaper, and the dark room looked like a cave. João Eduardo would lie down on the wickerwork couch or search out Agostinho's old guitar and strum a lighthearted *fado*. The journalist, meanwhile, resting his head on one fist, would labour on, 'the words just weren't flowing', and, when not even João Eduardo's *fado* inspired him, he would get up, go over to a cupboard, pour himself a glass of gin which he would gulp down noisily, then give an almighty stretch, light a cigarette and sing hoarsely to the guitar accompaniment:

> It was that tyrant Fate
> Who led me to this life,

And the guitar: dir-lin, din, din, dir-lin, din, don.

> To this life of black despair,
> where all around is strife.

This always brought back memories of Lisbon, because he would end by declaring bitterly:

'God, this is a dreary place!'

He could not stand the fact that he was living in Leiria, instead of drinking in Tio João's tavern in the old Moorish quarter of Lisbon, with Ana Alfaiata or Bigodinho, listening to João das Biscas, who, with a cigar in the corner of his mouth, one weeping eye half-shut against the smoke, would draw plangent notes from the guitar and sing of the death of Sofia!

Then, in order to comfort himself with the certainty of his own talent, he would read his articles out to João Eduardo in a very loud voice. And João became interested because these recent 'creations' were always giving the clergy 'a good dressing-down' and thus coincided with his own preoccupations.

It was around this time that, over the famous matter of the poorhouse, Dr Godinho had grown increasingly hostile towards the Cathedral chapter and to the priesthood in general. He had always hated priests; he suffered from a chronic liver disease and, because the Church made him think of the cemetery, he hated cassocks, since they seemed to him a reminder of the shroud. Thus, urged on by Dr Godinho, Agostinho, who had a great well of bile to plumb, stepped up his criticisms; however, given his weakness for literature, his vituperations were encrusted in such thick layers of rhetoric that, as Canon Dias said: 'he was more bark than bite'.

On one such night, João Eduardo found Agostinho all fired up about an article he had written that evening, and which was full of wit 'worthy of Victor Hugo himself'.

'Just wait – it's really something!'

As usual, it was a diatribe against the clergy and a eulogy of Dr Godinho. Having celebrated the virtues of the doctor, 'that highly respected family man', and his eloquence in the courts, which 'had saved so many unfortunates from the sword of the law', the article addressed Christ in raucous tones: 'Who would have thought (roared Agostinho), O Immortal One who died for us on the Cross, who would have thought, as you hung there exhausted and dying on Golgotha, who would have thought that one day, in Your name, in Your shadow, Dr Godinho would have been expelled from a charitable institution, Dr Godinho, a man so pure of soul, so talented . . .' And Dr Godinho's virtues paraded slowly by, solemn and sublime, leaving in their train a host of noble adjectives.

Then, momentarily ceasing in his contemplation of Dr Godinho, Agostinho addressed himself directly to Rome: 'Do you come here at the height of the nineteenth century to throw in the face of liberal Leiria the rules of the *Syllabus of Errors*? Fine, then. If you want war, you shall have it!'

'How about that, João?' he said. 'It's powerful stuff, don't you think, and philosophical too!'

Then he resumed his reading:

'"If you want war, you shall have it! We will raise high our flag, which you may be quite sure is not the flag of demagogy, and with strong arms we will hoist that flag above the highest bastion of public liberty, and we will cry out to Leiria, we will cry out to Europe: let us fight, children of the nineteenth century, let us fight for progress!" That'll show 'em!'

João Eduardo, who had remained silent for a moment, said, fitting his words to Agostinho's sonorous prose:

'The clergy want to drag us back to the dark days of obscurantism!'

Such a literary phrase took Agostinho by surprise; he looked at João Eduardo and said:

'Why don't you write an article yourself?'

João Eduardo replied, smiling:

'Oh, I'd tear those priests off a strip, Agostinho . . . I'd show their rotten underbelly, because I know what they're like . . .'

Agostinho urged him to put this reprimand in writing:

'It would be just the job!'

Why, only yesterday, Dr Godinho had said to him: 'Attack anything that smells of the priesthood! Any scandal you hear, print it! If there isn't any scandal, then make it up!'

And Agostinho added kindly:

'And don't worry about the style, I can always smarten it up for you.'

'We'll see, we'll see,' muttered João Eduardo.

From then on, Agostinho kept asking him:

'What's happened to that article of yours? Bring me that article.'

He really did want it, because he knew that João Eduardo had intimate knowledge of 'São Joaneira's little canonical clique' and imagined that he was privy to all kinds of infamies.

João Eduardo, however, was unsure. What if he was found out?

'Nonsense!' said Agostinho. 'I'll publish it under my name, as an editorial. Who will ever know?'

It happened that, on the following night, João Eduardo caught Father Amaro slipping a note to Amélia, and the next evening, with the pallor of one who has not slept, he turned up at the newspaper office bearing five long sheets of paper, written in the tiny, neat hand of a clerk. It was his article and was entitled: 'The New Pharisees'. After a few flowery thoughts about Jesus and Golgotha, João Eduardo's article was, beneath allusions which were about as diaphanous as cobwebs, a vengeful attack on Canon Dias, Father Brito, Father Amaro and Father Natário. Each of them got his just deserts, as Agostinho joyfully exclaimed.

'When will it come out?' asked João Eduardo.

Agostinho rubbed his hands and thought.

'It's strong stuff! It practically names names, but don't worry, I'll sort that out.'

He cautiously showed the article to Dr Godinho, who thought it 'a vile calumny'. Dr Godinho and the Church had merely had a slight difference of opinion; he acknowledged that, in general, religion was necessary for the masses; besides, his wife, the lovely Dona Cândida, was extremely devout and had commented of late that she was finding the newspaper's war on the clergy distinctly troubling; and Dr Godinho did not want to provoke unnecessary hatred amongst the priests, foreseeing that his love of domestic peace, order and his duty as a Christian would soon force him into some form of reconciliation, 'which was against his best instincts, but nevertheless . . .'

Thus he merely said to Agostinho:

'This cannot be published as an editorial, but merely as some sort of "personal statement". Those are your orders.'

So Agostinho told João Eduardo that the article would be published as a 'personal statement' and signed: 'A Liberal'. João Eduardo had wanted to end the article with the words: 'Mothers, you have been warned!' Agostinho suggested that this final warning might give rise to the jocular riposte: 'Warned or warmed?!' After long discussions, they decided to close with: 'You have been warned, you men in black!'

The following Sunday, the article appeared, signed: 'A Liberal.'

Father Amaro had spent all of that Sunday morning, on his return from the Cathedral, laboriously composing a letter to Amélia. Impatient, as he put it, 'with a relationship that never seemed to get anywhere, that never went beyond exchanging glances and squeezing hands', he had, one night at the lotto table, managed to pass her a note written in blue ink in his best handwriting: 'I want to see you alone. I have so much to tell you. Where would be a safe place? May God protect our love.' She had not replied, and Amaro, much put out and concerned too because he had not seen her that morning at nine o'clock mass, had resolved to 'set everything out clearly in a love letter'; and he paced about the house, strewing the floor with cigarette ends, poring over his *Dictionary of Synonyms*, as he set down the kind of deeply felt phrases that would touch her heart.

> My dearest Amélia (he wrote), I cannot understand what possible reasons can have kept you from replying to the note I gave you at your mother's house; for I gave it to you out of the great need I feel to talk to you alone, and my intentions were entirely pure and born out of the innocence of this soul that loves you so much and has no thought of sin.
>
> You must know that I feel for you a fervent affection, and for your part (if I am not deceived by those eyes which are the beacons of my life, like the star by which the sailor

steers his ship) it seems to me that you too, my Amélia, are fond of me, your adoring friend; for even the other day, when Libano won at lotto with his first six numbers and everyone made such a fuss, you squeezed my hand under the table so tenderly that it seemed to me that Heaven opened and I could hear the angels singing their Hosannas. Why, then, did you not reply? If you are worried that our affection might bring down upon us the disapproval of our guardian angels, then all I can say is that you commit a far greater sin by keeping me in this torment of uncertainty, because my thoughts are with you even when I celebrate mass, so that I cannot even lift up my soul during the divine sacrifice. If I believed that this mutual affection was the work of the Tempter, I would say to you: dearly beloved child, let us make this sacrifice to Jesus to pay back part of the blood that he spilled for us! But I have looked into my soul and I see in it the whiteness of lilies. And your love too is as pure as your soul that will one day be joined with mine in happiness amidst celestial choirs. If you only knew how much I love you, Amélia; sometimes I feel as if I could eat you up a bite at a time! Please reply, and tell me what you think about meeting one afternoon at Morenal. I am longing to express to you the fire burning inside me, as well as to talk to you about important things, and to feel your hand in mine, that hand which I hope will lead me along the path of love, to the ecstasy of celestial joy. Farewell, my bewitching angel; receive herewith the heart of your lover and spiritual father,

Amaro.

After supper, he copied out the letter in blue ink, placed it neatly folded in the pocket of his cassock and set off for Rua da Misericórdia. When he arrived, he could already hear from the stairs Natário's shrill voice raised in argument.

'Who else is here tonight?' he asked Ruça, who came to light his way, her shawl pulled tight around her.

'All the ladies are here, and Father Brito.'

'Excellent!'

He bounded up the stairs and, at the door of the living room, with his cape still on, but raising high his hat, he said:

'A very good evening to everyone, starting, of course, with the ladies.'

Natário immediately planted himself before him and exclaimed:

'What do you think about it then?'

'About what?' asked Amaro. Then noticing that everyone was silent and had their eyes fixed on him, he said: 'What's wrong? Has something happened?'

'Haven't you read it, Father?' they all exclaimed. 'Haven't you read *The District Voice*?'

He had never set eyes on it, he said. Then the indignant ladies burst out:

'It's absolutely appalling!'

'It's scandalous, Father Amaro!'

With his hands plunged in his pockets, Natário was studying Amaro with a sarcastic little smile, muttering:

'He hasn't read it! He hasn't read it! So what have you been up to, then?'

Terrified, Amaro suddenly noticed that Amélia was looking deathly pale and that her eyes were red. Then the Canon got heavily to his feet:

'Father Amaro, someone has given us a real roasting.'

'What?' cried Amaro.

'Oh, yes, good and proper.'

They all agreed that the Canon, who had brought the newspaper with him, should read it out loud.

'Read it, Dias,' said Natário. 'Read it so that we can all enjoy it!'

São Joaneira turned up the oil lamp. Canon Dias sat down at the table, unfolded the newspaper, carefully put on his spectacles and, with his snuff-stained handkerchief spread on his knees, began, in his usual slow way, to read the article.

The beginning was of no interest; it consisted of heartfelt phrases in which the 'Liberal' blamed the Pharisees for the crucifixion of Jesus: 'Why did you kill him? (he exclaimed). Answer!' And the Pharisees answered: 'We killed him because he represented freedom, emancipation, the dawn of a new era' etc. The 'Liberal' then described in broad terms the night on Calvary: 'There he is hanging on the cross, pierced by spears; soldiers have cast lots for his tunic, the will of the people has prevailed' etc. And the 'Liberal' again rounded on the unfortunate Pharisees with cutting irony: 'Regard your work!' The 'Liberal' then made a nimble transition from Jerusalem to Leiria. 'But do the readers of this article believe that the Pharisees are dead? You are much deceived! They live! We all know them. Leiria is full of them, and we are about to introduce them to our readers . . .'

'This is where it begins,' said the Canon, peering at everyone over the top of his spectacles.

This was indeed where it began; it was a gallery of crude ecclesiastical photographs: the first was of Father Brito: 'Regard him (exclaimed the 'Liberal') strong as an ox, astride his brown mare . . .'

'They even give the colour of the mare!' murmured Dona Maria da Assunção in pious indignation.

' . . . As ignorant as a melon, and he does not even know Latin . . .'

Father Amaro kept uttering astonished cries of: Oh! Oh! And Father Brito, scarlet-faced, fidgeted in his chair, slowly rubbing his knees.

'A bully,' continued the Canon, who read these cruel words with sweet serenity, 'rude in manner, but not averse to tenderness, who, according to well-informed sources, has chosen as his Dulcinea the administrator's legal spouse . . .'

Father Brito could control himself no longer:

'I'll tear the man in two!' he exclaimed, getting up, only to fall back heavily into his chair.

'Wait a moment, man!' said Natário.

'What do you mean, "wait a moment"?' I'll tear the man in two.'

But how could he when he did not even know who the 'Liberal' was?

'Forget the "Liberal"! The man I'm going to tear in two is

Dr Godinho. Dr Godinho owns the paper, and he's the man I'll tear in two!'

His voice had grown hoarse and he kept slapping himself furiously on the thigh.

They reminded him of the Christian duty of forgiveness. São Joaneira unctuously mentioned the blows Jesus Christ had had to bear. He should imitate Christ.

'Oh, forget Christ!' yelled Brito, apoplectic.

Such impiety provoked real horror.

'Please, Father Brito, please!' exclaimed the Canon's sister, pushing back her chair.

Libaninho, clasping his head in his hands, bowed before the impending disaster and murmured:

'Holy Mother of God, we might all be struck by lightning!'

And seeing that Amélia too was indignant, Amaro said gravely:

'Really, Brito, you go too far!'

'Well, they drove me to it!'

'No one drove you to it,' said Amaro firmly. And in a pedagogical tone, he added: 'I will only remind you, as is my duty, that in such cases of blasphemy, the Reverend Father Scomelli recommends general confession and two days' retreat on bread and water.'

Father Brito was muttering to himself.

'All right, all right,' said Natário. 'Brito may have committed a grave error, but he will ask God's pardon and God's mercy is infinite.'

There was a meaningful pause in which Dona Maria da Assunção was heard to murmur that she was 'completely drained'; and the Canon, who, during this crisis, had placed his spectacles on the table, picked them up again and calmly resumed his reading:

'You will be familiar with another such priest with a face like a ferret.'

All eyes fell on Father Natário.

'Do not trust him; he will not hesitate to betray you; he will take pleasure in harming you; his intrigues keep the Cathedral chapter in a state of constant uproar because he is the most venomous snake in the whole diocese, and yet he is very fond of gardening, for he carefully cultivates two little roses.'

'I say!' exclaimed Amaro.

'You see what I mean?' said Natário, standing up, his face ashen. 'What do you think? You all know how I often refer to my nieces as "my two little roses". It's just a joke. And yet he even attacks that!' And with a grim, embittered smile, he said: 'But tomorrow I'll find out who he is, oh yes, I'll find out all right.'

'Just treat it with the disdain it deserves, Father Natário,' said São Joaneira soothingly.

'Thank you, Senhora,' Natário responded, bowing with rancorous irony. 'Thank you so much. I'll do just that.'

But the Canon was reading on in his imperturbable voice. The next hate-filled thumbnail sketch was of him.

'A pot-bellied, gluttonous canon, and a former supporter of the usurper Prince Miguel, he was driven out of the parish of Ourém and once taught Moral Theology in a seminary; now, however, he teaches Immoral Theology in Leiria . . .'

'Disgraceful!' said Amaro, outraged.

The Canon put the newspaper down and said languidly:

'You don't really think this bothers me, do you?' he said. 'Certainly not. I've got enough to eat and drink, thank God. People can say what they like.'

'But, brother,' broke in his sister, 'we all have our pride.'

'Sister,' replied Canon Dias with all the bitterness of concentrated rage, 'no one asked you for your opinion.'

'I don't need to be asked!' she cried, drawing herself up. 'I can give my opinion when and how I choose. *You* may not feel ashamed, but I do.'

'Now, now . . .' everyone said, trying to calm her down.

'Hold your tongue, sister!' said the Canon, folding up his glasses. 'Your false teeth might fall out!'

'You rude man!'

She was about to say more, but the words would not come, and she began instead to sigh pitifully.

They were all concerned that she might faint. São Joaneira and Dona Joaquina Gansoso helped her into the bedroom, saying softly:

'Have you gone mad? Really, woman! Such a fuss! Pull yourself together!'

Amélia called for some orange flower water.

'Leave her be,' grumbled the Canon, 'just leave her be. It will pass. It's one of her hot flushes.'

Amélia exchanged a sad glance with Father Amaro and went into the bedroom with Dona Maria da Assunção and the deaf Gansoso sister, who were also going along 'to calm poor Dona Josefa down'. The priests were left alone, and the Canon turned to Amaro.

'Now it's your turn,' he said, taking up the newspaper again.

'And he really tears into you,' said Natário.

The Canon cleared his throat, brought the oil lamp closer and read:

'. . . But the real danger comes from certain dandified young priests who acquired their parish posting through the influence of certain aristocrats in Lisbon, and who, befriended by good families with pure young daughters who have no experience of the world, use the influence of their sacred ministry to plant in those innocent souls the burning seed of sin!'

'Outrageous!' murmured Amaro, deathly pale.

'Tell me, priest of Christ, what do you intend to do with that unsullied maid? Do you intend to drag her into the mire of vice? What are you doing in the bosom of that respectable family? Why are you stalking your prey the way a kite circles over the innocent dove? Fie on you, sacrilegist! You whisper seductive words in her ear in order to turn her from the path of honour; you condemn to disgrace and widowhood an honest girl who wishes only to offer you her hard-working hand, and you meanwhile are preparing for her a hideous future full of tears. And why are you doing all this? In order to sate the vile impulses of your sinful lust!'

'Disgraceful!' Father Amaro muttered between clenched teeth.

'But beware, evil priest!' And the Canon's voice took on cavernous tones as he spoke these words. 'The archangel is raising his sword of justice in readiness, and the enlightened inhabitants of Leiria can now view you and your accomplices with impartial eyes. Here we stand, we sons of toil, to mark your brow with the stigma of infamy. Therefore tremble, you supporters of the *Syllabus of Errors*. You have been warned, you men in black!'

'Extraordinary!' said the Canon, as he folded up the newspaper, beads of sweat standing out on his forehead.

Father Amaro's eyes were brimming with angry tears and he was breathing heavily; he slowly wiped his brow with his handkerchief, then, lips trembling, he said:

'I just don't know what to say, gentlemen. As God is my witness, that is the calumny of calumnies.'

'A shameless calumny,' they all rumbled.

'It seems to me,' went on Amaro, 'that we should go to the authorities about this.'

'That's exactly what I said,' broke in Natário, 'we need to talk to the secretary- general.'

'Oh, rubbish!' roared Father Brito. 'Go to the authorities? What the man needs is a good beating. I'll drink the fellow's blood!'

The Canon, who was deep in thought, stroking his chin, said:

'Natário, you're the one who should go to see the secretary-general. You've got a way with words and logic.'

'If that's what you want,' said Natário, bowing, 'I'll do it. I'll tell the authorities all about it'

Amaro was still sitting at the table, his head in his hands, utterly shaken. Libaninho murmured:

'I know that none of this has anything to do with me, but just listening to that whole diatribe made my knees knock. A scandal like this . . .'

But at that moment, they heard the voice of Dona Joaquina Gansoso as she came up the stairs, and the Canon said quietly and prudently:

'Gentlemen, it's best to say nothing more about this in front of the ladies. We've said all we need to say.'

A moment later, as soon as Amélia came into the room,

Amaro, declaring that he had a splitting headache, got to his feet and bade farewell to the ladies.

'Aren't you even stopping for tea?' asked São Joaneira.

'No, thank you, Senhora,' he said, wrapping his cape around him. 'I'm not feeling at all well. Goodnight. Meet me tomorrow, Natário, at one o'clock in the Cathedral.'

He squeezed Amélia's hand, which lay limp and passive in his. Then he left, shoulders hunched.

São Joaneira remarked sadly:

'Father Amaro looked dreadfully pale.'

The Canon got to his feet and said in an impatient, irritated voice:

'He may be pale now, but he'll be red enough in the face tomorrow. I just want to say one thing: this rant in the newspaper is the calumny of all calumnies. I don't know who wrote it or why, but it's just a lot of shameless nonsense. The person behind it is a fool and a rogue. We know what we have to do, and we've discussed the matter quite enough, so bring in the tea. What's done is done and let's hear no more about it.'

Everyone else still looked so cast down that the Canon added:

'One other thing: no one has died, and there is no need for anyone to look as if they had. Amélia, sit down at the piano and play me that tune I like, "Chiquita".'

The secretary-general, Gouveia Ledesma, a former journalist, and in his more expansive youth, the author of a sentimental volume entitled *Reveries of a Dreamer*, was running the district in the absence of the governor.

He was a young graduate and reputed to be a man of talent. When he was at Coimbra University, he had played the leading man in dramatic productions to great applause; and, at the time, he used to walk along the main street in the evening, wearing the same tragic air with which, on stage, he would pluck at his hair or, during love scenes, press his handkerchief to his eyes. Later, in Lisbon, he had frittered away a small inheritance on love affairs with various Lolas and Carmens, on lavish suppers at Mata's, on a great many pairs of trousers from Xafredo's the tailor and on pernicious literary friends; by the age of 30, he was poor, full of mercury and the author of twenty romantic serials published in the magazine *Civilisation*. He was so popular that he was known in brothels and cafés by the affectionate nickname of Bibi. However, judging that he had, by then, tasted life to the full, he let his sideboards grow, began to quote from Bastiat, hung around in political circles and set out on a career as an administrator; he now referred to the republic he had so praised in Coimbra as 'an absurd chimera', and Bibi was now a pillar of the establishment.

He detested Leiria, where people thought him terribly witty, and he would declare to the ladies at the soirées held by the local deputy Novais that he was 'tired of life'. It was whispered that dear old Novais' wife was mad about him, and it was true that Bibi had written to a friend in Lisbon: 'As for conquests, not much to report; the only one I have in my sights is Novais' little woman.'

He generally got up late, and on that particular morning, he was sitting in his dressing gown at the table, cracking open his boiled eggs, nostalgically reading a passionate account of a performance that had been booed off the stage at the Teatro São Carlos in Lisbon, when a servant – a Galician he had brought with him from the capital – came in to say that a priest wished to see him:

'A priest? Show him in!' And purely for his own benefit he murmured: 'The State should never keep the Church waiting!'

He got up and held out both his hands to Father Natário as he gravely entered the room in his long lustrine cassock.

'Bring another chair, will you, Trindade! Would you like a cup of tea, Father? Lovely morning, eh? I was just thinking about you, or, rather, about the clergy in general. I've been reading about the pilgrimages people are making to Our Lady of Lourdes . . . A splendid example to set! Thousands of people from the very best society . . . It's so reassuring to see this renewal of faith . . . As I was saying only yesterday at

Novais' house: "Faith, after all, is the real motive force in society." Do have a cup of tea! Ah, yes, it's such a comfort!'

'No, thank you, I've already had breakfast.'

'Ah, no, when I said it was a comfort, I was referring to faith not to the tea! Amusing, eh?'

And he laughed smugly. He wanted to please Natário, on the principle, as he often repeated with a knowing smile, that 'anyone in politics needs to have the priesthood on his side'.

'And of course,' he went on, 'as I was saying only yesterday at Novais' house, it's such a boon to the town itself! Lourdes, for example, was just a little village, but with the faithful arriving there in droves, it's become a city . . . Big hotels, boulevards, fine shops . . . Economic development going hand in hand with religious renewal.'

And he gave a grave, satisfied tug at his shirt collar.

'I've come to talk to you about an article that appeared in *The District Voice*.'

'Ah, yes,' said the secretary-general, 'absolutely, I've seen it already! A real tirade . . . But absolute rubbish in literary terms, as regards style and imagery . . .'

'And what do you intend to do about it, secretary-general?'

Senhor Gouveia Ledesma leaned back in his chair and asked in astonishment:

'Me? Do?'

Weighing his words, Natário said:

'The authorities have a duty to protect the state religion, and, by implication, its priests . . . Although, let us be clear about this, I have not come to see you on behalf of the clergy . . .'

And, placing one hand on his chest, he added:

'I am merely a poor priest with no influence . . . I have come, as a private individual, to ask the secretary-general if he can possibly allow respectable members of the diocesan Church to be libelled in this way.'

'It is certainly regrettable that a newspaper . . .'

Puffing out his chest indignantly, Natário broke in:

'A newspaper that should have been banned long ago, secretary-general!'

'Banned? Good heavens, Father! You surely don't want a return to the days when local magistrates acted for the king! Ban the newspaper? But the freedom of the press is a sacred principle! Besides, the publishing laws would not permit it . . . You can't present a legal action to the public prosecution service just because a newspaper publishes a few off-colour remarks about the Cathedral chapter – impossible! We would have to sue every newspaper in Portugal, apart from good Catholic papers like *The Nation* and *The Public Good*. It would put an end to freedom of thought, to thirty years of progress, to the very idea of government! We're not absolutists, my dear sir! We want light and plenty of it! Yes, that's what we want, light!'

Natário coughed very deliberately and said:

'Of course, but then, when the elections come around, and the authorities ask for our help, we, given that we receive no protection from them, will simply say: *Non possumus*!'

'Do you really think, Father, that for the sake of a few priestly votes we would be prepared to betray civilisation?'

And striking a noble pose, Bibi added:

'We are the children of liberty and we will not renounce our mother!'

'But Dr Godinho, who is behind the newspaper, is a member of the opposition,' remarked Natário. 'If you protect the newspaper, you are implicitly protecting his manoeuvrings . . .'

The secretary-general smiled.

'My dear Father, I'm afraid you don't quite understand how politics works. There is no real enmity between Dr Godinho and the district government, there is merely a slight difference of opinion . . . Dr Godinho is a very intelligent man. He is coming to the realisation that his Maia Group is achieving nothing. Dr Godinho appreciates the district government's policy and the district government appreciates Dr Godinho.'

Then, wrapping himself in the full mystery of the State, he added:

'I'm talking high politics here, Father.'

Natário stood up.

'So . . .'

'*Impossibilis est*,' said the secretary-general. 'Believe me, Father, as an individual, I find the article wholly repugnant, but as a representative of the authorities, I must respect the author's right to express his ideas . . . I can assure you – and please tell this to all the diocesan clergy – that the Catholic Church has no more fervent son than Gouveia Ledesma. However, I want a liberal religion, in keeping with progress and science . . . That is how I have always felt, and I have said as much in public, in the press, to the university and to the guilds. Indeed, I think there is no greater poetry than the poetry of Christianity! And I admire Pius IX: a great man. My only regret is that he does not wave the banner of civilisation!' And Bibi, pleased with the phrase, repeated it: 'Yes, my only regret is that he does not wave the banner of civilisation. The *Syllabus* is an impossibility in this century of electricity, Father. And we cannot sue a newspaper because it publishes a few humorous comments about the priesthood, nor, for political reasons, does it suit us to upset Dr Godinho. Those are my final thoughts on the matter.'

'Secretary-general . . .' said Natário, bowing.

'Your servant. I'm so sorry you won't have a cup of tea . . . And how is the precentor?'

'I believe that recently he has suffered a recurrence of the dizzy spells.'

'I'm so sorry. Another intelligent man, and a great Latinist too. Mind the step as you go out.'

Natário raced back to the Cathedral, in a state of high excitement, muttering angrily out loud to himself. Amaro was pacing slowly up and down outside the Cathedral, his hands behind his back; he looked very drawn and had dark shadows under his eyes.

'What happened?' he said, hurrying towards Natário.

'Nothing.'

Amaro bit his lip, and while Natário was excitedly recounting his conversation with the secretary-general and how he had argued with him and how 'the man had talked on and on', a shadow of sadness settled over Amaro's face, as, with the point of his umbrella, he kept angrily rooting out the bits of grass growing in the cracks of the paving stones.

'He's a pedantic fool,' Natário said, making a sweeping gesture. 'We won't get anywhere with the authorities. It's pointless. Now the matter is between me and the "Liberal". And I'm going to find out who he is, Father Amaro. And I will be the one to crush him, Father Amaro, me!'

João Eduardo, meanwhile, had been radiantly happy since Sunday. The article had caused an uproar; they had sold eighty copies of the newspaper, and Agostinho assured him that in the pharmacy in the main square, the view was that 'the "Liberal" knew the priesthood inside out and that he was absolutely right!'

'You're a genius, lad!' said Agostinho. 'Write me another one!'

João Eduardo was thrilled by 'the gossip going round the town'.

He re-read his article with paternal delight; had he not been afraid of upsetting São Joaneira, he would have liked to go round the shops declaring: 'I wrote that!' And he was already pondering another, even more terrifying article to be entitled: 'The priesthood of Leiria face-to-face with the nineteenth century!'

Dr Godinho had deigned to stop him in the main square to say:

'Your article has made quite a splash. You're a sly one. I especially liked that comment about Father Brito. I had no idea.. And they say the administrator's wife is very pretty too . . .'

'Didn't you know?'

'No, I didn't, but goodness I enjoyed it. Yes, you're certainly a sly one. I told Agostinho to publish it as a personal statement. You understand, I'm sure . . . I don't really want to have too many quarrels with the clergy . . . And there's my wife, of course, she's very devout. Well, she's a woman, and it's good for women to believe in something . . . . But I had a good

laugh to myself about it. Especially about Brito.
caused me so many problems in the last electioı
another thing, I've sorted out that little busin
about. You'll have your post in the district gove
within the month.'

'Dr Godinho . . . sir . . .'

'No, don't thank me. You deserve it.'

João Eduardo returned to the office, tremulous with joy. Senhor Nunes had gone out; João Eduardo slowly sharpened his quill and began drawing up a copy of a letter of attorney, then, suddenly, he grabbed his hat and ran to Rua da Misericórdia.

São Joaneira was sitting at the window alone, sewing; Amélia had gone to Morenal. João Eduardo announced from the door:

'Dona Augusta, I've just seen Dr Godinho and he said that I'll have that post I wanted within the month!'

São Joaneira took off her spectacles, let her hands fall into her lap and said:

'Really?'

'Yes, it's true, it's true . . .'

And João Eduardo rubbed his hands together, giggling nervously with joy.

'What luck, eh?' he exclaimed. 'So, if Amélia's agreeable . . .'

'Oh, João Eduardo,' said São Joaneira with a heavy sigh, 'that would take such a weight off my mind. I've been so . . . well, I've hardly slept.'

João Eduardo sensed that she was about to mention the article. He put his hat down on a chair in the corner and, returning to the window, his hands in his pocket, asked:

'But why? Why?'

'It's that shameless article in *The District Voice*. What do you think? Such calumnies! It's aged me overnight.'

João Eduardo had written the article in a fit of jealousy, in order to 'do for' Father Amaro; he had not foreseen the distress it might cause the two ladies, and seeing São Joaneira's eyes filling with tears, he felt almost sorry. He said ambiguously:

Yes, I read it, it is pretty bad . . .'

Then deciding to take advantage of São Joaneira's emotional state in order to advance his own romantic interests, he brought another chair over, sat down beside her and said:

'I never liked to say anything before, Dona Augusta, but . . . Well, Amélia has always been rather over-familiar with Father Amaro . . . And people might have got to know about it through the Gansoso sisters or Libaninho, quite unintentionally, of course, and rumours may have started . . . I know she saw no wrong in it, but . . . you know what Leiria is like, how people talk.'

São Joaneira declared a desire to speak to him frankly as to a son: the reason she had found the article so upsetting was because of him. After all, he might believe the gossip and want to withdraw his proposal of marriage! She could tell him, as a decent woman and as a mother, that there was absolutely nothing between Amélia and Father Amaro, nothing, absolutely nothing. Amélia was a natural chatterbox, and Father Amaro was always so kind, why, he was delicacy itself . . . She had always said that Father Amaro had a way with him that could touch people's hearts . . .

'Hm,' said João Eduardo, chewing one end of his moustache, his head bowed.

São Joaneira placed her hand lightly on João Eduardo's knee and looked into his eyes:

'It may not be my place to say so, but the girl really does love you, João Eduardo.'

His heart leaped with emotion.

'And I love her!' he said. 'You know how passionately I care about her. It doesn't matter what that article said.'

Then São Joaneira dried her tears on her white apron. She was so happy. She had always said that there was no more decent young man in the whole of Leiria!

'I love you like a son, you know.'

João Eduardo was touched.

'Well, let's sort things out, then, and silence those tongues once and for all . . .'

He stood up and with comic solemnity said:

'Dona Augusta, I have the honour of asking for your hand . . .'

She laughed, and in his happiness, João Eduardo planted a filial kiss on her head.

'Talk to Amélia tonight,' he said as he left. 'I'll come and see her tomorrow, and you'll see how happy we'll be . . .'

'The Lord be praised,' said São Joaneira, taking up her sewing again, with a great sigh of relief.

As soon as Amélia returned from Morenal, São Joaneira, who was laying the table, said to her:

'João Eduardo was here.'

'Oh, yes.'

'He came round to have a chat, poor thing . . .'

Amélia said nothing as she folded up her woollen shawl.

'He was upset . . .' her mother went on.

'What about?' Amélia asked, her face red.

'What do you think? Everyone talking about that article in *The District Voice* and asking who it meant by "young daughters who have no experience of the world" and the answer was, of course, "Who else? São Joaneira's daughter Amélia, in Rua da Misericórdia!" Poor João says he's been so worried, and he was too considerate to actually come and talk to you directly. And, well . . .'

'But what should I do, Mama?' exclaimed Amélia, her eyes suddenly full of tears at those words which fell on her torments like drops of vinegar on open wounds.

'I'm just telling you this for your own good. You do what you like, my dear. I know it's all lies. But you know how people talk. All I can tell you is that the boy didn't believe what the article said. That was what I was worried about. I couldn't sleep for thinking about it. But, no, he says he doesn't care about the article, that he loves you just the same, and that he can't wait to get married. If it was me, I would get married at once and put a stop to all the talk. I know you're not madly in love with him, but that will come with time. João's a good lad, and now he's got that new job . . .'

'Has he?'

'Yes, that's the other thing he came to talk to me about.

He's spoken to Dr Godinho and apparently he starts the new job within the month. So you do what you think best. But I'm not getting any younger, my dear, I could go at any moment . . .'

Amélia did not reply, staring out at the sparrows fluttering about on the rooftop opposite – far less troubled than were her own thoughts at that moment.

Since Sunday, Amélia had been living in a kind of daze. She knew that the 'pure young daughter' mentioned in the article was her, and the shame of having her love published in the newspaper like that was a torment to her. And, of course (she thought to herself, biting her lip in mute rage, her eyes full of tears), it would spoil everything. In the main square, in the arcade, people would smile mischievously and say: 'So São Joaneira's little Amélia has got herself involved with the parish priest, has she?' The precentor, who was very strict about anything to do with women, would reprimand Father Amaro. Her reputation would have been ruined as would their love, and all because they had exchanged a few glances and squeezed each other's hand.

On Monday, when she went to Morenal, she imagined that people were laughing at her behind her back, making fun of her; she sensed a rebuke in the curt wave that the respectable pharmacist Carlos gave her from his shop doorway; Marques from the ironmonger's had failed to take his hat off to her as she walked home, and as she entered the house, she felt that she had lost all credibility, forgetting that Marques was so short-sighted that, when he worked in the shop, he had to wear two pairs of spectacles, one on top of the other.

'What should I do? What should I do?' she muttered to herself from time to time, clutching her head. Her devout mind came up with only devout solutions – to go on a retreat, to make a promise to Our Lady of Sorrows 'to extricate herself from that situation', to go and make her confession to Father Silvério . . . And she would end up by taking her sewing and going and sitting resignedly by her mother's side, feeling very sorry for herself and thinking how unfortunate she had been all her life, ever since she was a child.

Her mother mentioned the article in only the vaguest, most ambiguous of terms:

'The person who wrote it has no shame . . . We should treat it with the disdain it deserves . . . As long as your conscience is clear, the rest is just gossip . . .'

But Amélia could see how upset she was – in her worn face, in her sad silences, in the sudden sighs she gave as she sat knitting by the window, her spectacles perched on the end of her nose; then Amélia was even more convinced that 'everyone' was talking about it, that her mother, poor thing, had been told about it by the Gansoso sisters and by Dona Josefa Dias, whose mouth produced tittle-tattle as naturally as it did saliva. The shame of it!

In that gathering of skirts and cassocks in Rua da Misericórdia, she had, up until then, thought that her love for Amaro was perfectly natural, but just as the colours of a portrait painted by the light of an oil lamp – and which, in that light, seemed true – look false and ugly when seen in the sunlight, so that same love seemed monstrous to her now, frowned upon as it was by people whom she had respected ever since she was a child – the Guedes, the Marqueses and the Vazes. And she almost wished that Father Amaro had not come back to Rua da Misericórdia.

And yet, with what longing she waited each night for his ring at the doorbell. But he did not come, and that absence, which her reason judged prudent, filled her heart with the despair of betrayal. On Wednesday night, she could contain herself no longer and, blushing over her sewing, she remarked:

'I wonder what's happened to Father Amaro?'

The Canon, who seemed to be dozing, shifted in his armchair, coughed loudly, and grunted:

'Too much to do . . . Besides it's much too early yet . . .'

And Amélia, who had turned white as chalk, was immediately gripped by the certainty that Father Amaro had decided to get rid of her, feeling terrified of the scandal created by the newspaper article and following the advice of his fearful fellow priests concerned for 'the good name of the clergy'. However, in front of her mother's friends, she wisely concealed her despair; she even went and sat down at the piano and pounded out such a thunderous mazurka that the Canon, once more stirring in his armchair, snorted:

'Less noise and more feeling, my girl!'

She spent the night in an agony of doubt, but she did not cry. Her passion for the priest flared up more fiercely, and yet she hated him for his cowardice. One remark in a newspaper and he shivered with fear in his cassock, not even daring to visit her, never thinking that her reputation too had been damaged, and that her love remained unsatisfied. And he was the one who had tempted her with his sweet words and his coquetry. The scoundrel! She wanted both to clutch him violently to her heart and to slap him hard. She had the ridiculous idea of going round to Rua das Sousas the very next day and throwing herself into his arms, installing herself in his room, and causing a scandal that would force him to flee the diocese. Why not? They were young and strong, they could live somewhere far away, in another town, and her imagination began to take hysterical pleasure in the delicious prospect of such an existence, in which she imagined herself constantly kissing him! In her overwrought state, that plan seemed to her perfectly practicable and easy: they would run away to the Algarve, where he would let his hair grow (and be even more handsome!), and no one would know that he was a priest; he could teach Latin and she would take in sewing; and they would live together in a little house whose greatest attraction for her was the bed with its two pillows side by side. And the one difficulty in this whole brilliant plan was how to get the trunk containing her clothes out of the house without her mother noticing. But when she woke, these foolish resolutions dissolved like shadows in the clear light of day; it all seemed utterly impracticable, and he seemed as far away from her as if the highest, most inaccessible mountains in the land now separated Rua da Misericórdia from Rua das Sousas. He really had abandoned her! He did not want to lose the money he earned from his parish or the esteem of his superiors. Poor her! She felt then that she would never be happy again and never again take an interest in life. Yet she still nurtured an intense desire to have her revenge on Father Amaro.

It occurred to her then, for the first time, that João Eduardo had not been to see her in Rua da Misericórdia since the publication of the article. So he too has turned his back on me, she thought bitterly. But what did it matter! In the midst of the distress caused by Father Amaro's abandonment of her, the loss of João Eduardo's dull, sentimental love, which was neither useful to her nor a source of pleasure, was a barely perceptible annoyance; this one misfortune had abruptly snatched all affections from her – both the one that filled her soul and the one that merely flattered her vanity; it annoyed her not to feel the clerk's love clinging to her skirts with all the docility of a dog, but all her tears were for the priest who now wanted nothing more to do with her! She only regretted João Eduardo's desertion because she thereby lost a ready means of enraging Father Amaro . . .

That is why on that afternoon as she stood by the window, silently watching the sparrows fluttering about on the rooftop opposite – having just learned that João Eduardo, assured now of his new job, had finally come to speak to her mother – she was thinking with satisfaction of the priest's despair when he saw her marriage banns published in the Cathedral. Moreover, São Joaneira's very practical words were quietly working away in her soul: the job with the district government brought in 25$000 *réis* per month; by marrying, she would immediately regain her respectability as a lady and, if her mother died, she could live quite decently on her husband's salary and the income from the farm at Morenal; they could even afford to go sea-bathing in the summer . . . And she could see herself in Vieira, much admired by all the gentlemen; she might even meet the wife of the district governor.

'What do you think I should do, Mama?' she asked suddenly. She had decided to seize on those perceived advantages, but her weak nature needed to be cajoled and persuaded.

'I would choose the safe option,' was São Joaneira's reply.

'Yes, it's usually best,' murmured Amélia, going into her

room. And she sat down very sadly at the foot of her bed, because the melancholy of evening made her longing for 'the good times with Father Amaro' seem all the more painful.

It rained heavily that night, and the two ladies were alone. São Joaneira, free now from her anxieties, grew sleepy and kept nodding off, her knitting in her lap. Amélia put her sewing down then, and leaning one elbow on the table, twirled the shade on the oil lamp and thought about her marriage: João Eduardo was a decent enough fellow, poor thing; he was exactly the kind of husband the petit bourgeois admired – he wasn't bad-looking and he had a job; asking for her hand in marriage, despite the libels in the newspaper, did not seem to her, as her mother had said, 'a generous gesture', but she was flattered by his devotion, especially after Amaro's cowardly abandonment of her; and poor João had been in love with her for two years . . . She then began laboriously recalling all the things about him that she liked – his seriousness, his white teeth, his clean clothes.

Outside, the wind was blowing hard, and the rain, coldly flailing the window panes, awoke in her an appetite for comfort, a good fire, a husband by her side, a little baby boy sleeping in the cradle – because the child was sure to be a boy and he would be called Carlos and would have Father Amaro's dark eyes. Ah, Father Amaro! Once she was married, she would doubtless meet Father Amaro again. And then an idea pierced her whole being, made her sit up suddenly and forced her instinctively to seek out the dark of the window to hide her flaming cheeks. No, not that! That would be terrible! But the idea took implacable hold of her like a very strong arm simultaneously suffocating her and inflicting on her the most delicious pain. And then her old love, which spite and necessity had driven down into the depths of her soul, burst forth and flooded through her. Wringing her hands, she passionately repeated Amaro's name again and again; she hungered for his kisses – oh, how she adored him! And it was all over, all over! And she, poor thing, would have to marry. Standing at the window, her face pressed against the darkness of the night, she wept softly.

Over tea, São Joaneira suddenly said:

'If you're going to do it, my dear, you should do it now. Start getting your trousseau together and, if possible, get married before the month is out.'

Amélia said nothing, but her imagination grew agitated at these words. Married before the month was out! Despite her indifference towards João Eduardo, the idea of living and sleeping with a passionate young man stirred her whole being.

And as her mother was going down to her bedroom, Amélia said:

'What do you think, Mama? I feel a bit awkward about discussing it all with João Eduardo and accepting his proposal. It might be best to write him a letter . . .'

'I agree, my dear, write to him. Ruça will take it round in the morning. Write him a nice letter, one that will please him.'

Amélia stayed up until late in the dining room writing a draft letter. It said:

Senhor João Eduardo,

Mama has informed me of the conversation she had with you. And if your feelings are genuine, and you have given me every proof that they are, I willingly accept your proposal, for you already know my feelings. As regards the trousseau and the papers to be drawn up, we can talk about that tomorrow. We will expect you for tea. Mama is very pleased and I hope that everything works out well for our happiness, as I am sure, with God's help, it will. Mama sends her best wishes, as does your loving

Amélia Caminha

As soon as she had signed the letter, the sight of the sheets of white paper scattered before her made her feel like writing to Father Amaro. But what? To confess her love to him with the same quill still wet with the same ink with which she had just accepted another man as her husband? To accuse him of cowardice and to show her displeasure would be humiliating. And yet, although she had no reason to write to him, her hand nonetheless languorously wrote the first words: 'My darling Amaro . . .' She stopped, realising that there was no one who could deliver the letter for her. Ah, so they would have to separate like this, in silence, for ever. But why should they separate? she thought. Once she was married, she could still see Father Amaro. And the same idea returned, surreptitiously this time, and in such an honest guise that it did not alarm her: Father Amaro could be her confessor; he was the one person in all Christendom who could best guide her soul, her will, her conscience; there would be between them a constant, delicious exchange of confidences, of sweet admonishments; every Saturday, she would go to confession to receive in the light of his eyes and in the sound of his words a portion of happiness; and that would be chaste, exciting and to the glory of God.

She felt rather pleased with the impression, which she could not quite define, of an existence in which the flesh would receive its legitimate satisfactions, and her soul would enjoy the charms of an amorous devotion. Everything would turn out well after all . . . And soon afterwards, she was sleeping peacefully, dreaming that she was in *her* house, with *her* husband, and that she was sitting on Father Amaro's knees, playing cards with her old friends, to the great contentment of the entire Cathedral.

The following day, Ruça took the letter to João Eduardo, and the two women spent the whole morning sewing by the window and talking about the wedding. Amélia did not want to leave her mother, and, since the house was large enough, the newlyweds would live on the first floor and São Joaneira would sleep in the room upstairs; the Canon would doubtless help with the trousseau; and they could spend their honeymoon on Dona Maria's farm. And at this happy prospect, Amélia blushed beneath the eyes of her mother, who gazed at her adoringly over her spectacles.

When the Angelus rang, São Joaneira shut herself up in her bedroom downstairs to say her rosary, leaving Amélia alone 'to sort things out with her young man'. Shortly afterwards, João Eduardo rang the doorbell. He was very nervous and had donned black gloves and drenched himself in eau-de-cologne. When he reached the door of the dining room, there was no light on, and Amélia's pretty figure was silhouetted against the bright window. He placed his cloak down in one corner, as he usually did, and rubbing his hands, he went over to her, for she had still not moved. He said:

'I got your note, Miss Amélia . . .'

'Yes, I sent Ruça round with it first thing so as to catch you at home,' she said, her cheeks burning.

'I was on my way to the office, I was coming down the stairs . . . It must have been nine o'clock . . .'

'Yes, it must have been . . .' she said.

They fell silent, embarrassed. Then he delicately took her hands and said softly:

'You still want to, then?'

'I do,' murmured Amélia.

'And as soon as possible?'

'Yes.'

He sighed, utterly happy.

'I'm sure we'll get on well, I'm sure we'll get on very well!' he said. And his hands, tenderly squeezing her arms, grasped them from the wrists to the elbows.

'Mama says that we can all live here together,' she said, trying to speak calmly.

'Of course, and I'll have some sheets made,' he added, very agitated.

He suddenly drew her to him and kissed her on the lips; she gave a little sob, and then, weak and languid, abandoned herself to his arms.

'Oh, my love!' murmured João Eduardo.

They heard her mother's shoes come squeaking up the stairs, and Amélia walked briskly over to the sideboard to light the oil lamp.

São Joaneira stood in the doorway and uttered her first words of motherly approval, saying kindly:

'Are you sitting up here in the dark, my dears?'

It was Canon Dias who told Father Amaro about Amélia's

wedding, one morning in the Cathedral. He spoke of the appropriateness of the marriage and added:

'I'm pleased, because it's what the girl wants and it's a relief to her poor mother . . .'

'Of course, of course,' muttered Amaro, who had gone very white.

The Canon cleared his throat loudly and said:

'So you can go round there again, now that everything's in order . . . That unpleasant business in the newspaper is all water under the bridge . . . What's done is done.'

'Of course, of course . . .' grunted Amaro. He flung his cape about him and left the church.

He was so furious that he had to stop himself cursing out loud as he walked along. On the corner of Rua das Sousas, he almost collided with Natário, who grabbed him by the sleeve in order to whisper in his ear:

'I haven't found out anything yet.'

'About what?'

'About the "Liberal", about the article. But I'm working on it, oh yes!'

Amaro, anxious to talk to someone, said:

'Have you heard the news? About Amélia's marriage . . . . What do you think?'

'Yes, that fool Libaninho told me. He says the lad's got the job. Through Dr Godinho, of course. He's another one. What a bunch of scoundrels: Dr Godinho at loggerheads in his newspaper with the district government and the district government throwing jobs to Dr Godinho's favourites . . . There's no understanding them! We're a country of rogues!'

'Apparently everyone's thrilled at São Joaneira's house,' said Amaro blackly.

'Well, good luck to them! I haven't got time to go round there . . . I haven't got time for anything. I know what my goal is, to find out who this "Liberal" is and to crush him! I can't stand these people who take a beating, say nothing and turn the other cheek. I'm not like that, oh no. I never forget.' A rancorous shudder ran through him, curling his fingers into claws, narrowing his bony chest, and he said through clenched teeth: 'When I hate, I really hate!'

He was silent for a moment, enjoying the taste of his own bile.

'If you go to Rua da Misericórdia, give them my congratulations . . .' And he added, fixing Amaro with his beady eyes: 'That fool of a clerk is making off with the prettiest girl in town, the lucky so-and-so!'

Amaro bade him a brusque farewell and shot off down the road.

After that first terrible Sunday when the article had appeared, Father Amaro, had at first, very selfishly, thought only about the consequences – 'the fatal consequences, dear God' – that the scandal could have for him. What if it got around that he was the 'dandified priest' the 'Liberal' was addressing? He spent two days in terror, fearfully expecting to see Father Saldanha appear at any moment, with his child-like face and mellifluous voice, telling him: 'The precentor requires your presence!' He spent that time preparing explanations, clever answers, flattering remarks. But when he saw that, despite the outspoken nature of the article, the precentor seemed ready 'to turn a blind eye', only then, feeling calmer, did he stop to consider his violently interrupted love affair. Fear made him astute, and he decided not to go back to Rua da Misericórdia for a while.

'We'll just let the storm pass,' he thought.

In a fortnight or three weeks, when the article had been forgotten, he would go back to São Joaneira's house; he would make it clear to the girl that he still adored her, but he would avoid their old familiarity, the whispered conversations, the chairs pushed cosily together at the card table; then, through Dona Maria da Assunção or through Dona Josefa Dias, he would arrange for Amélia to leave Father Silvério and take him as her confessor instead; they could reach some arrangement in the secrecy of the confessional; they would find some discreet modus vivendi, cautious meetings here and there, letters sent via the maid; and, if prudently conducted, there would be no danger of that love affair ever being one day revealed in the newspaper. And he was already congratulating himself on the cleverness of this plan when he received that terrible blow – the girl was getting married!

After his initial despair, which he vented by stamping on the floor and uttering blasphemies for which he immediately asked pardon from Our Lord Jesus Christ, he tried to calm himself and to think the matter through rationally. Where was that passion leading him? Into scandal. And once she was married, they each would follow their legitimate, sensible destinies, she with her family and he with his parish. When they met afterwards, they would exchange friendly greetings, and he could walk the streets of the town with his head high, without fear of gossip in the arcade, insinuations in the press, the precentor's harsh words or any prickings of conscience. And his life would be happy. No, dear God, his life could not be happy without her. Without the excitement of visiting Rua da Misericórdia, of squeezing her hand, of hoping for even greater delights, what was there left to him? He would vegetate, like the mushrooms that grew in the damp corners of the Cathedral courtyard. And she, who had driven him mad with her flirtatious looks and manners, had simply turned her back on him as soon as another man appeared, someone who would make a good husband with a salary of 25$000 *réis* per month. All that sighing and blushing – pure mockery! She had toyed with him.

How he hated her, although not as much as he hated the clerk, who had triumphed because he was a man and had his freedom and his hair and his moustache, and an arm to offer her in the street. He lingered rancorously over visions of the clerk's happiness: he saw him bringing her triumphantly home from the church; he saw him kissing her throat, her breasts . . . And these ideas made him stamp his feet furiously on the floor, startling Vicência downstairs in the kitchen.

Then he tried to get a grip on himself and all his faculties and to apply them to finding the best way to have his revenge. And then the old despair returned that he was not living in the times of the Inquisition and could not therefore pack them off to prison on some accusation of irreligion or black magic. Ah, a priest could have enjoyed himself then. But now, with the liberals in power, he was forced to watch as that wretched clerk earning six *vinténs* a day made off with the girl, whilst he, an educated priest, who might become a bishop or even Pope, had to bow his shoulders and ponder his grief alone. If God's curses had any value, then let them be cursed. He hoped to see them overrun with children, with no bread in the cupboard, their last blanket pawned, gaunt with hunger, cursing each other – then he would laugh, oh, how he would laugh!

By Monday, he could contain himself no longer and he went to Rua da Misericórdia. São Joaneira was downstairs in the sitting room with Canon Dias. As soon as she saw him, she said:

'Father Amaro, how good to see you! I was just talking about you. We wondered where you had got to, what with our good news.'

'Yes, I heard,' murmured Amaro, looking very pale.

'It had to happen some time,' said the Canon jovially. 'May God make them happy and not give them too many children because meat is very expensive.'

Amaro smiled, hearing the piano upstairs.

It was Amélia playing, as she used to, 'The Waltz of Two Worlds'; and João Eduardo, sitting very close to her, was turning the pages of the music.

'Who was that, Ruça?' she called, hearing Ruça coming up the stairs.

'Father Amaro.'

The blood rushed to her face, and her heart beat so fast that for a moment her fingers hung motionless over the keys.

'Oh, that's all we needed,' muttered João Eduardo.

Amélia bit her lip. She hated the clerk; she suddenly found everything about him repugnant, his voice, his manner, his body close to hers; she thought with delight of how, after she was married (since she had to get married), she would confess everything to Father Amaro and would never stop loving him! She felt no scruples at that moment, and almost wanted the clerk to notice the passion lighting up her face.

'Honestly!' she said. 'Move over a bit, you don't leave me enough room to play.'

She abruptly stopped playing the waltz and instead began singing 'The Farewell'.

> Ah, farewell, farewell!
> Gone now are the days
> When I lived happy by your side . . .

Her voice rose up ardently, sending the song down through the floorboards, straight to the heart of Amaro in the room below.

And Amaro, sitting on the sofa, his walking stick resting between his knees, devoured each note, while São Joaneira chattered on, describing the lengths of cotton she had bought for the sheets and the alterations she was going to make to the newly-weds' bedroom, and the advantages of them all living together . . .

'Won't we be happy,' broke in the Canon sourly, heaving himself to his feet. 'We'd better go upstairs, we shouldn't really leave the engaged couple alone like that.'

'Oh, I've no worries on that account,' said São Joaneira, smiling, 'I trust him, he's a very proper young man.'

Amaro was trembling as he went up the stairs and, as soon as he entered the room and saw Amélia's face lit by the candles on the piano, he felt dazzled, as if the imminence of the wedding had made her even more beautiful, as if separation had made her even more enticing. He went over and, eyes downcast, gravely shook her hand and that of the clerk, mumbling:

'Congratulations . . . Congratulations . . .'

He turned then and joined the Canon who had flopped down in his armchair complaining that he was tired and wanted his tea.

Amélia seemed abstracted, running her fingers dreamily over the keys. Father Amaro's manner confirmed her suspicions: he wanted to be rid of her at all costs, the ungrateful wretch. He behaved as if nothing had happened, the scoundrel. In his priestly cowardice, terrified of the precentor, the newspaper, the gossip in the arcade, of everything, he had removed her from his imagination, from his heart and from his life, as one would remove a poisonous insect. Then, in order to enrage him, she began talking in a low tender voice to João Eduardo; she leaned languidly against his shoulder, giggling and whispering; they tried, with loud hilarity, to play a piece for four hands; then she pinched him, and he gave a piercing shriek. And São Joaneira gazed on them dotingly, while the Canon dozed, and Father Amaro, relegated, as once João Eduardo had been, to a corner of the room, sat leafing through the old scrapbook.

A sudden ring on the doorbell startled them all; coming up the stairs was the sound of rapid footsteps which paused in the living room below, then Ruça came in to say that it was Father Natário, who preferred not to come up, but would like a word with the Canon.

'This is an odd time to deliver private messages,' grumbled the Canon, levering himself reluctantly out of the comfortable depths of his armchair.

Amélia closed the piano, and São Joaneira put down her knitting and went to the top of the stairs to listen; outside, the wind was blowing hard and they could hear the retreat being sounded on the other side of the square.

Then the Canon called up:

'Father Amaro!'

'Yes, Master.'

'Come down here, will you, and tell São Joaneira that she can come too.'

São Joaneira went slowly down the stairs, much alarmed; Amaro assumed that Father Natário must have found out who the 'Liberal' was.

The little room seemed very cold and was lit only by the feeble light of the candle on the table; and on the wall, from an old, very dark painting – which the Canon had recently given to São Joaneira – loomed the pale face of a monk and a large skull.

Canon Dias had sat down on one end of the sofa and was reflectively taking a pinch of snuff; Natário, who was striding about the room, exclaimed:

'Good evening, Senhora! Hello there, Amaro! I have come with news! I didn't want to come upstairs because I assumed the clerk would be there, and these things are strictly between ourselves. As I was saying to Canon Dias . . . Father Saldanha has been to see me, and things are looking bad.'

Father Saldanha was the precentor's confidant. And Father Amaro asked with some concern:

'Bad for us, you mean?'

Natário solemnly raised one arm and said:

'*Primo*: Father Brito has been moved to the parish of Amor near Alcobaça, to the mountains, to the back of beyond . . .'

'No!' exclaimed São Joaneira.

'It's all the doing of that so-called "Liberal". Our worthy precentor took his time to ponder that article in *The District Voice*, and now he's acted. Poor old Brito has been exiled.'

'Well, you know what people said about the administrator's wife . . .' murmured São Joaneira.

'Now then!' the Canon broke in severely. 'Now then, Senhora! This is not a gossip shop . . . Continue, Father Natário.'

'*Secundo*,' went on Natário, 'as I was about to say to Canon Dias, the precentor, in view of the article and other attacks in the press, has decided, as Father Saldanha put it, "to review the behaviour of the diocesan clergy". He very much disapproves of priests socialising with women . . . He wants an explanation regarding these dandified priests tempting pretty young girls . . . In short, in His Excellency's words, he is determined "to cleanse the Augean stables", which, put plainly, Senhora, means that there's going to be an almighty fuss.'

There was a shocked silence. And Natário, standing in the middle of the room, his hands in his pockets, asked loudly:

'So what do you think of that, eh?'

The Canon got slowly to his feet:

'Look, Father Natário, things may not be as bad as they seem . . . And don't you stand there looking like a Mater Dolorosa either, São Joaneira. Off you go and order the tea, that's what matters.'

'As I said to Father Saldanha . . .' began Natário, about to launch into another peroration.

But the Canon stopped him abruptly in his tracks:

'Father Saldanha is a pedant and a fool! Let's go upstairs and have some toast, and remember, not a word of this to the young people.'

Tea was a silent affair. The Canon, frowning deeply, uttered an outraged sigh with every mouthful of toast; São Joaneira, having mentioned that Dona Maria da Assunção had a bad cold, grew sad and leaned her head on her hands; Natário paced about, creating quite a breeze in the room with the skirts of his long coat.

'So when's this wedding to be?' he said suddenly, stopping in front of Amélia and João Eduardo, who were having their tea by the piano.

'Soon,' she said, smiling.

Then Amaro got up slowly and, consulting his silver fob watch, said dully:

'It's time I was getting back to Rua das Sousas.'

But São Joaneira wouldn't hear of it. Honestly, anyone would think someone had died. Why didn't they have a game of lotto to distract them? The Canon, however, emerged from his torpor to say severely:

'You're quite wrong, Senhora, no one here is in the least bit sad. We only have reasons to be glad. Isn't that so, João Eduardo?'

João Eduardo fidgeted and smiled:

'Well, I certainly only have reasons to be glad.'

'Of course,' said the Canon. 'Now I'll bid you all good night. I'm off to play lotto in the land of Nod. And so is Amaro.'

Amaro went over and silently shook Amélia's hand, then the three priests went down the stairs in silence.

In the sitting room below, the candle was burning down.

The Canon went in to get his umbrella, and then, beckoning to the others, slowly closed the door. He said quietly:

'I didn't want to frighten São Joaneira, but this business with the precentor and all the gossip that's flying around could prove disastrous.'

'We must take great care,' counselled Natário in a low voice.

'Yes, it certainly looks bad,' murmured Amaro sombrely.

They were standing up in the middle of the room. Outside, the wind was howling; the skull in the painting was thrown first into darkness then into light by the flickering candle flame; and upstairs Amélia was gaily singing 'Chiquita'.

Amaro recalled other happy nights when he, carefree and triumphant, would make the ladies laugh, and Amélia would turn her languid gaze on him as she sang: 'Ay, chiquita que sí' . . .

'As you know,' said the Canon, 'I have enough to eat and drink, so I'm all right, but what matters is upholding the honour of the priesthood.'

'There's no doubt,' added Natário, 'that if there's another article and more gossip, the thunderbolt will fall . . .'

'Poor old Brito,' muttered Amaro, 'exiled to the back of beyond.'

Someone must have made a joke upstairs because they could hear the clerk laughing.

Amaro snorted bitterly:

'Well, they're certainly enjoying themselves.'

They went downstairs. As Natário opened the front door, a gust of fine rain struck him full in the face.

'What a night!' he exclaimed angrily.

The Canon was the only one with an umbrella, and opening it slowly, he said:

'Well, it looks like we're in for a soaking . . .'

From the brightly lit upstairs window came the sounds of the piano, the accompaniment to 'Chiquita'. The Canon huffed and puffed, clinging on to his umbrella in the wind; beside him, Natário ground his teeth furiously and drew his coat about him; Amaro walked along, head bowed, exhausted and defeated; and as the three priests, huddling together under the Canon's umbrella, squelched through the puddles along the dark street, the loud, drenching rain beat ironically against their backs.

XI

A few days later, the gentlemen who used to gather at the pharmacy in the square were astonished to see Father Natário and Dr Godinho standing at the door of the ironmonger's shop engaged in harmonious conversation. The tax-collector – to whom everyone deferred on matters of foreign policy – observed them closely through the glass door of the pharmacy and declared in grave tones that he could not be more surprised than if he had seen Victor Emmanuel and Pius IX out walking arm in arm.

The town's surgeon, however, was unsurprised by that 'exchange of friendship'. According to him, the last article in *The District Voice*, which had obviously been written by Dr Godinho himself (it was his incisive style, so full of logic, so crammed with erudition!), showed that the members of the Maia Group wanted closer links with those running the poorhouse. Dr Godinho (as the surgeon put it) was currying favour with the district government and the diocesan clergy; the closing words of the article were significant – 'it is not our place to argue with the clergy over how best they should carry out their divine mission'.

The truth was (as an obese fellow called Pimenta remarked) that, although they had not yet made their peace, they were in negotiations, for, very early the previous morning, he had seen with his own eyes Father Natário leaving the office of *The District Voice*.

'Come on, Pimenta, you're making it up!'

Pimenta drew himself up majestically, gave a grave tug at the waistband of his trousers, and was just about to deliver an indignant riposte, when the tax-collector came to his aid:

'No, no, Pimenta's quite right. The other day I saw that rascal Agostinho doff his hat to Father Natário. Natário is up to something, that's for sure. I'm a great one for watching people . . . For example, Father Natário, who never used to come here to the arcade, is always nosing around the shops now. Then there's his sudden friendship with Father Silvério . . . They're always to be seen together in the square when the Angelus is rung. And it's all to do with Dr Godinho and his followers. Father Silvério is Godinho's wife's confessor. You see, it all fits!'

Father Natário's recent friendship with Father Silvério had indeed been much commented upon. Only five years earlier in the Cathedral sacristy there had been scandalous scenes between the two clergymen. Natário had launched himself at Father Silvério, brandishing an umbrella, and was only stopped by good Canon Sarmento, who, his face bathed in tears, had grabbed Natário's cassock and cried: 'No, dear colleague, this will be the ruin of religion!' Natário and Silvério had not spoken since, much to Silvério's dismay, for he was a kindly, dropsically obese fellow, and, according to his confessants, 'he was all affection and forgiveness'. But small, gaunt Natário clung to his rancour. When Precentor Valadares took over the running of the See, he called them in and, having eloquently reminded them both of the need to 'maintain peace in the Church' and having mentioned the touching example of Castor and Pollux, he had propelled Natário gravely and tenderly into the arms of Father Silvério, who, much moved, held him for a moment clasped to his vast chest and stomach, murmuring:

'We are all brothers, we are all brothers!'

But Natário, whose hard, coarse nature, like cardboard, never lost its folds, always spoke to Father Silvério in sullen tones; if they met in the Cathedral or the street, he would slip past him with a curt nod, muttering: 'At your service, Father Silvério!'

One rainy afternoon, two weeks ago, however, Natário had paid an unexpected visit to Father Silvério, on the pretext of sheltering from a sudden downpour.

'I also wanted to ask you for your remedy for earache because one of my nieces is being driven almost mad with it!'

Overjoyed to be able to put to use his studies in household remedies, and doubtless forgetting that he had seen Natário's two nieces that very morning, looking as healthy and happy as two house sparrows, good Silvério quickly wrote down the recipe and said with a broad smile:

'What a pleasure it is to see you here again in what I hope you consider to be your house!'

This reconciliation was so public that the Barão de Vila-Clara's brother-in-law, a graduate with considerable poetic gifts, wrote on the subject in one of his many satires, which he called *Barbs*, and which were passed around in manuscript form from house to house, much savoured and much feared; he entitled the poem 'The Famous Reconciliation between the Monkey and the Whale', obviously having in mind the physical appearance of the two priests. It was indeed a common sight now to see Father Natário's slight figure gesticulating and hopping about beside Father Silvério's enormous, slow bulk.

One morning, even the employees standing on the balcony of the municipal council offices (which were, at the time, opposite the Cathedral) had great fun observing the two priests strolling about on the square in the warm May sunshine. The administrator – who spent his office hours gazing from his balcony through a pair of binoculars at the wife of Teles the tailor – had suddenly burst out laughing; the notary Borges immediately ran to the balcony, quill in hand, to see what the administrator was laughing at, and then, snorting with amusement, he, in turn, called to Artur Couceiro, who was busily copying out a song from a magazine in order to practise it later on the guitar; even the stern and dignified amanuensis Pires joined them, pulling his silk cap down over his ears, terrified as he was of draughts; and the whole group gazed, wide-eyed, at the two priests, who were standing outside the Cathedral. Natário seemed very excited about something; he was clearly trying to persuade or incite Father Silvério to action, and he stood there on tiptoe in front of him, frantically waving his bony hands about. Then, suddenly, he grabbed Father Silvério by one arm and dragged him the length of the paved square; when they reached the end, he drew back, made a sweeping gesture of utter desolation, as if attesting to the possible ruin not only of himself, but of the Cathedral beside them, the city and the whole universe; kindly Silvério, eyes bulging, looked absolutely terrified. And then they resumed their walk. But Natário again grew agitated; he would abruptly step back or poke Silvério's vast stomach with one bony finger, then stamp furiously on the polished flagstones, and just as suddenly, arms hanging loose by his sides, slump into despair. Then good Silvério spoke for a moment, his hand pressed to his bosom; immediately, Natário's sallow face lit up; he gave a little skip, patted his colleague joyfully on the shoulder, and the two priests went into the Cathedral, arm in arm and laughing softly.

'Ridiculous creatures!' said Borges, who hated priests.

'I bet you it's about that newspaper article,' said Artur Couceiro, resuming his lyrical work. 'Natário won't rest until he's found out who wrote it; he said so at São Joaneira's house. And he's on to a good thing with Silvério, because he's confessor to Dr Godinho's wife.'

'Scum!' growled Borges in disgust. And he continued slowly writing the document he was composing, despatching to Alcobaça the numbed and hopeless prisoner sitting on a bench at the far end of the room between two soldiers, his wrists manacled, his face bearing the marks of hunger.

Some days later, a service was held in the Cathedral for the lying in state of the rich landowner Morais, who had died of an aneurism, and to whom his wife was giving, as people said, 'a funeral fit for a king' (doubtless as a penance for the grief she had caused him by her unbridled passion for lieutenants in the infantry). Amaro had removed his vestments and, by the light of an old brass oil lamp in the sacristy, was catching up on some paperwork, when the oak door creaked open and Natário's agitated voice said:

'Amaro, is that you?'

'Yes, what's wrong?'

Father Natário closed the door, threw wide his arms and said:

'Great news! It's the clerk!'

'What clerk?'

'João Eduardo! It's him. He's the "Liberal"! He was the one who wrote the article!'

'Are you sure?' asked Amaro, astonished.

'I've got proof, my friend. I saw the original written in his own hand. I actually saw it. Five whole sheets of paper.'

Amaro was staring at Natário, wild-eyed.

'It was hard work,' said Natário, 'but I've found out everything! Five sheets of paper! And he wants to write another one. Senhor João Eduardo, our dear friend Senhor João Eduardo!'

'Are you quite sure?'

'Sure? I'm telling you I saw it, man!'

'And how did you find out, Natário?'

Natário bowed, and with his head down, he said very slowly:

'Ah, as for that, my friend . . . The whys and wherefores . . . You understand I'm sure. *Sigillus magnus*!'

And then, his voice shrill with triumph, he strode up and down the sacristy.

'But that's not all! The Senhor João Eduardo we used to see in São Joaneira's house, apparently such a nice lad, is and always has been a complete rogue! He's a close friend of Agostinho, the scoundrel who edits *The District Voice*. He's there at the office until the early hours of the morning . . . An orgy of wine and women . . . And he boasts that he's an atheist . . . He hasn't been to confession for six years. He refers to us as a "priestly rabble". He's a republican. A brute, dear Amaro, an utter brute!'

As he listened to Natário, Amaro, with trembling hands, was fumblingly putting away papers in the drawer of his desk.

'And now what?' he asked.

'Now?' replied Natário. 'Now we destroy him!'

Amaro closed the drawer and, nervously dabbing at his dry lips with his handkerchief, said:

'The brute . . . And the poor girl . . . how can she marry a man like that . . . a libertine!'

The two men looked at each other hard. In the silence, the

old sacristy clock continued its sad tick-tock. Natário took his snuff box from his trouser pocket and with his eyes still fixed on Amaro, the pinch of snuff between his fingers, he said with a cold smile:

'We should stop the marriage, don't you think?'

'Do you think so?' asked Amaro urgently.

'My dear colleague, it's a matter of conscience . . . For me, it's a question of duty. We can't let the poor young thing marry a scoundrel, a freemason, an atheist . . .'

'Of course we can't,' murmured Amaro.

'Happened just in time, eh?' said Natário, and he took a long sniff of snuff.

Then the sacristan came in; it was time to close the church; he wanted to know if they would be much longer.

'We'll be finished shortly, Senhor Domingos.'

And while the sacristan was closing the heavy bolts on the door that opened onto the courtyard, the two priests stood very close, talking in low voices.

'You go and talk to São Joaneira,' Natário was saying. 'No, wait, it would be best if Dias spoke to her; yes, he should speak to São Joaneira. That would be safest. You talk to Amélia and tell her quite simply that she should put him out of the house!' And he whispered in Amaro's ear: 'Tell her that he lives with a woman of easy virtue!'

Amaro drew back.

'But I don't even know if that's true!'

'It's bound to be. He's capable of anything. And besides it's a way of convincing the girl . . .'

And following in the wake of the sacristan, who was jingling his bunch of keys and loudly clearing his throat, they left the church.

The chapels were hung with black cloth embroidered with silver; the bier stood in the centre, between four large candleholders in which the candles were burning low; the broad velvet cloth covering Morais' coffin fell in fringed folds; at the head was a wreath of everlasting flowers, and at the foot, suspended on a large scarlet ribbon, hung the habit of a Knight of Christ.

Father Natário stopped and, smugly taking Amaro's arm, he said:

'And, my friend, I've got another little surprise for the gentleman . . .'

'What's that?'

'I'm going to cut off his supplies!'

'Cut off his supplies?'

'The fool was all ready to take up his job with the district government, as chief clerk. Well, I'm going to spoil that little arrangement. And Nunes Ferral, who is on my side and is a man of excellent ideas, will throw him out of the office where he now works . . . Then let him go and write articles for *The District Voice*!'

Amaro was horrified by this bitter intriguing.

'God forgive me, Natário, but that will ruin the boy . . .'

'I won't be happy until I see him begging for bread in the streets, Amaro.'

'Natário, please, that is most uncharitable, most un-Christian. And to say that in the Cathedral where God can hear you . . .'

'Don't you worry about that, my friend. This is how one serves God, not by mumbling paternosters. There is no charity for the impious. The Inquisition used fire on them, so it seems quite reasonable to me to use hunger. Everything is permitted to those who serve the holy cause. That will teach him to meddle in my affairs!'

As they were leaving the church, Natário glanced back at the coffin and, pointing at it with his umbrella, he asked:

'Who's in there?'

'Morais,' said Amaro.

'The fat fellow with the pock-marked face?'

'That's right.'

'The great fool.'

And then after a silence:

'So the service was for Morais. I didn't even realise, I was so caught up in my campaign. His widow will be very wealthy. She's generous too, always giving presents. And Silvério's her father confessor. That old elephant has all the luck.'

They left. Carlos' pharmacy was closed; the sky was very dark.

In the square, Natário stopped.

'To sum up then: Dias will talk to São Joaneira, and you will talk to Amélia. I'll sort things out with the people at the district government offices and with Nunes Ferral. You two will take care of the marriage and I'll take care of the job!' And clapping Amaro jovially on the shoulder, he said: 'That's what I call attacking him through the heart and through the stomach! Now I must be off, my nieces will be expecting me for supper. Rosa has had the most terrible cold. The girl's not strong, and I worry about her a lot. I just have to see her looking a bit peaky and I can't sleep. Well, what can one expect when one has a good heart . . . . See you tomorrow, Amaro.'

'Yes, see you tomorrow, Natário.'

And the two priests parted as the Cathedral clock was striking nine.

Amaro was still trembling slightly when he reached home, but he was feeling determined and happy too; he had a delicious duty to perform. And in order to drive home that great responsibility, he said out loud, as he walked gravely about the house:

'It's my duty! It's my duty!'

As a Christian, as a parish priest, as a friend to São Joaneira, it was *his duty* to go to Amélia and, quite simply, with not a glimmer of self-interest, tell her that João Eduardo, her fiancé, was the one who had written the article.

It was him! He had defamed the family's friends, those erudite, respected priests; he had discredited her; he spends his nights in debauchery in Agostinho's pigsty of a house; in private he insults the clergy and boasts of his lack of religion; he hasn't been to confession for six years! As Father Natário says, the man's a brute! Poor girl! No, she can't possibly marry a man who would prevent her from leading the 'perfect life' and who would ridicule her beliefs! He would not allow her to pray or to fast or to seek out healthy guidance from a confessor; as St John Chrysostom says, 'he would ripen her soul for Hell'! He was not her father or her guardian, but he was her parish priest, her shepherd, and if he did not save her from that heretical fate through his grave counsel and through the influence of her mother and her friends, he would be like someone who, asked to tend another's sheep, cruelly opens the gate to the wolf. No, Amélia could not possibly marry that atheist!

And, at that hope, his heart beat fast with excitement. No, the other man would not have her. Just as he was about to take legal possession of that waist, those breasts, those eyes, of Amélia herself, he, the parish priest, was there to declare: Back, you scum! This woman belongs to God!

And he would take great care to guide Amélia to salvation. The article would be forgotten and the precentor reassured: in a few days he would be able calmly to return to Rua da Misericórdia, to resume those delicious evening gatherings – to regain his power over that soul and to shape it for Paradise.

It was not a plot to take her away from her fiancé, good heavens, no; his motives (and he said this out loud the better to convince himself) were honest and pure; it was his holy duty to drag her back from Hell; he did not want her for himself, he wanted her for God! True, his interests as a lover did coincide with his duties, but even if she were squint-eyed, ugly and stupid, he would still, in the service of Heaven, go to Rua da Misericórdia and unmask Senhor João Eduardo as a slanderer and an atheist!

And reassured by that argument, he went to bed happy.

But he dreamed all night of Amélia. He had run away with her and was leading her along a road that led to Heaven! The Devil was after him, he could see him, and he looked like João Eduardo, snorting hard and tearing with his horns at the delicate hearts of the clouds. So he hid Amélia beneath his priest's cloak, devouring her with kisses. But the road to Heaven had no end. 'Where is the gate to Paradise?' he asked the golden-haired angels who passed with a rustle of wings, bearing souls in their arms. And they all replied: 'In Rua da Misericórdia. At number 9, Rua da Misericórdia!' Amaro felt lost; a vast, milky sky, as soft and giving as a bird's plumage, wrapped around him, and he looked in vain for the sign of an inn. Sometimes a shining globe would slide past, inside which he could hear the sound of God in the process of creation; or a squadron of archangels, wearing diamond cuirasses and brandishing swords of fire, would gallop nobly by . . .

Amélia was cold and hungry. 'Be patient, my love, be patient!' he would say. Walking on, they came across a white figure holding a green palm leaf. 'Where is God, our Father?' Amaro asked him, still clasping Amélia to his breast. The figure said: 'I was a confessor and now I'm a saint; the centuries pass and immutably, sempiternally, I hold this palm leaf in my hand and am bathed in constant ecstasy. No colour ever touches this white light; no feeling shakes my eternally immaculate being; and fixed as I am for ever in good fortune, I feel the monotony of Heaven weigh on me like a cloak of bronze. Ah, if only I could stride about amongst Earth's many forms of shamelessness, or plunge into the many varieties of pain, amidst the flames of Purgatory.'

Amaro muttered: 'We did well to sin.' But Amélia was fainting with weariness. 'Let us sleep, my love!' And they lay down and watched a floating, dusty cloud of stars falling like tares shaken through a sieve. Then the clouds began to arrange themselves around them, like the folds of curtains, giving off the delicate perfume of lavender sachets; Amaro placed his hand on Amélia's breast; they swooned in tender ecstasy; they embraced and their hot, wet lips met. 'Oh, Amélia!' he murmured. 'I love you, Amaro, I love you!' she sighed. But suddenly the clouds drew back like the curtains round a bed, and Amaro saw the Devil approaching, talons on hips, his mouth open in a silent laugh. There was someone else with him, a man as old as the earth; whole forests grew in the coils of his hair; his eyes had the blue vastness of an ocean; and along the fingers with which he smoothed his endless beard walked rows and rows of human beings of all races, as if along a road. 'These are the two individuals,' the Devil said to him, lashing his tail. And behind them Amaro saw legions of saints, male and female, beginning to gather. He recognised St Sebastian with the arrows stuck in him, St Cecilia playing the organ, and, in their midst, he heard the bleating of St John's flocks; and towering above them all stood the good giant, St Christopher, leaning on his pine tree. They were watching and whispering. Amaro could not free himself from Amélia, who was crying softly; their two bodies seemed unnaturally bound together; and in great distress, Amaro saw that her skirts were lifted to reveal her white knees. 'These are the two individuals,' the Devil said to the old man, 'and since all of us here are lovers of female beauty, notice what pretty legs the girl has!' Venerable old saints stood eagerly on tiptoe, craning necks that bore the scars of martyrdom; and the eleven thousand virgins clapped their wings and flew away like startled pigeons. Then the old man, rubbing his hands from which whole universes fell, said gravely: 'I see, my friend, I see. So, Father, you go to Rua da Misericórdia, you destroy the happiness of Senhor João Eduardo (a gentleman), tear Amélia away from her mother and seek out a corner of Eternity where you can sate your lustful desires. I am old, this voice that once rang out so wisely over valleys has grown hoarse. But do you think I am afraid of the Conde de Ribamar, your protector, even if he is a pillar of the Church and a column of the Order? Pharaoh was a great king, but I drowned him, his captive princes, his treasures, his war chariots and his hordes of slaves! That is what I am like. And if the ecclesiastical gentlemen continue to scandalise Leiria, I am still capable of burning a city as if it were a scrap of useless paper, and I have plenty of water left for floods.' Then turning to two angels armed with swords and lances, he roared: 'Clap the father in irons and take him to abyss number seven!' And the Devil whined: 'Behold the consequences of your actions, Father Amaro!' He felt himself plucked by fiery hands from Amélia's breast, and he was about to struggle and cry out against the judge who had sentenced him, when a prodigious sun rising in the East fell full on the old man's face, and, with a scream, Amaro recognised his Eternal Father!

He woke up bathed in sweat. A ray of sunlight was coming in through the window.

That night, João Eduardo, walking from the square to São Joaneira's house, was astonished to see appear at the far end of the street, coming from the Cathedral, a procession bearing the Sacrament.

It was heading for São Joaneira's house. Amongst the old ladies with their shawls over their heads, the torches picked out the scarlet cloth of copes; beneath the canopy glinted the gold of the parish priest's stole; a bell was being rung ahead of the procession, lights came on in windows, and in the dark night the Cathedral bell tolled ceaselessly.

Alarmed, João Eduardo ran to join the procession, where he learned at once that the last rites were being carried to São Joaneira's paralysed sister.

An oil lamp had been placed on a chair on the stairs. The servers rested the poles of the canopy against the wall, and Amaro went in. João Eduardo followed, feeling very nervous. He was thinking about that death; the period of mourning would delay the marriage; he felt troubled by Amaro's presence there and by the power he would acquire at such a moment; and in the downstairs sitting room he asked Ruça almost querulously:

'So what happened then?'

'The poor woman started growing weak this evening and the doctor came and said she was dying and the mistress sent for the sacraments.'

João Eduardo judged it would be polite to attend the ceremony.

The old lady's room was next to the kitchen and had, at that moment, a gloomy solemnity about it.

The table was covered by an appliqué table cloth on which stood a plate containing five cotton wool balls and two wax candles. The old lady's white head and waxen face were barely distinguishable from the linen pillow case; her eyes were wildly dilated, and she kept tugging slowly and persistently at the top of the embroidered sheet.

São Joaneira and Amélia were kneeling by the bed, praying; Dona Maria da Assunção (who had happened to drop by on her way back from the farm) had remained in the doorway, terrified, sitting back on her heels, murmuring hail Marys. João Eduardo silently knelt down beside her.

Father Amaro, bent over the bed, almost whispering into the old lady's ear, was exhorting her to abandon herself to divine mercy, but realising that she could not hear him, he knelt instead and rapidly recited the *Misereatur*; in the silence, his voice, which rose on the stressed syllables of the Latin words, had a touching sense of finality that made the two ladies weep. Then he got up, dipped one finger in the holy oils and, murmuring the ritual penitent words, he anointed eyes, chest, mouth and hands – the hands that for ten years had only moved to reach for the spittoon – and the soles of those feet that had only stirred to feel for the warmth of the hot water bottle. And then, having burned the cotton wool balls soaked in oil, he knelt down again, and remained there, unmoving, his eyes fixed on his breviary.

João Eduardo tiptoed back into the dining room and took a seat on the piano stool. Amélia would probably not play again for four or five weeks. Seeing the sweet progress of his love abruptly interrupted by death and its ceremonies, he felt overwhelmed by melancholy.

Much distressed by the scene, Dona Maria came out into the dining room, followed by Amélia whose eyes were red with weeping.

'Ah, thank heavens you're here, João Eduardo,' the old woman said. 'Would you be kind enough to accompany me back to my house? I'm all of a tremble. It took me completely by surprise, and God forgive me, but I cannot bear the sight of people dying. Even though she's fading away like a little bird . . . and she certainly has no sins . . . Let's walk together across the square, that's the quickest way. Do forgive me. And forgive me, Amélia, but I simply cannot stay . . . My pains are beginning . . . It's so very sad! Although it's better for her in a way. Oh dear, I feel quite faint.'

Amélia had to take her downstairs to São Joaneira's room and charitably comfort her with a glass of fortified wine.

'Amélia,' João Eduardo said. 'If you need me to do anything . . .'

'No, thank you. The poor thing won't last much longer . . .'

'Don't forget, Amélia,' Dona Maria da Assunção reminded her, 'place the two holy candles at her head. It brings great relief to the dying. And if the death rattle goes on too long, add another two unlit candles to form a cross. Good night. Oh, dear, I can barely think straight . . .'

At the front door, as soon as she saw the canopy and the men with the torches, Dona Maria clutched João Eduardo's arm and clung to him in terror – although this may also have had something to do with the fortified wine she had drunk, which always made her feel unusually affectionate.

Amaro had promised to return later, 'to keep them company, as a friend, throughout that difficult time'. And informed of this kind undertaking on Amaro's part, the Canon (who had arrived when the procession was going back round the corner towards the Cathedral) declared at once that, since his colleague Amaro would be spending the night there, he would go home and rest his bones, because, God knows, these upsets played havoc with his health.

'And you wouldn't want me to catch something and find myself in the same situation . . .'

'Please, Canon,' exclaimed São Joaneira, 'don't even say that!' And she began to weep pitifully.

'Well, good night, then,' said the Canon, 'and don't upset yourself too much. After all, the poor creature didn't have much of a life, and since she has no sins, she won't be bothered to find herself in the presence of God. It's for the best really, all things considered. Anyway, I'll be off now, I'm not too good myself . . .'

São Joaneira was not feeling well either. The shock, so soon after supper, was threatening to bring on a migraine, and when Amaro returned at eleven o'clock, it was Amélia who opened the door and showed him up to the dining room, saying:

'I'm sorry, Father, Mama has got a migraine, poor thing. She was in a terrible state. She went to bed, took a sedative and went to sleep.'

'Let her sleep then!'

They went into the dying woman's room. Her face was turned to the wall; from her open lips came a faint, continuous moaning. On the table now stood a thick candle which gave off a sad light; and in one corner, numb with fear, Ruça was saying the rosary as São Joaneira had told her to. Amélia said softly:

'The doctor says that she can't feel anything. He says that she'll just moan and moan like that and then die suddenly like a little bird . . .'

'May God's will be done,' Amaro murmured gravely.

They went back into the dining room. The whole house lay in silence; outside, the wind was blowing hard. They had not been together like this for weeks. Amaro felt intensely embarrassed and went over to the window; Amélia leaned against the sideboard.

'It's going to be a wet night,' Amaro said.

'And it's cold too,' she said, wrapping her shawl around her. 'I've been so afraid.'

'Have you never seen anyone die before?'

'No.'

They fell silent, he standing at the window, she leaning against the sideboard, her eyes cast down.

'It really is rather cold,' said Amaro, and his voice sounded odd, so troubling to him was her presence there at that hour of the night.

'The brazier's lit in the kitchen,' said Amélia. 'We'd better go in there.'

'Yes, all right.'

They went into the kitchen. Amélia brought the brass oil lamp, and Amaro, going over to stir the contents of the brazier with a pair of tongs, said:

'It's ages since I've been in the kitchen! Have you still got the plant pots out on the window sill.'

'Yes, and I've got a carnation now too.'

They sat down on low chairs beside the brazier. As she leaned towards the fire, Amélia could feel Father Amaro's eyes silently devouring her. He was sure to speak! Her hands were trembling; she did not dare to move or look up for fear that she might burst into tears, but she longed for his words be they bitter or sweet.

At last the words came, grave words.

'Miss Amélia, I wasn't expecting to have this opportunity to speak to you alone, but since that is how things have turned out, it must be God's will. And then you've changed so much towards me . . .'

She turned suddenly, her face scarlet, her lips trembling:

'But you know perfectly well why!' she exclaimed, almost crying.

'I know. If it hadn't been for the lies told in that wretched article nothing would have happened, and our friendship would be the same and everything would be fine . . . That's precisely what I wanted to talk to you about.'

He drew his chair nearer to hers, and very gently, very calmly he said:

'You know that article in which all our friends were insulted, in which my reputation was dragged through the mud, in which even your honour was besmirched? You remember, don't you? Well, do you know who wrote it?'

'Who?' asked Amélia in astonishment.

'Senhor João Eduardo!' Amaro said quietly, folding his arms.

'No, it can't be!'

She had stood up. Amaro tugged gently at her skirt to make her sit down again, and his voice went on, patiently, softly:

'Listen. Sit down. He was the one who wrote it. We only found out yesterday. Natário saw the original written in João Eduardo's hand. It was Natário who uncovered the truth. By perfectly honourable means, of course, and because it was God's will that the truth should emerge. Now listen. You don't know what that man is like.' Then he told her everything Natário had learned about João Eduardo, about the nights he spent with Agostinho, his insulting remarks about priests, his lack of religion . . .

'Ask him if he has been to confession in the last six years, and ask him for his confession certificate.'

With her hands fallen limply in her lap, she murmured:

'Good God, good God!'

'Then I realised that as a friend of the family, as parish priest, as a Christian and as your friend, Miss Amélia ... Because, believe me, I do love you ... Anyway, I realised that it was my duty to warn you. If I were your brother, I would simply say: "Amélia, drive that man from this house!" I am not, alas, your brother. But I come with a devout heart to say: "The man whom you want to marry gained your good opinion and that of your mother on false pretences; he came here looking for all the world like a decent young man, but deep down he's ..."'

He got up as if too indignant to go on.

'Miss Amélia, he is the man who wrote the article! He is the one who had poor Brito sent off to the wilds of Alcobaça! Who called me a seducer! Who called Canon Dias a libertine! A *libertine*! Who tried to poison relations between your mother and the Canon! And who accused you, in the plainest of terms, of allowing yourself to be seduced! Do you still want to marry that man?'

She did not reply, her eyes fixed on the fire, two silent tears running down her cheeks.

Amaro paced angrily up and down, then returning to her side, he went on in mellifluous tones and with affectionate gestures:

'But just suppose that he is not the author of the article and that he did not insult in print your mother, the Canon and your friends, there still remains his lack of piety. Imagine your future if you were to marry him. You would either have to accept his opinions, abandon your devotions, break with all your mother's friends, never set foot in church again, be a cause of scandal to decent folk, or else you would have to oppose him, and your home would become a hell. You would have to justify everything. Fasting on Fridays, going to Exposition of the Blessed Sacrament, keeping Sunday as a day of rest .... And the quarrels you would have if you wanted to go to confession ... Terrible. And having to put up with him ridiculing the mysteries of the faith. I can still remember the first night I came here, the disparaging remarks he made about the Holy Woman of Arregaça! And I remember too a night when Father Natário was talking about the sufferings of our Holy Father Pius IX, who would be taken prisoner if the liberals entered Rome . . . He laughed the idea to scorn, said it was a wild exaggeration. As if it were not true that, if the liberals had their way, we would see the Head of the Church, Christ's Vicar, forced to sleep in a prison cell on a few bits of straw. These are his opinions, of which he makes no secret. Father Natário says that João Eduardo and Agostinho were overheard in the café near the main square saying that baptism was an abuse because everyone should be free to choose the religion they want, and not be forced, as a child, to be a Christian. What do you think of that? I say this to you as your friend . . . For the good of your soul, I would rather see you dead than bound to that man! Marry him and you will lose for ever the grace of God!'

Amélia raised her hands to her head and slumped back in her chair, murmuring sadly:

'Oh, my God, oh, my God!'

Amaro sat down next to her, almost touching her dress with his knee, speaking now with paternal kindness:

'And do you think, my child, that a man like that could have a good heart, could respect your virtue and love you as a Christian husband should? If a man has no religion, he has no morality. If a man does not believe, he cannot love, says one of our holy fathers. Once the first fire of passion is over, he will become cold and irritable, he will go back to Agostinho and to those women of easy virtue, he might even mistreat you . . . You would live in constant fear. A man who does not respect religion has no scruples: he lies, steals, slanders . . . . Just look at that article. He comes here and shakes the Canon by the hand, then goes off to the newspaper and calls him a libertine. What remorse you would feel at the hour of your death! It's all right as long as you're young and healthy, but when the final moment comes, when, like the poor creature next door, you find yourself in the last agony, how terrible it would be to appear before Jesus Christ, having lived in sin at that man's side! He might even refuse to let them give you the last rites! To die without the sacrament, to die like an animal!'

'Please, Father, stop!' exclaimed Amélia bursting into hysterical sobs.

'Don't cry,' he said, taking her hand in his own two tremulous hands. 'Listen, you can be open with me . . . It's all right, calm down, we'll find a solution. No banns have been published. Just tell him that you do not want to marry him, that you know everything, that you hate him . . .'

He was slowly squeezing and stroking Amélia's hand. Then in a voice grown suddenly ardent, he said:

'You don't really care for him, do you?'

With her head fallen forward on her chest, she said very softly:

'No.'

'There you are, then!' he said excitedly. 'And tell me, do you love someone else?'

She did not reply, but she was breathing hard, staring, wide-eyed, into the flames.

'Do you? Tell me!'

He put his arm around her shoulder, gently drawing her to him. Her hands lay limply in her lap; without moving, she slowly turned to look at him, her eyes shining beneath a mist of tears, then, pale and weak, she slowly half-opened her lips. Trembling, he put his lips to hers and they remained motionless, locked in one long, deep kiss, teeth touching teeth.

'Miss Amélia! Miss Amélia!' came Ruça's terrified voice.

Amaro leaped to his feet and ran into the next room. Amélia was shaking so much that she had to lean against the kitchen door for a moment, her hand pressed to her heart, her knees buckling. Only when she had recovered did she go down to wake her mother.

When they went into the dying woman's room, Amaro was kneeling in prayer, his face almost resting on the bed; the two women fell to their knees; the old woman's chest and sides were shaken by rapid breathing; and the more stertorous the breathing became, the more quickly the priest prayed. Suddenly the agonising sound stopped; they looked up; the old woman lay still, her eyes bulging and opaque. She was dead.

Father Amaro immediately led the two women into the dining room, and there, cured of her migraine by the shock, São Joaneira burst into tears, remembering the days when her poor sister had been young and pretty! And how she had been about to be married to the heir to the Vigareira estate!

'And she had such a generous nature, Father. A saint! When Amélia was born and I was so ill, she didn't move from my bedside day or night! And she was always so cheerful. Oh, dear God!'

Amélia was leaning against the dark window, staring dully out at the black night.

The door bell rang at that point. Amaro went downstairs with a candle. It was João Eduardo, who, on seeing the priest there at that hour of the night, stood dumbstruck at the open door. At last he managed to say:

'I just came to see if there was any news . . .'

'I see.'

The two men looked at each other for a moment.

'Well, if I'm not needed . . .' said João Eduardo.

'No . . . thank you. The ladies are about to go to bed.'

João Eduardo turned pale with anger at Amaro's proprietorial manner. He stood a while longer, hesitating, but seeing the priest shielding the flame with his hand from the wind in the street, he said:

'Good night, then.'

'Good night.'

Father Amaro went back upstairs, and having left the two ladies in São Joaneira's bedroom (for they were too frightened to sleep alone), he returned to the room where the dead woman lay, relit the candle on the table, settled himself in a chair and began to read the breviary.

Later, when the house was in silence, the priest, feeling sleep overwhelm him, went into the dining room where he consoled himself with a glass of port that he found on the sideboard; and he was just enjoying a cigarette when he heard the sound of heavy boots outside, walking back and forth beneath the windows. The night was too dark for him to be able to make out who 'the walker' was. It was a furious João Eduardo keeping watch on the house.

XII

Early the next day, shortly after Dona Josefa Dias had got back from mass, she was most surprised to hear the maid call up to her from where she was cleaning the steps downstairs:

'Father Amaro's here, Dona Josefa!'

He had visited the Canon's house only rarely of late, and so, flattered and curious, Dona Josefa shouted down:

'Tell him to come up. There's no need for formality. He's like one of the family! Tell him to come straight up!'

She was in the dining room, arranging slabs of quince jelly on a tray; she was wearing a pair of blue-tinted spectacles and a black woollen dress which was frayed at the sides and pushed out above her ankles by the single hoop of a crinoline; she shuffled out onto the landing in her hideous felt slippers, and, for the benefit of the parish priest, she prepared a pleasant face beneath the black scarf pulled tight over her head.

'What a nice surprise!' she exclaimed. 'I've only just got in from my first mass of the day. I went to the Chapel of Our Lady of the Rosary. Father Vicente was saying mass today. Oh, it did me so much good, Father. It makes such a difference. Now, don't sit there, you'll be in a draught. So the poor little cripple has passed away . . . Tell me what happened, Father . . .'

Father Amaro had to describe the death agony and São Joaneira's grief, and how, after death, the old woman's face appeared to grow young again, and what São Joaneira and Amélia had decided to do as regards a shroud . . .

'Between you and me, Dona Josefa, it's a great relief to São Joaneira . . .' Then suddenly, shifting forwards in his chair, placing his hands on his knees, he said: 'And what about Senhor João Eduardo, eh? He was the one who wrote that article!'

The old woman cried out, putting her hands to her head:

'Oh, don't even talk to me about it, Father, don't even talk about it. The whole business has made me positively ill.'

'Oh, so you know?'

'Oh, yes, Father. I owe that to Father Natário; he came to see me yesterday and told me everything. Oh, the scoundrel, the reprobate!'

'And you know, too, that he's a close friend of Agostinho, that they sit drinking in Agostinho's office into the early hours and go to the billiard room off the main square and make mock of religion.'

'Please, Father, not another word. Yesterday, when Father Natário was here, it quite upset me to hear about such sinful behaviour . . . Father Natário was good enough to tell me about it as soon as he heard. He's so thoughtful. But you know, Father, I always had my doubts about that man. I never said so, oh no, I've never been one to meddle in other people's lives, but I had a feeling inside. He went to mass, kept the fasts, but I always had a suspicion that he was only doing that in order to deceive São Joaneira and Amélia. And now we see what he's really like! I never really cared for him, Father, never.' Then, her eyes glinting with wicked joy, she said: 'And it looks as if the marriage is off too!'

Father Amaro leaned back in his chair and said very deliberately:

'It would be unthinkable for a girl of good principles to marry a freemason who hasn't been to confession for six years.'

'Absolutely, Father. I would rather see her dead. She must be told everything . . .'

Father Amaro broke in, pulling his chair closer to hers:

'That is precisely why I came to see you, Senhora. I spoke to Amélia yesterday . . . but, of course, in the midst of such misfortune, with the poor lady dying in the next room, I could hardly insist. I merely told her what had happened, advised her as best I could, told her that she risked losing her soul and leading a life of misery, etc. In short, I did what I could, Senhora, as a friend and as her parish priest. And, as was my duty (although I found this very hard to do, very hard indeed), I reminded her that as a Christian and as a woman, she had an obligation to break with the clerk.'

'And what did she say?'

Amaro pulled a rueful face.

'She didn't say anything. She just looked sad and started crying. Naturally, she was very upset about the death in the house, and it's clear that she's not madly in love with him, but she wants to get married, she's afraid that if her mother died, she would be left all alone. Well, you know what girls are like. My words obviously hit home, and she was very angry, etc., but I think it would be best if you spoke to her. You're a friend of the family, you're her godmother, you've known her ever since she was a child . . . You will doubtless bequeath her a tidy sum in your will . . . These are all important factors . . .'

'You leave it to me, Father!' exclaimed the old woman. 'I'll tell her what's what!'

'The girl needs guidance. Between you and me, she needs a confessor. Her current confessor is Father Silvério, and, far be it from me to criticise, but Father Silvério, poor old thing, really isn't up to much as a confessor. Oh, he's very charitable, very virtuous, but he hasn't really got what it takes. For him confession is a matter of form. He asks the usual questions about doctrine, then he takes the confessant through the ten commandments . . . you know the kind of thing. Obviously the girl doesn't steal or murder or covet her neighbour's wife! That sort of confession is of no use to her; what she needs is a confessor who will be firm with her, who will say to her – go that way! – and accept no rebuttals. The girl has a weak nature and, like most women, she simply cannot cope on her own; that's why she needs a confessor who will rule her with a rod of iron, someone she will obey, someone to whom she will tell everything, someone she is afraid of . . . That is what a confessor should be . . .'

'You're the sort of confessor she needs, Father.'

Amaro smiled modestly:

'You may be right. I would certainly advise her well. I'm a friend of her mother's and I think Amélia is a good girl worthy of the grace of God. And whenever I talk to her, I always give her any advice I can. But you understand, there are some things you can't discuss in the dining room, with other people about. That's where the confessional is so important. That is what I lack, opportunities to talk to her alone. But I can't possibly go to her and say: "Right, from now on you're going to confess to me!" I'm always very scrupulous about such things . . .'

'I'll tell her, Father, I'll tell her.'

'That would be most kind of you. You would be doing that soul a great good. Because if the girl looks to me to guide her soul, then all her difficulties will be over, she will be set fair on the road to Grace. When do you think you'll talk to her, Dona Josefa?'

Dona Josefa felt it would be a sin to delay the matter and was determined to speak to her that very night.

'I think not, Dona Josefa. People will be there paying their condolences . . . The clerk, of course, will also be there . . .'

'Good heavens, Father! Do you mean that I and the other women will have to spend the night under the same roof as that heretic?'

'I'm afraid so. After all, at the moment, the boy is still considered one of the family. Besides, Dona Josefa, you, Dona Maria and the Gansosos are people of great virtue, but we must not be proud of being virtuous. Indeed if we are, we risk losing all the fruits of that virtue. Mingling occasionally with bad people is an act of humility most pleasing to God; it is like a great nobleman standing side by side with a farm labourer . . . It is as if we were saying: "I am superior to you in virtue, but compared with what I must be in order to enter into glory, who knows, perhaps I am as great a sinner as you!" And that humility of soul is the best possible gift we can offer to Jesus.'

Dona Josefa was listening to him, rapt. Then she said admiringly:

'Ah, Father, it almost makes one virtuous just to listen to you!'

Amaro bowed.

'God, in His kindness, sometimes inspires me with the right words. But I mustn't take up any more of your time. We're agreed, then. You will speak to Amélia tomorrow and if, as is likely, she agrees to hear my advice, then bring her to the Cathedral on Saturday, at eight o'clock. And be firm with her, Dona Josefa!'

'You leave it to me, Father. But aren't you going to taste my quince jelly?'

'I certainly am,' said Amaro, and, picking up one of the slabs, he graciously took a bite.

'I made it from Dona Maria's quinces. It's turned out much better than the jelly the Gansoso sisters made.'

'Goodbye, then, Dona Josefa. By the way, what has the Canon to say about this business with the clerk?'

'My brother?'

At that moment, the bell downstairs rang furiously.

'That will be him now,' said Dona Josefa. 'And he's obviously angry about something.'

The Canon had just returned from the farm, furious with the tenant, with the farm manager, the Government and the general perversity of men. Someone had stolen some onion sets, and he was venting his rage by gleefully repeating over and over the name of the Evil One.

'Please, brother, it's not nice!' exclaimed Dona Josefa, seized by scruples.

'Now, sister, you can leave such nonsense for Lent. I say "Devil take it!" and I'll say it again. But I've told the tenant that if he sees or hears anyone on the farm, then he should load his shotgun and shoot them!'

'People just don't respect other people's property these days,' said Amaro.

'People don't respect anything!' said the Canon. 'And they were such lovely onion sets too, it did you good just to look at them. But that's the way things are. That's what I call sacrilege, utter sacrilege!' he added earnestly, because the theft of his onion sets, a Canon's onion sets, seemed to him as black an act of impiety as if someone had filched the holy vessels from the Cathedral.

'It shows a lack of the fear of God and a lack of religion,' remarked Dona Josefa.

'What do you mean "a lack of religion"!' retorted the Canon, exasperated. 'A lack of policemen, more like!' And turning to Amaro, he said: 'It's the old girl's funeral today, isn't it? So I've got that to deal with too! Oh, sister, go and get me a clean collar, will you, and my buckled shoes.'

Father Amaro returned then to his main concern:

'We were just talking about this business with João Eduardo and the article in *The District Voice*!'

'There's another bit of knavery,' the Canon riposted. 'Honestly, there are some terrible people about, terrible.' And he stood, arms crossed, eyes wide, as if contemplating a legion of monsters roaming the universe and blithely attacking reputations, the principles of the Church, the honour of families and the clergy's onion sets.

As he left, Father Amaro went over the recommended plan of action with Dona Josefa, who accompanied him out onto the landing.

'So today, it being a time for condolences, we'll do nothing. Tomorrow, you'll talk to Amélia and then bring her to me at the Cathedral on Saturday. Fine. And do your best to persuade the girl, Dona Josefa, and try to save that soul. God is watching you. Speak to her firmly . . . firmly, do you hear! And our Canon will explain things to São Joaneira.'

'Don't worry, Father. I'm her godmother, and whether she likes it or not, I'm going to set her on the road to salvation.'

'Amen,' said Father Amaro.

That night, Dona Josefa did indeed do nothing. It was the night of condolences in Rua da Misericórdia. They were all in the downstairs living room, which was dimly lit by a single candle hidden beneath a dark green shade. São Joaneira and Amélia, all in black, sat sadly on the sofa in the middle; on chairs ranged around the walls, their friends, sad-faced and dressed in deep mourning, sat in a dumb torpor, maintaining a funereal stillness; occasionally there would be the murmur of two voices, or a sigh would emerge from the shadows in one corner of the room; then Libaninho or Artur Couceiro would tiptoe over to trim the wick of the candle; Dona Maria da

Assunção would mournfully clear her throat; and, in the ensuing silence, they would hear only the clatter of clogs over the cobbles or the poorhouse clock chiming the quarter hours.

At intervals, Ruça, who was also dressed in black, came in bearing a tray of cakes and tea; the shade would be removed from the candle, and the old ladies, whose eyelids were already drooping, would, in response to the sudden brightness in the room, immediately press their handkerchiefs to their eyes and then, sighing, help themselves to cakes.

Ignored by everyone, João Eduardo sat in one corner, near the deaf Gansoso sister, who was asleep with her mouth open; all night, in vain, his eyes sought those of Amélia, who did not move, her head bowed, her hands in her lap, alternately crumpling up and smoothing out her fine chambray handkerchief. Father Amaro and Canon Dias arrived at nine o'clock. Amaro went solemnly over to speak to São Joaneira:

'It is a great blow, Senhora, but let us console ourselves with the thought that your excellent sister is now enjoying the company of Our Lord Jesus Christ.'

There was a ripple of sobbing, and since there were no chairs left, the two clerics sat down on the sofa, on either side of São Joaneira and Amélia, who were both in tears. They were thus acknowledged as members of the family. Dona Maria da Assunção said quietly to Dona Joaquina Gansoso:

'Isn't it nice to see all four of them together.'

And so until ten o'clock, the evening continued in somnolent gloom, disturbed only by constant coughing from João Eduardo, who had a bad cold, although Dona Josefa Dias told everyone afterwards that 'he was only doing it in order to make a mockery of the whole thing and out of a lack of respect for the dead'.

Two days later, at eight o'clock in the morning, Dona Josefa Dias and Amélia entered the Cathedral, having first spoken to Amparo, the pharmacist's wife, whom they met outside; one of Amparo's children had measles, and although it wasn't anything very grave, she had come 'just in case, to make a promise'.

It was a misty day, and the Cathedral was filled by grey light. Amélia, pale beneath her lace mantilla, stopped in front of the altar to Our Lady of Sorrows, fell to her knees and remained there motionless, her face resting on her prayer-book. Dona Josefa Dias, having first prostrated herself before the chapel of the Sacrament and before the high altar, padded over to the sacristy door and pushed it slowly open. Father Amaro was pacing about inside, shoulders bowed, hands behind his back.

'Is she here?' he asked at once, looking up at Dona Josefa, his restless eyes glittering in his closely shaven face.

'She's here,' said Dona Josefa with quiet triumph. 'I went to fetch her myself. I spoke to her firmly, Father, I didn't spare her. Now it's up to you.'

'Thank you, thank you, Dona Josefa!' said Amaro, squeezing both her hands hard. 'God will not forget this.'

He looked about him nervously; he patted his pockets for his handkerchief and his notebook, then, quietly closing the door behind him, he went into the church. Amélia was still kneeling, a motionless black shape against the white pillar.

'Psst,' said Dona Josefa.

Amélia, very red-faced, got to her feet, tremulously arranging the folds of her mantilla around her face and neck.

'I'll leave her to you, Father,' said Dona Josefa. 'I'm going to see Amparo now, and I'll come back for Amélia later. Off you go, child, off you go. And may God bring enlightenment to your soul.'

And she left, curtseying before all the altars as she went.

Carlos the pharmacist – who was one of the Canon's tenants and rather behind with the rent – made a great show of doffing his cap when Dona Josefa appeared at the door, and he led her immediately upstairs to the curtained room where Amparo was sitting at the window sewing.

'Don't you worry about me, Senhor Carlos,' said Dona Josefa. 'Don't let me keep you from your work. I've just left my goddaughter at the Cathedral and have popped in here to have a rest.'

'Then if you'll excuse me . . . How's the Canon by the way?'

'He hasn't had any more pain, but he has had some dizzy spells.'

'It's the spring,' said Carlos who was once more his majestic self, standing in the middle of the room, his thumbs hooked in his waistcoat. 'I've had the same thing. Sanguine people, like the Canon and myself, tend to suffer from what one might term the rising of the sap. There are many humours in the blood, which, if they are not eliminated through the proper channels, can, if I may put it like this, make various inroads into the body in the form of boils or pimples that often occur in the most uncomfortable places, and although, in themselves, insignificant, they are always accompanied, so to speak, by . . . But forgive me, it's the practitioner in me speaking. Now if you'll excuse me . . . My best regards to the Canon, and tell him to use James's magnesium!'

Dona Josefa asked to see the little girl with the measles. But she did not go beyond the door of the room, urging the child, who stared at her from amidst the blankets with wide, feverish eyes, not to neglect her prayers morning and night. She suggested various miracle cures to Amparo, adding that if that promise of Amparo's had been made with faith in her heart, then the child could consider herself as good as cured. Ah, every day she gave thanks to God that she had never married. Children bring nothing but work and worry, and what with the problems they cause and the time they take up, they were often the very reason why women neglected their religious duties and thus risked going to Hell . . .

'You're quite right, Dona Josefa,' said Amparo. 'They are a burden. And I've got five of them! Sometimes they drive me so wild that I just sit down here on this chair and have a good cry all by myself.'

They had gone back to the window and were enjoying themselves hugely by spying on the administrator who was in his office peering through his binoculars at the tailor's wife. It was scandalous! They never used to have civil servants like that in Leiria. And then there was the secretary-general's outrageous behaviour with Novais' wife! But what could you expect from men with no religion, who had been brought up in Lisbon and who, according to Dona Josefa, were predestined to be consumed like Gomorrah by the fires of Heaven? Amparo continued her sewing, head bowed, ashamed perhaps, in the presence of such pious anger, of her longing to visit the Passeio Público in Lisbon and to hear the singers in the Teatro São Carlos.

But Dona Josefa quickly moved on to the subject of João Eduardo. Amparo knew nothing about it, and Dona Josefa had the satisfaction of giving her a blow-by-blow account of the history of the article, of the unfortunate events at Rua da Misericórdia, and Natário's campaign to unmask the 'Liberal'. She went into particular detail when it came to describing João Eduardo's character, his lack of piety, his orgies . . . And, considering it her Christian duty to destroy the atheist utterly, she even implied that certain robberies committed recently in Leiria were also the work of João Eduardo.

Amparo declared herself to be 'flabbergasted'. And what about his marriage to Amélia?

'Oh, that's all in the past now,' declared Dona Josefa gleefully. 'They're going to put him out of the house! I wouldn't be surprised if he wasn't hauled up before the magistrates. I think he should be myself, and so do my brother and Father Amaro . . . There are more than enough reasons to clap him in jail.'

'But I thought Amélia was fond of him.'

Dona Josefa grew indignant. Amélia was a sensible, virtuous girl. The moment she had found out about his outrageous behaviour, she had been the first to reject him! She hated him now. And lowering her voice to a confidential whisper, Dona Josefa went on to say that it was a well-known fact that he lived with a woman of easy virtue over by the barracks.

'Father Natário told me,' she said. 'And he is a man who only ever speaks the purest truth. He was considerateness itself with me . . . As soon as he knew, he came to see me at once to ask my advice. So thoughtful . . .'

Carlos reappeared at this point. There was no one in the

pharmacy just then (he had barely been able to draw breath all morning!) and he had come up to keep the ladies company.

'I suppose you've heard, Senhor Carlos,' Dona Josefa said, 'about this João Eduardo and the article in *The District Voice*?'

The pharmacist opened large, astonished eyes. What relation could there be between a vile article like that and an apparently honest young man?

'Honest!' wailed Dona Josefa. 'He was the one who wrote it, Senhor Carlos!'

And seeing Carlos bite his lip in surprise, she again launched enthusiastically into the story of the 'scandal'.

'What do you think to that, Senhor Carlos?'

The pharmacist gave his opinion in a drawling voice laden with the authority of one possessed of vast knowledge.

'I would say, as would all decent people, that it brings shame on Leiria. When I first read that article, I remarked then that religion is the basis of society, and to undermine it is, so to speak, to shake the very foundations of that edifice. It is a disgrace that we have living in this town these materialists and republicans, who, as everyone knows, want to destroy everything that exists; they say that men and women should behave as promiscuously as dogs . . . (Forgive me for expressing myself like that, but facts are facts.) They want the right to come into my house and take away my money and the sweat from my brow; they don't believe in authority and, if you let them, they would spit on the sacred Host itself . . .'

Dona Josefa gave a little shriek and recoiled, shuddering.

'And those people dare to speak of freedom. I myself am a liberal, though not, to be frank, a fanatical one. Just because a man is a priest, I don't regard him as a saint, no . . . For example, I could never stand Father Miguéis. He was like a boa constrictor. I'm sorry, Dona Josefa, but he was. I told him so to his face. After all, we do have freedom of speech in this country . . . We spilt our blood in the trenches at Oporto precisely so that we could. I told him to his face. Sir, I said, you are a boa constrictor! Nevertheless, a man in a cassock does, generally speaking, deserve our respect. And that article, as I said, brings shame on Leiria. I'll say this too: one should show no mercy to these atheists and republicans. I'm a peaceable man – Amparo here can vouch for that – but if I had to make up a prescription for a declared republican, I wouldn't hesitate, instead of giving him one of those beneficial compounds that are the pride of our profession, I would send him a dose of prussic acid. No, no, I wouldn't, of course . . . . But if I was on a jury I would make sure the full weight of the law fell on him.'

And he swayed for a moment on the tips of his slippered toes, flinging out his arm as if expecting the applause of a district or municipal council in session.

However, the slow chimes of eleven o'clock came from the Cathedral, and Dona Josefa hurriedly wrapped herself up in her shawl in order to go and fetch Amélia, the poor thing, who must be tired of waiting.

Carlos accompanied her to the door, again doffing his hat, telling her (as if he were sending the Canon some choice gift):

'Tell the Canon what I had to say on the matter . . . Tell him that as regards that article and attacks on the clergy in general, I am heart and soul behind the clergy. Your servant, Senhora . . . The weather looks like it's closing in.'

When Dona Josefa went into the church, Amélia was still in the confessional. Dona Josefa coughed loudly, knelt down, and with her hands covering her face, immersed herself in a prayer to Our Lady of the Rosary. The church was utterly still and silent. Then Dona Josefa turned to the confessional, peeping between her fingers; Amélia had not moved, she had her mantilla pulled forward over her face, and the skirt of her black dress trailed on the floor around her. Dona Josefa returned to her prayers. A fine rain was now beating against the windows of one of the side windows. At last, from the confessional came the creak of wood and the rustle of skirts on flagstones, and, turning around, Dona Josefa saw Amélia standing before her, her cheeks aflame and her eyes shining.

'Have you been waiting long, Dona Josefa?'

'Not very long. Are you ready, then?'

She got up, crossed herself, and the two women left the Cathedral. The fine rain was still falling, but Artur Couceiro, who had letters to deliver to the district government offices, accompanied them back to Rua da Misericórdia under his umbrella.

XIII

It was growing dark as João Eduardo was about to set off to Rua da Misericórdia with a roll of wallpaper samples under his arm for Amélia to choose from, when he found Ruça outside his door, about to ring the bell.

'What's wrong, Ruça?'

'My mistresses won't be at home tonight, and this is a letter from Miss Amélia.'

João Eduardo felt his heart contract, and he followed Ruça with wild eyes as she clacked down the street in her clogs. He went over to the lamp post opposite and opened the letter.

> Senhor João Eduardo.
>
> When I agreed to marry you it was in the belief that you were a good man who could make me happy; but now that everything has come out, and now that we know that you were the person who wrote that article in *The District Voice* and who slandered our friends and insulted me, and since your habits give me no guarantee of a happy married life, you must, from today, consider everything between us at an end, for no banns have been published and no expenses incurred. And I hope, as does my mother, that you will have the decency not to visit our house or to pursue us in the street. I tell you all this on my mother's orders, and remain
>
> Your servant,
> Amélia Caminha

João Eduardo stood stock still, staring foolishly at the wall lit by the street lamp, with his roll of wallpaper under his arm. Mechanically, he went back into the house. His hands were shaking so much that he could barely light the oil lamp. Standing by the table, he re-read the letter. Then he stayed there, burning his eyes on the flame of the lamp, filled by a chilling sense of immobility and silence, as if suddenly, with no warning, the whole world had become still and mute. He wondered where they would have gone to spend the night. Memories of happy evenings at the house in Rua da Misericórdia paraded slowly through his mind: Amélia working, head bent, and affording, between dark hair and white collar, a glimpse of her pale neck softened by the light . . . Then the idea that he had lost her for ever pierced his heart like the cold thrust of a dagger. Stunned, he clasped his head in his hands. What should he do? What should he do? Sudden decisions flashed momentarily inside him, only to fade at once. He wanted to write to her! To kidnap her! To go to Brazil! To find out who had revealed that he was the author of the article! And since that was the only practicable thing to be done at that hour, he ran to the office of *The District Voice*.

Agostinho was stretched out on the sofa, with a candle burning on a chair nearby, enjoying the Lisbon newspapers. The look of distress on João Eduardo's face alarmed him.

'What's wrong?'

'You've ruined me, you scoundrel!'

And without pausing for breath, João Eduardo accused Agostinho of having betrayed him.

Agostinho got up slowly and felt placidly in his jacket pocket for his tobacco pouch.

'Don't make such a fuss,' he said. 'I give you my word of honour that I did not tell a soul who wrote that article. Not that anyone asked me . . .'

'Well, who was it, then?' yelled the clerk.

Agostinho shrugged.

'All I know is that the priests have been frantically trying to find out who wrote it. Natário came in one morning about a piece concerning a widow in need of charity, but he didn't say a word about the article. Dr Godinho knew, go and see him! But what have they done to you?'

'They've killed me,' said João Eduardo bleakly.

He stood for a moment staring at the floor, utterly defeated, then left, slamming the door. He walked around the main square and wandered the streets until, attracted by the darkness, he headed for the road out to Marrazes. He was breathing hard and was aware of an unbearable dull pounding in his head; the wind was whistling in across the fields, yet he felt as if wrapped in a universal silence; occasionally, the full force of his misfortune would tear at his heart, and then the whole landscape seemed to tremble and the road ahead to turn to soft mud. By the time he had walked back to the Cathedral, the clock was striking eleven, and he found himself in Rua da Misericórdia, his eyes fixed on the dining room window, where a light was still burning; then a light appeared in Amélia's bedroom too; she was probably going to bed . . . He was gripped by a furious desire for her beauty, her body, her kisses. He ran home and fell, utterly exhausted, onto his bed; then he was seized by a deep, indefinite longing for what he had lost and he cried for a long time, touched by the sound of his own sobbing, until he fell asleep, face down, an inert mass.

Early next morning, Amélia was walking down Rua da Misericórdia to the main square, when João Eduardo ambushed her.

'I need to talk to you, Miss Amélia.'

She recoiled in fear and said, trembling:

'You have nothing to say to me.'

But he stood before her, very determined, his eyes red as glowing coals.

'I just want to say . . . About the article, it's true, I did write the wretched thing, but you were driving me mad with jealousy . . . . But what you said about me being a man of bad habits is pure lies. I have always been a decent man.'

'Father Amaro knows all about you! Now please let me pass.'

Hearing the priest's name, João Eduardo turned white with rage:

'Oh, so it was Father Amaro, was it? The scoundrel! Well, let me tell you . . .'

'Please let me pass!' she said angrily and so loudly that a fat man in a cloak stopped to look at them.

João Eduardo drew back, doffing his hat, and she took shelter in Fernandes' shop.

Then, in despair, he ran to Dr Godinho's house. The previous night, in between crying fits, feeling utterly abandoned, he had thought about going to see Dr Godinho. He had worked for him as a clerk once, and since it was through him that he had got his present job with Nunes Ferral, and through his influence that he had secured the post in the district government office, he judged him to be a prodigal and inexhaustible fount of good fortune. More than that, ever since he had written the article, he had considered himself part of the editorial board of *The District Voice* and of the Maia Group; now that he was being attacked by the priesthood, it was clear that he should seek the strong protection of his boss, Dr Godinho, the enemy of all reactionary forces, the Cavour of Leiria, as the satirist Azevedo described him, rolling his eyes. And so, on his way to the yellow mansion, near the main square, where the doctor lived, João Eduardo felt abuzz with hope, glad to be able to take refuge, like a beaten dog, between the legs of that colossus.

Dr Godinho had already gone down to his office and, leaning back in his large yellow-studded armchair, staring up at the dark oak ceiling, he was taking one last blissful puff of his breakfast cigar. He received João Eduardo's 'Good morning' majestically.

'So what can I do for you, my friend?'

As always, João Eduardo felt intimidated by the tall shelves filled with grave folios, by the reams of legal documents, by the magnificent painting depicting the Marquês de Pombal looking out over the Tagus, driving away the English with the wave of an admonitory finger, and in a constrained voice he said that he had come in order to ask the good doctor for a solution to the misfortune that had befallen him.

'Have you been in a fight? Has someone beaten you?'

'No, sir, it's about a family matter.'

He then launched into a prolix account of his story since the publication of the article; with great emotion, he read Amélia's letter; he described his meeting with her that morning . . . And there he was, driven out of Rua da Misericórdia by the manoeuvrings of the parish priest! He might not be a graduate from Coimbra University, but it seemed to him that there should be laws against a priest who insinuated his way into a family, misled a pure young woman, used intrigue to make her break her engagement and assumed dominion over her in the home.

'I don't know, sir, but it seems to me there should be laws against it!'

Dr Godinho seemed most put out.

'Laws?' he boomed, smartly crossing his legs. 'What laws do you think there should be? Do you want to sue the priest? Why? Did he hit you? Did he steal your watch? Did he insult you in the press? No. So what then?'

'But, sir, he lied about me to the ladies! I have never been a man of bad habits, sir, never. He slandered me!'

'Do you have witnesses?'

'No, sir.'

'Exactly.'

And resting his elbows on his desk, Dr Godinho declared that, as a lawyer, there was nothing he could do. The courts did not deal with such matters, with these moral dramas which, so to speak, took place in the bedroom . . . He could not intervene as a man, as an individual, as plain Alípio de Vasconcelos Godinho, because he did not know Father Amaro or the ladies in Rua da Misericórdia . . . He regretted this because, after all, he too had been young once, he too had experienced the poetry of youth, and he too (alas!) had known the pain of heartbreak . . . But that was all he could do – feel regret. Why had João Eduardo given his affections to such an over-religious young woman in the first place?

João Eduardo broke in:

'It isn't her fault, sir. It's the fault of that priest who is trying to lead her astray! It's the fault of those rascally canons!'

Dr Godinho held up his hand severely at this and advised João Eduardo to take care when making such assertions. There was no proof that the priest had had any more influence in that household than any other skilful spiritual director. And with the authority bestowed on him by his age and by his position in the country, he recommended that João Eduardo should not, out of spite, spread accusations that would only serve to destroy the prestige of the priesthood, which was indispensable in any well-constituted society. Without it, everything would be anarchy and orgy!

And he leaned back, satisfied, thinking that he certainly had a way with words that morning.

But the concerned face of the clerk, who did not move from beside the desk, made him impatient, and so, picking up a volume of legal documents, he said sharply:

'What more do you want, then, my friend? As you see, I cannot provide you with a remedy.'

João Eduardo retorted in a sudden rush of desperate courage:

'I thought you might be able to do something for me . . . because I was, after all, a victim . . . All this comes from the discovery that I wrote that article. And we had agreed it would remain a secret. Agostinho didn't tell anyone, and you were the only other person who knew . . .'

Dr Godinho started indignantly in his chair.

'And what are you implying? Are you suggesting that I was the one who revealed the secret? Well, I didn't . . . or, rather, I did; I told my wife, because in any well-constituted family, there should never be secrets between man and wife. She asked me, and I told her. But let's just suppose that I did spread that rumour. One of two things is possible: either the article was a calumny, in which case I should accuse you of besmirching an honourable newspaper with a pack of defamatory lies, or it was true, in which case what kind of man are you to be ashamed of the truths you told, to be afraid to uphold in the broad light of day opinions that you wrote in the dark of night?'

João Eduardo's eyes filled with tears. And confronted by that look of defeat, pleased to have crushed João Eduardo with the power and logic of his argument, Dr Godinho softened:

'But let's not quarrel. Let us talk no more of points of honour. One thing is certain, I sincerely regret the position you find yourself in.'

He offered him advice in a paternal, solicitous manner. He

should not be too cast down; there were plenty more young women in Leiria, principled young women who were not under the sway of the priesthood. He should be strong and console himself thinking that even Dr Godinho – yes, even he – had suffered for love in his youth. He should shun the dominion of the passions, since that could prove prejudicial to him in any public career. And if he would not do so for his own sake, then do it for him, for Dr Godinho!

João Eduardo left the office, feeling angry and judging that he had been betrayed by the doctor.

'This is happening to me,' he muttered, 'because I'm just a nobody, my vote doesn't count in elections, I don't go to Novais' soirées, I'm not a member of the club. What a world! But if I had money . . .'

He was filled then by a furious desire to avenge himself on priests, on the rich, and on the religion that justifies them. With determined step, he returned to Dr Godinho's office and half-opening the door, said:

'Would you at least allow me to give vent to my feelings in the newspaper. I would like to write about this whole scandalous business and give those wretches the reply they deserve . . .'

Such boldness on the part of the clerk enraged Dr Godinho. He drew himself up in his chair and, ominously folding his arms, said:

'Now you're going too far, Senhor João Eduardo! Are you asking me to transform a newspaper of ideas into a mere scandal sheet? No, don't hold back. Why don't you ask me to insult the principles of religion, to belittle the Redeemer, to repeat Renan's drivel, to attack the fundamental laws of the State, to defame the king, to scorn the institution of the family! Are you drunk, sir?'

'Please, Dr Godinho!'

'You must be drunk. Be careful, my friend, be very careful, you are on a very slippery slope. That way lies a complete loss of respect for authority, the law, for all things holy and for the home. That way lies a life of crime. And don't you look at me like that. A life of crime, I say. I have twenty years' experience in the courts. Get a grip on yourself, man! Restrain your passions. Good heavens! How old are you now?'

'I'm twenty-six.'

'Well, a man of twenty-six has no excuse having such subversive ideas. Goodbye, and please close the door behind you. And listen, don't even think of sending another article to another newspaper. I won't allow it, I who have always protected you. You just want to cause a scandal. Don't deny it, I can see it in your eyes. Well, I won't allow it! It's for your own good, to save you from committing an evil act against society!'

He struck a grand pose in his chair, and repeated vigorously:

'An evil act against society! Where do you gentlemen want to lead us with your materialism and your atheism? When you have destroyed the religion of our fathers, what do you have to put in its place? What? Show me!'

The embarrassed expression on João Eduardo's face (who did not have to hand a religion with which to replace the religion of our fathers) provoked a cry of triumph from Dr Godinho.

'You have nothing! You have mud to sling, you have, at most, empty words! But as long as I am alive, Faith and the Principle of Order will continue to be respected, at least in Leiria! You may fill the rest of Europe with fire and blood, but in Leiria you will not dare to raise your heads. I will be on guard in Leiria, and I swear to you that I will prove merciless!'

João Eduardo received these threats with bowed shoulders, without even understanding them. How could his article and the intrigues in Rua da Misericórdia produce social catastrophes and religious revolutions? Such severity defeated him. He was sure now to lose Dr Godinho's friendship as well as his job in the district government office . . . He tried to placate him:

'But surely, sir, you can see . . .'

Dr Godinho interrupted him with a grand gesture:

'Oh, I see perfectly. I see that passion and vengeance are carrying you off along a fateful path . . . I only hope that my advice will hold you back. Now goodbye. And close the door. Close the door, man!'

João Eduardo left, feeling humiliated. What should he do now? That colossus, Dr Godinho, had driven him away with terrifying words. And what could he, a poor clerk, do against Father Amaro who had on his side the clergy, the precentor, the chapter of canons, the bishops, the Pope, the compact, close-knit class that rose before him like an awesome citadel of bronze reaching up to the sky? They were the ones who had made Amélia change her mind and write that letter, they were behind her harsh words. It was a plot by parish priests, canons and religious fanatics. If he could only drag her away from that influence, then she would soon revert to being the Amélia who used to embroider slippers for him and wait blushing at the window to see him pass by. The suspicions he had once nursed had vanished in the happy evenings spent together after they had decided to marry, when she would sit sewing by the lamp, talking about the furniture they would buy and the decorating work to be done in the house. She loved him then, he was sure. But what did that matter? They had told her that he was the author of the article, that he was a heretic and a libertine; and Amaro, in his pedantic tones, had threatened her with Hell; the enraged Canon, all-powerful in Rua da Misericórdia because he contributed to the household expenses, had spoken to her sternly, and the poor girl, frightened, overwhelmed, with that terrifying pack of priests and religious fanatics whispering in her ear, had, poor thing, given in. She perhaps truly believed that he was a bad person. And at that hour, while he was out wandering the streets, rejected and unhappy, Father Amaro would be lounging, legs crossed, in the armchair in the sitting room in Rua da Misericórdia, jabbering away, master of the house and of Amélia! The scoundrel! And there were no laws to avenge him. And he could not even cause a scandal now that *The District Voice* was also closed to him.

He was then filled by a passionate desire to knock Father Amaro down with all the brute force of a Father Brito. But what would bring him far greater satisfaction would be a series of thunderous articles in a newspaper revealing the intrigues in Rua da Misericórdia, articles that would mobilise public opinion, fall like catastrophes upon Father Amaro, and force him, Canon Dias and all the others to be driven from São Joaneira's house! Yes, Amélia, once free of those intriguers, would then surely run into his arms, weeping tears of reconciliation.

Thus he struggled to convince himself that 'it was not her fault'; he remembered the months of happiness before the arrival of Father Amaro; he came up with natural explanations for the way she used to flirt with Amaro, and which had aroused in him desperate pangs of jealousy: it was just a desire, poor thing, to be pleasant to a guest, to a friend of Canon Dias, to keep him there to the advantage of her mother and the household! Besides, she had seemed so happy once a decision about their marriage had been taken. Her indignation at the article was clearly not entirely hers – it had been provoked in her by the parish priest and by those over-pious women. And he found consolation in the thought that he had not been rebuffed as a lover or a husband, but was merely a victim of the intrigues of the vile Father Amaro, who wanted his fiancée and hated him because he was a liberal. All this filled his soul with a wild rancour against Father Amaro; as he walked along the street, he racked his brain for some means of vengeance, letting his imagination roam freely, but he always came back to the same idea, another article of denunciation in a newspaper! He rebelled against his own evident weakness and vulnerability. If only he had some important figure on his side.

A farm labourer, his face as yellow as cider, was walking slowly along with one arm held to his chest, and he stopped João Eduardo to ask where Dr Gouveia lived.

'First street on the left, the green door by the street lamp,' said João Eduardo.

And a sudden immense hope illuminated his soul: Dr Gouveia was the man who could save him! The doctor was his friend; he had treated him as such ever since he had cured him of pneumonia three years before; he had heartily approved of

João Eduardo's marriage to Amélia; only a few weeks ago, he had stopped him in the square to ask him: 'So, when are you going to make that young woman happy, eh?' And he was feared and respected in Rua da Misericórdia! They and their friends were all his patients and, while scandalised by his lack of religion, they were humbly dependent on his knowledge to treat their various aches and pains and nervous attacks and to dole out medicine. And Dr Gouveia, who was the declared enemy of the priesthood, was sure to be angered by their plot against him; and João Eduardo could already imagine himself following Dr Gouveia into São Joaneira's house and hearing the doctor rebuke São Joaneira, humiliate Father Amaro and convince the old ladies of their mistake; and then his happiness, unshakeable now, would be restored.

'Is the doctor in?' he asked almost gaily of the maid who was hanging out clothes in the courtyard.

'He's in his surgery, Senhor Joãozinho. Go straight in.'

On market days, there were always a lot of patients up from the country. But at that hour – when the folk from the neighbouring parishes gathered together in the taverns – the only people waiting in the low-ceilinged room furnished with benches, pots of marjoram and a large engraving of Queen Victoria's coronation were an old man, a woman with a baby and the man with his arm held to his chest. Despite the bright sunlight streaming in from the courtyard and the fresh green leaves of the lime tree brushing against the window, the room seemed terribly sad, as if the walls, the benches and even the marjoram plants were saturated with the melancholy of all the illnesses that had passed through there. João Eduardo went in and sat down in one corner.

It was gone midday, and the woman kept complaining about how long she had been waiting: she was from a remote parish, had left her sister at the market, and the doctor had been closeted with two other women for a whole hour now. Every few minutes the child would start crying and the woman would bounce her up and down in her arms, until, at last, they both fell silent; the old man rolled up one trouser leg and gazed with satisfaction at the wound on his shin which was bandaged with rags; the other man kept yawning disconsolately and this only made his long, sallow face seem even more lugubrious. The waiting left the clerk feeling enervated and weak; he gradually began to wonder whether it was right to bother Dr Gouveia; he had prepared his story carefully, but it now seemed to him unlikely to be of sufficient interest to the doctor. His despondency grew and was made worse by the bored faces of the other patients. Perhaps life really was a sad affair, filled only with misery, treachery, affliction and illness. He got to his feet and, hands behind his back, stood gloomily studying Queen Victoria's coronation.

Occasionally the woman with the baby would half-open the green baize door that led into the doctor's room to see if the two ladies were still in there. They were, and their slow voices could be heard droning on.

'You could waste the whole day in here!' grumbled the old man.

He too had tethered his horse outside the tavern and left his daughter in the market square . . . And then there would be the long wait at the pharmacy afterwards! And it was three leagues back to his parish! Being ill is fine if you're rich and have plenty of time on your hands.

The idea of illness and of the loneliness it brings made losing Amélia seem even more unbearable to João Eduardo. If ever he fell ill, he would have to go to the hospital. That wretched priest had taken everything from him – fiancée, happiness, family comforts, sweet companions.

At last, the two ladies were heard leaving. The woman with the child picked up her basket and hurried in. The old man moved to the bench nearest the door and said with satisfaction:

'My turn next!'

'Will you be long with the doctor?' João Eduardo asked.

'No, I've just got to pick up a prescription.'

He immediately launched into the story of his wound: a wooden beam had fallen on him; he had thought no more about it, but then the wound had turned septic, and now there he was with only one good leg and in terrible pain.

'What about you, have you got anything seriously wrong with you?' he asked.

'No, I'm not ill,' said João Eduardo, 'I have some business with the doctor.'

The other two men eyed him enviously.

At last it was the turn of the old man and then of the sallow-faced fellow holding his arm to his chest. Left alone, João Eduardo paced nervously up and down the room. It now seemed to him extremely difficult simply to walk in unannounced and ask the doctor for his protection. What right did he have? He considered complaining first of pains in the chest or of some stomach upset, and then, by the by, telling him of his misfortunes . . .

But just then the door opened, and there before him stood the doctor, drawing on a pair of woollen gloves, his long, grey beard spilling over his black velvet jacket, his broad-brimmed hat on his head.

'Ah, it's you, young man! Has something happened at São Joaneira's house?'

João Eduardo blushed.

'No, Doctor, I wanted to talk to you in private.'

He followed him into his office. Dr Gouveia's famously dusty office, with its chaos of books, its panoply of Indian arrows and its two stuffed storks had the reputation in Leiria of being 'an alchemist's cell'.

The doctor took out his watch.

'A quarter to two. You'll have to be brief.'

The look on the clerk's face made it clear that he would have great difficulty in condensing an extremely complex narrative.

'All right,' said the doctor, 'just take your time. There's nothing harder than being clear and brief; you need genius to achieve that. Now, what's the matter?'

João Eduardo then gave a garbled account of events, emphasising the priest's treachery and Amélia's innocence.

The doctor listened, stroking his beard.

'So you and the priest,' he said, 'both want the girl. Since he is more intelligent and more determined than you, he has got her. It's the law of nature; the strongest one pounces and eliminates the weaker one; he gets both the woman and the prey.'

João Eduardo thought this was a joke. He said in a tremulous voice:

'You're making fun of me, Doctor, when my heart has been cut to pieces.'

'No, I'm not,' said the doctor kindly. 'I'm merely philosophising, not making fun . . . But what do you want me to do about it?'

It was exactly what Dr Godinho had said to him, only more pompously.

'I'm sure that if you spoke to her . . .'

The doctor smiled.

'I can prescribe this or that medicine to the girl, but not this or that man. Do you expect me to go and say: "Miss Amélia, you must choose João Eduardo"? Do you expect me to go and say to the priest, a scoundrel I have never even met: "Please desist from seducing this young woman"?'

'But they slandered me, Doctor, they described me as a man of bad habits, a rogue . . .'

'No, they didn't slander you. In the eyes of the priest and of those ladies who spend the evenings playing lotto in Rua da Misericórdia, *you* are the rogue; a Christian who writes articles attacking parish priests and canons, people who are vital to them in their attempts to communicate with God and to save their souls, *is* a rogue. They didn't slander you, my friend.'

But, Doctor . . .'

'Listen. In obeying the instructions given her by Father whoever-he-is and getting rid of you, the girl is merely behaving like a good Catholic. That's my view. The entire life of a good Catholic, her thoughts, her ideas, her feelings, her words, how she spends her days and nights, her relationships with her family and her neighbours, what she has for supper, her clothes and her amusements, are all regulated by ecclesiastical authority (parish priest, bishop or canon), approved or censured by her confessor, under the advice and guidance of her spiritual director. A good Catholic, like your Amélia, has no life of her own: she has no reason, no desire, no will, no feelings of her own; her priest thinks, wants, decides and feels for her. In this world, her sole task, which is at once her sole right and her sole duty, is to accept that guidance, to accept it without argument and to obey him regardless of the consequences; if she disagrees with his ideas, it means that her ideas are false; if she wounds his feelings, then her feelings are to blame. Given these facts, if the priest says to the young woman that she should not marry or even talk to you, she proves, by obeying him, that she is a good Catholic, a true devotee, logically following the moral rule she has chosen. And that is that; and forgive the sermon.'

João Eduardo listened with mingled respect and horror to these words, lent even greater authority by the doctor's placid face and fine grey beard. It seemed to him almost impossible now to win back Amélia, if it was true that she did belong so absolutely, with all her soul and all her senses, to the priest who confessed her. But why then was he considered to be a bad husband?

'I could understand it,' he said, 'if I was a man of bad habits, Doctor. But I'm well-behaved; I work hard; I don't frequent taverns or lead a dissolute life; I don't drink, I don't gamble; I spend my evenings at Rua da Misericórdia or at home doing work for the office . . .'

'My dear boy, you might well possess all the social virtues, but, according to the religion of our country, any values that are not Catholic values are by definition useless and pernicious. Being hard-working, chaste, honest, fair, truthful are great virtues, but to the priests and to the Church they don't count. You could be the very model of kindness, but if you didn't go to mass, didn't fast or go to confession, didn't doff your hat to the priest, you would be considered a rogue. Other people far greater than you, whose souls were perfect and who lived impeccable lives, have been judged to be out-and-out scoundrels because they were not baptised. You've probably heard of Plato, Socrates, Cato, etc. They were all men famous for their virtue. Well, a certain Bossuet, who is a great authority on doctrine, said that Hell is full of such men's virtues. This proves that Catholic morality is different from natural morality or social morality. But these are difficult things for you to understand. Shall I give you an example? According to Catholic doctrine, I am one of the most shameless men to walk the streets of Leiria; my neighbour Peixoto, who beat his wife to death and is in the process of doing the same to his ten-year-old daughter, is held by the clergy to be an excellent man because he fulfills his duties as a Catholic and plays the bass tuba at sung masses. That, my friend, is the way things are. And it must be good, because thousands of respectable people think it is, and the State thinks so and spends a fortune on keeping things the way they are, and forces us to respect the way things are, and I myself pay 1,200 *réis* a year so that things remain the same. You, of course, pay less.'

'I pay seven *vinténs*, Doctor.'

'But you at least go to the festivals, hear the music and the sermons, you get something in return for your seven *vinténs*. My 1,200 *réis* is totally lost; my only consolation is that the money is going towards maintaining the splendour of the Church, the same Church that considers me an outlaw while I'm alive and has a first-class Hell ready for me when I die. Anyway, I think we've talked enough. What else can I say?'

João Eduardo was utterly downcast. Listening to the doctor, it seemed to him, more than ever, that if a man of such wise words and such a superfluity of ideas were to take an interest in him, then the intrigue would easily be undone and his happiness and his place in Rua da Misericórdia recovered for ever.

'You can't help me, then?' he said gloomily.

'I could cure you of another bout of pneumonia. Have you got any pneumonia for me to cure? No? Well, then . . .'

João Eduardo sighed:

'But I'm a victim, doctor!'

'No, you're wrong. There should be no victims, except when it comes to preventing tyrants from seizing power,' said the doctor, putting on his broad-brimmed hat again.

'But in the end,' João Eduardo exclaimed, clinging to the

doctor with the desperation of a drowning man, 'in the end, what that scoundrel of a priest wants, regardless of what pretexts he invents, is the girl. If she was an ugly old woman, he wouldn't care how impious I was. What he wants is the girl!'

The doctor shrugged.

'It's only natural, poor thing,' he said, grasping the door handle. 'What do you expect? As regards women, he has the same passions and organs as any other man; as a confessor, he has the importance of a God. He will obviously use that importance to satisfy those passions, and the fact that he has to disguise the fact with the appearances and pretexts of the divine office is, well, natural . . .'

When João Eduardo saw him opening the door and saw the hope that had brought him there about to vanish, he said angrily, thrashing the air with his hat:

'Damn all priests! I've always hated the whole lot of them! I'd like to see them wiped from the face of the Earth, Doctor!'

'That's just more foolishness,' said the doctor, resigned to listening further and so pausing in the doorway. 'Listen. Do you believe in God? In God in his Heaven, in the God who is up there in Heaven and who rules from on high over justice and truth?'

Surprised, João Eduardo said:

'Yes, I do.'

'And in original sin?'

'Yes.'

'And in a life hereafter and in redemption, etc.?'

'I was brought up in those beliefs . . .'

'So why do you want to wipe priests from the face of the Earth? You should, on the contrary, feel that there are too few of them. As far as I can see, you are a rationalist liberal at the outer limits of the Constitution . . . But if you believe in God in Heaven, who guides us from above, and in original sin and in the hereafter, you need a class of priests who will explain doctrine and God-revealed morality to you, who will help you to cleanse yourself of that original stain and prepare you for your place in Paradise! You need priests. And it strikes me as a terrible lack of logic on your part to discredit them in the newspapers . . .'

Astonished, João Eduardo could only stammer:

'But, Doctor . . . Forgive me, Doctor, but you . . .'

'Speak up, man! I what?'

'You have no need for priests in the world.'

'Nor in the next. I have no need for priests in the world because I have no need for a God in his Heaven, which means, my boy, that I have my own God inside me, a principle that guides my actions and my judgements: common conscience. Perhaps you don't quite understand. I'm expounding subversive doctrines here . . . And now I really must go, it's three o'clock . . .'

And he showed him his watch.

At the door into the courtyard, João Eduardo said again:

'Forgive me, Doctor . . .'

'That's quite all right. And forget all about Rua da Misericórdia.'

João Eduardo said passionately:

'That's easy enough to say, Doctor, but when passion is gnawing away at you inside . . .'

'Ah,' said the doctor, 'passion is a great and fine thing! Love is one of the great forces of civilisation. Used well it can build a world and would be enough for us to carry out a moral revolution.' Then changing his tone: 'But listen. Love is not always passion and it does not always have its seat in the heart. The heart is the term we ordinarily use, out of decency, to designate another organ. And in matters of sentiment that is usually the only organ involved. And in those cases, the unhappiness does not last. Goodbye, and I very much hope that you fall into the latter category.'

XIV

João Eduardo walked down the road, rolling a cigarette. He had been left weak and drained by his night of despair, by that morning spent in futile wanderings, and by his conversations with Dr Godinho and Dr Gouveia.

'It's over,' he was thinking. 'I can do nothing more. I'll just have to accept it.'

His soul was exhausted by all that passion, hope and anger. He would like to go and lie down in some isolated place, far from lawyers, women and priests, and to sleep for months. But since it was already after three, he hurried to the office. He would probably be given a lecture for arriving so late. Ah, but his was a sad life!

He had turned the corner into the main square, when just outside Osório's eating house, he bumped into a young man wearing a light-coloured jacket edged with black ribbon; the young man's moustache was so dark that, against his extremely pale skin, it looked false.

'Hello, João Eduardo! How are things?'

It was Gustavo, the typesetter from *The District Voice*, who had gone to Lisbon two months before. According to Agostinho, he was an intelligent lad and very learned, 'but with some alarming ideas'. He would sometimes write articles on foreign affairs, full of resonant, poetic phrases, cursing Napoleon III, the Czar and all oppressors of the people, bemoaning the enslavement of Poland and the misery of the proletariat. The friendship between himself and João Eduardo had grown out of conversations they had had on religion, in which both gave vent to their hatred of the clergy and their admiration for Jesus Christ. Events in Spain had so inspired him that he had even had hopes of joining the International; and his desire to live amongst the workers, where there would be associations, speeches and fraternity, had taken him to Lisbon. He had found a good job there and good comrades.

But since he had to care for his infirm old mother and it was cheaper if they lived together, he had returned to Leiria. Besides, with the elections looming, *The District Voice* was doing so well that the three typesetters were to be given a wage increase.

'So here I am back with Agostinho.'

He had been just about to have lunch and he immediately invited João Eduardo to join him. For heaven's sake, the world wouldn't end if he missed one day at the office.

João Eduardo remembered then that he had not in fact eaten anything since the previous evening. Perhaps it was lack of food that had left him in this stupefied, easily discouraged state. He accepted at once, glad, after all the emotions and exhaustions of the morning, to sit down on a tavern bench with a full plate in front of him and with a friend who shared his antipathies. Besides, the buffetings he had suffered had created in him a real craving for sympathy, and so he said warmly:

'It's good to see you, man. I couldn't have met you at a better moment. The world's such a terrible place that if it wasn't for the times spent with your friends, life wouldn't be worth living.'

Gustavo was taken aback by these unprecedented words from the normally reticent João Eduardo.

'Why, what's wrong? Aren't things going well? Not getting on with that beast Nunes, eh?' he asked.

'No, just suffering from a bit of spleen.'

'Spleen's an English phenomenon! Oh, but you should have seen Taborda in *A London Love*! Anyway, forget about spleen! What you need is a bit of ballast inside you and plenty of wine to wash it down with!'

He took João Eduardo's arm and guided him into the tavern.

'Hello there, Osório! Fraternal greetings!'

Osório, the owner of the tavern, was leaning on the bar; he was a plump, contented personage, with a fat, mischievous face and with his shirtsleeves rolled up almost to his shoulders to reveal very white, bare arms; he immediately expressed his pleasure at seeing Gustavo back in Leiria. He thought he looked thinner. It must be the bad water in Lisbon and the additives in the wines . . . Now what could he do for the two gentlemen?

Gustavo planted himself before the bar, his hat pushed back on his head, and prepared to make the joke that had so amused him in Lisbon:

'Osório, bring us a king's liver and some priest's kidneys, grilled!'

Quick as a flash, as he wiped down the zinc counter with a rag, Osório said:

'I'm afraid we don't have that here, Senhor Gustavo, that's a Lisbon delicacy.'

'Well, I must say you're very backward! I had that for breakfast every day in Lisbon. Never mind, just bring us some liver – well done – and some potatoes!'

'You will be served like friends of the house.'

They sat down at the 'table for the timid', between two pine partitions closed off by a cotton curtain. Osório, who thought Gustavo 'a clever, serious-minded lad', brought them a bottle of red wine and a dish of olives and, as he polished the glasses on his filthy apron, he said:

'So what news from the capital, Senhor Gustavo? How are things there?'

Gustavo immediately grew grave, smoothed his hair with his hand and uttered a few enigmatic phrases:

'Very unstable . . . A lot of charlatans in politics . . . The working classes are beginning to organise . . . A lack of unity at the moment . . . They're just waiting to see how things turn out in Spain . . . It could all turn very nasty . . . Everything depends on Spain . . .'

But Osório, who had saved a bit of money and bought a small farm, had a horror of upheavals. What the country needed was peace. He was particularly against anything that depended on the Spanish. Surely they knew the saying: from Spain expect neither a good wind nor a good wedding.

'We are all brothers!' exclaimed Gustavo. 'When it comes to bringing down Bourbons and emperors, political cliques and the nobility, there are no Spanish or Portuguese, we are all brothers! Fraternity, Osório!'

'Well, you'd better drink its health, then, and drink heartily, because that's what makes the world go round,' said Osório placidly, heaving his great bulk out of the cubicle.

'Elephant!' snorted Gustavo, shocked at Osório's indifference to the Brotherhood of the People. But what could you expect from a landowner and an election agent?

He hummed a bit of the Marseillaise, filled their glasses with wine, pouring it from on high, and asked what João Eduardo had been up to. Didn't he go to *The District Voice* any more? According to Agostinho, there was no dragging him away now from Rua da Misericórdia.

'So when's this wedding, then?'

João Eduardo blushed and said vaguely:

'We haven't quite decided yet . . . There have been a few problems . . .' And he added with a wry smile: 'We've had a couple of spats.'

'Over nothing, I suppose,' said Gustavo, with a shrug expressive of his revolutionary scorn for such sentimental frivolities.

'Well, I don't know about that,' said João Eduardo. 'I just know that it's most upsetting. They bring a man very low, Gustavo.'

He fell silent, biting his lip, to emphasise the emotions shaking him.

But Gustavo found anything to do with women ridiculous. It wasn't the time for love . . . The man of the people, the working man who clung on to some woman's skirts, was of no use to anyone. He was a traitor! This was no time to be thinking about love affairs, but about restoring freedom to the people, taking work out of the claws of the wealthy, putting an end to monopolies and working towards a republic! It wasn't self-pity that was needed, but action, strength!' And he emphasised the final word, brandishing his scrawny, tubercular wrists over the large plate of fried liver that the waiter had just brought.

Listening to him, João Eduardo remembered the days when

Gustavo had been madly in love with Júlia from the bakery and would turn up at work with eyes as red as coals and fill the place with terrible, thunderous sighs. Every sigh would be greeted by his colleagues with a mocking clearing of the throat. One day, Gustavo and Medeiros even came to blows in the courtyard.

'Look who's talking,' João Eduardo said at last. 'You're just like everyone else. You're full of talk, but when it's your turn, you're just the same as all of us.'

Gustavo was shocked – ever since he had started frequenting the Alcântara Democratic Club in Lisbon and helped to draw up a manifesto for their brothers on strike at the cigarette factory, he considered himself to be devoted exclusively to the service of the Proletariat and the Republic. Him? Like all the others? Waste his time on women?

'I'm afraid you're very much mistaken,' he said and retreated into a shocked silence, furiously cutting up the fried liver on his plate.

João Eduardo feared that he might have offended him.

'Come on, Gustavo, be reasonable. A man can have his principles and work for a cause, but also get married, enjoy a bit of comfort and have a family.'

'Never!' exclaimed Gustavo passionately. 'A man who marries is lost. From then on all he cares about is earning his daily bread, staying in his burrow, getting up in the night to tend to his screaming, teething babies, without a moment to spare for his friends . . . Useless! A traitor! Women understand nothing about politics. They're afraid of their man getting caught up in riots or having problems with the police. He's a patriot bound hand and foot. And when he has some secret to keep . . . well, a married man can't keep a secret. Sometimes a whole revolution has been compromised because of that. To hell with the family! Osório, more olives!'

Osório's belly appeared between the partition walls.

'What are you two gentlemen arguing about? You sound like the Maia Group disrupting a municipal council meeting.'

Gustavo leaned back on his bench, his legs outstretched, and asked him loftily:

'Osório, you can decide this. Tell my friend here. Would you be prepared to change your political opinions to please your wife?'

Osório rubbed the back of his neck and said in a playful tone:

'I'll tell you this much, Gustavo. Women are far more intelligent than we are. When it comes to politics and business, if you do what they say, you won't go far wrong. I always consult my wife, and, if you must know, I've been doing so for twenty years and it's worked so far.'

Gustavo leaped up from the bench:

'Traitor!' he yelled.

Osório, who was used to that favourite expression of Gustavo's, was not in the least put out; with his love of sharp ripostes, he even joked:

'I don't know about traitor, but trader certainly. Just you wait until you get married, Senhor Gustavo, and then we'll talk again.'

'Come the revolution, we'll march in here with rifles on our shoulders and haul you up before a court martial, you capitalist!'

'But meanwhile the best thing to do is to drink up,' said Osório making a slow retreat.

'Hippopotamus!' grumbled Gustavo.

And since he loved arguments, he started up again, maintaining that any man infatuated with a woman could not be relied on to stand firm on his political beliefs . . .

João Eduardo was smiling sadly, in mute disagreement, thinking to himself that, despite his passion for Amélia, he had not been to confession for the last two years.

'I've got proof,' bawled Gustavo.

He cited a freethinker of his acquaintance who, in order to keep the peace at home, fasted on Fridays and raked the path to the chapel every Sunday . . .

'And that's what will happen to you! You have pretty sound ideas about religion, but one day I'll see you in a red habit and carrying a candle in the Easter procession. Philosophy and atheism are cheap when you're talking over billiards with the boys, but putting it into practice in the family, when you've got a pretty wife who's religious too, that's very difficult indeed. And that's what will happen to you, if it isn't happening already. You'll throw your liberal convictions in the ash can and doff your hat to the confessor.'

João Eduardo turned scarlet with indignation. Even in the days of his happiness, when he was sure that Amélia was his, that accusation (which Gustavo only made in order to provoke an argument) would have scandalised him. But now when he had lost Amélia for having declared out loud, in a newspaper, his horror of priests! Now, with his heart broken, bereft of joy, precisely because of his liberal opinions!

'It's ironic that you should say that to me of all people,' he said sombrely and bitterly.

Gustavo guffawed:

'Why, I didn't know you'd become a martyr to freedom!'

'Don't make fun of me, Gustavo, please,' João Eduardo said, very shocked. 'You don't know what's been happening. If you did, you wouldn't say that . . .'

He then told him the story of the article in *The District Voice*, not mentioning that he had written it while aflame with jealousy, but presenting it instead as a pure affirmation of principles. And he pointed out to him that, at the time, he had been about to marry a very devout young woman from a household that saw more priests than the Cathedral sacristy.

'And did you sign it?' asked Gustavo, aghast at the revelation.

'Dr Godinho didn't want me to,' João Eduardo said, blushing slightly.

'And you tore them off a strip, did you?'

'Oh, yes, I really went for them.'

In his enthusiasm, Gustavo yelled for 'another bottle of red!'

He joyfully filled their glasses and drank a toast to João Eduardo.

'I'd love to read it! Can I send it to the boys in Lisbon? What effect did it have?'

'It caused an almighty scandal.'

'And the priests?'

'They were furious!'

'But how did they find out it was you?'

João Eduardo shrugged. Agostinho hadn't told anyone. He suspected Godinho's wife, who had found out from her husband and then passed it on to Father Silvério, her confessor, the one who lives in Rua das Teresas . . .

'A big fat chap, looks as if he had dropsy?'

'That's the one.'

'The brute!' roared Gustavo furiously.

He now regarded João Eduardo with new respect, the João Eduardo who had been so unexpectedly revealed to him as a champion of free thought.

'Drink, my friend, drink!' he said, affectionately filling his glass, as if João Eduardo's heroic effort on behalf of liberalism still required a great deal of encouragement, even several days after the event.

And what had happened? What had the inhabitants of Rua da Misericórdia had to say about it?

Touched by such intense interest, João Eduardo blurted out his secret. He even showed him Amélia's letter which, poor thing, she had doubtless been driven to write in mortal terror of Hell, under pressure from the furious priests . . .

'And here I am, Gustavo, a victim of events!'

He was indeed, and Gustavo regarded him with growing admiration. He was no longer shy little João Eduardo, Nunes' clerk, the importunate suitor of Rua da Misericórdia, he was the victim of religious persecution. He was the first such victim Gustavo had seen, and he found João Eduardo suddenly interesting, even though he did not appear in the traditional poses of propaganda posters, tied to a post in the middle of a bonfire or fleeing with his terrified family, pursued by soldiers galloping out from the surrounding shadows. He secretly envied him that social honour. The boys in Alcântara would certainly be impressed. It was pretty clever too to be a victim of reactionary forces without being obliged to give up the pleasure of eating Osório's fried liver and having your wages paid promptly each Saturday. But it was the priests' behaviour that angered him most. In order to revenge themselves on a liberal, they had intrigued against him and taken his fiancée from him. What scoundrels! And forgetting his recent sarcastic remarks about Marriage and the Family, he fulminated against the clergy who always strive to ruin that perfect social institution of divine origins.

'This calls for a truly fiercesome revenge! They must be crushed!'

Vengeance was precisely what João Eduardo thirsted after. But what form should it take?

'Why, you should reveal everything in another forthright article in *The District Voice*!'

João Eduardo told him what Dr Godinho had said: from thenceforth *The District Voice* was closed to all freethinkers.

'The ass!' roared Gustavo.

But he had an idea, damn it! They would publish a pamphlet, a pamphlet of twenty pages, what in Brazil was called a 'smear sheet', written in an ornate style (he would take care of that) and which would fall upon the clergy like an avalanche of mortal truths.

João Eduardo warmed to the idea. Encouraged by Gustavo's active sympathy for his plight, seeing in him a brother, he shared with him his last, most painful secrets. What lay at the bottom of the intrigue was Father Amaro's passion for Amélia, and it was in order to get her that he had driven João Eduardo out . . . The enemy, the villain, the bully – was the priest.

Gustavo clutched his head; such a case (which, in the places where he worked, was pretty small beer) happening to a friend of his and to a fellow democrat who was sitting there before him drinking, seemed to him monstrous, on a par with the senile madness of Tiberius, who, in perfumed baths, violated the delicate flesh of patrician young men.

He could not believe it. João Eduardo provided him with more proof. And then Gustavo, whose lunch of fried liver had been drowned in vast amounts of red wine, raised two clenched fists and, with scarlet face and through gritted teeth, he roared out:

'Down with religion!'

From the other side of the partition wall a mocking voice croaked a response:

'Long live Pius IX!'

Gustavo got to his feet in order to punch the interloper, but João Eduardo restrained him. Gustavo meekly resumed his seat and drank down the last drop of wine in his glass.

Then, elbows on the table, face to face, the bottle between them, they discussed in low voices their plan for the pamphlet. Nothing could be easier; they would write it together. João Eduardo wanted to write it in the form of a novel with a dark plot, giving the parish priest all the vices and perversions of Caligula and Heliogabalus. Gustavo, however, preferred to take a philosophical angle as regards style and principles, which would demolish absolute Papal authority once and for all! He would take responsibility for printing it, in the evenings, and for free, of course. Then they foresaw a sudden problem.

'Paper, how will we get the paper?'

It meant an expenditure of nine or ten *mil réis*, which neither of them had, nor did they have a friend who shared their principles and would advance them the amount.

'Ask Nunes for an advance on your salary!' Gustavo suggested brightly.

João Eduardo scratched his head disconsolately. He was imagining Nunes' devout fury – as a member of the parish council and a friend of the precentor – when he read the pamphlet. And if he ever found out that his clerk had written it, using the office quills and the best office paper . . . He could see him now, apoplectic with rage, raising his vast body up onto the tips of his white shoes, and declaring shrilly: 'Get out of here, you freemason, get out!'

'Then I really would be in a mess,' said João Eduardo, 'no fiancée and no bread.'

This reminded Gustavo too of the certain anger of Dr Godinho, the owner of the printing press. For Dr Godinho, after his reconciliation with the personnel of Rua da Misericórdia, had publicly resumed his considerable position as pillar of the Church and protector of the Faith . . .

'Damn it, it could cost us very dear,' he said.

'It's impossible!' said João Eduardo.

Then they both cursed roundly. Fancy losing an opportunity like that to expose the clergy for what they were!

Just as a fallen column seems larger than when erect, so their plan for a pamphlet, now that it was not to be, seemed to them of colossal size and importance. It was no longer a matter of demolishing one bad parish priest, it would have been the ruin, far and wide, of the clergy, of the Jesuits, of temporal power and of other terrible things. Damnation! If it wasn't for Nunes, if it wasn't for Godinho, if it wasn't for the nine *mil réis'* worth of paper . . .

Those perpetual obstacles to the poor, lack of money and dependence on an employer, which even prevented them from publishing a pamphlet, made them turn on society.

'There has to be a revolution!' declared Gustavo. 'Everything must be torn down, everything!' And his grand sweeping gesture over the table indicated, in one formidable act of social levelling, the destruction of churches, palaces, banks, barracks and buildings owned by the likes of Godinho. 'Another bottle of red, Osório!'

But Osório did not appear. Gustavo hammered as hard as he could with his knife handle on the table. Furious, he was finally forced to go out to the bar 'to puncture the belly of that traitor who dared keep a citizen waiting like that'.

He found Osório with his hat off, smiling radiantly and chatting to the Barão de Via-Clara, who, as the elections drew near, had descended on the local taverns to shake hands with his friends. And the Baron looked magnificent in his gold-rimmed spectacles and his patent leather shoes, as he stood there on the tavern's dirt floor, choking slightly at the acrid smell of boiled oil and sedimented wine.

When he saw him, Gustavo withdrew discreetly into the cubicle.

Finding João Eduardo in despair, his head in his hands, Gustavo called on him not to weaken. What did it matter? He had, after all, escaped marriage to a religious zealot . . .

'But I want revenge on that villain!' burst out João Eduardo, pushing his plate away from him.

'Don't you worry,' promised Gustavo solemnly, 'revenge cannot be far off!'

In a low voice he told him of 'things being planned in Lisbon'. He had been told of the existence of a republican club whose membership included some very important people – that was in itself, he felt, a guarantee of triumph. The workers were also taking action . . . He himself – and he was so close to João Eduardo, who was now sprawled on the table, that his breath almost touched his face – had been chosen to join a section of the International that a Spaniard in Madrid was organizing; he had never actually seen the Spaniard, who went about in disguise because of the police, and the thing had failed because of a lack of funds . . . But there was a man who owned a butcher's shop who had promised them a hundred *mil réis* . . . The army was in on it too: a chap with a big belly had been seen at a meeting and he'd been told on good authority that the man was a Major, and he certainly looked the part . . . All in all, taking all these elements into account, Gustavo was of the opinion that, within a matter of months, the government, the king, the aristocracy, the capitalists, the bishops and all those other monsters would be blown sky high!

'And then we will be like little kings, my lad! Godinho, Nunes, the whole pack of them will be clapped in jail. I'll throw Godinho in there myself. We'll beat the priests into submission. And the people will at last be able to breathe freely!'

'Yes, but until that happens . . .' sighed João Eduardo, who was thinking bitterly that by the time the revolution arrived it would be too late to get Amélia back . . .

Osório came into the cubicle with a bottle of wine.

'And about time too, my noble sir!' said Gustavo sarcastically.

'I may not belong to the same class, but at least they treat me with respect,' Osório retorted, and his satisfaction seemed to make his belly swell.

'What, for half a dozen votes?'

'Eighteen in the parish and with hopes for nineteen. Can I get you gentlemen anything else? No? Well, never mind. Drink up!'

And he drew the curtain, leaving the two friends sitting before a full bottle of wine, dreaming of a revolution that would allow one of them to see Miss Amélia again and the other to give Dr Godinho a good drubbing.

It was nearly five o'clock when they finally left the cubicle. Osório, who took an interest in them because they were educated fellows, noticed at once, from the corner of the bar where he was poring over his newspaper, that they were both a bit tipsy, especially João Eduardo, with his hat pulled down and a scowl on his face: a man who couldn't hold his drink, thought Osório, who did not know him well. But Gustavo, after his three litres of wine, was his usual jubilant self. A great lad! He was the one who was paying the bill and so he swayed over to the bar and clapped his two coins down on the bar.

'Stick that in your coffers, Fatso!'

'What a pity there are only two of them, Senhor Gustavo.'

'Ah, you rascal! Do you imagine that the sweat of the people and their hard-earned cash is intended to fill the bellies of Philistines? Make sure you don't lose them. For come the great settling of accounts, the man who will have the honour of piercing that great stomach of yours is Bibi here . . . Yes, I am Bibi . . . *I* am Bibi! Tell them, João, tell them who Bibi is . . . .'

But João Eduardo wasn't listening; with an angry frown on his face, he was mistrustfully eyeing a drunk seated before an empty litre bottle of wine at a table at the rear; with his chin resting on the palm of one hand and his pipe between his teeth, he was staring at the two friends open-mouthed.

Gustavo dragged João over to the bar.

'Tell Osório here who Bibi is. Who is Bibi? Take a good look at this lad, Osório. The boy's got talent and he's one of the best. I'll tell you something. He could put a stop to absolute Papal authority with just two strokes of his quill. He's one of us! And we're friends for life, we are! Stop working out the bill, my fat friend, and listen to what I'm saying. He's one of the best. And if he should ever come back here and want two litres of wine on credit, be sure to give it to him . . . Bibi here will take care of everything.'

'Right,' began Osório, 'so it was two fried livers, two salads . . .'

But the drunk had managed to heave himself up from his bench, and, pipe in mouth, belching loudly, he came and stood unsteadily in front of Gustavo and held out his hand.

Gustavo looked down at him with some distaste.

'What do you want? I bet it was you who shouted out: "Long live Pius IX" a while ago. You traitor . . . Remove your hand!'

Finding himself rejected, the drunk merely grunted, and bumping into João Eduardo, offered him his outstretched hand instead.

'Go away, you brute!' said João Eduardo roughly.

'Just wanna be friends . . .' mumbled the drunk.

And he did not go away, but stood there still proffering his five fingers and filling the air with his foul breath.

Furious, João Eduardo pushed him hard against the bar.

'Now, I'll have no fist-fights in here!' exclaimed Osório sternly. 'I want no violence.'

'Well, he should leave me alone, then,' growled João Eduardo. 'I'll do the same to you if you don't watch it . . .'

'Anyone who doesn't behave himself will be thrown out,' said Osório very gravely.

'Who's going to be thrown out?' João Eduardo roared, drawing himself up and shaking his fist. 'Go on, tell me, who? Who do you think you're talking to?'

Osório did not reply; he was leaning on the bar, revealing the two enormous arms which ensured that his tavern remained a peaceful place.

Gustavo took charge and placed himself between them, declaring that they should both behave like gentlemen. This was no time for arguments and harsh words. It was all right to make fun and to joke with your friends, but always in a gentlemanly fashion. And, after all, they were all of them gentlemen.

He dragged a grumbling, resentful João Eduardo off into a corner.

'Come on, João!' he said, gesticulating wildly, 'that's no way for an educated man to behave!'

Manners must be maintained! Impulsive, drunken behaviour meant an end to jollity, society and fraternity.

He turned to Osório, speaking to him nervously over his shoulder:

'I'll answer for him, Osório. He's a gentleman, but he's had a few upsets lately and he's not used to drinking, that's all it is! But he's one of the best . . . really. Please accept my apologies on his behalf.'

He led João Eduardo back to the bar and persuaded him to shake Osório's hand. Osório declared warmly that he had not wanted to insult him. They shook hands vehemently. To consolidate their reconciliation, Gustavo ordered three white rums. João Eduardo, in generous mood, ordered a round of brandies too. And with the drinks lined up on the bar, they exchanged friendly words and addressed each other as 'gentleman'. Meanwhile, forgotten in his corner, sprawled on the table, head on his fists, nose pressed against the wine bottle, the drunk was quietly dribbling, his pipe still clenched between his teeth.

'That's what I like to see!' said Gustavo, whom the brandy had made maudlin. 'Harmony! I just love harmony. Harmony amongst friends and amongst all humanity. I'd like to see the whole human race sit down to a banquet, with no guns, but with plenty of jokes, and make decisions together on all the important social questions. And that day is not far off, Osório. They're preparing for it right now in Lisbon. And Osório will supply the wine! A nice little deal, eh? You have to admit I'm a good friend.'

'Thank you, Senhor Gustavo, thank you . . .'

'That's just between you and me, eh, gentlemen's agreement and all that. And as for him,' he embraced João Eduardo, 'he's like a brother to me! Friends for life, we are! Enough of being sad, boy. We've got that pamphlet to write. Godinho and Nunes . . .'

'That Nunes, just let me at him!' yelled João Eduardo who, after drinking the rum toasts, seemed in a more sombre mood.

Two soldiers came in, and Gustavo judged that it was time he was getting back to the printing press. Otherwise, they'd be there all day, for the rest of their lives! But work is duty, work is virtue.

After shaking hands once more with Osório, they finally left. At the door, Gustavo again swore his brotherly loyalty to João Eduardo, made a gift to him of his tobacco pouch, then, hat pushed back on his head, he disappeared round the corner, singing 'The Hymn to Work'.

Left alone, João Eduardo immediately set off to Rua da Misericórdia. When he reached São Joaneira's door, he carefully stubbed out his cigarette on the sole of his shoe, then tugged fiercely at the rope on the door bell.

Ruça came running down.

'Where's Amélia? I want to talk to her.'

'The ladies have gone out,' said Ruça, alarmed by Senhor João's manner.

'You're lying, you hussy!'

Terrified, the girl slammed the door shut.

João Eduardo went and leaned against the wall opposite, arms folded, watching the house; the windows were closed, as were the curtains; two of the Canon's snuff handkerchiefs were drying on the balcony.

He returned to the front door and knocked gently this time. Then he again rang the bell furiously. No one came, and so he stalked off to the Cathedral.

As he emerged into the square in front of the church, he stopped and looked around him, frowning; but the square seemed empty; a small boy sitting on the front step outside Carlos' pharmacy was holding the bridle of a mule laden with grass; chickens wandered about here and there pecking voraciously at the ground; the door of the church was closed, and all one could hear was the sound of hammering from a nearby house undergoing renovations.

João Eduardo was just about to walk on down to the Alameda when, from the sacristy side of the church appeared Father Silvério and Father Amaro, engaged in quiet conversation.

The clock struck the quarter hour, and Father Silvério paused to check his watch. Then the two priests both looked knowingly up at the administrator's open window, where, in the shadows, they could make out the figure of the administrator with his binoculars trained on the house of Teles the tailor. They went down the Cathedral steps, shoulder to shoulder, laughing, amused by that passion which was the talk of Leiria.

Just then Father Amaro saw João Eduardo standing in the middle of the square. He turned, doubtless intending to go back into the Cathedral in order to avoid the encounter, but seeing that the door was shut, he decided to continue on, eyes lowered, beside Father Silvério, who was calmly taking out his box of snuff. Without a word, João Eduardo leaped forward and dealt Father Amaro a forceful blow on the shoulder.

Stunned, Father Amaro feebly brandished his umbrella.

'Help!' shouted Father Silvério, stepping back, his arms in the air. 'Help!'

A man came running over from the municipal council offices and grabbed João Eduardo's collar.

'I've got him!' he roared. 'I've got him!'

'Help! Help!' shouted Father Silvério from a safe distance.

Windows round the square were flung open. A startled Amparo wearing a white petticoat appeared on the balcony above the pharmacy; Carlos, still in his slippers, rushed out from his laboratory; and the administrator gesticulated from his window, binoculars in hand.

Then Domingos, the notary, emerged from the municipal council building, looking very sombre, still with his oversleeves on, and he and a policeman led a pale, unresisting João Eduardo back into the office.

Carlos was quick to usher Father Amaro into the

pharmacy; he made a great fuss about mixing up some orange flower and ether, shouted up to his wife to prepare a bed . . . He wanted to examine Father Amaro's shoulder, was there any swelling?

'Thank you, it's nothing,' said Amaro, who was very white. 'It's nothing, just a scratch. A drink of water will be fine . . .'

Amparo, however, thought a glass of port would do him more good, and she ran upstairs to fetch it, saying repeatedly 'Oh dear, oh dear!', tripping over the children who were clinging to her skirts, and explaining on the stairs to the maid that someone had tried to kill the parish priest!

People had gathered round the pharmacy door to gawp; one of the carpenters who was working nearby said that it had definitely been a knife attack; and an old lady at the back was pushing and shoving and craning her neck in order to see the blood. Finally, at the request of Father Amaro, who feared a scandal, Carlos went over to the door and said majestically that he did not want a riot outside his premises. Father Amaro was feeling better. It had merely been a punch, a scratch . . . He would take care of him.

And when the mule outside began to bray, Carlos turned indignantly to the small boy looking after it and said:

'Aren't you ashamed after a distressing incident like this – distressing for the whole town – to be sitting there with a creature that does nothing but bray? Go away, you insolent boy, go away!'

He advised the two priests to go upstairs to the sitting room, away from 'the prying eyes of the populace'. And Amparo soon appeared with two glasses of port, one for Father Amaro, the other for Father Silvério, who flopped down on one end of the sofa, still terrified and emotionally exhausted.

'I'm fifty-five years old,' he said, having drained the last drop of port from his glass, 'and this is the first time I have ever been involved in a fracas.'

Father Amaro, who was feeling calmer now, put on a brave front and said jokingly to Father Silvério:

'Oh, it wasn't such a tragedy, my friend . . . And I don't

know about it being your first time either . . . Everyone knows that once you came to blows with Father Natário.'

'Ah, yes,' exclaimed Silvério, 'but that was between priests, my friend!'

Amparo, who was still shaking, refilled Father Amaro's glass and wanted to know 'the details, all the details'.

'There are no details, Senhora, I was walking along with my colleague, chatting, and the man came over to me, caught me unawares, and punched me on the shoulder.'

'But why? Why?' exclaimed Amparo, clasping her hands in amazement.

Then Carlos gave his opinion. Only a matter of days ago, he had said, in the presence of Amparo and Dona Josefa, the excellent Canon Dias' sister, that all these materialistic, atheistic ideas were leading young people to dangerous extremes . . . Little had he known then how prophetic his words would prove to be!

'Look at this young man, for example! He begins by forgetting all Christian duty (so Dona Josefa told us), he associates with ne'er-do-wells, he sits in bars and makes fun of dogma, he publishes abject attacks on religion in the newspapers . . . Finally, in an atheistic rage, at the very doors of the Cathedral, he hurls himself upon an exemplary priest (and I'm not just saying that because you're here, Father) and tries to murder him! Now what, I ask, lies at the bottom of all this? Hatred, pure hatred for the religion of our fathers!'

'Yes, I'm afraid that's the truth of the matter,' sighed Father Silvério.

But Amparo, who was indifferent to the philosophical causes of the crime, was burning with curiosity to know what would be going on at the municipal council buildings, what João Eduardo would say, whether they would have put him in irons . . . Carlos immediately offered to go and find out.

Besides, he said, it was his duty as a man of science to explain to the magistrate the possible consequences of a blow to the delicate clavicle area (although, God be praised, there appeared to have been no fracture or swelling), and he wanted, above all, to assure the authorities, so that they could take appropriate action, that the attempted beating was not an act of personal revenge. What could Father Amaro possibly have done to Nunes' clerk? It was the result of a vast conspiracy of atheists and republicans against the priesthood of Christ!

'Seconded! Seconded!' said the two priests gravely.

'And that is what I intend to prove to the administrator.'

In his zeal as indignant conservative, he was about to set off in the slippers and jacket he wore in the laboratory, but Amparo caught up with him in the corridor.

'At least put your frock coat on; you know how formal the administrator is!'

She herself helped him on with it, while Carlos, his imagination working furiously (that wretched imagination of his which, as he himself said, often gave him headaches), prepared his statement, which would cause an enormous stir in the town. He would stand up to speak. The room in the municipal council building would be crammed with the paraphernalia of justice; the administrator would be sitting gravely at his desk, the personification of Order; around him would be the amanuenses busy with official papers; and the prisoner would be standing opposite them in the traditional attitude of all political prisoners, arms folded, head held high, defying death. Then he, Carlos, would enter and say to the administrator: 'I have come here spontaneously to place myself at the service of social justice!'

'I will prove to them, with an iron logic, that it is all the result of a rationalist conspiracy. You may depend upon it, Amparo, that it is all a rationalist conspiracy,' he said, with a little groan, as he pulled on his high boots.

'And see if he says anything about Amélia or São Joaneira . . .'

'I'll take notes. But this has nothing to do with São Joaneira. This is a purely political trial.'

He strode majestically across the square, convinced that all the neighbours would be at their doors, murmuring: 'There goes Carlos to make his statement.' Yes, he was going to make a statement, but not about the blow to Father Amaro's shoulder. What did that matter? What mattered was what lay behind the blow – a conspiracy against Order, the Church, the Constitution and Property! That is what he would prove to the administrator. That blow, sir, is the first violent expression of a great social revolution!

And pushing open the baize door that led into the council offices, he stood for a moment grasping the handle, filling the doorway with the magnificence of his person. Alas, there was none of the paraphernalia of justice he had imagined. There was the prisoner, poor João Eduardo, but he was sitting on the edge of a bench, staring stupidly at the floor, his ears bright red. Artur Couceiro, in order not to look at João Eduardo, had his nose in a vast register of official letters on which he had spread out yesterday's evening paper, deeply embarrassed by the presence on the prisoner's bench of that fellow frequenter of evenings at São Joaneira's house. The amanuensis, Pires, eyebrows anxiously raised, was absorbed in sharpening his quill pen with his fingernail. The notary Domingos, on the other hand, positively buzzed with activity. He was scribbling furiously; the trial was obviously moving on apace. It was time for Carlos to introduce his idea . . . He stepped forward.

'Gentlemen, is the administrator available?'

At precisely that moment, the administrator called from inside his office.

'Senhor Domingos!'

The notary stood to attention, placing his spectacles on top of his head.

'Yes, sir!'

'Have you got any matches?'

Domingos searched frantically in his pocket, in the drawer, amongst his papers . . .

'Have any of you gentlemen got any matches?'

Various hands scrabbled over desks. No, there were no matches.

'Senhor Carlos, have you got any matches?'

'No, I'm afraid I haven't, Senhor Domingos.'

Then the administrator himself appeared, adjusting his tortoiseshell glasses.

'So no one has any matches, eh? Why are there never any

matches here? An office like this and no matches . . . What do you do with them? Go out and buy half a dozen boxes.'

The employees exchanged concerned glances at this flagrant lack of essential office apparatus. And Carlos, taking advantage of the administrator's presence and attention, said:

'Sir, I have come here . . . I have come here spontaneously, out of a genuine concern you might say . . .'

'Tell me something, Senhor Carlos,' the administrator said, interrupting him. 'Are the two priests still in your shop?'

'Father Amaro and Father Silvério remained with my wife in order to recover from the distressing . . .'

'Would you be kind enough to tell them that they are needed here.'

'I am, of course, at the disposal of the law.'

'Tell them to come as soon as possible. It's half past five, and we want to go home. It's been like this all day, just one thing after another! We're supposed to close at three!'

And with that, he turned on his heel and went out onto the balcony in his office – the same balcony on which, every day, between eleven and three, he defiled Teles' wife with his gaze, all the while twirling his blond moustaches and smoothing his blue cravat.

Carlos was already opening the baize door when a 'Pst' from Domingos stopped him.

'Oh, Carlos,' he said, and there was something touchingly supplicatory about the little smile he gave, 'forgive me, but would you mind bringing back a box of matches too?'

At that moment, Father Amaro appeared at the door, and behind him came the enormous bulk of Father Silvério.

'I wish to speak to the administrator in private,' said Amaro.

All the employees stood up, as did João Eduardo, whose face was as white as the whitewashed wall. Father Amaro crossed the office with subtle, ecclesiastical steps, followed by Silvério, who, as he passed the prisoner, made an oblique, cautious, semicircular gesture, as if fearfully warding him off; the administrator came out to greet the priests, and his office door closed discreetly behind them.

'There's some compromise afoot,' muttered the worldly-wise Domingos, winking at his colleagues.

Carlos sat down glumly. He had gone there to enlighten the authorities on the social dangers threatening Leiria, the Province and Society as a whole in order to play his part in that trial which he believed to be a political trial, and yet there he was silent, forgotten, sitting next to the prisoner on the bench. They had not even offered him a chair. It would be absolutely intolerable if the parish priest and the administrator reached some agreement without consulting him! For he was the only one who had seen in that blow to the priest's shoulder not the clerk's fist, but the hand of rationalism. This disdain for his perceptions seemed to him a grave error on the part of the municipal council. The administrator clearly lacked the ability to save Leiria from the dangers of revolution! The gossip in the arcade was quite right – the man was a nincumpoop!

The door opened a crack to reveal the administrator's glittering glasses.

'Senhor Domingos, would you mind coming in?' he said.

The notary bustled importantly over, and the door was once more discreetly closed. Ah, how that door, as it closed in his face, leaving him outside, how it angered Carlos! There he sat with Pires, with Artur, amongst those subaltern intellects, he who had promised his Amparozinho that he would speak plainly to the administrator. And who had the administrator's ear, who was called? Domingos, an utter dimwit, who spelled 'satisfaction' with a 'ph' in the middle. And what could one expect of a man who spent his mornings, binoculars in hand, dishonouring a family? Poor Teles, his neighbour and friend. Yes, he really ought to speak to Teles.

But his indignation only grew the more when he saw Artur Couceiro, an office employee, in the absence of his boss, get up from his desk and walk familiarly over to the prisoner and say to him sadly:

'Oh, João, what were you thinking of? But don't worry, things will work out, you'll see.'

João Eduardo gloomily shrugged his shoulders. He had

been there for half an hour, sitting on the edge of that bench, not moving, not taking his eyes off the floor, feeling as empty of ideas as if his entire brain had been removed. All the wine, which, in Osório's tavern and in the Cathedral square, had lit flames of anger in his soul and filled his pulses with a desire for violence, seemed to have been suddenly eliminated from his organism. He felt now as harmless as when he sat carefully sharpening his quill in the office. He was overwhelmed by a great weariness, and there he waited on the bench, physically and mentally inert, thinking dully that he would be sent to a prison cell in São Francisco, sleep in a straw cape, eat at the poorhouse . . . He would never again walk by the river nor ever see Amélia . . . The little house he lived in would be rented out to someone else . . . And who would take care of his canary? Poor thing, it would probably die of hunger. Unless Eugénia, his neighbour, took it in . . .

Suddenly, Domingos emerged from the administrator's office and, rapidly closing the door behind him, declared triumphantly:

'What did I say? A compromise! Everything's been sorted out.'

And to João Eduardo:

'You lucky so-and-so! Congratulations!'

Carlos thought that this was the greatest administrative scandal since the days of the Cabrals! And he was just about to retire in high dudgeon (like the Stoic, in the classical painting, leaving a patrician orgy), when the administrator opened the door of his office. Everyone stood up.

His Excellency stepped out into the office and, very gravely, weighing every word, his glasses fixed on the prisoner, said:

'Father Amaro, who is the kindest and most charitable of priests, came to tell me . . . that is, he came to ask me to take this matter no further. He, understandably, does not wish his name to be dragged through the courts. Besides, as Father Amaro so rightly said, his religion, of which, I may say, he is a most honourable example, preaches the forgiveness of all wrongs . . . He recognises that, although brutal, the attack came to nothing. It seems too that you were drunk.'

All eyes fixed on João Eduardo, who blushed scarlet. This, it seemed to him, was infinitely worse than prison.

'Anyway,' the administrator went on, 'having considered the matter carefully, I hereby release you. Make sure you behave yourself now. We'll have our eye on you. Off you go.'

And the administrator withdrew into his office. João Eduardo seemed too stunned to move.

'C-can I go, then?' he stammered.

'You can go to China, wherever you want! *Liberus, libera, liberum*!' exclaimed Domingos, who hated priests and was delighted with the outcome.

João Eduardo looked around at the other employees, at the frowning Carlos; his eyes brimmed with tears, then he picked up his hat and left.

'Well, that saves a lot of work!' said Domingos, gleefully rubbing his hands.

The necessary paperwork was hastily patched together. After all, it was late. Pires took off his oversleeves and put away his aircushion. Artur rolled up his sheet music. Standing sulkily at the window, Carlos stared sombrely out at the square.

At last, the two priests left, accompanied to the door by the administrator, who, now that his public duties were over, was once more the man of society. Why had friend Silvério not been to the Baronesa de Via-Clara's house lately? They had had the most furious game of ombre! Peixoto lost twice. How the man cursed! Your servant, gentlemen. I'm so glad that everything has been sorted out. Mind the step, now.

However, when he was returning to his office, he deigned to pause by Domingos' desk and, growing solemn again, said:

'Things worked out well. It's slightly irregular, but sensible. There are quite enough attacks on the clergy in the press without this kind of thing . . . It could have caused a great scandal. The lad could have said that he was jealous of Father Amaro, that he was trying to lead the girl astray, etc. It's much better to hush things up. Especially since, as Father Amaro told me, the only influence he has had in Rua da Misericórdia or wherever has been in freeing the girl from marrying that lad, who, as we see, is a drunk and a bully!'

Carlos was in torment. All these explanations were addressed to Domingos. And to him, not a word! There he stood, forgotten by the window.

But no! The administrator was beckoning to him mysteriously from inside his office.

At last! He rushed radiantly in, suddenly reconciled with the administrator.

'I was going to drop in at the pharmacy,' the administrator said quietly and, with no further ado, handed him a folded piece of paper, 'to get you to send this round to my house later today. It's a prescription from Dr Gouveia. But since you're here . . .'

'I came in order to make a statement . . .'

'Oh, that's all over with!' said the administrator briskly. 'Don't forget now, send that round to me before six. I have to take it tonight. Goodbye. And don't forget.'

'I won't,' said Carlos sharply.

As he walked into the pharmacy, he was ablaze with anger. He would send a furious letter to the newspaper, or his name wasn't Carlos! But Amparo, who had spied his return from the balcony, ran down to him, full of questions.

'So what happened? Did they let the lad go? What did he say? What was it like?'

Carlos looked at her with fire in his eyes.

'Through no fault of mine, materialism triumphed. But they'll pay for it!'

'But what did you say?'

Seeing Amparo and his assistant wide-eyed and eager to devour every word of his statement, Carlos, needing to salvage his dignity as husband and his superiority as employer, said laconically:

'I merely made my views clear.'

'And what did the administrator say?'

It was then that Carlos remembered the crumpled prescription in his hand and read it. He was struck dumb with indignation; that piece of paper was all he had got from his great interview with the administrator!

'What's that?' asked Amparo urgently.

What was it, indeed? In his rage, and throwing confidentiality and the good name of the administrator to the winds, he exclaimed:

'It's a prescription for a bottle of Gibert's syrup for the administrator. There's the prescription, Senhor Augusto!'

Amparo, who had some experience in the pharmacy and knew what mercury was used for, turned as red as the gaudy ribbons adorning her false topknot.

All that evening, the town buzzed with talk of the 'attempt on Father Amaro's life'. Some people criticised the administrator for taking the matter no further, especially the gentlemen of the opposition, who saw in the weakness of that particular civil servant incontestable proof that the government, with its profligacy and its corruption, was leading the country into the abyss.

Father Amaro, though, was admired as a saint. What piety! What gentleness! The precentor sent for him at dusk and received him paternally with a 'Greetings, my paschal lamb!' And having heard the story of the attack and of his generous intervention . . .

'My son,' he exclaimed, 'you combine the youth of Telemachus and the prudence of Mentor! Father Amaro, you would have been worthy to be a priest of Minerva in the city of Salento!'

When Amaro went to São Joaneira's house that night, he did so as if he were a saint who had survived the wild beasts in the Roman circus or Diocletian's plebs! Amélia made no attempt to disguise her joy and, trembling, she clutched his hands in hers for a long time, her eyes wet with tears. As in happy former days, they gave him the Canon's green armchair to sit in. Dona Maria da Assunção even tried to give him a cushion to rest his bruised shoulder on. Then he had to give a detailed description of the scene, from the moment when, as he was chatting to Father Silvério (who had acquitted himself very well), he had seen the clerk in the middle of the square, brandishing his walking stick with the air of a bullyboy.

These details angered the ladies. The clerk seemed to them worse than Longinus or Pilate. The wretch! Father Amaro should have trampled him under foot! What a saint he was to have forgiven him!

'I did as my heart bade me,' he said, lowering his eyes. 'I remembered the words of Our Lord Jesus Christ. He tells us that if someone smites us on our right cheek, we should turn to him the other also.'

The Canon coughed loudly and remarked:

'I'll tell you something, if someone smote me on my right cheek . . . But those are the orders of Our Lord Jesus Christ, and I would, of course, offer my left cheek. Orders from above! But after I'd done my duty as a priest, ladies, I'd thrash the rascal!'

'Did it hurt very much, Father?' a faint and unfamiliar voice asked from the corner.

An extraordinary event! Dona Ana Gansoso had spoken after ten long years of somnolent taciturnity! The torpor that had remained unshaken by parties or funerals was not, after all, devoid of human feeling and had been broken at last by sympathy for Father Amaro. All the women smiled at him gratefully, and Amaro, flattered, responded kindly:

'Scarcely at all, Dona Ana, scarcely at all, Senhora. Not that he didn't hit me hard, mind. But I'm made of sterner stuff than that.'

'The monster!' cried Dona Josefa Dias, enraged at the idea of the clerk's fist unleashed against that saintly shoulder. 'The monster! I would like to see him clapped in irons and set to building roads! I knew what he was like. I was never taken in by him. I always thought he had the face of a murderer!'

'He was drunk, and you know what men are like when they've been drinking . . .' observed São Joaneira timidly.

There was uproar at this. She must not find excuses for him. It was almost sacrilege to do so. The man was an animal, an animal!

And there was exultation when Artur Couceiro turned up

and immediately gave them the latest news: Nunes had sent for João Eduardo and had said to him (and these were his exact words): 'I won't have thugs or criminals working in my office, so get out!'

São Joaneira was moved to sympathy.

'The poor boy won't have anything to eat . . .'

'Well, let him drink, then, let him drink!' shouted Dona Maria da Assunção.

Everyone laughed. Only Amélia, bent over her sewing, turned very pale, terrified at the thought that João Eduardo might starve.

'I'm sorry, but I don't consider it a laughing matter!' said São Joaneira. 'I won't be able to sleep for thinking about the boy having nothing to eat . . . Oh, no, it's not right. Forgive me, Father Amaro, but . . .'

But Father Amaro did not wish poverty on the boy either. He wasn't a man to bear a grudge. And if the clerk came to his door in need, he would give him some money (not much, because he wasn't rich), but he would gladly give him something.

Such saintliness drove the women wild. What an angel! They gazed on him adoringly, their hands almost raised in prayer. His presence, like that of a St Vincent de Paul, exuding charity, gave the room a chapel-like sweetness, and Dona Maria da Assunção sighed with devout pleasure.

Then Natário appeared, looking radiant. He first vigorously shook everyone's hand, then burst out in triumph:

'You've heard then? The scoundrel and murderer has been driven away like a dog! Nunes has thrown him out, and Dr Godinho told me just now that he won't let him set foot in the district government offices. So that's him, dead and buried! It's a relief to all decent people!'

'And we owe it all to you, Father Natário!' cried Dona Josefa Dias.

Everyone agreed. It had been his skill and cunning that had uncovered João Eduardo's treachery and saved Amélia, Leiria and Society.

'Whichever way the scoundrel turns, I'll be there to block

his path. I won't let go of him as long as he's in Leiria. What did I tell you, ladies? I said I would crush him and I have!'

His sallow face glowed. He leaned back in his armchair, taking a much-deserved rest after a difficult victory. Then turning to Amélia, he said:

'Anyway, what's done is done. All I can say is that you've rid yourself of an utter scoundrel!'

Then the congratulatory comments – which had been repeated over and over at length ever since she broke off her engagement to 'the scoundrel' – began with renewed enthusiasm.

'It was the most virtuous thing you've done in your whole life!'

'You were touched by the grace of God!'

'You're in a state of grace, child!'

'Oh, so it's St Amélia now, is it?' said the Canon, getting up, bored with all this glorification. 'I think we've talked about the scoundrel long enough. What about ordering the tea, eh?'

Amélia had said nothing, but was sewing rapidly, occasionally glancing anxiously up at Amaro; she was thinking about João Eduardo and about Natário's threats; and she imagined João Eduardo gaunt with hunger, exiled, sleeping in doorways . . . And while the ladies were settling around the tea table, chatting, she managed to say quietly to Amaro:

'I can't bear the idea of him suffering. I know he's acted wrongly, but . . . It's like a thorn inside me. It makes me unhappy just to think of it.'

Father Amaro, revealing himself to be superior to the injury inflicted, said very kindly and in a lofty spirit of Christian charity:

'My dear child, that's nonsense. The man won't die of hunger. No one dies of hunger in Portugal. He's a healthy young man and not unintelligent; he'll sort something out for himself. Don't worry about it. That's just bluster on Father Natário's part. The man is sure to leave Leiria, and then we'll hear no more about him. He'll find a job somewhere. As for me, I've forgiven him and I'm sure God will bear that in mind.'

These generous words spoken in a low voice and accompanied by a loving look succeeded in reassuring her completely. Father Amaro's clemency and charity seemed to her better than anything she had heard or read about in the lives of saints and pious monks.

After tea, over lotto, she sat next to him. She felt suffused by a sense of delicious happiness. Everything that had bothered and frightened her up until then: João Eduardo, marriage, duty, had finally disappeared from her life. João Eduardo would go away and find a job somewhere, and Father Amaro was there, entirely hers, utterly in love with her. Sometimes, beneath the table, their knees would tremulously touch; at one point, everyone protested loudly against Artur Couceiro, who had won for the third time running and was brandishing his winning card, and their hands met caressingly; their chests lifted with a slight simultaneous sigh, drowned out by the old ladies' cackling; and they sat out the rest of the night, silently marking their cards, their faces ablaze, under the terrible pressure of a shared desire.

While the ladies were putting on their coats, Amélia went over to the piano and ran her fingers over the keys, and Amaro managed to murmur in her ear:

'Oh, my dear, I love you so much . . . if only we could be alone together . . .'

She was about to reply when Natário, who was standing by the sideboard putting on his cloak, said in harsh, booming tones:

'Why, I'm surprised you ladies allow such a book in the house!'

Surprised, everyone turned to look at the large bound volume that Natário was pointing at with the tip of his umbrella, as if at something truly abominable. Eyes glinting, Dona Maria da Assunção immediately came closer, imagining that it must be one of those novels she had heard about, describing immoral goings-on. Amélia joined her and, amazed at Natário's reproving words, said:

'But it's a copy of *Panorama*, it's an educational magazine . . .'

'I can see that,' said Natário sharply. 'But I can see this too.' And he opened the volume at the first blank page and read out loud: '"This book belongs to me, João Eduardo Barbosa, and helps to fill my leisure hours." You don't understand, do you? It's quite simple really. You obviously don't realise that ever since that man laid hands on a priest, he is *ipso facto* excommunicated, as are all the things that belong to him.'

The women instinctively drew back from the sideboard on which the fatal copy of *Panorama* lay open, huddling together with a shudder of fear at the idea of excommunication, which they imagined to be an unleashing of catastrophes, a shower of thunderbolts hurled from the hands of a vengeful God; and there they stood, dumbstruck, in a terrified semicircle around Natário, who, with his cloak over his shoulders and his arms folded, was enjoying the effect of his revelation.

Then São Joaneira, despite her fear, ventured to ask:

'Are you serious, Father Natário?'

Natário grew indignant.

'Am I serious? Please, São Joaneira! Would I joke about a case of excommunication, Senhora? Ask the Canon if I'm joking.'

All eyes turned on the Canon, that inexhaustible fount of all ecclesiastical knowledge.

Adopting the pedagogical air of his seminary days, which he always adopted when he spoke of doctrinal matters, he declared that Natário was absolutely right. Anyone who struck a priest, knowing that he was a priest, was *ipso facto* excommunicated. It is accepted doctrine. It is what is called automatic excommunication; it does not require a declaration from the Pope or from the bishop nor any ceremony for it to be considered valid and for all the faithful to consider the offender as excommunicated. They should, therefore, treat him as such, avoiding him and everything that belongs to him. Indeed, the Canon continued in sombre tones, this matter of laying sacrilegious hands on a priest was considered so special that the bull issued by Pope Martin V, which was intended to limit the number of cases of tacit excommunication, preserves it for anyone ill-treating a priest. He cited further papal bulls, the Constitutions of Innocence IX and of Alexander VII, the Apostolic Constitution, and other terrifying bits of legislation; he muttered Latin phrases that struck fear into the ladies' hearts.

'That is doctrine,' he concluded, 'but I think it might be best not to make too much of a fuss about it . . .'

Dona Josefa Dias said at once:

'But we cannot put our souls at risk by coming across excommunicated objects on the tops of tables.'

'We must destroy them!' exclaimed Dona Maria da Assunção. 'We must burn them, burn them!'

Dona Joaquina Gansoso dragged Amélia over to the window, asking if she had anything else belonging to the man. Amélia, confused, said that somewhere, though she couldn't quite remember where, she did have a handkerchief, a single glove and a raffia cigarette case.

'Onto the fire with them!' shouted Dona Joaquina, greatly agitated.

The room echoed now with the shrill cries of the women, in the grip of a holy fury. Dona Josefa Dias and Dona Maria da Assunção, filled by an inquisitorial desire for an act of devout extermination, spoke eagerly about 'the fire', rolling the words around in their mouths. Amélia and Dona Joaquina were in Amélia's bedroom hunting through drawers, through underwear, ribbons and bloomers for the 'excommunicated items'. And São Joaneira was a frightened and astonished witness to this call for an auto-da-fé that had suddenly rung out in her own peaceful living room, and she clung to the Canon, who, after muttering something about 'a private Inquisition', had sunk back comfortably into his armchair.

'I just want to make them aware that no one who shows disrespect for a priest goes unpunished,' said Natário quietly to Amaro.

Amaro nodded silently, contented with that pious rage which was the noisy affirmation of the ladies' love for him.

But Dona Josefa was growing impatient. She was holding the copy of *Panorama* with the corners of her shawl so as to avoid contagion, and she called into the bedroom, where the furious search through drawers was continuing:

'Have you found them yet?'

'Here they are!'

Dona Joaquina emerged triumphant, bearing the cigarette case, the old glove and the cotton handkerchief.

The clamouring women raced into the kitchen. Even São Joaneira followed them, as a good hostess, to watch over the bonfire.

Left alone, the three priests looked at each other and laughed.

'Women are the very devil,' said the Canon philosophically.

'No, Father,' said Natário, growing suddenly serious. 'I'm laughing because although, seen from outside, it may look ridiculous, the sentiment behind it is good. It proves their true devotion to the priesthood, their horror of impiety. And that, after all, is an admirable sentiment.'

'Oh, admirable,' agreed Amaro, equally seriously.

The Canon got up.

'And if they got hold of the man himself, they would be capable of burning him as well. I'm not joking; my sister has it in her to do that . . . She's a veritable Grand Inquisitor in skirts that one.'

'Yes, you're right there,' said Natário.

'I can't resist going to watch the execution,' exclaimed the Canon. 'I want to see it with my own eyes.'

And the three priests went to the kitchen door. There the ladies were, standing round the fire, still in their heavy outdoor clothes, caught in the violent light of the flames, in eerie silhouette. Ruça was on her knees, blowing feebly into the flames. They had used a large knife to slit the binding of the magazine, and the curled and blackened pages crackled and flew up the chimney, borne aloft on pale tongues of fire. Only the kid glove refused to burn. In vain they used tongs to push it into the hottest part of the fire: the flames merely charred it, reducing it to a shapeless, scorched lump, but it would not burn. Its resistance to the fire terrified the ladies.

'It's because it belonged to the very hand with which he committed the offence!' declared Dona Maria da Assunção angrily.

'Blow on it, girl, blow on it!' advised the Canon from the doorway, vastly amused.

'Please don't make mock of serious things!' cried Dona Josefa.

'Sister, are you trying to give advice to a priest on burning a heretic? What arrogance! I'm telling you that you have to blow!'

Then, trusting in the Canon's superior knowledge, Dona Joaquina and Dona Maria da Assunção crouched down and blew on the flames. The other women watched, silently smiling, their eyes shining and cruel, enjoying the sight of that extermination so pleasing in the eyes of the Lord. The fire, full of elegant energy, crackled and leapt, glorying in its old job as purifier of sins. Until at last, amongst the burning logs, nothing remained of the heretic's copy of *Panorama*, the handkerchief or the glove.

At that same hour, the heretic, João Eduardo, was in his room, sitting at the foot of his bed, sobbing, his face bathed in tears, thinking about Amélia and the happy evenings spent in Rua da Misericórdia, about the city he was bound for, about the clothes he would have to pawn, and wondering vainly why they were doing this to him, when he had always been so hardworking, had never intended to harm anyone and so utterly adored Amélia.

XV

There was a sung mass at the Cathedral the following Sunday, and São Joaneira and Amélia walked across the square to fetch Dona Maria da Assunção, who never went out alone on market days or when there were a lot of 'working people' about, for fear that they might steal her jewels or insult her chastity.

On that morning, large crowds had indeed come in from the villages and were filling the square: serious-looking men with close-shaven faces and with their jackets slung over their shoulders stood around in groups, blocking the street; there were women in pairs, wearing a fortune in gold chains and gold hearts on their plump bosoms, and in the shops, the assistants bustled about behind counters laden with linen goods and fabrics; coarse voices emerged from the packed taverns; endless haggling went on in the market, amongst the sacks of flour, the piles of china and the baskets of corn bread; crowds of people flocked around the stalls that glinted with small round mirrors and overflowed with bunches of rosaries; old women sitting by trays of cakes cried their wares; and on street corners, the poor of the parish said mournful paternosters.

Ladies were already heading for mass, grave-faced and all dressed in silk, and the arcade was full of gentlemen, very erect in their new cashmere suits, smoking expensive cigarettes and enjoying their Sunday.

Amélia drew everyone's eyes: the tax-collector's bold son, who was with a group of friends, even said out loud: 'Ah, she's stolen my heart!' As the two ladies were hurrying on down Rua do Correio, they saw Libaninho, wearing black gloves and a carnation in his buttonhole. He had not seen them since the 'disgraceful incident outside the Cathedral' and he immediately burst out in exclamations: Ladies, how terrible! That wicked clerk! He himself had been so busy that he had only been able to offer his commiserations to Father Amaro that very morning; the saintly creature had been putting on his vestments, but had received him with such kindness; he had asked to see Father Amaro's shoulder and, praise God, there was not even a mark on it . . . And if only they could have seen for themselves what delicate flesh the Father has, such white skin . . . the skin of an archangel!

'But do you know, ladies, I found him greatly upset.'

The two ladies were much alarmed. Why, Libaninho?

His maid Vicência had not been feeling well for some days and had been admitted into hospital early that morning with a high fever.

'And there he is with no maid, nothing. Imagine! He's all right today, because he's having lunch with the Canon (I saw *him* today as well – what a saint!), but what about tomorrow and the day after? Vicência's sister, Dionísia, is there at the moment, but I mean, Dionísia, really! That's what I said to him: Dionísia could be a saint for all I know, but her reputation . . . the worst in Leiria. A shameless hussy who never sets foot in church. I'm sure the precentor wouldn't approve.'

The two ladies agreed that Dionísia (a woman who ignored all the Church's teachings and who had even performed in amateur theatricals) was definitely not a suitable maid for the parish priest . . .

'Now, São Joaneira,' said Libaninho, 'do you know what I think? I've already said as much to Father Amaro . . . I think he should move back in with you. That way he will be somewhere comfortable with people who care about him, who will look after his clothes, who know his tastes and where he will be surrounded by virtue. Now, he didn't say no and he didn't say yes. But I could tell from his face that he was dying to do just that. You ought to talk to him yourself, São Joaneira!'

Amélia turned as red as her Indian silk scarf. And São Joaneira merely said ambiguously:

'Oh, no, I couldn't mention it . . . I'm very discreet in such matters . . . I'm sure you understand . . .'

'But it would be like having a saint living in your house,' urged Libaninho. 'Just think of that! And it would suit everyone. I'm sure that even Our Lord would be happy to see it.

Anyway, ladies, I must rush. Don't delay now, it's nearly time for mass.'

The two ladies walked on in silence to Dona Maria da Assunção's house. Neither of them wanted to risk being the first to speak about the grave and unexpected possibility of Father Amaro returning to Rua da Misericórdia. It was only when they had stopped and São Joaneira was ringing the doorbell, that she said:

'Father Amaro really can't have Dionísia as his housekeeper . . .'

'No, just the thought of it is horrific!'

And that was exactly what Dona Maria da Assunção said when they told her briefly about Vicência's illness and Dionísia's temporary installation as housekeeper: horrific!

'Not that I've met her, of course,' said the excellent lady. 'I'd even rather like to, because they say she is encrusted in sin from head to toe!'

São Joaneira then mentioned 'Libaninho's idea'. Dona Maria da Assunção said at once that it was an inspiration from Our Lord Himself, that Father Amaro should never have left Rua da Misericórdia! It was almost as if, as soon as he left, God had withdrawn His grace from the household . . . There had been nothing but problems – the article in *The District Voice*, the Canon's stomach ache, the death of São Joaneira's sister, that unfortunate marriage (which, oh horror, so very nearly took place), the incident outside the Cathedral . . . It was as if the house had been bewitched! And it was almost a sin to allow that sainted man to live amongst such disorder with that filthy woman Vicência, who didn't even know how to darn a sock!

'The best possible place for him is in your house. He has everything he needs there. And it's a real honour for you, like being in state of grace with God. As I've always said, if I wasn't on my own, I'd have him here as my lodger. This is the place for him . . . what a room, eh?'

And her eyes shone as she gazed around at her precious things.

The room was indeed crammed with a vast collection of

holy objects and pious bric-a-brac: the tops of the two copper-hinged rosewood sideboards were crowded with Our Ladies dressed in blue silk, either protected under glass domes or poised on pedestals, as well as with curly-headed Baby Jesuses with fat bellies and one hand raised in blessing, St Anthonies in their habits, St Sebastians bristling with arrows, and bearded St Josephs. There were exotic saints, who were her pride and joy, and which she had had specially made in Alcobaça – St Paschal Baylon, St Didacus, St Chrysolius, St Gorislano . . . Then there were the scapulars, the rosaries made out of metal or olive stones and coloured beads, yellowing lace from ancient albs, hearts made from scarlet glass, cushions with the initials J.M. embroidered in sequins, palms from Palm Sunday, martyrs' palms, packets of incense. The walls were entirely covered by pictures of Virgins of every devotion – balanced on orbs, kneeling at the foot of crosses or pierced by swords. And hearts dripping blood or on fire, hearts from which lightning sprang forth; framed prayers for certain much-loved festivals – 'The Marriage of Our Lady', 'The Invention of the Holy Cross', 'The Stigmata of St Francis', and, above all, 'The Holy Virgin's Confinement', the most holy of all, which was suitable for Ember Days. The tables were full of small oil lamps ready lit so that they could be placed immediately in front of a particular saint when the good lady had a bout of sciatica or her catarrh got worse or she suffered from cramp. She herself tidied, dusted and polished that holy, heavenly population, that pious arsenal, which was barely enough for the salvation of her soul and the relief of any aches and pains. Her main concern was the positioning of the different saints; she was constantly changing them around because sometimes, for example, she sensed that St Eleutherius did not like being next to St Justin, and so she would hang his picture in a spot where he was in more sympathetic company. And there was a hierarchy amongst them too (drawn up according to the precepts of the ritual explained to her by her confessor) which bestowed on each of them different degrees of devotion, with less respect being due to St Joseph II than to St Joseph I. Such wealth was the envy of her friends and an edifying experience for curious visitors, and whenever Libaninho came to visit, he would cast a languorous look around the room and say: 'Oh, my dear, it's like the Kingdom of Heaven!'

'It's true, isn't it?' the excellent lady continued, her face radiant. 'The saintly Father Amaro would be at home here, don't you think? It's like holding heaven in your hand!'

The two other ladies agreed. She, of course, could afford to have her house decorated with such devotion, she was rich . . .

'I don't deny it, I've spent a few hundred *mil réis* on this room, not counting what I spent on the reliquary . . .'

Ah, the famous reliquary made out of sandalwood and lined with satin. It contained a sliver of wood from the actual Cross, a fragment from the Crown of Thorns and a scrap of material from the Baby Jesus' nappy. Amongst the devout in Leiria, there were bitter mutterings that such precious items, being of divine origin, should be in the shrine in the Cathedral. Dona Maria da Assunção, fearful that the precentor would find out about that seraphic treasure, only showed it to a few close friends, in great secrecy. And the holy priest who had obtained it for her had made her swear on the Gospel not to reveal its provenance, 'in order to avoid gossip'.

São Joaneira, as usual, drooled over the scrap of material from the nappy.

'Wonderful!' she murmured. 'Wonderful!'

And Dona Maria da Assunção said in a low voice:

'There's none better. It cost me thirty *mil réis*, but I would have given sixty or a hundred for it. I would have given everything!' she stammered, in raptures over the precious scrap of cloth. 'My lovely little Baby's nappy!' she said, almost in tears.

She gave it a resounding kiss and put the reliquary away in a large drawer.

But the clock was striking noon, and the three ladies hurried to the Cathedral to get seats near the high altar.

Outside they met Dona Josefa Dias, who was also rushing to church, desperate to attend mass, her cape all awry and one feather in her hat coming loose. She had been in a positive frenzy with the maid all morning. She had had to do all the preparation for lunch herself. She was in such a state, she wasn't sure even a mass could make her feel better.

'Father Amaro's coming today. You'll have heard about his maid falling ill. Oh, and I forgot to say, my brother would like you to lunch with us too, Amélia. So that there are two ladies and two gentlemen, he says.'

Amélia gave a joyful laugh.

'And you can come and fetch her in the evening, São Joaneira. Goodness, I had to get dressed so quickly, I think my petticoat is falling down!'

When the four ladies went into the Cathedral, the church was already full. It was a sung Eucharist. Although it went against the strict letter of the ritual, diocesan custom (of which good Silvério, who was very strict on liturgical matters, had always disapproved) required that whenever the Blessed Sacrament was exposed there was also to be music for violin, cello and flute. The highly decorated altar, with its relics on display, stood out in festive white: the dossal, the frontal, and the paraments for the missals were white with raised embroidery in pale gold; pyramids of white flowers and foliage filled the vases; swathes of decorative white velvet cloth had been hung like curtains on either side of the tabernacle and looked like two vast white wings, reminiscent of the Dove of the Holy Spirit; and twenty candlesticks topped by yellow flames flanked the steps leading up to the monstrance, in which was displayed on high, in a glitter of gold, the round, opaque host. Subdued whispers filled the packed church; now and again someone cleared their throat or a baby cried; the air was growing thick with mingled breath and the smell of incense; and from the choir, where the figures of the musicians could be seen moving about behind the necks of bass fiddles and behind the music stands, came the occasional moan of a violin being tuned or a high note from a piccolo. The four friends had only just found their seats near the high altar when the two acolytes entered from the sacristy, one tall and straight as a pine tree, the other flabby and dishevelled, each carrying one of the two tall consecrated candlesticks; behind them came squint-eyed Pimenta bearing the silver censer and wearing a voluminous surplice from beneath which appeared his huge flapping feet taking slow stately steps; then, accompanied by the rustle in the nave of people kneeling down and leafing through prayer books, came the two deacons; and finally, vested in white, eyes lowered and hands clasped in prayer, displaying the humble meditative quality demanded by the ritual and expressive of Jesus' own meekness on the road to Calvary, came Father Amaro – still red in the face after the furious row he had just had in the sacristy, before donning his vestments, about the state of the albs.

And the choir immediately launched into the Introit.

Amélia spent the mass gazing in rapt amazement at Father Amaro, who was, as the Canon said 'a real artist when it came to sung masses'; everyone in the chapter agreed, as did all the ladies. What dignity, what chivalry in the ceremonial greetings he addressed to the deacons! How well he prostrated himself before the altar, humble and submissive, as if he were mere ashes or dust before the Lord, who was watching from nearby, surrounded by His court and by His heavenly family! But he was especially admirable during the blessings; he passed his hands slowly over the altar as if to pluck up and gather in the grace that fell from Christ's presence there, and then, with a broad, charitable gesture, he scattered it the length of the whole nave, over the vast expanse of white headscarves, to where the men from the country stood crowded together at the back, walking sticks in hand, staring in astonishment at the glittering monstrance! That was when Amélia loved him most, thinking to herself that those hands bestowing the blessing had passionately squeezed her hands beneath the table when they were playing lotto; that voice, with which he addressed her as 'my love', was now reciting ineffable prayers and it seemed to her far better than the moaning of the violins, and stirred her more deeply than the bass notes from the organ! She imagined proudly that all the women there probably admired him too, but the only time she felt jealous, the jealousy of a devotee aware of the charms of Heaven, was when he stood before the altar in the ecstatic position required by the ritual, as still as if his soul had soared high up into the Eternal and beyond the senses. However, she preferred him, because he felt more human and accessible, during the Kyrie or the reading of the Epistle, when he sat with the deacons on the red damask bench; she would have liked to have caught his glance then, but he kept his eyes modestly lowered.

Sitting back on her heels, smiling radiantly, Amélia admired his profile, his well-made head, his gold-embroidered vestments, and she remembered the first time she had seen him coming down the stairs in Rua da Misericórdia, cigarette in hand. How much had happened since that night. She remembered Morenal, the leap from the wall, her aunt's death, that kiss by the fire . . . How would it all end? She tried to pray then and began leafing through her prayer book, but she suddenly remembered what Libaninho had said that morning about Father Amaro having skin as white as an archangel's. It must indeed be very delicate and tender. She burned with intense desire, and imagined it must be a tempting visitation by the Devil; to drive it away she fixed wide eyes on the shrine and on the altar where Father Amaro, flanked by the deacons, was making semicircles of incense which signified everlasting praise, while the choir bawled out the Offertory . . . Then as he stood on the second altar step, hands in prayer, he himself was wafted with incense; squint-eyed Pimenta made the silver chains of the thurible creak loudly and the smell of incense rolled forth like a celestial annunciation; the shrine was shrouded in white volutes of smoke; and Father Amaro seemed to Amélia almost divine! Oh, how she adored him!

The church shook to the clamour of the organ at full blast; mouths wide open, the choir were singing at full pelt; above them, rising above the necks of the violins, the director of music, in the white heat of performance, was desperately waving a baton made from a rolled-up sheet of plainsong.

Amélia left the church feeling exhausted and looking very pale.

Over lunch at the Canon's house, Dona Josefa told her off repeatedly for 'not saying a word'.

Though she did not speak, under the table, her small foot was constantly brushing and pressing against that of Father Amaro. It got dark early now and so they had lit the candles; to accompany the dish of milk pudding which almost filled the middle of the table and on which Father Amaro's initials had been traced in cinnamon, the Canon had opened a bottle, not of his famous 1815 *duque* wine, but of the 1847 vintage; it was, as the Canon explained, 'a small homage' by his sister to her guest. With his glass of 1847 wine Amaro immediately drank to the health of 'the worthy lady of the house'. Dona Josefa positively glowed, a hideous sight in her green woollen dress. She was just sorry the meal had been so awful . . . Gertrudes was getting so careless. She had nearly burned the duck *and* the milk pudding!

'But it was delicious, Senhora!' protested Amaro.

'Now you're being kind. I did manage to step in just in time. A little more milk pudding, Father?'

'No, thank you, Senhora, I've had quite enough.'

'We'd better finish off this wine,' said the Canon. 'Have another glass.'

He himself drank it down slowly in one, uttered a satisfied 'Ah!' and settled back in his chair.

'A good drop of wine that! Makes life worth living!'

His face was flushed and with his thick flannel jacket on and a napkin tied round his neck, he looked even fatter than usual.

'Yes, a good drop of wine that!' he said again. 'Better than the stuff you had today at mass . . .'

'Please, brother!' exclaimed Dona Josefa, scandalised at his irreverence, her mouth still full of milk pudding.

The Canon shrugged scornfully.

'And what's wrong with that? It's time you learned not to meddle in things you don't understand. If you must know, the quality of wine at mass is of great importance. The wine should be good because . . .'

'It contributes to the dignity of the holy sacrifice,' said Amaro gravely, meanwhile stroking Amélia's knee.

'And not just that,' said the Canon, immediately adopting a pedagogical tone. 'If the wine is not good and contains additives, it leaves a deposit, and if the sacristan is not scrupulous about cleaning the chalice, it can start to smell really terrible. And then do you know what happens? The priest goes to drink the blood of Our Lord Jesus Christ and, taken by surprise, he pulls a face. Now do you see?'

And he planted a kiss on his glass. But he was in garrulous mood that night and, after uttering a leisurely belch, he again addressed Dona Josefa, who sat in awe of his knowledge.

'Since you're such a know-all, sister, tell me something else: should the communion wine be white or red?'

Dona Josefa felt that it should be red so as to resemble Our Lord's blood.

'You put her right, Miss Amélia,' boomed the Canon, wagging his finger at her.

Amélia declined with a giggle. Since she wasn't a sacristan, how could she possibly know?

'And you, Father?'

Amaro said laughingly that since it obviously wasn't red, it had to be white.

'Why?'

Amaro had heard tell that it was the custom in Rome.

'But why?' persisted the Canon in rumbling, pedantic tones.

Amaro did not know.

'Because when our Lord Jesus Christ first consecrated the wine, he did so with white wine. And the reason is very simple, it is because, as everyone knows, at that time in Judaea they did not make red wine. Give me a little more milk pudding, will you?'

Then, apropos of the wine and the cleansing of the chalices, Father Amaro began complaining about Bento, one of the sacristans. That morning before donning his vestments – just before the Canon had come into the sacristy – Amaro had had to reprimand him about the state of the albs. In the first place, Bento sent them to be laundered by one Antónia who, to general scandal, lived out of wedlock with a carpenter and was not fit to touch holy vestments. That was the first thing. Secondly, the woman returned them in such a filthy state that it would be an insult to wear them during holy communion.

'Oh, send them to me, Father, send them to me,' said Dona Josefa. 'I'll give them to my washerwoman, who is a person of great virtue and returns the clothes looking absolutely immaculate. It would be an honour. I myself would iron them and we could even have the iron blessed . . .'

But the Canon (who really was in loquacious mode that night) interrupted her, and turning to Father Amaro, he fixed him with a stern look and said:

'Regarding my visit to the sacristy, I meant to say, dear friend and colleague, that today you committed a punishable error.'

Amaro looked troubled.

'What error was that, Master?'

'After vesting,' the Canon continued slowly, 'when the deacons were already there beside you and you bowed to the cross in the sacristy, instead of making a low bow, you only made a half bow.'

'Now just a moment, Master!' exclaimed Amaro. 'That's what it says in the rubric. *Facta reverentia cruci*, bow to the cross, that is, a simple bow, a slight lowering of the head.'

And to demonstrate, he made just such a bow to Dona Josefa, who beamed and wriggled with glee.

'Not so!' declared the Canon who, in his own house and at his own table, was used to imposing his opinions. 'And I have my authors to support me.' And he let fall from on high, like great boulders of authority, the venerable names of Laboranti, Baldeschi, Merati, Turrino and Pavonio.

Amaro had pushed his chair back, ready for argument, glad, in front of Amélia, to be able to trounce the Canon, that master of moral theology and colossus of liturgical practice.

'I maintain,' he exclaimed, 'I maintain, along with Castaldus . . .'

'Stop, thief!' roared the Canon, 'Castaldus is one of mine!'

'No, Castaldus is mine, Master!'

And they grew angry, each one claiming the venerable

Castaldus and his eloquent authority. Dona Josefa bounced gleefully up and down in her chair, her face all creased with laughter, and she murmured to Amélia:

'Isn't it lovely to see them like this! The saints!'

Amaro went on, his head held high:

'More than that, I have good sense on my side too, Father. *Primo*, the rubric, as I said initially. *Secundo*, the priest, while in the sacristy with the biretta on his head, should not make a deep bow because the biretta might fall off, and then where would we be? *Tertio*, it would lead to the absurdity of the priest making a deeper bow to the cross in the sacristy than to the cross on the altar!'

'But the bow to the cross on the altar . . .' bawled the Canon.

'Is only a half bow. Read the rubric: *Caput inclinat*. Read Gavantus, read Garriffaldi. And that is how it should be! Do you know why? Because the priest is at his most dignified after mass since he has inside him the body and blood of our Lord Jesus Christ. The point, therefore, is mine!'

And standing up, he vigorously rubbed his hands together in triumph.

The Canon was sitting slumped, like a stunned ox, his double chins resting on the folds of his napkin. Then after a moment, he said:

'Yes, you're quite right. I just wanted to find out what your response would be. He's an honour to me, my student,' he added, winking at Amélia. 'Anyway, drink up, drink up! And then bring in some nice hot coffee, Josefa.'

However, at that point, they were startled by a loud ringing at the doorbell.

'That'll be São Joaneira,' said Dona Josefa.

Gertrudes came in wrapped in a shawl and a woollen cape.

'It's a message from Miss Amélia's house. The Senhora sends her regrets, but she can't come, she's not feeling well.'

'Who shall I go home with, then?' asked Amélia anxiously.

The Canon reached across the table and patted her hand:

'If the worst comes to the worst, I'll take you. Your virtue will be quite safe with me . . .'

'Brother, really!' cried Dona Josefa.

'Oh, hush, sister. Out of a saintly mouth come only saintly words.'

Amaro agreed fulsomely:

'The Canon's absolutely right. Out of a saintly mouth come only saintly words. Your health, Master!'

'And yours!'

And they clinked glasses, their eyes bright, entirely reconciled after their argument.

But Amélia was worried.

'Oh dear, whatever can be wrong with Mama?'

'A bout of laziness most likely,' said Father Amaro, laughing.

'Now don't distress yourself, child,' said Dona Josefa. 'I'll go with you, we all will.'

'We'll carry her on a dais like a holy image,' muttered the Canon, peeling a pear.

Then he suddenly put down his knife, looked wildly around him and, running his hand over his stomach, said:

'I'm not feeling very well either as it happens . . .'

'What is it? What's wrong?'

'Just a bit of a pain. It's gone now. It was nothing.'

Much alarmed, Dona Josefa tried to stop him eating the pear. The last time this had happened it had been brought on by eating fruit.

But he obstinately bit into the pear.

'The pain's gone now,' he grumbled.

'It was in sympathy with your Mama,' said Amaro quietly to Amélia.

Then the Canon abruptly pushed back his chair and slumped to one side:

'I'm not at all well, not at all! Oh, dear God! Oh, my Lord. Oh, I'm dying!'

Everyone rushed to his side. Dona Josefa took his arm and helped him to his room, calling to the maid to fetch the doctor. Amélia ran into the kitchen to heat up a towel to place on his stomach. But there was no towel. A terrified Gertrudes was bumping into chairs, looking for a shawl to put on.

'Go without it, you fool,' Amélia shouted.

The girl left. In his bedroom the Canon was howling with pain.

Amaro, genuinely concerned now, went into the room. Dona Josefa was on her knees by the dressing table saying mournful prayers to a large lithograph of Our Lady of Sorrows, and the poor Canon was lying face down on the bed, biting the pillow.

'Senhora,' said Amaro severely, 'this is no time for praying. We must do something. What do you usually do?'

'Ah, Father, there's nothing we can do,' said Dona Josefa tearfully. 'The pain comes and goes so quickly. There's no time to do anything. Sometimes some limeflower tea helps, but I haven't any in the house. Oh, dear Lord!'

Amaro ran to his house to fetch some tea, and returned, panting, shortly afterwards, along with Dionísia, who had come to offer her energy and her experience.

But, fortunately, the Canon had suddenly felt much better!

'Thank you so much, Father!' Dona Josefa said. 'Such excellent tea! You're most kind. He'll go to sleep now. That's what always happens after one of his attacks. If you'll excuse me, I'll go and sit with him . . . This was the worst attack yet. It's those wretched . . .' But she stopped herself, terrified. 'It's the Dear Lord's fruit that does it. It's His divine will . . . Will you excuse me?'

Amélia and Amaro were left alone in the room. Their eyes shone with the desire to touch each other, to kiss, but all the doors were open, and they could hear the old woman's slippers in the next room. Father Amaro said loudly:

'The poor Canon! The pain must be terrible.'

'He gets it about every three months,' said Amélia. 'Mama had a feeling it would happen now. She said so only the day before yesterday: "I'm worried," she said, "the Canon's due for another one of his attacks" . . .'

Amaro sighed and said softly:

'I don't have anyone to worry about me like that . . .'

Amélia rested her lovely, tender eyes on him:

'Don't say that.'

Their hands were about to meet passionately across the table, but Dona Josefa appeared, wrapped in her shawl. Her brother had gone to sleep, and she could barely stand for exhaustion. These upsets were ruining her health. She had lit two candles to St Joachim and made a promise to Our Lady of Good Health. It was the second time this year. And Our Lady had not failed her . . .'

'She never fails those who pray to her with faith, Senhora,' said Father Amaro piously.

The hollow chimes of the tall grandfather clock struck eight. Amélia again said how worried she was about her mother. It was getting later and later.

'And when I went out it was starting to rain,' said Amaro.

Amélia ran anxiously to the window. The paving stones outside, under the street lamp, gleamed wetly. The sky was dark.

'It looks set in for the night.'

Dona Josefa was most upset about this unforeseen difficulty, but, as Amélia could see, she couldn't possibly leave the house; Gertrudes had gone for the doctor, but, of course, had not found him and would doubtless be going from house to house looking for him, who knows when he would turn up . . .

Amaro then suggested that Dionísia (who had come with him and was waiting in the kitchen) could accompany Miss Amélia to her house. It was only a few steps away, and there was no one about in the streets. He would go with them as far as the corner of the square. But they should hurry before the rain got too bad.

Dona Josefa went and found an umbrella for Amélia. She asked her to be sure to tell her mother what had happened, but that she wasn't to worry, because her brother was better now.

'Oh, and tell her,' she shouted from the top of the stairs, 'tell her that we did all we could, but that the pain was over in a flash!'

'I'll tell her. Goodnight.'

When they opened the street door, the rain was falling

heavily. Amélia thought they should wait, but Amaro tugged impatiently at her arm.

'It's all right, it's all right.'

They walked down the deserted street, huddled beneath the umbrella, with Dionísia beside them, saying nothing, her shawl over her head. All the windows in the houses were dark, and in the silence they could hear the water filling the gutters.

'Goodness, what a night!' said Amélia. 'My dress will be ruined.'

They had reached Rua das Sousas.

'Now it's really coming down,' said Amaro. 'I think it would be best if we just stopped at my house for a moment and waited . . .'

'No! No!' cried Amélia.

'Don't be silly!' he exclaimed impatiently. 'You're going to ruin your dress. It's only for a moment, it's just a shower. Look, it's clearing up over there. It'll be over soon. Don't be silly. Your mother would be furious with you if she saw you out in this downpour, and quite right too!'

'No! No!'

But Amaro had already stopped, rapidly opened the door and was gently pushing Amélia inside:

'Just for a moment, it'll soon pass, go in . . .'

And there they stayed, in silence, in the dark hallway, watching the threads of rain glistening in the light of the street lamp opposite. Amélia felt utterly bewildered. Both the blackness of the hallway and the silence frightened her, but it also seemed to her delicious to be standing next to him in the darkness, unbeknown to anyone else. Involuntarily drawn to him, she rubbed against his shoulder, only to draw back immediately, startled to hear his agitated breathing, to feel him pressed up against her skirts. She could sense behind her the stairs that led up to his room, and she felt an intense desire to go upstairs and see what his room was like . . . She felt embarrassed by the presence of Dionísia, who was hunched silently by the door; she kept glancing across at her, wishing she would go away, wishing she would vanish into the darkness of the hallway or the night.

Then Amaro started stamping his feet on the floor, rubbing his hands and shivering.

'We'll catch our deaths standing here,' he said. 'The flagstones are icy cold. It would be much better if we waited upstairs in the dining room.'

Oh, no!' she said.

'Nonsense! Your mother would be angry if we didn't. Go on, Dionísia, light a lamp upstairs.'

Dionísia immediately ran up the stairs.

He took Amélia's arm and in a low voice said:

'Come on, why not? What do you think? Don't be silly now. Just until the rain stops. What do you say?'

She said nothing, but was breathing hard. Amaro placed his hand on her shoulder, on her breast, holding her close, stroking the silk of her dress. A shudder ran through her. And she followed him then up the stairs, as if in a daze, her ears burning, stumbling with each step on the hem of her dress.

'Go in there, into my room,' he whispered.

He ran to the kitchen. Dionísia was lighting a candle.

'Dionísia . . . I'm going to hear Miss Amélia's confession. It's an urgent matter. Come back in half an hour. Here you are.'

And he placed three coins in her hand.

Dionísia took off her shoes, tiptoed downstairs and shut herself in the coal cellar.

He went back into the room carrying the candle. Amélia was there, utterly still and pale. Amaro closed the door and went silently towards her, teeth clenched, almost snorting like a bull.

Half an hour later, Dionísia coughed discreetly on the stairway. Amélia came down at once, well wrapped up in her cape: as they opened the street door, two drunks were passing, talking loudly. Amélia withdrew quickly into the dark. A little while later, Dionísia peered out and, seeing that the street was empty, said:

'The coast's clear now, my dear.'

Amélia covered her face and they hurried back to Rua da Misericórdia. The rain had stopped, the stars had come out, and a dry coldness announced the coming of the north wind and the good weather.

XVI

The following morning, when Amaro saw that, according to the clock by his bed, it was nearly time for mass, he leaped joyfully out of bed. And as he pulled on the old overcoat that served him as a dressing gown, he was thinking about the morning in Feirão when he had woken up terrified because, the night before, for the first time since he had become a priest, he had sinned grossly with Joana Vaqueira on the straw in the barn. And he had not dared to say mass with that sin on his soul, for it weighed on him like a heavy stone. According to all the holy fathers and the sublime Council of Trent, he was contaminated, filthy, ripe for Hell. Three times he went up to the church door and three times he drew back in fear. He was convinced that if he were to touch the Eucharist with the same hands that had lifted Joana Vaqueira's petticoats, the chapel would fall in on him or he would stand paralysed as he watched, rising up before the shrine, sword in hand, the glittering figure of St Michael the Avenger! He had got on his horse and ridden for two hours, past the claypits to Gralheira, to confess to good Father Sequeira. Those were the days of his innocence, the days of exaggerated piety and novice terrors! Now his eyes had been opened to the human reality around him. Parish priests, canons, cardinals and monsignors did not sin on the straw of barn floors, no, they did so in comfortable bedrooms, with their supper to hand. And the churches did not fall in on them, and St Michael the Avenger did not leave the comforts of Heaven for such trivial matters.

That was not what was worrying him, what was worrying him was Dionísia, whom he could hear moving around in the kitchen, clearing her throat; he did not even dare ask her for water so that he could shave. He disliked knowing that she had become a party to his secret. He did not doubt her discretion, that, after all, was her profession, and a few coins would ensure her loyalty. But it was repugnant to his priestly modesty to know that this old woman, who had been the concubine of both civil and military authorities, whose fat body had wallowed in the town's murkiest secular goings-on, knew his weaknesses, knew of the physical desire that raged beneath his priest's cassock. He would have preferred it if Silvério or Natário had been the ones to see him last night aflame with lust; that at least would have been between priests! What made him most uncomfortable was the idea of those little cynical eyes observing him, as unimpressed by the austerity of the cassock as by the respectability of uniforms, because they knew that underneath both lay the same wretched bestiality of the flesh.

'That's it,' he thought, 'I'll give her a *libra* and send her away.'

There was a discreet knocking on the bedroom door.

'Come in!' said Amaro, sitting down at his desk, as if absorbed in some paperwork.

Dionísia came in, placed the jug of water on the stand, coughed and, addressing Amaro's back, said:

'Sir, things can't go on like this. Yesterday someone nearly saw the girl leaving. That's very bad. For everyone's sake, secrecy is essential.'

No, he couldn't dismiss her. The woman was forcing herself into his confidences. Those words, whispered in case the walls might hear, revealed the prudence of a professional and showed him the advantages of having such an experienced accomplice.

Red-faced, he turned round.

'Someone saw, did they?'

'Yes, it was only two drunks, but it could easily have been two gentlemen.'

'That's true.'

'And given your position, Father, and the girl's position . . . Everything must be done with the utmost secrecy. Not even the furniture in the room should know. In any affairs that come under my protection, I demand as much care as if we were dealing with a death!'

Amaro made a sudden decision to accept Dionísia's protection.

He felt around in the drawer and placed half a *libra* in her hand.

'May God bless you and keep you, my dear,' she murmured.

'So what do you think we should do next, Dionísia?' he asked, leaning back in his chair, awaiting her expert advice.

She said quite naturally and without mystery or malice.

'I think the best place to meet the young lady would be at the sexton's house.'

'The sexton's house?'

She calmly reminded him how convenient the place was. As he himself knew, one of the rooms next to the sacristy gave onto a courtyard where a large shed had been built while the renovation work was being carried out. Well, the sexton's house backed on to that. Senhor Esguelhas's kitchen door opened onto the courtyard; it was just a matter of coming out of the sacristy, across the courtyard and there he would be in his lovenest!

'And what about her?'

'She can come in through the sexton's front door, through the street door that opens onto the churchyard. No one ever goes by there, it's a desert. And if someone did see her, she could say that she was taking a message to the sexton. That's a very rough plan, but we can sort it out properly later.'

'Yes, I see, so it's more of a sketch,' said Amaro, who was walking up and down the room, thinking.

'I know the place well, Father, and, believe me, there's not a better place for an ecclesiastical gentleman in your situation.'

Amaro stopped in front of her and said, laughing:

'Tell me frankly, Dionísia, this isn't the first time you've recommended the sexton's house, is it?'

She stoutly denied this. She did not even know Senhor Esguelhas. But the idea had come to her in the night, when she was tossing and turning in bed. First thing in the morning, she had gone to look at the place and realised that it was ideal.

She cleared her throat, padded noiselessly over to the door, then turned to offer one last piece of advice:

'All this depends, of course, on your coming to an arrangement with the sexton.'

This was exactly what was worrying Father Amaro now.

Amongst the servers and sacristans at the Cathedral, Esguelhas was thought of as 'a miseryguts'. He had had one leg amputated and used a crutch to get around on. And certain priests, who wanted the job for one of their favourites, even said that, according to the Rule, this defect rendered him unfit to serve the Church. However, the former parish priest, José Miguéis, in obedience to the Bishop, had kept him on at the Cathedral, arguing that the disastrous fall that had occasioned the amputation had occurred in the belltower on the occasion of a religious festival and, thus, while Esguelhas was taking part in the ritual: *ergo* Our Lord had clearly indicated his intention not to get rid of Esguelhas. And when Amaro had taken over the parish, Esguelhas had used the influence of São Joaneira and Amélia to keep hold of the bell rope, as he put it. Apart from that (and this had been the view in Rua da Misericórdia), it was a charitable deed. Esguelhas was a widower and had a fifteen-year-old daughter who had been paralysed in the legs since she was a child. 'The Devil certainly had it in for my family's legs,' Esguelhas used to say. It was doubtless this misfortune that made him seem so sad and withdrawn. It was said that the girl (whose name was Antónia, but whom her father called Totó) tormented him with her moods, her bad temper and her appalling stubbornness. Dr Gouvéia declared her an 'hysteric', but all people of good principles were sure that Totó was possessed by the Devil. There had even been a plan to have her exorcised: the vicar general, however, always concerned about what the press might say, had hesitated to give his permission for the ritual to take place, and they had merely sprinkled her with some holy water, without any result. Otherwise, it was not known what form the girl's 'possession' took: Dona Maria da Assunção had heard that she howled like a wolf; in another version, Dona

Joaquina Gansoso assured everyone that the poor unfortunate tore her own flesh with her nails. Esguelhas, on the other hand, when asked about the girl, said only:

'Well, she's still here.'

Any hours not taken up with his work for the church were spent with his daughter in his little house. He only crossed the square to go to the pharmacy for some medicine or to buy cakes at Teresa's shop. All day, that part of the Cathedral, the courtyard, the shed, the high wall beside it overgrown with nettles, the house at the rear, with its black-shuttered window set in a leprous wall, was sunk in silence, in dank shadow; and the choirboys, who sometimes risked tiptoeing across the courtyard to spy on Esguelhas, invariably found him bent over the fire, his pipe in his hand, spitting sadly into the ashes.

He respectfully heard mass every day with Father Amaro. And, on that particular morning, as Amaro was putting on his vestments and listening for the sound of Esguelhas' crutch on the flagstones outside, he was already pondering the story he would tell Esguelhas, because he could not simply ask to use his room without explaining, somehow, that he required it for some religious purpose. And what other purpose could that be but to prepare, in secret and far from worldly distractions, some tender soul for the convent and for a life of holiness?

When Amaro saw Esguelhas come into the sacristy, he greeted him with a friendly 'Good morning'. Esguelhas, he said, was looking the picture of health! Hardly surprising really, because, according to the holy fathers, the act of consecration gives bells a special quality, and being in the company of bells induces a sense of joy and well-being. He then jovially told Esguelhas and the two sacristans that, as a small boy living in the house of the Marquesa de Alegros, his one great wish had been to be a sexton . . .

They all laughed heartily, enchanted by the Father's joke.

'No, don't laugh, it's true. And I wouldn't have been far off. In earlier days, it used to be the clerics of the minor orders who rang the bells. Our holy fathers consider them one of the most efficient routes to piety. There's a poem about it, in which the bell itself speaks:

Laudo Deum, populum voco, congrego clerum,
Defunctum ploro, pestem fugo, festa decoro . . .

Which means, as you know: I praise God, I summon the people, I bring together the clergy, I mourn for the dead, I drive away plagues, I gladden festivals.'

He was already in his amice and alb, standing in the middle of the sacristy as he carefully recited these lines, and Esguelhas drew himself up on his crutch at these words which bestowed on him such unexpected authority and importance.

The sacristan was standing ready with the purple chasuble. But Amaro had not quite finished his glorification of bells; he went on to explain their ability to dispel storms (despite what some presumptuous sages may say to the contrary), not just because they communicate to the air the unction they receive from the blessing, but because they scatter any demons that might be wandering about amongst the gales and the thunderbolts. The holy Council of Milan recommends that the bells be rung whenever there is a storm.

'Although in such cases, Esguelhas,' he added, smiling solicitously at the sexton, 'I would advise you not to take the risk. After all, it does involve being high up and close to the storm itself . . . Right, come on then, Matias.'

And as the chasuble was placed over his shoulders, he murmured gravely:

'*Domine, quis dixisti jugum meum* . . . Tie it a bit tighter behind, Matias. *Suave est, et onus meum leve* . . .'

He bowed to the cross and went into the church in the prescribed manner, eyes lowered and body erect, while Matias, scuffing one foot, bowed briefly to the crucifix in the sacristy, then hurried after Amaro with the ciborium, coughing loudly to clear his throat.

During mass, as he turned to the nave during the Offertory at the *Orate fratres*, Father Amaro (with a benevolence permitted by the ritual) addressed himself always to the sexton, as if the Sacrifice had been made especially for him, and Esguelhas, with his crutch resting beside him, plunged into a more than usually respectful devotion. Even at the *Benedicat*, having begun the blessing facing the altar to draw from the well of God's mercy, Amaro completed the Blessing and turned slowly back again to Esguelhas, as if to present to him alone the Graces and Gifts of Our Lord.

'Esguelhas,' he said quietly as they went back into the sacristy, 'go and wait for me in the courtyard, will you. I need to talk to you.'

He soon rejoined him, looking suitably grave.

'Put your hat back on, Esguelhas. I have a serious matter to discuss with you. I'd actually like to ask you a favour.'

'Father!'

No, it was not a favour exactly, because when it came to serving God, we all had a duty to do our utmost to help. There was a young woman who wanted to become a nun. In fact, to show what confidence he had in him, he would tell him her name.

'It's São Joaneira's Amélia!'

'Really, Father?'

'She has such a strong vocation, Esguelhas! She has clearly been marked out by the finger of God! It's quite extraordinary . . .'

He then told him a long story which he laboriously made up as he went along, depending on the feelings he imagined he could see on the sexton's astonished face. The girl had lost interest in life after the disagreement she had had with her fiancé. But her mother, who was getting on in years and who needed her to look after the house, was withholding her consent, assuming this interest to be just a passing fancy. But it was no fancy, it was her true vocation. He was sure of it. Unfortunately, when there was any kind of opposition, a priest had to tread very carefully. Every day, the heretical newspapers (which were, alas, the majority) inveighed against the influence of the clergy. The authorities, even more heretical than the newspapers, put obstacles in their way. There were some truly draconian laws . . . If they knew that he was instructing the girl so that she could take the veil, they would lock him up! What could one expect? We were living in heretical, atheistic times! He needed to have many long conversations with the girl, to test her, to understand her temperament, to see if she was best suited to Solitude and Penance or to helping the sick, to Perpetual Adoration or to teaching. In short, he must know her inside and out.

'But where can I do this?' he exclaimed, opening wide his arms as if distraught to find himself frustrated in his saintly duty. 'Where? It couldn't be in her mother's house, because they were already suspicious. Meeting in the church would be tantamount to meeting in the street. She's still only a young girl, and so we couldn't possibly meet at my house . . .'

'Of course not.'

'And so, Esguelhas . . . and I'm sure you'll thank me for this . . . I thought of your house.'

'Oh, Father,' said the sexton, 'I, my house and everything in it are at your disposal.'

'It's to help a soul and will be a source of great joy to Our Lord . . .'

'And to me, Father, and to me!'

Esguelhas' only concern was that the house was not worthy and not comfortable enough . . .

'Really!' said Amaro, smiling, as if renouncing all human comforts. 'As long as there are two chairs and a table on which to place the prayer book . . .'

On the other hand, said the sexton, if they wanted a quiet, private house, it was perfect. He and his daughter lived there like two monks in the desert. On the days when Father Amaro was there, he would go off for his walk. They couldn't use the kitchen, of course, because poor Totó's room was next to it, but there was always his bedroom upstairs.

Father Amaro struck his head with his hand. He had forgotten about Totó.

'That spoils our little plan, Esguelhas!' he exclaimed.

But the sexton was quick to reassure him. He was now caught up in this conquest of a bride for Our Lord; he wanted his roof to provide shelter for the holy preparation of that young girl's soul . . . Perhaps it would draw down God's pity on him. He warmly recommended the house's many advantages and facilities. Totó wouldn't be in the way. She never left her bed. Father Amaro would come in through the kitchen from the sacristy and Amélia through the street door; they could then go upstairs and shut themselves in his room.

'And what does Totó do?' asked Father Amaro, still hesitant.

The poor thing spent all her time in bed . . . She went through phases: sometimes she would make dolls and lavish such love on them that she gave herself a fever; at others she lay in terrible silence, staring at the wall. But then again she could be cheerful and chatty . . . It really was a great misfortune.

'She should entertain herself, she should read,' said Father Amaro, just to show interest.

The sexton sighed. She did not know how to read, she had never learned. That was exactly what he said to her: if she could read, life would weigh less heavily on her. But she had a horror of applying herself to anything. Perhaps Father Amaro would be so kind as to try and persuade her when he came to the house.

But Amaro was not listening, absorbed in an idea that had lit up his face with a smile. He had stumbled upon a natural pretext to give to São Joaneira and her friends for Amélia's visits to the sexton's house: she was teaching the paralysed girl to read. She was educating her! Opening her soul to the beauties of holy books, to the stories of the martyrs and to prayer!

'It's decided then, Esguelhas,' he declared, gleefully rubbing his hands. 'Your house will be the place where we will make the girl a saint. But,' and he lowered his voice, 'this is our secret.'

'Please, Father!' said the sexton, almost offended.

'I'm counting on you,' said Amaro.

He went straight back to the sacristy to write a note that he would pass secretly to Amélia and in which he would explain in detail the arrangements he had made 'to enable them to enjoy new and divine joys'. He warned her that the pretext for her to visit the sexton's house every week would be the education of Esguelhas' paralysed daughter; he would put forward the idea that night when he came to the house. 'After all,' he said, 'there is a grain of truth in it, for it would indeed be pleasing to God if the darkness of that soul could be illuminated with some religious instruction. And thus, my dear, we would kill two birds with one stone.'

Then he went home. He sat down at the breakfast table feeling very pleased with himself, with life and with the sweet facilities with which life furnished him. The jealousy, the torments of desire, the solitude of the flesh, everything that had consumed him for months and months, first in Rua da Misericórdia and then in Rua das Sousas, had passed. He was at last comfortably installed in happiness! And in a state of dumb enchantment, his fork forgotten in his hand, he remembered the previous night and the whole of that half hour, pleasure by pleasure, mentally savouring them, one by one, gorging himself on the certainty of possession – the way a farmer walks the small newly acquired field that his eyes have coveted for years. He would no longer cast bitter sideways glances at the gentlemen out strolling by the river with their ladies on their arm! He now had his own lovely lady, all his, body and soul, who adored him, who wore good linen, and whose breasts smelled of eau-de-cologne! He was, it is true, a priest . . . but he had an argument for that too: as long as a priest's behaviour was not a cause for scandal amongst the faithful, then it in no way damaged the efficacy, usefulness and grandeur of religion. All the theologians teach that the order of priests was instituted to administer the sacraments; what mattered was that the people should receive the inner, supernatural sanctity contained in the sacraments, and provided that these were dispensed according to the consecrated formulae, what did it matter whether the priest was a saint or a sinner? The sacrament still carried within it the same beneficial qualities. It did so not through the merits of the priest, but through the merits of Jesus Christ. If someone was baptized or anointed, it mattered not if it was by pure hands or soiled, they would still be washed clean of original sin or well prepared for eternal life. This is clear in the writings of all the holy fathers, and was established by the lofty Council of Trent itself. As regards their soul or their salvation, the faithful lose nothing through the unworthiness of the parish priest. And if that priest repents at the final hour, the gates of Heaven will not be closed to him. In short, all's well that ends well. These were Father Amaro's thoughts as he happily sipped his coffee.

After lunch, Dionísia came in, all smiles, to find out if he had spoken to Esguelhas.

'Yes I did mention it, just in passing,' he said ambiguously. 'But nothing's decided yet. Rome wasn't built in a day you know.'

'Ah,' she said.

And she withdrew to the kitchen, thinking that the parish priest lied like a heretic. Not that she cared. She had never liked working with ecclesiastical gentlemen – they paid badly and were always so mistrustful . . .

And when she heard Amaro going out, she ran to the stairs and reminded him that she did, in fact, have her own house to look after, and so when he found another maid . . .

'Dona Josefa Dias is sorting that out for me, Dionísia. I hope to have someone tomorrow. But drop round now and then . . . now that we're friends.'

'If you ever need me, you just have to call down to me in the yard,' she said from the top of the stairs. 'Anything at all . . . I know a little about a lot of things, even removing any problems, shall we say, or helping with a birth . . . Indeed, while we're on the subject . . .'

But Amaro was not listening: he slammed the door and fled, incensed by that clumsy, immodest offer of help.

He first brought up the matter of the sexton's daughter in São Joaneira's house a few days later.

He had given the note to Amélia the previous evening and, now, while the others were chatting loudly in the living room, he went over to the piano where Amélia was lazily running her fingers up and down the scales. Bending down to light his cigarette on the candle, he murmured:

'Did you read it?'

'Yes, it's an excellent idea!'

Amaro immediately rejoined the circle of ladies, where Dona Joaquina Gansoso was describing the disaster that had taken place in England and which she had read about in the newspaper: a coal mine had collapsed, burying 120 workers. The old ladies shuddered in horror. Pleased at the effect her words had had, Dona Joaquina Gansoso piled on more details: the people outside had struggled to free the unfortunate miners; they could hear their moans beneath the earth; it all took place in the encroaching darkness in the middle of a snow storm . . .

'Most unpleasant!' grunted the Canon, snug in his armchair, enjoying the warmth of the room and the safety of a roof.

Dona Maria da Assunção declared that all those mines and those foreign machines filled her with fear. She had seen a factory near Alcobaça and it had seemed to her to be an image of Hell. She was sure that Our Lord did not view them kindly . . .

'It's like railways,' said Dona Josefa. 'I'm convinced they're the Devil's work. I'm not joking. The howls, the flames, the noise! It sends shivers down my spine!'

Father Amaro laughed out loud, assuring Dona Josefa that they were a wonderfully comfortable way to travel at speed. Then he immediately grew serious and added:

'There's no question, though, that these inventions of modern science do have a touch of the Devil about them. That is why our Holy Church blesses them, first with prayers and then with holy water. Surely you know about this custom. The holy water exorcises them and drives out the Enemy Spirit, and the prayers redeem them from the original sin which exists not only in man, but also in everything he makes. That is why locomotives are always blessed and purified . . . So that the Devil cannot use them for his own ends.'

Dona Maria da Assunção immediately demanded an explanation. How exactly did the Enemy use railways for his own ends?

Father Amaro kindly enlightened her. The Enemy had many ways of doing so, but what he usually did was to derail the train, thus killing the passengers, and since those souls had not received the last rites, the Devil took immediate possession of them, right there and then.

'The villain!' snorted the Canon, feeling a secret admiration for the Enemy's wiles.

Dona Maria da Assunção fanned herself languorously, her face bathed in a beatific smile.

'Ah, ladies,' she said slowly to those around her, 'that won't ever happen to us. We won't be caught unprepared.'

It was true, and they all savoured for a moment the delicious certainty that they would be prepared and would thus thwart the Tempter's malicious intentions.

Father Amaro coughed as if about to say something, and then, resting both hands on the table, he said in a very practical tone:

'One must be constantly vigilant if one is to keep the Devil at bay. I was thinking about this only today (indeed it was the subject of my meditation) in respect of a most unfortunate case almost on the Cathedral's doorstep. The sexton's little daughter . . .'

The ladies had drawn their chairs closer, drinking in his words, their curiosity suddenly aroused, hoping to hear some piquant story about the Devil's misdeeds. Amaro continued speaking in a voice made more solemn by the surrounding silence.

'The girl spends the whole day in bed. She cannot read, she performs no religious devotions, she is not in the habit of meditating, and, as a consequence, she is, to use St Clement's phrase, "a defenceless soul". So what happens? The Devil, who is always on the watch and never misses a trick, makes himself at home there. That is the origin, as poor Esguelhas was telling me today, of her fits of fury and despair, of her motiveless rages . . . The poor man has a truly wretched life.'

'And just two steps away from the Lord's church!' exclaimed Dona Maria da Assunção, enraged by Satan's impudence in installing himself in a body and in a bed that were separated from the Cathedral walls by only a narrow courtyard.

Amaro said:

'You're quite right. It's an absolute scandal. But if the girl cannot read, if she knows no prayers, if she has no one to instruct her or to bring the word of God to her, no one to give her strength and teach her how to frustrate the Enemy . . .'

He got resolutely to his feet and paced about the room, shoulders bowed, like a shepherd grieving over the fact that a force greater than him has snatched away a beloved sheep. Exalted by his own words, he was filled by genuine pity and compassion for that poor child for whom the agony of immobility must be made even worse by the lack of any consolation.

The ladies looked at him, saddened by that unfortunate example of a neglected soul, especially since it was clearly a source of pain to Father Amaro.

Dona Maria da Assunção rapidly ran through her abundant arsenal of devotional objects and suggested placing a few saints at her bedhead, St Vincent, for example, or Our Lady of the Seven Wounds . . . But her friends' silence eloquently expressed the inadequacy of that devout gallery.

'You may say to me,' said Father Amaro, sitting down again, 'that she is merely the daughter of the sexton. But she has a soul, she has a soul like ours!'

'Everyone has a right to the grace of God,' said the Canon gravely and impartially, acknowledging the equality of the classes as long as it was only in respect of Heaven's comforts and not material goods.

'As far as God is concerned, there are no rich and poor,' sighed São Joaneira. 'In fact it's better to be poor, for theirs is the Kingdom of Heaven.'

'Better to be rich you mean,' said the Canon, holding out one hand to halt that false interpretation of divine law. 'For Heaven is also for the rich. You have misunderstood the precept. *Beati pauperes*, blessed are the poor, means that the poor should be content with their poverty and not covet the property of the rich, nor want more than the mouthful of bread that they have, nor aspire to share the wealth of others, for if they do, they will no longer be blessed. That is why, Senhora, the rabble that preaches that the workers and the lower classes should live better than they do are going against the express will of the Church and of Our Lord and deserve to be horsewhipped like the excommunicants that they are! Uf!'

And he lay back in his chair, exhausted by this long speech. Father Amaro, meanwhile, said nothing, leaning one elbow on the table and slowly rubbing his head. He was about to launch his idea, as if it were a divine inspiration, and suggest that Amélia should carry out the religious education of the poor paralysed child. But his entirely carnal, concupiscent motive made him pause superstitiously. The sexton's daughter appeared to him now in exaggerated form, plunged in a dark abyss of agony. He felt the thrill of charity in consoling her, entertaining her, making her days less bitter. Surely that action would redeem many sins, would delight God, if done in the pure spirit of Christian brotherhood. He felt a kind young man's sentimental compassion for the wretched body pinned to that bed, never seeing the sun or the street. And he sat there, awkward and undecided, scratching his neck, wishing he had never mentioned Totó to the ladies . . .

But Dona Joaquina Gansoso had an idea:

'What if we sent her that book full of paintings of the lives of the saints, Father? They're so edifying. I found them terribly touching . . . You've got it, haven't you, Amélia?'

'No, I haven't got it,' Amélia said, without glancing up from her sewing.

Then Amaro looked at her. He had almost forgotten about her. She was on the other side of the table to him, hemming a duster: the slender parting in her hair was almost lost amongst her thick, abundant locks, on which the oil lamp beside her cast a line of lustrous light; her eyelashes seemed longer and blacker against the warm brown skin of her cheek, flushed with rose; her close-fitting dress formed a crease at the shoulder and rose amply over the round shape of her breasts, which he saw rise and fall with her regular breathing . . . That was the part of her beauty he loved most; he imagined her breasts to be round and full and the colour of snow; he had held her in his arms, but she had been clothed, and his urgent hands had met only cold silk. But in the sexton's house, they would be his, with no obstacles, no clothes, at the entire disposal of his lips. Dear God! And there was nothing to prevent them consoling Totó's soul at the same time! He hesitated no longer. And raising his voice above the babble of old ladies now discussing the disappearance of *The Lives of the Saints*.

'No, ladies, it is not books that the girl needs. Do you know what I think? One of us, the one with most time to spare, should take the word of God to her and educate her soul!' And he added, smiling: 'And if truth be told, the person with most time on her hands here is Miss Amélia.'

What a surprise! It seemed like the will of Our Lord himself had come to him in a revelation. The ladies' eyes lit up with devout excitement at the idea of that charitable mission having its origins right there in Rua da Misericórdia . . . Enraptured, they greedily anticipated the praise of both the precentor and the Cathedral chapter. Each one proffered her advice, eager to take part in the holy work and to share the rewards that Heaven would doubtless shower down upon them. Dona Joaquina Gansoso declared warmly that she envied Amélia and was very shocked when Amélia burst out laughing.

'Do you think I would not do it with the same devotion? You're already proud that you will be the one carrying out the good work . . . That kind of attitude will do you no good, you know!'

But Amélia was in the grip of hysteria, leaning back in her chair, struggling to choke back her laughter.

Dona Joaquina's eyes flashed.

'It's indecent,' she cried, 'positively indecent!'

They calmed her down, and Amélia had to swear on the Holy Gospels that she had merely had a silly thought and was generally in a nervous state . . .

'Well,' said Dona Maria da Assunção, 'she's quite right to be proud. It's an honour for the house. When people find out . . .'

Amaro said severely:

'But they mustn't find out, Dona Maria! Of what use, in

the eyes of God, are good works that are a cause of boasting and vanity?'

Dona Maria bowed her shoulders, humbling herself before the reprimand. And Father Amaro went on gravely:

'It must go no further than this room. It is between God and us. We want to save a soul, to console someone who is sick, not to be praised in the newspapers. Isn't that so, Canon?

The Canon sat up slowly:

'You have spoken tonight with the golden tongue of St John Chrysostom. I am greatly edified, and now I could do with some toast.'

While Ruça was preparing the tea, they decided that, in secret, so that the action would prove more valuable in the eyes of God, Amélia would go once or twice a week, according to the degree of her devotion, to spend an hour at the paralysed girl's bedside in order to read to her from *The Lives of the Saints*, to teach her some prayers and to inspire her with virtue.

'One thing is certain,' said Dona Maria da Assunção, turning to Amélia, 'you're a very lucky girl!'

Ruça came in with the tray, in the midst of the laughter provoked by 'Dona Maria's foolishness' as Amélia put it, Amélia having blushed scarlet. And thus it was that she and Father Amaro were able to see each other freely, to the greater glory of God and the humiliation of the Enemy.

They met every week, sometimes once, sometimes twice, so that, by the end of the month, their charitable visits to Totó had reached the symbolic number of seven, which should, in the minds of the devout, have corresponded to The Seven Sorrows of Mary. Father Amaro would warn Esguelhas the night before, and Esguelhas would leave the street door ajar, having first swept the whole house and prepared the bedroom for the priest's work. On those days, Amélia got up early: she always had a white petticoat to starch or a bow to make; her mother was bemused by these affectations and by the quantity of eau-de-cologne with which she drenched herself; but Amélia explained that it was 'in order to inspire Totó with ideas of cleanliness and freshness'. Once dressed, she would sit and wait for eleven to strike, looking very serious, her face flushed, her eyes fixed on the hands of the clock, responding distractedly to her mother's remarks; at last, the old contraption would grind out a cavernous eleven o'clock and then, with one last glance in the mirror, she would leave, planting a large kiss on her mother's cheek.

She was always apprehensive, afraid that someone might see her. Every morning, she prayed to Our Lady of Safe Journeys to keep her from unfortunate encounters, and if she saw a poor person, she would invariably give them alms, to placate the Good Lord, friend to beggars and vagabonds. The most frightening part was the Cathedral square over which Amparo in the pharmacy kept an incessant vigil as she sat at the window, sewing. Amélia would shrink into her cape then and keep her sunshade low over her face as she went into the Cathedral, always right foot first.

She found the silence of the church, deserted and drowsing in the wan light, equally terrifying; the taciturn saints and crosses seemed to be chiding her for her sin; she imagined that the glass eyes of the images and the painted pupils of the pictures were fixed on her with cruel insistence and that they noticed how her breast rose and fell at the thought of the pleasure to come. Sometimes, in the grip of superstition and in order to fend off the disapproval of the saints, she would even promise to devote the whole morning to Totó and to give all her charitable attentions only to her, and not to allow Father Amaro so much as to touch her dress. But if, when she went into the sexton's house, she did not find Amaro there, she would not even pause at the foot of Totó's bed, but go straight to the kitchen window, to keep watch on the thick sacristy door, every one of whose black iron studs she now knew individually.

He would arrive at last. It was the beginning of March; the swallows had returned; they could be heard twittering in the melancholy silence as they flew amongst the buttresses of the Cathedral. Here and there, plants that favour dank places clothed the corners in dark green. Amaro would sometimes gallantly pick her a flower, but Amélia would grow impatient and tap on the window. He would hurry then, and they would stand for a moment at the door, hands clasped, their shining eyes devouring each other; and then they would go in and see Totó and give her the cakes that Amaro always brought for her in the pocket of his cassock.

Totó's bed was in the small bedroom next to the kitchen. Her scrawny body was barely visible on the sagging mattress, beneath filthy blankets the edges of which she spent her time unpicking. On those days, she had taken to wearing a white dressing gown, and her hair gleamed with oil, for lately, since Father Amaro's visits, 'she had got it into her head that she wanted to look proper' as a delighted Esguelhas put it, to the point that she would not be parted from the mirror and comb that she hid under her pillow, and she had instructed her father to stow under the bed, amongst the dirty bedclothes, the dolls which now she scorned.

Amélia would sit down for a moment at the foot of the bed and ask Totó if she had studied her ABC, making her pronounce the occasional letter. Then she would ask her to repeat correctly the prayer she had been teaching her, while the priest waited on the threshold, his hands in his pockets, bored and embarrassed by the paralysed girl's shining eyes, which never left him for a moment, penetrating him, exploring his body with ardour and astonishment, eyes that seemed even larger and more brilliant in her dark face, so gaunt that her cheekbones were clearly visible beneath the skin. He felt neither compassion nor charity for Totó; he hated that delay; he found the girl coarse and irritating. These moments dragged for Amélia too, when she resigned herself to talking to the girl, in order not to scandalise Our Lord too much. Totó seemed to hate her and either responded irritably or else lay in rancorous silence, her face turned to the wall; one day, she even tore up the alphabet, and she would shrink away angrily if Amélia tried to rearrange the shawl around her shoulders or smooth the bedclothes.

Finally, Amaro would grow impatient and make a sign to

Amélia, and she would set before Totó the picture book of *The Lives of the Saints*.

'There you are, now you look at the pictures. There's St Matthew, and that's St Virginia. Bye-bye now. I'm going upstairs with Father Amaro to pray to God to give you good health and to help you to walk . . . No, don't spoil the book, that's naughty.'

And when they went upstairs, Totó would crane her neck after them, eyes flashing then filling with angry tears as she listened to the stairs creaking. The room above was very low with no ceiling, just the black beams on which the tiles rested. Beside the bed hung a small oil lamp that left a stain on the wall like a black plume of smoke. And Amaro always used to laugh at the preparations Esguelhas had made – the table in one corner with a copy of the New Testament on it, and a jug of water and two chairs on either side.

'It's for our class, so that I can teach you the duties of a nun,' he said, laughing.

'Teach me, then!' she would murmur, as she stood before Amaro, a warm smile on her lips revealing her white teeth, and her arms flung wide, offering herself up to him.

He would shower voracious kisses on her neck and hair; sometimes he would bite her ear and she would utter a little yelp, after which they would both stand for a moment utterly still, listening, afraid of the paralysed girl downstairs. Then Amaro would close the shutters and the door, which was so stiff he had to press hard against it with his knee. Amélia would slowly get undressed and would remain for a moment immobile, her petticoats fallen around her feet, a white shape in the darkness of the room. Amaro, nearby, would be breathing hard. Then she would hurriedly make the sign of the cross and give a sad little sigh as she climbed onto the bed.

Amélia could only stay until midday, which is why Amaro hung his watch on the nail holding the oil lamp in place. But even when they did not hear the chimes of the clock, Amélia could tell the time from the crowing of a neighbouring cockerel.

'I must go now, my love,' she would say wearily.

'Stay. You're always in such a hurry.'

They would lie in silence for a while longer, cuddled up close to each other, in sweet lassitude. Through the spaces between the roof beams they could see cracks of light; sometimes they heard a cat padding across, occasionally catching a loose tile as it passed; or a bird would alight, singing, and they would hear the rustle of its wings.

'It's time I went,' Amélia would say.

Amaro wanted to make her stay longer and would keep kissing her ear.

'Greedy thing!' she would murmur. 'Stop it!'

Then she would get dressed quickly in the dark, open the window, once more embrace Amaro, who lay stretched out on the bed, and, finally, she would move the table and the chairs, so that the paralysed girl downstairs would hear and know that their class was over.

Amaro would not stop kissing her, and so, to draw things to a close, she would run away from him and fling open the door; Amaro would go down the stairs, stride through the kitchen without so much as a glance at Totó and walk across to the sacristy.

Amélia, on the other hand, would go and see Totó to find out if she had liked the pictures. Sometimes she would find her hiding with her head under the blankets, which she held down with her hands; at other times, sitting up in bed, Totó would scrutinise Amélia with eyes that flickered with lewd curiosity; she would put her face up close to Amélia's, her nostrils dilated as if to sniff her; troubled, Amélia drew back, blushing; it was getting late, she would say, then pick up her *Lives of the Saints* and leave, cursing that creature and her malicious silence.

When she crossed the square at that hour, she always saw Amparo at her window. She had even thought it prudent to tell her in confidence of her charitable visits to Totó. As soon as Amparo saw her, she would call down and, leaning over the balcony, ask:

'So how is Totó?

'Oh, she's coming along.'

'Can she read yet?'

'She can spell.'

'And what about the prayer to Our Lady?'

'Oh, she can say that already.'

'Such devotion, my dear!'

Amélia would modestly lower her eyes. And Carlos, who was also in on the secret, would leave the counter to come to the door and admire Amélia.

'Back from your great mission of mercy, eh?' he would say with wide, admiring eyes, as he swayed back and forth on the toes of his slippered feet.

'Oh, I just spend a bit of time with her, to distract her . . .'

'Marvellous!' murmured Carlos. 'The work of a true apostle! Off you go, my saintly girl, and give my regards to your mother.'

Then he would go back inside and say to his assistant:

'Do you see that, Senhor Augusto? Instead of wasting her time on love affairs like other girls, she makes herself a guardian angel. She spends the flower of her youth with a cripple! Do you think philosophy, materialism and all that other rubbish could inspire such actions? No, only religion could, my dear sir. I wish all the Renans of this world and that whole band of philosophers could see this! Don't get me wrong, sir, I admire philosophy when it goes hand in hand with religion . . . I'm a man of science and I admire Newton and Guizot, but, mark my words, in ten years' time, Senhor Augusto, philosophy will be dead and buried!'

And he continued pacing about the pharmacy, hands behind his back, pondering the death of philosophy.

XVII

This was the happiest period of Amaro's life.

'I am in God's grace,' he would sometimes think at night as he got undressed, when, out of ecclesiastical habit, he examined his days and found that they followed easily, comfortably and pleasurably one upon the other. In the last two months, there had been no frictions or difficulties in his service of the parish; everyone, as Father Saldanha put it, was in a positively saintly mood. Dona Josefa Dias had found him a cheap and excellent cook called Escolástica. He had a devoted and admiring court in Rua da Misericórdia; once or twice each week came that delicious, heavenly hour in Esguelhas' house; and to complete this picture of harmony, the weather was so warm that the roses were already starting to bloom in Morenal.

But what enchanted him most was that no one – not the old ladies, not the other priests, nor anyone in the sacristy – knew anything about his regular rendezvous with Amélia. The visits to Totó had become part of the household customs; they referred to them as 'Miss Amélia's devotions', and they did not ask her for details on the devout principle that such devotions are a secret to be shared only with Our Lord. Very occasionally one of the ladies would ask Amélia how the patient was getting on, and Amélia would assure her that Totó was much changed and that she was beginning to open her eyes to God's law; then, very discreetly, they would change the subject. There was merely a vague plan one day, later on, once Totó knew her catechism by heart and had been cured by the efficacy of prayer, to make a pilgrimage to admire Amélia's holy work and the shaming of the Enemy.

Given their generous confidence in her virtue, Amélia even suggested to Amaro that it might be a good idea to tell the ladies that he was occasionally present when she was carrying out her pious work with Totó.

'That way, if anyone did see you going into the sexton's house, no one would suspect anything.'

'That doesn't seem necessary,' he said. 'God is clearly on our side, my love. We don't want to interfere in his plans. He sees further than we do . . .'

She agreed immediately, as she did with his every utterance. From the very first morning in Esguelhas' house, she had abandoned herself to him absolutely and entirely, body, soul, will and feeling: there was not a hair on her head, not an idea, however small, in her mind that did not belong to Father Amaro. That possession of her whole being had not been a gradual process, it had happened as soon as his strong arms closed around her. It was as if his kisses had sucked up and consumed her soul; now she was like an inert accessory of his person. And she did not hide the fact; she enjoyed humbling herself before him, offering herself up, feeling that she was all his, his slave; she wanted him to think for her and to live for her; she had gladly unloaded onto him the burden of responsibility that had always weighed so heavily on her in life; her views came to her ready-formed from Amaro's brain, as naturally as if the blood running through her veins sprang from his heart. 'Father Amaro wanted . . .' or 'Father Amaro said . . .' were for her all-sufficient, all-powerful reasons. She lived with her eyes fixed on him, in a state of animal obedience; she only looked away and down when he spoke or when the moment came to unbutton her dress.

Amaro took prodigious pleasure in this domination; it was a revenge for a whole past life of dependencies – his uncle's house, the seminary, the white salon of the Conde de Ribamar . . . His entire existence as a priest was one long humble bow that wearied his soul; he lived in obedience to the bishop, to the ecclesiastical council, to the canons, to the Rule that did not even allow him to have a will of his own in how he treated the sacristan. And now, at last, there at his feet, he had that body, that soul, that living being over whom he reigned despotically. As a priest, he spent his days praising, adoring and sending up incense to God, and now he too was the God of that creature who feared him and who punctually offered up her devotions to him. For her, at least, he was handsome and better than any count or duke, and as worthy of a mitre as the wisest of men. She herself had once said to him, after thinking for a moment:

'You could become Pope!'

'I am certainly the stuff that Popes are made of,' he replied gravely.

And she believed him, fearing only that such lofty posts would take him away from her and carry him far from Leiria. That passion, in which she was so absorbed and steeped, had made her stupid and obtuse about anything that was not to do with Father Amaro and with her love. Indeed, Amaro did not allow her other interests or curiosities about anything other than him. He even forbade her to read novels or poetry. What did she need knowledge for? What did it matter to her what went on in the world? One day when she had spoken with some enthusiasm about a dance that was being held in Vias-Claras, he was as offended as if she had actually betrayed him. In the sexton's house he rained down the most terrible accusations upon her: she was vain, a fallen woman, a daughter of Satan!

'I'll kill you, do you hear? I'll kill you!' he exclaimed, grabbing her wrists and fixing her with burning eyes.

He was tormented by the fear that she might escape from his dominion, might lose her mute and absolute adoration of him. He thought sometimes that she might, with time, grow weary of a man who could not satisfy a woman's vanities and tastes, who always wore the same black cassock and had a shaven face and tonsure. He imagined that colourful cravats, well-waxed moustaches, a fine horse or a lancer's uniform were things that held a real fascination for women. And if he heard her mention an officer at the barracks or some gentleman of the town, he would become immediately and irrationally jealous:

'Do you like him? Is it because of the clothes he wears, or his moustache?'

'Like him? I've never even seen the man!'

Well, she shouldn't talk about him then. Feelings of

curiosity and thoughts about other men . . . why, it was just such a lack of vigilance over one's soul and will that the Devil could seize upon.

He began to hate everything about the secular world simply because it might attract her and draw her away from the shadow cast by his cassock. On complicated pretexts, he forbade all communication with the town. He even convinced her mother not to let Amélia go to the arcade or to the shops alone. And he was always representing men to her as monsters of impiety, stupid and false, encrusted in sin, marked out for Hell! He told her the most terrible stories about the various young men of Leiria. Terrified but nevetheless intrigued, she would ask him:

'How do you know that?'

'I cannot say,' he would reply and nothing more, indicating that his lips were closed by the seal of confession.

At the same time, he would hammer into her the glories of the priesthood. He would make a great display of erudition drawn entirely from his old schoolbooks, praising the work of priests and their superiority. In Egypt, which, in ancient times, had been a great nation, a man could only be king if he were also a priest. In Persia and Ethiopia, a simple priest had the power both to crown kings and to oust them. Who enjoyed an equivalent authority? No one, not even in the Court of Heaven. The priest was superior to the angels and to the seraphim because, unlike the priest, they were not given the marvellous power to forgive sins. Even the Virgin Mary did not have greater power than he, Father Amaro. With all due respect for the majesty of Our Lady, he could say, along with St Bernardino of Siena: 'The priest is greater than thee, beloved mother!', because although the Virgin had incarnated God in her chaste womb, she had done so only once, whereas the priest, in the holy sacrifice of mass, incarnated God every day! And this was not just some subtle argument of his own, all the holy fathers agreed.

'What do you think?'

'Oh, my love!' she would murmur, full of wonder, swooning with sensual pleasure.

Then he would dazzle her with venerable quotations: St Clement, who called the priest 'the earthly God'; eloquent St John Chrysostom, who said that 'the priest is the ambassador who brings orders from God'. And St Ambrose who wrote: 'There is a greater difference between the role of king and the role of priest than there is between lead and gold.'

'And I am the gold,' said Amaro, patting himself on the chest. 'What do you think?'

She would hurl herself into his arms, bestowing voracious kisses on him, as if to touch and possess in him 'St Ambrose's gold', 'the ambassador of God', everything that is most high and most noble on earth, the being who exceeds the arch-angels in grace!

As much or even more than his voice, it was this divine priestly power, this familiarity with God, that made her believe the promises which he repeated over and over: being loved by a priest would call down upon her God's interest and friendship; when she died, two angels would come and take her by the hand and resolve any doubts that St Peter, the keeper of the keys to Heaven, might have; white roses would spontaneously spring up on her grave, as had happened in France with a young girl loved by a priest, as celestial proof that, in the holy arms of a priest, virginity remains unspoiled.

She was enchanted by this image. When she thought of her grave perfumed by white roses, she would grow suddenly thoughtful, as if anticipating mystical joys, and utter little sighs of pleasure. Pouting, she would say that she wanted to die now.

Amaro would laugh.

'How can you talk about death when you're growing plumper all the time?'

She had indeed grown fatter. Hers was now an ample and homogeneous beauty. She had lost the restless look that had made her lips seem tight and her nose too pointed. Her lips were of a warm, moist red; there was laughter in her calm, liquid eyes; her whole person exuded mature fecundity. She had grown lazy: at home, she kept pausing in her work to sit staring into space, wearing a fixed, silent smile; and then everything seemed to fall asleep for a moment, her needle, the piece of cloth she was sewing, her whole being . . . She was imagining the sexton's bedroom, the bed, and Father Amaro in his shirtsleeves.

She spent her days waiting for eight o'clock, which was when Amaro would arrive with the Canon. But the evenings dragged for her now. He had recommended great reserve, and she, in an excess of obedience, exaggerated this to the point of never sitting next to him when tea was served, never even offering him a cake. She hated the presence of the old ladies, their cackling voices, the tedium of lotto; everything in the world seemed unbearable to her, except being alone with him. But what a change when she was in the sexton's house! Her contorted face, her wild breathing, her agonized cries, followed by a deathly stillness, sometimes frightened Amaro. He would raise himself up on one elbow and ask, concerned:

'Are you all right?'

And she would open startled eyes, as if she were returning from somewhere far away; and then she looked truly lovely, folding her bare arms over her naked breasts, and nodding slowly.

XVIII

An unexpected circumstance arose to spoil those mornings in the sexton's house. This was Totó's eccentric behaviour. As Father Amaro said: 'The girl's turned out to be a real monster.'

She had taken a violent dislike to Amélia. As soon as Amélia approached the bed, Totó would pull the covers up over her head and writhe about frantically if she so much as felt the touch of her hand or heard the sound of her voice. Amélia would flee, gripped by the idea that the Devil, catching a whiff of the church on her clothes, impregnated as they were with incense and sprinkled with holy water, was thrashing about inside Totó's body.

Amaro had tried to reprimand Totó with high-sounding words, tried to make her aware of her demoniacal ingratitude towards Miss Amélia, who had come to pass the time with her and to teach her to converse with Our Lord . . . But Totó had merely burst into hysterical sobs and then, suddenly, gone utterly still and rigid, her eyes rolled back and bulging, her lips flecked with foam. It gave them both a terrible fright; they frantically splashed the bed with water. As a precaution, Amaro recited the words of exorcism. But, since then, Amélia had decided 'to leave the creature in peace'. She gave up trying to teach her the alphabet or the prayers to St Anne.

Out of conscience, though, they always looked in for a moment to see her. They did not go beyond the door to the bedroom, merely asking her how she was. She never replied. Then they would immediately withdraw, terrified of those wild, shining, devouring eyes that moved from one to the other, studying their bodies with an avid curiosity that made her nostrils flare and her pale lips draw back, eyes that fixed with a metallic glitter on Amélia's clothes and Father Amaro's cassock, as if trying to guess what lay underneath. What troubled them most, however, was her obstinate, rancorous silence. Amaro, who did not much believe in demonic possession, saw symptoms of insanity in her. Amélia grew more and more frightened. It was just as well that Totó's paralysed legs kept her pinned to the mattress. Good God, if not, she might come into the room upstairs and attack them!

She told Amaro that 'after that spectacle' she did not even enjoy the morning's pleasure, and so they decided, from then on, to go up to the room without speaking to Totó.

This only made matters worse. When Totó saw Amélia walk from the street door to the stairs, she would lean out from the mattress, her hands gripping the edge, desperate to see her and follow her, her face contorted with despair at her own immobility. And as Amélia went into the room, she would hear a short laugh drift up from downstairs or a long 'Ooh!' or a chilling howl.

She was petrified now: it occurred to her that God had placed there, side by side with her love for Amaro, an implacable demon to mock and deride her. In order to reassure her, Amaro told her that Pope Pius IX had recently declared it a sin to believe in demonic possession.

'Why do they have special prayers and exorcisms then?

'That's from the old religion. Everything's going to change now. After all, science is science . . .'

She sensed that Amaro was deceiving her, and Totó was spoiling their happiness. Finally, Amaro found a way of escaping from the 'wretched girl', and that was for both of them to enter through the sacristy. They only had to cross the kitchen in order to go up the stairs, and Totó's bed was positioned in such a way that she could not see them when they cautiously tiptoed past. Besides, between eleven o'clock and midday, which was the hour chosen for their rendezvous, the sacristy was empty.

But even when they entered on tiptoe, holding their breath, their footsteps, however light, would still make the old stairs creak. Then Totó's voice would emerge from the bedroom, a hoarse, harsh voice screaming:

'There's a dog outside! There's a dog outside!'

Amaro felt a furious desire to strangle her. Amélia would turn pale and tremble.

And the creature would keep howling out:

'There go the dogs! There go the dogs!'

They took refuge in the room, bolting the door behind them. But they could not escape that baleful, desolate voice that seemed to them to come from Hell itself.

'The dogs are fighting! The dogs are fighting!'

Amélia would fall onto the bed, almost fainting with terror. She swore she would never again visit that accursed house.

'But what the devil do you want?' he would ask angrily. 'Where would we see each other? Do you want us to lie down on the benches in the sacristy?'

'But what did I do to her? What did I do?' exclaimed Amélia, clasping her hands.

'Nothing. She's mad. And poor Esguelhas is a most unfortunate man. But what do you want me to do about it?'

She did not reply. But at home, as the day for their next rendezvous approached, she would begin to tremble at the thought of that voice which thundered constantly in her ears and which she could hear even in her dreams. And that horror began slowly to awaken her from the sleep that had overtaken her whole being as soon as she had fallen into Father Amaro's arms. She asked herself questions now: Was she not committing an unpardonable sin? She was no longer consoled by Amaro's assurances that God would forgive her. When Totó howled, she saw Amaro turn pale, as if a glimpse of Hell had sent a shudder through him. And if God truly forgave them, why did he allow the Devil to hurl scorn and abuse at them through the mouth of Totó?

She would kneel down then at the foot of her bed and pray endlessly to Our Lady of Sorrows, asking Her to enlighten her, to tell her the reason behind Totó's persecution of her, asking if it was Her divine intention to send her a dreadful warning. But Our Lady did not answer. Amélia did not feel Our Lady descend from Heaven to hear her prayers as once she had, nor feel in her soul that sweet tranquillity, like a milky wave, which was a visitation from Our Lady. She would wring her hands, feeling utterly defeated and bereft of grace. She would promise then not to go back to the sexton's house, but when the day came, the idea of Amaro, of the bed, of those kisses that carried away her very soul, of the fire that filled her, she would feel too weak to resist temptation. She would get dressed, swearing that it would be the very last time, and at the stroke of eleven, she would leave, her ears burning, her heart pounding at the thought of Totó's voice, her belly aflame with desire for the man who would lay her down on the mattress.

She did not pray as she went into the church, for fear of the saints.

She would run to the sacristy to take refuge in Amaro, to find shelter in the sacred authority of his cassock. Seeing her arrive so pale and upset, he would try to calm her down by laughing it off. What nonsense! Surely she wasn't going to let the presence of a mad girl in the house spoil the gift of those mornings together. He promised her too that he would look for another place for them to meet and sometimes, just to distract her, and taking advantage of the deserted sacristy, he would show her all the different robes, chalices and vestments, try to interest her in a new antependium or some antique lace on a surplice, proving to her, by the familiarity with which he touched these relics, that he was still the parish priest and had not lost his credit in Heaven.

And so it was that, one morning, he showed her the cloak of Our Lady that had arrived only days before, a present from a rich devotee in Ourém. Amélia thought it wonderful. It was made of blue satin embroidered with stars to represent the sky, and blazing forth from its centre was an exquisitely worked golden heart surrounded by golden roses. Amaro unfolded the cloak and held it up to the window, so that the heavy embroidery caught the light.

'Beautiful, eh? It must be worth hundreds of *mil réis*. They tried it on the image yesterday. It fits perfectly. Although it is a bit long . . .' And looking at Amélia, comparing her tall figure with the rather dumpy image of Our Lady, he said: 'It would look really good on you, though. Let me see.'

She recoiled.

'Good grief, no, please, that would be a sin!'

'Nonsense,' he said, approaching with the cloak spread wide, revealing the white satin lining, white as morning mist. 'It hasn't been blessed yet. It's just as if it had come straight from the dressmaker's.'

'No, no,' she said feebly, her eyes now shining with desire.

Then he got angry. Was she saying that she knew better than he did what was and was not a sin? Was she trying to teach him how much respect was or was not due to the vestments of the saints?

'Don't be silly. Let me see . . .'

He placed it over her shoulders and fastened the engraved silver clasp over her breast. Then with a smile of devout, ardent pleasure, he stood back to admire her as she stood wrapped in the cloak, frozen and afraid.

'Oh, my love, you look so beautiful!'

Moving with solemn caution, she walked over to the mirror – an old tarnished mirror in a carved dark oak frame crowned by a cross. She looked at herself for a moment entirely wrapped in that sky-blue silk, glittering with stars of an almost celestial beauty. She felt the rich weight of it. The holiness it had acquired from contact with the image filled her with a voluptuous, pious pleasure. A fluid sweeter than air flowed about her, caressing her body with the ether of Paradise. She felt like a saint on a platform, or even higher than that, in Heaven itself . . .

Amaro said in stammering, rapturous tones:

'Oh, my love, you're even lovelier than Our Lady!'

She gave a quick glance at the mirror. Yes, she was beautiful, though not as beautiful as Our Lady . . . But with her red lips and with her brown skin lit by her dark, shining eyes, if she had been placed on the altar, with the organ playing and the murmur of mass being said around her, she would certainly have made the hearts of the faithful beat faster . . .

Amaro came up behind her, folded his arms over her chest and clasped her to him, then he leaned over and placed his lips on hers in a long, silent kiss. Amélia closed her eyes and her head lolled back, heavy with desire. Amaro's lips remained avidly pressed to hers, sucking out her soul. Her breathing quickened, her legs shook, and with a moan she fainted on Amaro's shoulder, white and overwhelmed with pleasure.

She came to at once and looked at Amaro, blinking as if summoned from some far distant place; then a wave of blood rushed to her cheeks:

'Oh, Amaro, how dreadful, how sinful!'

'Don't be silly!' he said.

But she was already taking off the cloak, in great distress.

'Take it off, take it off!' she cried as if the silk were burning her.

Then Amaro grew very serious. One really should not play with sacred things.

'But it hasn't been blessed yet, honestly,' he said.

He carefully folded up the cloak, wrapped it in a white sheet and silently replaced it in the drawer. Amélia was watching him, petrified, her pale lips moving in prayer.

When he said to her that it was time to be going to the sexton's house, she drew back, as if he were the Devil calling to her.

'No, not today!' she said imploringly.

He insisted. This really was taking piety too far. She knew it wasn't a sin when the things had not yet been blessed. She was being very narrow-minded. What the devil did it matter, it would only be half an hour, or even a quarter of an hour!

She said nothing, moving towards the door.

'So you don't want to, then?'

She turned and looked at him with supplicant eyes:

'No, not today!'

Amaro shrugged. And Amélia walked quickly back through the church, her head down, her eyes fixed on the flagstones, as if she were running a gauntlet of threatening looks from the indignant saints.

The following morning, as soon as São Joaneira, who was in the dining room, heard the Canon come panting up the stairs, she went out to meet him and closeted herself with him in the downstairs parlour.

She wanted to tell him about the worrying incident that had taken place early that morning. Amélia had woken up screaming that Our Lady was standing with her foot on her throat and was trying to suffocate her, that Totó was standing behind her, burning her, and that the flames from the fires of Hell reached higher than the towers of the Cathedral. Absolutely terrible. She had gone in to find Amélia running about the room like a mad thing. Then she had collapsed in hysteria. The whole house had been in an uproar. The poor child was in bed now and had only had a spoonful of broth all morning.

'Just nightmares,' said the Canon. 'Caused by indigestion!'

'No, Canon, that's not what it is!' exclaimed São Joaneira, who was sitting opposite him, perched on the edge of a chair, looking exhausted. 'It's something else. It's those wretched visits to the sexton's daughter!'

And then she unburdened herself with the effusiveness of one opening the floodgates of a long accumulated discontent. She had never wanted to say anything before because, after all, it was a great work of charity, but, ever since it had begun, Amélia had been a different person. She had been so moody lately. One moment, she was happy for no apparent reason, the next she looked miserable enough to make the furniture feel depressed. She would hear her pacing about until late at night and opening the windows . . . Sometimes she had felt quite afraid of the strange look in her eyes. Whenever she came back from the sexton's house, she was as white as chalk and almost faint with hunger, so much so that she always had to have a bowl of broth as soon as she arrived home. Well, people did say that Totó was possessed by the Devil. And the precentor, the one who had died (may he rest in peace) used to say that the two things in this world that women were most prone to were tuberculosis and demonic possession. She felt that she could not allow Amélia to continue visiting the sexton's house, not until she was sure that it wasn't doing any harm to her health or to her soul. What she wanted, in short, was for someone with good judgement and experience to go and examine Totó . . .

'In a word,' said the Canon, who had listened to this

somewhat tearful outpouring with his eyes closed, 'you want me to go and see Totó and find out exactly what is going on.'

'It would be such a relief if you could, my sweet!'

The Canon was touched by this endearment, which São Joaneira, given her grave matronly state, normally reserved for the intimacy of the siesta. He stroked São Joaneira's plump neck and promised kindly that he would look into the matter.

'Tomorrow, when Totó will be on her own,' said São Joaneira.

But the Canon preferred Amélia to be present. He could then see how the two of them got on, and if there was any evidence of the Evil Spirit's presence . . .

'But I'm only doing this to please you, you know . . . I've got quite enough troubles of my own without getting mixed up in the Devil's affairs.'

São Joaneira rewarded him with a resounding kiss.

'Ah, you women are such sirens!' said the Canon philosophically.

He did not like this particular assignment at all. It meant disrupting his habits, it meant ruining a whole morning; and having to exercise his judgement was bound to prove tiring; apart from that, he hated the sight of sick people or anything to do with death. However, true to his word, a few days later, on the morning that Amélia was due to visit Totó, he reluctantly dragged himself off to Carlos' pharmacy and installed himself there, with one eye on the newspaper and the other on the door, waiting for Amélia to cross the Cathedral square. His friend Carlos was not there; Senhor Augusto was filling in time seated at his desk, head on his hand, poring over the sentimental poetry of Soares de Passos; outside, the already hot late April sun was making the stones in the square glitter; no one was about; the only sound to break the silence was the hammering from the work being done on Dr Pereira's house. Amélia was late. And the Canon, having considered for a long time, with the newspaper fallen open on his knees, the enormous sacrifice he was making for São Joaneira, was just beginning to feel his eyelids droop, in the grip of that fatigue that can so easily overwhelm one in the quiet of noon, when another cleric came into the pharmacy.

'Father Ferrão, what are you doing in town?' exclaimed the Canon, roused from his exhaustion.

'Oh, just a flying visit, Canon,' said Ferrão, carefully setting down on a chair two large tomes tied together with string.

Then he turned and respectfully doffed his hat to Senhor Augusto.

Father Ferrão's hair was completely white; he must have been over sixty, but he was a robust man with bright, sparkling eyes and magnificent teeth, which his iron constitution ensured remained in good condition; his one disfigurement was his enormous nose.

He asked the Canon in a kindly way if he was there on a visit or, alas, for reasons of ill health.

'No, I'm just waiting for someone. I'm on a special mission, my friend.'

'Ah,' said Ferrão discreetly. And while he was methodically removing from a thick file of papers a prescription to give to Senhor Augusto, he told the Canon the latest parish news. The Canon's farm, Ricoça, was in Ferrão's parish of Poiais. Father Ferrão had passed the house that morning and been surprised to see that the outside was being painted. Was the Canon considering spending the summer there?

No, not at all. But since he had been having some decorating work done inside and the front was a disgrace, he had told them to give that a lick of paint too. Well, one had to keep up appearances, especially when one's house was passed each day by the heir to the Poiais estate, a braggart who imagined that his was the only decent house for ten leagues around . . . He was only doing it to annoy that atheist . . . 'A good idea, don't you think, Father?'

Father Ferrão, who was just thinking to himself how regrettable it was to find such feelings of vanity in a priest, hastily agreed, out of Christian charity and so as not to annoy his colleague:

'Of course, of course. Cleanliness is next to godliness, after all . . .'

The Canon, spotting a dress and shawl crossing the square, went to the door to see if it was Amélia. It was not. He came back, conscious once more of his immediate concerns, and when Senhor Augusto went out to the back, to the dispensary, he whispered to Ferrão:

'Yes, I'm on a very special mission indeed! I'm going to see a case of demonic possession!'

'Oh, dear,' said Ferrão, grave-faced at the thought of such a responsibility.

'Would you like to come with me? It's just near here.'

Ferrão excused himself politely. He had been to see the vicar general, then gone to visit Silvério to ask him for the two books, had then come here to sort out a prescription for one of his older parishioners, and he had to be back in Poiais at the stroke of two.

The Canon pressed him; it would only take a moment and it did seem a most curious case . . .

Ferrão then confessed to his dear colleague that he preferred not to examine such matters. He approached them with a sceptical mind, with distrust and suspicion, and was therefore far from impartial.

'But miracles do happen!' said the Canon. Despite his own doubts, he disliked the fact that Ferrão should be unconvinced about a supernatural phenomenon in which he, Canon Dias, was interested. He said rather abruptly: 'I have some experience myself, and I know that miracles happen.'

'Of course they do,' said Ferrão. 'To deny that God or the Queen of Heaven could appear to a child goes against the very doctrine of the Church. To deny that the Devil can inhabit the body of a man would be a grave error. It happened to Job, for example, and to Sara's family. Of course miracles happen. But how rare they are, Canon!'

He fell silent for a moment, watching the Canon, who was quietly taking some snuff, then he went on in a low voice, his eyes bright and intelligent:

'Have you ever noticed that it always happens to women? Miracles only ever happen to women, who are so astute even Solomon could not resist them, and whose temperament is so highly-strung and so contradictory that not even doctors can understand them. Have you ever heard of Our Lady appearing to a respectable notary public? Have you ever heard of a worthy judge being possessed by the Evil Spirit? No. That gives me pause for thought, and I conclude that it's just malice, illusion, imagination, sickness, etc. Don't you think so? My rule in these cases is to treat them as lightly and with as much indifference as I can muster.'

But the Canon, who was watching the door, suddenly brandished his parasol and called out:

'Hey! Hey there!'

It was Amélia. She stopped at once, annoyed by an encounter that would only delay her further. Father Amaro must already be getting worried.

'So,' said the Canon, standing at the door opening his parasol, 'as soon as you smell a miracle . . .'

'I immediately suspect a scandal.'

The Canon looked at him for a moment with new respect.

'You, Ferrão, could outdo Solomon himself in prudence!'

'Please, Canon!' cried Ferrão offended by that injustice done to Solomon's incomparable wisdom.

'Yes, Solomon himself!' said the Canon from the street.

He had concocted a clever story to justify his visit to Totó, but during his conversation with Ferrão it had completely slipped his mind, as did everything that he left for a moment in the reserves of his memory; and so he simply said to Amélia:

'Come along then, I want to see this Totó girl as well.'

Amélia froze. Father Amaro would already be there. But her protectress, Our Lady of Sorrows, to whom she immediately turned in that moment of affliction, did not desert her. And the Canon, who was walking beside her, was surprised to hear her say with a smile:

'Well, this is obviously Totó's day for visitors. Father Amaro told me that he might visit today too. Indeed, he may already be there.'

'Ah, our friend Amaro too! Good, very good. We'll have a consultation with Totó.'

Pleased by her own guile, Amélia chattered on about Totó. The Canon would see for himself . . . She was utterly incomprehensible . . . She hadn't wanted to say anything at home, but lately Totó had taken against her. And she said odd things, talked about dogs and animals; it quite made her shudder. It was a task that was beginning to weigh on her. The girl didn't listen to the lessons or the prayers or any advice. She was little better than a wild beast.

'What a terrible smell!' grumbled the Canon as they went in.

What did he expect? The girl was a pig and it was impossible to clean her up. Her father was a sloven too.

'It's through here, Canon,' she said, opening the door to the bedroom, which, in obedience to Father Amaro's orders, Esguelhas always left shut.

They found Totó propped up in bed, her face ablaze with curiosity at the Canon's unfamiliar voice.

'How are you, Senhora Totó?' he said from the door, without actually going in.

'Go on, say hello to the Canon,' said Amélia, immediately beginning, with unaccustomed kindness, to straighten the bedclothes and tidy the room. 'Tell him how you are . . . Now don't sulk!'

But as Totó scrutinised that fat, grizzled priest, so different from the parish priest, she remained as silent as the image of St Bento that stood above her bed. And her eyes, which grew brighter each day as her face grew gaunter, glanced, as they always did, from the man to Amélia, eager to understand why she had brought him there, that fat old man, and wondering if Amélia would go upstairs with him too.

Amélia was trembling now. What if Father Amaro came in, and, right there, in front of the Canon, Totó burst out into her frenzied shouting and started calling them 'dogs' again? On the pretext of putting something away, she went to the kitchen to watch the courtyard. She would signal to Father Amaro from the window, as soon as he appeared.

And the Canon, alone in Totó's bedroom, preparing to make his observations, was about to ask her how many people formed the Holy Trinity, when she leaned forward and said in a voice as subtle as a sigh:

'Where's the other one?'

The Canon did not understand. Speak up! What was she trying to say?

'The other man who comes with her.'

The Canon drew nearer, ears straining with curiosity.

'Which other man?'

'The handsome one. The one who goes upstairs with her to the room. The one who pinches her . . .'

But Amélia came back into the room at that point, and Totó immediately fell silent and lay absolutely still, her eyes closed, breathing easily as if she had received sudden relief from her suffering. The Canon, immobilised by shock, had remained where he was, bent over the bed in order to hear what Totó was saying. He finally straightened up, huffing and puffing as if it were a hot day in August, took a large pinch of snuff and stood there with the box open in his hand, his bloodshot eyes fixed on Totó's bed.

'So, Canon, what do you think of my patient?' asked Amélia.

Without looking at her, he said:

'Hm, fine. Yes, she's seems fine. Odd, though . . . Anyway, I'd better be going. Goodbye.'

He left, muttering something about having things to do, and went straight back to the pharmacy.

'Give me a glass of water!' he exclaimed, collapsing on a chair.

Carlos, who had returned, bustled over with some orange-flower water, asking if the Canon was unwell.

'No, just worn out,' he said.

He picked up the newspaper from the table and sat there, motionless, absorbed in his reading. Carlos tried to discuss the politics of the day, events in Spain, the danger of revolution threatening Society, the deficiencies of the municipal council of which he was now a fierce adversary . . . All in vain. The Canon merely grunted a few gloomy monosyllables. In the end, Carlos withdrew in shocked silence, and with an inner disdain that traced sarcastic lines around his mouth, he compared the glum obtuseness of that priest with the inspired words of a Lacordaire or a Malhão. That was why in Leiria, as in all of Portugal, materialism was raising its Hydra head.

The tower clock was striking one when the Canon, who was keeping a weather eye open on the square, saw Amélia walk past; he threw down the paper, left the pharmacy without a word and strode off to Esguelhas' house as swiftly as his large body would allow. Totó shook with fear to see that bulbous figure reappear at her bedroom door. But the Canon smiled and called her Totozinha and promised her some money to buy cakes with; and he even sat down with a delighted 'Ah!' at the foot of her bed, saying:

'Now we're going to have a talk, my little friend. This is your bad leg, isn't it? Poor thing. You'll get better one day. I'll pray to God . . . You leave it to me.'

She turned first white and then red, glancing anxiously from side to side, embarrassed to be alone with this man, who was sitting so close she could smell his sour breath.

'Now, listen,' he said, leaning towards her, making the bed creak beneath his weight. 'Who is this other man? Who is it who comes here with Amélia?'

She replied immediately, in one breath:

'He's the handsome one, the thin one, they go upstairs, shut themselves in, they're like dogs.'

The Canon's eyes bulged.

'But who is he? What's his name? What did your father tell you?'

'He's the other one, the parish priest, Amaro,' she said impatiently.

'And they go up to the room, do they? And what do you hear? Tell me everything, little one!'

Totó told him, with a fury that lent sibilant tones to her hoarse voice, how they came into the house, looked in to see her, and how they would rub against each other and then rush off to the room upstairs, where they would spend an hour shut up together.

But the Canon, whose dull eyes flickered with lubricious curiosity, wanted to know all the awful details.

'And what do you hear, Totozinha? Can you hear the bed creak?'

She nodded, very pale now, her teeth clenched.

'And have you seen them kissing and embracing? Go on, tell me, I'll give you some money.'

She kept her mouth shut, and to the Canon her contorted face looked almost savage.

'You don't like her, do you?'

She shook her head fiercely.

'And you say you've seen them pinching each other?'

'They're like dogs!' she said through gritted teeth.

The Canon sat up, again blew out his breath and scratched his head vigorously.

'Right,' he said, getting up. 'Goodbye, then, little one. Wrap up warm. You don't want to catch cold.'

He left and as he slammed the door, he said out loud:

'This is the villainy to beat all villainies! I'll kill him! I'll murder him!'

He stood for a moment lost in thought, then bustled off to Rua das Sousas, parasol at the ready, his face apoplectic with rage. In the Cathedral square, however, he paused to think a while, and turning on his heel, he went into the church. He was so enraged that, forgetting the habit of forty years, he forgot to genuflect to the Sacrament. He headed straight for the sacristy, just as Father Amaro was coming out, carefully drawing on the black leather gloves which he always wore now to please Amélia.

He was shocked by the Canon's agitated state.

'What's wrong, Master?'

'What's wrong?' exclaimed the Canon. 'You villain! It's your depraved behaviour that's wrong!'

And he said nothing more, overcome by anger.

Amaro had turned very pale.

'Wh-what are you saying, Master?'

The Canon drew breath:

'Don't you "Master" me! You have ruined the girl! These are the actions of an utter scoundrel.'

Father Amaro frowned, as if he had failed to understand a joke.

'What girl? You're having me on . . .'

He even smiled, affecting confidence, but his white lips trembled.

'I saw you, man!' bawled the Canon.

Then Amaro drew back, suddenly terrified:

'You saw me?'

It flashed upon his mind that he had somehow been betrayed and the Canon had perhaps been hidden in some corner of Esguelhas' house.

'I didn't actually see anything, but I might as well have,' said the Canon in ominous tones. 'I know everything. I've just come from there. Totó told me. You spend hours and hours shut up in that bedroom. She can even hear the bed creaking from downstairs. It's disgusting!'

Finding himself caught, Amaro, like some pursued and cornered animal, made one last desperate effort at resistance.

'And what has it got to do with you?'

The Canon started.

'What has it got to do with me? How can you talk to me like that? I'll tell you what it's got to do with me, I'm going straight to the vicar general and report the whole matter to him.'

Father Amaro, deathly pale, went over to him, fists clenched:

'You scoundrel!'

'Steady on, now, steady on!' exclaimed the Canon, brandishing his parasol. 'You're not going to hit me, are you?'

Father Amaro took a step back; he closed his eyes and drew one hand across his forehead, which was beaded with sweat; then, after a moment, and speaking with apparent calm, he said:

'Look here, Canon. I saw you once in bed with São Joaneira.'

'You're lying!' bellowed the Canon.

'I did, I did!' said Amaro fiercely. 'When I came back one evening . . . You were in your shirtsleeves, and she had just got up and was fastening her stays. You even called out: "Who's there?" I saw you as clearly as I can see you now. You say one word, and I'll tell everyone that São Joaneira has been your mistress for the last ten years, right under the noses of the whole clergy. What do you say now?'

The Canon's fury had long since waned and, at those words, he stood stock still like a bewildered ox. After a while, he managed to say in a faint voice:

'What a rogue you've turned out to be!'

Father Amaro, almost calm now, and assured of the Canon's silence, said cheerily:

'What do you mean "a rogue"? Why? We've both blotted our copybooks, that's all. And I didn't go snooping around or try to bribe Totó . . . I just happened to come home at the wrong time. And don't talk to me about morality – don't make me laugh. Morality is for school and for sermons. This is what I choose to do, you do something else, and the others do what they can. You're getting on a bit now and so you grab yourself an old lady; I'm still young and so I choose Amélia. It's a sad state of affairs, but that's the way things are. It's Nature! We're men. And as priests, and out of respect for our class, what we have to do is to back each other up.'

The Canon was listening, nodding in dumb acceptance of these truths. He had slumped down in a chair, resting from all that pointless rage; then, looking up at Amaro, he said:

'But you're only at the beginning of your career!'

'And you're at the end of yours!'

They both laughed and immediately withdrew the offensive words they had said one to the other and gravely shook each other's hand. Then they talked.

What enraged the Canon was that he should have chosen Amélia. If it had been some other girl, he would have been almost pleased for him, but Amélia! If her poor mother found out, she would die of grief.

'But there's no reason why her mother should find out,' said Amaro. 'This is between you and me, Father. This is a secret between you and me. Her mother must know nothing, and I won't say a word to Amélia about what has passed between us today. Things will remain as they were, and the world will continue to turn. But remember, Master, not a word to São Joaneira. No treachery now.'

The Canon, with his hand on his breast, gravely gave his word of honour as a gentleman and a priest that the secret would remain forever buried in his heart.

Then they affectionately shook hands again.

The tower clock struck three. It was nearly time for the Canon's high tea.

As they left, he clapped Amaro on the back and gave him a knowing look:

'You clever young rascal!'

'Well, what do you expect? It all just started as a bit of fun . . .'

'Young man,' said the Canon sententiously, 'these are precisely the things that count in life.'

'You're quite right, Master, they are.'

From that day on, Amaro enjoyed almost complete tranquillity of soul. Up until then, he had occasionally been troubled by the thought that this was cruel repayment for all the trust and kindness that had been lavished on him in Rua da Misericórdia. But the Canon's tacit approval had, as he put it, removed that thorn from his conscience. After all, the Canon was the head of the household, a respectable gentleman, the boss. São Joaneira was merely his mistress. And Amaro even sometimes jokingly addressed Dias as 'his dear father-in-law'.

Something else happened to cheer him up. Totó suddenly fell ill; the day after the Canon's visit she had started vomiting blood; Dr Cardoso was called in and spoke of galloping consumption, a matter of weeks, a hopeless case . . .

'The sort of thing, my friend,' he had said, 'which is over in a trice,' and he had made a whistling noise with his lips. This was his way of depicting death, which, when in a hurry, concludes its work with a swift scything movement.

The mornings spent at Esguelhas' house were peaceful now. Amélia and Amaro no longer tiptoed in, trying to slink by to their pleasures upstairs, unnoticed by Totó. They slammed the doors and talked loudly, knowing that Totó was downstairs prostrated by fever, in sheets wet from her constant sweating. Amélia still guiltily said a Hail Mary every night for Totó to get better. And sometimes, when she was undressing upstairs in the sexton's bedroom, she would stop suddenly and pull a sad face.

'Oh, my love, it does seem wrong for us to be up here enjoying ourselves while the poor creature is down there battling with death.'

Amaro would shrug. What could they do about it if it was the will of God?

And Amélia, resigning herself entirely to God's will, would step out of her petticoats.

She was now often subject to such bouts of sentiment, which annoyed Father Amaro. She often seemed cast down; she always had some awful dream to tell him about, one that had tormented her all night, and in which she saw warnings of impending doom.

Sometimes she would say to him:

'If I were to die, would you be very sad?'

Amaro would get angry. It was ridiculous! They only had one hour to spend together, so why spoil it with gloomy thoughts?

'You don't know what it's like,' she would say, 'my heart is as black as the night.'

Her mother's friends had noticed the change in her. Sometimes, she would not say a word all evening, bent over her sewing, desultorily plying her needle; or else, too tired to sew, she would sit by the table twirling the green shade on the oil lamp, her eyes vacant, her soul far away.

'Leave that lampshade alone!' the ladies would say to her irritably.

She would smile, give a weary sigh and slowly take up the white petticoat she had been hemming for weeks now. Her mother, seeing how pale she always was, thought of calling in Dr Gouveia.

'It's nothing, Mama, just my nerves, it will pass.'

Proof to everyone that her nerves were on edge was the

way in which the slightest thing made her jump; she would even scream out, almost faint, if a door suddenly banged. On some nights, she would ask her mother to sleep in her room, for fear of nightmares and visions.

'It's just as Dr Gouveia always said,' São Joaneira remarked to the Canon, 'she's one of those girls who needs to get married.'

The Canon cleared his throat.

'She's got everything she needs,' he muttered. 'Absolutely everything. More than enough it would seem.'

The Canon believed that the girl was (as he put it to himself) 'brimming with happiness'. On the days when he knew she had visited Totó, he would look at her all the time, peering at her from the depths of his armchair with his lewd, heavy-lidded eyes. He showered her with displays of paternal affection. Whenever he met her on the stairs, he would always stop her and tickle her or pat her cheek. He repeatedly asked her over to his house in the mornings, and while Amélia was chatting to Dona Josefa, he would shuffle around her in his slippers like an old cockerel. Amélia and her mother talked endlessly about the Canon's sudden friendly interest in her, convinced that he would leave her a good dowry.

When the Canon was alone with Amaro, he would roll his eyes and say: 'You lucky devil. She's a dish fit for a king that one!'

Amaro would reply arrogantly:

'And a very tasty one, Master, very tasty indeed!'

That was one of Amaro's great pleasures – to hear his colleagues praise Amélia, who was known amongst the clergy as 'the flower of the devotees'. Everyone envied him his confessant. He always insisted that she dress up in her best clothes for mass on Sunday; he had even got annoyed with her lately because she always wore the same dark woollen dress which made her look like an old penitent.

Amélia, however, no longer felt a lover's need to please Amaro in everything. She had awoken almost completely from that foolish sleep into which Amaro's first embrace had thrown her. She was becoming painfully aware of her guilt. A dawn of reason was breaking over the darkness of that devout, slavish spirit. What was she after all? The parish priest's mistress. And that idea, put bluntly, was terrible to her. Not that she regretted the loss of her virginity, her honour or her good name. She would sacrifice far more than that for him and for the delirious pleasures he gave her. But there was something more frightening than the disapproval of the world, and that was the vengeance of the Lord. What she quietly wept for was the possible loss of Paradise or, worse still, some punishment from God, not a transcendent punishment that would torture her soul beyond the grave, but some torment in life that would afflict her health, her well-being, her body. She had a vague fear of illness, leprosy, paralysis, poverty or hunger or any of the other penalties in which she believed the God of the catechism to be prodigal. When she was a little girl and forgot to pay the Virgin her regular tribute of Hail Marys, she would be afraid that the Virgin would make her fall down the stairs or get slapped by the teacher; now she went cold with fear at the idea that God, to punish her for going to bed with a priest, would send her some disease that would disfigure her or reduce her to begging for alms in the alleyways. She had been unable to rid herself of these ideas ever since the day in the sacristy when she had committed the sin of lust while wearing Our Lady's cloak. She was sure that the Holy Virgin hated her and ceaselessly complained about her; in vain did she try to win her round with an endless flow of humble prayers; she could sense that Our Lady, inaccessible and disdainful, had turned her back on her. That divine face had never again smiled on her; those hands had never again opened gratefully to receive her prayers as if they were congratulatory bouquets. There was only a cutting silence, the icy hostility of a divinity offended. She knew how powerful Our Lady's influence was in the councils of Heaven; she had been taught this as a child; everything she wants she gets, as a recompense for the tears she shed on Calvary; her Son sits smiling on her right hand side, God the Father speaks into her left ear. And Amélia understood that there was no hope for her, and that some terrible thing was being prepared for her up above, in Paradise, that would one day fall upon her body and upon her soul, crushing her in its calamitous collapse. What would it be?

She would have ended her relationship with Amaro if she dared, but she feared his wrath almost as much as God's. What would become of her if she had both Our Lady and the parish priest against her? Besides, she loved him. In his arms, all terror of Heaven, even the idea of Heaven, vanished; safe in his arms, she felt no fear of divine anger; like a strong wine, desire and the fury of the flesh filled her with fierce courage; it was like a brutal challenge to Heaven coiling furiously about her body. The terror came later, when she was alone in her room. It was that struggle that drained the colour from her face, traced hard lines at the corners of her dry, parched lips, and gave her the faded air of weariness that so irritated Father Amaro.

'What's wrong with you? It's as if someone had squeezed all the juice out of you,' Father Amaro would say when she lay cold and inert beneath his first kisses.

'I didn't sleep well. It's my nerves.'

'Damn your nerves!' Amaro would grumble impatiently.

Then she would ask him strange questions that would drive him to despair, the same questions every day. Had he said mass that morning with real fervour? Had he read his breviary? Had he said his prayers?

'Stop it!' he would say angrily. 'Damnation! Anyone would think I was still a seminarian and you were the examining father, making sure I had kept the Rule. Don't be so ridiculous!'

'It's important to be at peace with God,' she would murmur.

She was genuinely concerned now that Amaro should be 'a good priest'. In order to be saved and to be exempted from Our Lady's wrath, she was relying now on Amaro's influence at the court of God, and she feared that if he neglected his devotions, he would ruin her, and that any diminishment of his fervour would diminish her in the eyes of the Lord. She wanted him to remain a holy favourite in Heaven, in order to reap the benefits of his mystical protection.

Amaro referred to this as 'the obsessions of an old nun'. He hated it because he thought it frivolous and because it took up precious time during those mornings at the sexton's house.

'Look, we haven't come here to be miserable,' he would say sharply. 'Close the door, will you.'

She would obey and then, when he kissed her in the darkness of the closed room, he would at last recognise his Amélia, the Amélia of their first encounters, the delicious body that trembled passionately in his arms.

He desired her more each day with a continuous, tyrannical desire which those few hours could not satisfy. There really was no other woman like her. He was sure that not even in Lisbon, not even amongst the nobility, was there another woman like her. She had her moments of silliness, it was true, but they weren't to be taken seriously, it was a matter of enjoying things while he was young.

Oh, and he did enjoy himself. His life was furnished on every side with sweet comforts, as if it were a room of cushioned walls, where there were no sharp corners to the furniture, where the body found only pillowy softnesses wherever it alighted.

The mornings spent in Esguelhas' house were, of course, the best part, but there were other pleasures too. He ate well; he smoked good cigarettes and used a cigarette-holder; his underwear was all new and all made of linen; he had bought some furniture; and he no longer had to worry about money because Dona Maria da Assunção, his best confessant, was always ready to open her purse. And recently, he had had a piece of luck: one night at the house of São Joaneira, the excellent Dona Maria had expressed the view, regarding an English family whom she had seen pass by in a char-à-banc en route to Batalha, that the English were all heretics.

'They are baptised just as we are,' remarked Dona Joaquina Gansoso.

'Yes, my dear, but it's a laughable affair really, it's not like *our* baptism, and doesn't really count.'

The Canon, who enjoyed tormenting her, said gravely that Dona Maria had just uttered a blasphemy. It was determined in Canon 4, Session 7 of the Holy Council of Trent that 'anyone who declared that the baptism given to heretics, in the name of the Father, the Son and the Holy Ghost, was not a true baptism would be excommunicated'. According to the Holy Council, Dona Maria was thenceforth excommunicated!

The excellent lady had an attack of hysterics. The following day she threw herself at the feet of Father Amaro, who, as a penance for the offence committed under Canon 4, Session 7 of the Holy Council of Trent, ordered her to pay for three hundred masses for the benefit of the souls in Purgatory, for which Dona Maria paid five *tostões* each.

He was thus sometimes able to enter the sexton's house with an air of mysterious satisfaction and with a small package in his hand. It would be some present for Amélia, a silk handkerchief, a coloured scarf, a pair of gloves. She would go into raptures over these proofs of Amaro's affection for her, and while the darkened room filled with the delirium of love, below them, tuberculosis was busily wielding its scythe above Totó.

XIX

'Is the Canon in? I need to talk to him urgently.'

The maid showed Father Amaro into the office and ran upstairs to tell Dona Josefa that the parish priest had come to see the Canon and that he looked so upset that something terrible must surely have happened.

Amaro flung open the door of the office, then slamming it shut again without even a 'Good morning', exclaimed:

'The girl's pregnant!'

The Canon, who had been at his desk writing, fell back in his chair, shocked rigid.

'What?'

'She's pregnant!'

And in the ensuing silence the floorboards creaked beneath the priest's furious pacings between window and bookshelf.

'Are you absolutely sure?' the Canon asked, horrified.

'Absolutely. She's been worrying about it for days. She's done nothing but cry. But there's no doubt now. Women know these things, they don't make mistakes. All the signs are there. What should I do, Father?'

'What a dreadful nuisance!' muttered the Canon, stunned.

'Can you imagine the scandal? Her mother, the whole neighbourhood . . . And what if they suspect me? I'm ruined. I just don't want to know. I'll run away!'

The Canon was dazedly scratching his head, his mouth hanging open. He could already imagine the screams in the house on the night of the birth, São Joaneira ever after bathed in tears, his tranquil life dead and buried . . .

'Say something!' yelled Amaro desperately. 'What do you think? Try and come up with something. I'm just too stunned to think, I don't know, I'm lost.'

'These are the consequences of your actions, my dear colleague.'

'Oh, go to Hell! This is nothing to do with morality. It was stupid of me, fine, but it's done now.'

'What do you want, then?' asked the Canon. 'You don't want someone to give the girl some drug to finish her off, do you?'

Amaro shrugged, impatient with such a ridiculous idea. The Canon was obviously raving . . .

'Well, what do you want?' asked the Canon again in a cavernous voice, dragging the words up from the depths of his chest.

'What do I want? I want there to be no scandal. What else would I want?'

'How many months gone is she?'

'How many? Well, just over a month . . .'

'Then we should marry her off!' Canon Dias declared. 'We must marry her off to the clerk!'

Father Amaro started in admiration and surprise.

'Devil take it, you're right! That's a masterly idea!'

The Canon agreed, nodding gravely, that it was indeed a masterly idea.

'Marry her off now, while there's still time. *Pater est quem nuptiae demonstrant* . . . Whoever is the husband is the father.'

The door opened at this point and Dona Josefa's blue-tinted spectacles and black bonnet appeared. Gripped by a real frenzy of curiosity, she had been unable to wait any longer upstairs in the kitchen; she had tiptoed downstairs and pressed her ear to the keyhole of the office door; but the thick baize portière had been drawn inside, and the rumble of firewood being unloaded in the street had further muffled the voices of Amaro and the Canon. The good lady had decided then to go in and say 'Good morning' to the parish priest.

But from behind the smoked lenses, her beady eyes scoured in vain her brother's fat, inscrutable face and Amaro's pale countenance. The two priests were as impenetrable as two shuttered windows. Amaro even spoke lightly of the precentor's rheumatism, of the rumours going round about the secretary-general's marriage . . . Then, after a pause, he got up, saying that he was having an excellent pork stew for supper that night – and much to Dona Josefa's chagrin, he rushed off, calling back to the Canon from behind the curtain:

'I'll see you tonight at São Joaneira's house, Master.'

'Yes, see you there!'

And the Canon continued writing earnestly. Dona Josefa could contain herself no longer and, having shuffled around her brother's desk in her slippers for a moment, she asked:

'Any news?'

'Oh, yes!' he said, shaking his quill. 'Dom João VI is dead!'

'Insolent creature!' she bellowed, turning on her heels, cruelly pursued by her brother's mocking laughter.

That night, in São Joaneira's downstairs parlour, while upstairs, Amélia, with death in her soul, was hammering out 'The Waltz of Two Worlds', the two priests, cigarettes clenched between their teeth, sat hatching their plan in whispers, huddled on the sofa beneath the gloomy painting in which the vague hand of the anchorite hung poised like a claw above the skull: first, they had to find João Eduardo, who had disappeared from Leiria; Dionísia, who had a nose for these things, was searching every corner of the town in order to find the hole in which the beast was hiding; then, because time was pressing, Amélia would write to him . . . Just a few simple words: that she knew he had been the victim of an intrigue; that she had never ceased being his friend; that she owed him an apology; that he should come and see her . . . If the lad hesitated, which was unlikely (the Canon was quite sure of this), they could dangle before him the prospect of a job at the district government office, easy enough to obtain through Godinho, who was entirely ruled by his wife, who was, in turn, enslaved to Father Silvério . . .

'But what about Natário?' said Amaro. 'Natário hates the clerk. What will he have to say about this revolution?'

'Ah!' cried the Canon, slapping his thigh, 'I forgot to tell you! Haven't you heard what happened to poor Natário?'

Amaro had not.

'He's broken his leg! He fell off his horse!'

'When?'

'This morning. I only found out about it this evening. I was always telling him that animal would do for him one day. And it has, and done a proper job of it too. He'll be out of circulation for a long time. I'd completely forgotten about it. The ladies upstairs don't know anything about it either!'

There was great sadness when they found out upstairs. Amélia closed the piano lid. They all thought of various remedies they could send him, there was a positive cackle of offerings: ligatures, threads, an unguent made by the nuns in Alcobaça, half a bottle of liqueur made by a group of anchorites who live near Córdoba . . . It was important too to ensure Heaven's intervention, and each lady volunteered to use her influence with her particular saints: Dona Maria da Assunção promised to pray to St Eleutherius, whom she had been trying out recently; Dona Josefa Dias undertook to interest Our Lady of the Visitation; Dona Joaquina Gansos swore by St Joachim . . .

'And what about you, Amélia?' asked the Canon.

'Me?'

And she turned pale, suddenly overwhelmed by all the sadness in her soul, thinking that she, with her sins and her passions, had lost the valuable friendship of Our Lady of Sorrows. And being unable to add her influence in Heaven in order to mend Natário's leg was a cause of great sorrow to her, perhaps the worst punishment she had experienced since she had first begun to love Father Amaro.

It was a few days later, in the sexton's house, that Amaro shared the Canon's plan with Amélia. He prepared her first, telling her that the Canon knew everything . . .

'It's all under the seal of the confessional,' he added to comfort her. 'Besides, he and your mother have their own guilty secrets. It's all in the family.'

Then he took her hand and, looking at her tenderly, as if pitying her already for the bitter tears she would weep, he said:

'Now listen, my love. Don't get too upset about what I am about to say to you, because it's necessary for our salvation . . .'

At the first mention of marriage to the clerk, however, Amélia protested loudly:

'Never, I would rather die.'

He had got her into that state and now he just wanted to pass her on to someone else! Was she just a rag that one uses and then throws to a pauper? Having driven the man from her house, was she then supposed to humiliate herself, write to him and fall into his arms? No! She had her pride too! Slaves were exchanged and sold, but that was in Brazil!

She grew tearful then. He didn't love her any more, he was tired of her. Oh, she was a poor, poor wretch! She flung herself face down on the bed and broke into strident sobs.

'Be quiet, woman, they can hear you out in the street!' said Amaro desperately, shaking her by the arm.

'I don't care! Let them hear! I'll go into the street and shout out that I'm in this state thanks to Father Amaro who now wants to leave me!'

Amaro went white with rage and felt a furious desire to hit her. He controlled himself, however, and with a tremulous voice that belied his apparent serenity:

'You're not yourself, my love. Anyway, how can I marry you? I can't. So what do you want me to do? If people see that you're pregnant, if you have the child at home, you can imagine the scandal! You'll be ruined for ever. And what will happen to me? I'll be ruined too, suspended, perhaps put on trial. How do you expect me to live? Do you want me to die of hunger?'

He himself was moved to tears by the idea of the privations and miseries suffered by the interdicted priest. She was the one who did not love him; he had been so affectionate and kind to her, and now she wanted to repay him with scandal and disgrace . . .

'No, no!' cried Amélia, sobbing and throwing her arms around his neck.

And they remained locked in an embrace, trembling with the same emotion – she making his shoulder moist with her tears, he biting his lip, his eyes shining and wet.

At last, he slowly pulled away and, drying his tears, said:

'No, my dear, this is a great misfortune for us, but it has to be. If you will suffer, imagine how I will suffer too. Seeing you married and living with another man . . . Let's not even talk about it. It's fate, it's God's ordinance.'

She sat, utterly overcome, on the edge of the bed, still shaken by great sobs. The punishment had arrived, Our Lady's revenge, which she had felt building in the depths of Heaven for some time, like a complicated storm. There it was now, worse than all the fires of Purgatory. She had to leave Amaro whom she imagined she loved even more now, and had to go and live with that other man, with the excommunicate. How could she ever again enter into God's grace once she had slept and lived with a man whom canon law, the Pope and the whole of Earth and Heaven considered to be damned. And he would be her husband, possibly the father of other children. Ah, Our Lady was taking vengeance too far.

'But how can I marry him, Amaro, if the man has been excommunicated?'

Amaro then hastened to reassure her, coming up with all kinds of arguments. They must not exaggerate. The lad hadn't really be excommunicated . . . Natário and the Canon had misinterpreted church law and the papal bulls . . . According to certain authors, striking a priest when he was not in his vestments was not *ipso facto* a reason for excommunication . . . He himself shared that view . . . . Eventually the excommunication could be lifted.

'You understand, don't you? As the Holy Council of Trent says, and as you know yourself, "we tie and we untie". The lad was excommunicated . . . but we can lift the excommunication order. He will be as clean as he was before. Don't you worry about that.'

'But what will we live on if he's lost his job?'

'You didn't let me finish. A job will be found for him. The Canon will find him a job. It's all been arranged, my dear.'

She said nothing, exhausted and deeply sad, two tears running down her cheeks.

'Your mother doesn't suspect anything, does she?'

'No, not yet,' she said with a great sigh.

They sat in silence: she wiping away her tears, trying to calm herself before going out into the street again; he, head down, gloomily pacing the floor, thinking of the happy mornings they used to enjoy there, when there were only kisses and smothered laughter; everything had changed now, even the weather had turned cloudy, a late summer day, threatening rain.

'Is it obvious I've been crying?' she asked, smoothing her hair at the mirror.

'No. Are you leaving?'

'Yes, Mama's expecting me.'

They exchanged a sad kiss, and she left.

Meanwhile, Dionísia was sniffing about the town on João Eduardo's trail. She had intensified her search as soon as she found out that the rich Canon Dias was also involved. And every day at dusk, she would slip through Father Amaro's front door to give him the latest news: she knew that the clerk had gone first to Alcobaça to stay with a cousin who was a pharmacist, and then on to Lisbon; there, with a letter of recommendation from Dr Gouveia, he had found work in a procurator's office; however, only days later, as ill luck would have it, the procurator had died of apoplexy; since then, João Eduardo had vanished into the confusion and chaos of the capital. There was one person who should know his whereabouts, and that was the typographer, Gustavo. Unfortunately, Gustavo had had a quarrel with Agostinho, had left *The District Voice* and he too had disappeared. No one knew where he had gone, and, alas, his mother could not help either because she had died.

'Oh, no!' said the Canon, when Father Amaro brought him these snippets of information. 'This seems to be a tale in which everyone dies. A veritable hecatomb!'

'You may laugh, Father, but it's serious. Looking for a man in Lisbon is like looking for a needle in a haystack. It's hopeless.'

Then, growing increasingly anxious as the days passed, he wrote to his aunt, asking her to scour Lisbon for a certain João Eduardo Barbosa. He received a scrawled three-page letter in which she complained about her Joãozinho, who had made her life a hell, getting so drunk on gin that he had frightened away all her lodgers. She was slightly less worried now, though, because a few days ago, poor Joãozinho had sworn on his mother's life to drink nothing thenceforth but lemonade. As for that João Eduardo fellow, she had asked in the neighbourhood and asked Senhor Palma of the Ministry of Public Works, who knew everyone, but had gleaned nothing. There was a Joaquim Eduardo who owned a shop locally selling knicknacks and if he was the man he was looking for, he was on to a good thing, because he was a very decent fellow . . .

'Pure gossip!' said the Canon impatiently.

He then resolved to write a letter himself. And urged on by Father Amaro (who was constantly emphasising to the Canon how he and São Joaneira would suffer if the scandal broke), the Canon eventually authorised his friend in Lisbon to pay out the necessary money to employ the police. The response was some time in coming, but when it did, it was both promising and magnificent. The wily policeman Mendes had found João Eduardo! Except that he did not know his address yet, having only seen him in a café; but in two or three days' time Mendes promised to have more precise information.

Imagine then the despair of the two priests when, a few days later, the Canon's friend wrote to say that the man whom the wily Mendes had taken for João Eduardo in a café in central Lisbon, basing himself on an incomplete description, was, in fact, a young man from Santo Tirso who was in town to apply for a job as a civil servant . . . The expenses so far amounted to three *libras* and seventeen *tostões*.

'Seventeen *tostões*, damn it!' roared Canon Dias, turning furiously to Amaro. 'You were the one who had all the pleasure and fun, and here I am ruining my health with all these toings-and-froings, not to mention spending money like water!'

Amaro, who was entirely dependent on the Canon, bowed before these insults.

But all was not lost, thank God. Dionísia was on the trail!

Amélia received all this news disconsolately. After her initial tears, the inevitability of the solution had imposed itself on her. What else could she do? Given her regrettably slender waist and hips, in two or three months' time she would be unable to conceal her state. And what would she do then? Run away from home, go to Lisbon like Mr Stork's daughter, to get beaten up by English sailors in the Bairro Alto, or, like Joaninha Gomes, who had been Father Abílio's mistress, to have rats thrown in her face by soldiers. No. She would have to marry . . .

Then she would give birth after only seven months (it happened often enough!), legitimised by the sacrament, by the law and by Our Lord God . . . And her child would have a father, would receive an education and would not be an orphan . . .

Ever since Father Amaro had sworn to her that the clerk was not really excommunicated and that a few prayers would suffice to remove that excommunication, her devout scruples had faded like dying embers. After all, the only motivating forces behind the clerk's errors were jealousy and love: it was as a scorned lover that he had written the article in *The District Voice* and in a fury of betrayed passion that he had struck Father Amaro. She could never forgive him for that brutal act, but how he had been punished! With no job, no home, no wife, and so lost in the anonymous misery of Lisbon that not even the police could find him! And all for her sake. Poor boy! And after all, he wasn't bad-looking . . . People talked about his lack of piety, but he had always seemed attentive at mass and, every night, he used to say a special prayer to St John that she had presented to him on an embroidered card.

With his job in the district government, they could afford a little house and a maid. Why shouldn't she be happy at last? He wasn't a man to go to taverns, nor was he idle. She was sure that she would prevail and impose on him her tastes and devotions. And it would be pleasant to go to mass on Sunday in her best clothes, with her husband by her side, greeted by everyone, and to be able to go out walking with her baby resplendent in lace bonnet and fringed shawl. Who knows, perhaps the affection she lavished on her little one and the comfort with which she surrounded her husband would serve to make Heaven and Our Lady soften towards her! Ah, she would do anything to achieve that, to have again that friend in Heaven, her beloved Virgin, friend and confidante, always ready to ease her pain, to deliver her from misfortune, busily preparing for her a bright and cosy corner in Paradise.

She spent hours over her sewing thinking such thoughts, even on her way to the sexton's house; there, having spent a moment with Totó, who was very quiet now, worn down by the slow fever, she would go up to the sexton's bedroom where her first question to Amaro was always:

'Any news?'

He would frown and mumble:

'Dionísia's still looking . . . Why, are you in a hurry?'

'Of course I'm in a hurry,' she would reply gravely, 'after all, I'm the one who will be shamed.'

He said nothing then, but there was as much hatred as there was love in the kisses he gave to that woman who resigned herself so easily to sleeping with another man.

His jealousy had been growing ever since she had come to accept that odious marriage. Now that she no longer wept, he was beginning to grow angry at her lack of tears, and privately it drove him to despair that she did not prefer shame with him to rehabilitation with another man. It would not have been so bad if she had continued to protest and sob loudly; that would have been genuine proof of her love, in which, in his vanity, he would delightedly bathe; but her acceptance of the clerk with no show of repugnance, no horrified gestures, seemed to him tantamount to betrayal. He began to suspect that, deep down, *she did not mind.* João Eduardo was, after all, a man; he had a fine moustache and the strength of his twenty-six years. She would experience the same delirious pleasure in João Eduardo's arms as she had in his. If the clerk had been a rheumaticky old man, she would not be so resigned to her fate. Then, to avenge himself, to 'spoil the arrangement', he hoped that João Eduardo would not turn up; and often when

Dionísia came to report to him on her findings, he would say with a little smile:

'Don't worry. He's obviously not going to turn up. Just leave it. It's not worth wearing yourself out . . .'

But Dionísia was made of sterner stuff and, one night, she arrived to say triumphantly that she was on the man's trail. She had seen Gustavo, the typographer, going into Osório's tavern. She would go and talk to him the next day and then she would know everything.

That was a bitter moment for Amaro. Now that the marriage for which he had so longed in those first terrifying hours seemed certain, he felt it to be the greatest catastrophe of his life.

He would lose Amélia for ever! By one of those malign twists in which Providence takes such delight, the man whom he had driven out, whom he had suppressed, was coming to take his woman away from him quite legitimately. And it enraged him to think that João Eduardo would hold her in his arms, that she would give João Eduardo the same fiery kisses that once she had given to him, and cry out 'Oh, João!' as now she murmured 'Oh, Amaro!' But the marriage was inevitable; everyone wanted it, Amélia, the Canon, even Dionísia in her venal zeal.

What use was it to him to be a man with blood in his veins and with a healthy body full of strong passions? He had to say goodbye to the girl, to see her go off arm in arm with the Other, with her husband, to their house where they would play with the child, his child. And he would stand helplessly by and watch the destruction of his happiness, trying to smile; he would go back to living alone, eternally alone, re-reading the breviary. If only he still lived in the days when one could get rid of a man by denouncing him as a heretic! If only the world could go back two hundred years; then Senhor João Eduardo would know what it meant to humiliate a priest and marry Miss Amélia.

And in his excitable, feverish state, that absurd idea took such a powerful hold on his imagination that he had a vivid dream which he often laughingly recounted to the ladies. He was in a narrow street seared by a burning sun; a rabble of people were pressed against the great studded doors of the houses on either side; on balconies, ornately dressed noblemen twirled their moustaches; beneath the folds of mantillas, eyes burned with holy fervour. And the procession of the auto-da-fé came slowly down the street, accompanied by an enormous hubbub and the clamour of the neighbouring bells all tolling the death knell. At the front went the half-naked flagellants, white hoods covering their faces, whipping themselves and howling out the *Miserere*, their backs caked in blood; on a donkey rode João Eduardo, stupid with terror, his legs dangling, his white shirt daubed with fiery devils, and on his chest a sign on which was written – HERETIC; behind came a terrifying servant of the Holy Office furiously goading the donkey on; nearby, a priest, holding a crucifix on high, was bellowing at him to repent. And he, Amaro, was walking beside him singing the *Requiem*, his breviary open in one hand, while with the other he blessed the old ladies, his friends in Rua da Misericórdia, who all knelt to kiss his alb. Sometimes he would look back to enjoy the melancholy spectacle, and then he would see the long line of members of the Fraternity of Noblemen: here a pot-bellied, apoplectic fellow, there someone with the face of a mystic and a fierce moustache and fiery eyes; each one bore a lighted torch in one hand and, in the other, a hat whose black plume hung down to the ground. The helmets of the harquebusiers glittered brightly; the starving features of the rabble were contorted with devout rage; and the cortège wound along the twisting streets, to the loud accompaniment of plainsong and fanatical cries, the thunderous ringing of the bells and the clink of weaponry, which, together, created a horror that filled the entire city as they approached the brick platform on which the bundles of firewood were already lit.

He was terribly disappointed when, after the ecclesiastical glory of that dream, he was woken early by the maid bringing him hot water for his morning shave.

This was the day when they were expecting to find out where João Eduardo was and to write him the letter. He had arranged to meet Amélia at eleven, and the first thing he said to her, as he bad-temperedly pushed open the door, was:

'They've found him, or, rather, they've found his best friend, the typographer, who knows where the creature is . . .'

Amélia who was feeling utterly discouraged and terrified, exclaimed:

'At least this torment will be over.'

Amaro gave a bitter laugh.

'So you're pleased, are you?

'What do you expect after the fear I've been living in . . .'

Amaro made a gesture of despair and impatience. Fear! What hypocrisy! Fear of what? Why her mother would let her do anything. What she really wanted was to get married. She wanted someone else. She no longer liked their bit of fun in the morning, so quickly over . . . She wanted to have it in comfort at home. Did she imagine she could deceive him, a man of thirty with four years of experience of the confessional? He could see through her. She was just like all the others, she wanted a change of man.

She did not reply, she merely turned very pale. And Amaro, furious at her silence, said:

'You see, you say nothing. What could you say? It's the honest truth! After all my sacrifices . . . after all I've suffered for you, someone else turns up, and off you go!'

She got up, stamping her foot in despair.

'You were the one who wanted it like this, Amaro!'

'No wonder! You don't imagine I would ruin myself for you, do you? Of course I wanted it.' And looking loftily down on her, making her feel all the scorn of a very upright soul. 'But you don't even attempt to hide your happiness, your eagerness to go to him. You're a whore, that's what you are!'

Without a word, white as a sheet, she picked up her shawl to leave.

In desperation, Amaro grabbed her violently by the arm.

'Where are you going? Look at me. You're a whore I say. You can't wait to sleep with him.'

'Yes, you're right, I can't!' she said.

Amaro lost all control then and slapped her hard.

'Don't kill me!' she cried. 'It's your child!'

He stood before her, confused and trembling: at that word, at the idea of his child, he was filled by pity and desperate love; and hurling himself on her, in a crushing embrace, as if wanting to bury her in his own breast, to absorb her entirely into himself, he showered her face and hair with furious, painful kisses.

'Oh, forgive me, Amélia, forgive me! I must be mad!'

She was sobbing hysterically, and they spent the whole of that morning in the sexton's room in a delirium of love to which that sense of maternity, binding them together like a sacrament, lent an added tenderness, a constantly renewed desire, which threw them ever more eagerly into each other's arms.

They forgot the time, and Amélia only leapt from the bed when she heard the sound of Esguelhas' crutch down below in the kitchen.

While she was hurriedly getting dressed in front of the fragment of mirror on the wall, Amaro stood looking at her sadly, watching her running the comb through her hair, a sight that soon he would never see again, and he gave a deep sigh and said sweetly:

'Our good times together are nearly over, Amélia. That's how you want it. But do sometimes think of these wonderful mornings together . . .'

'Oh, don't say that!' she said, her eyes filling with tears.

And suddenly throwing her arms around his neck, with the old passion of their happy times together, she murmured:

'I will always be yours. Even after I am married.'

Amaro grasped her hands passionately:

'Do you swear?'

'I swear.'

'On the sacred host?'

'I swear on the sacred host, I swear by Our Lady!'

'Whenever you can?'

'Yes!'

'Oh, Amélia, oh, my love! I would not exchange you for a queen!'

She went downstairs. As he straightened the sheets, Amaro heard her talking calmly to Esguelhas, and he thought to himself what a wonderful girl she was, capable of deceiving the Devil himself, and what a dance she would lead that fool of a clerk.

That 'pact', as Father Amaro called it, became so binding between them that they even calmly discussed the details. They considered the marriage to the clerk as one of society's necessary impositions which suffocate independent souls, but from which nature escapes through the smallest crack, like some irreducible gas. Before Our Lord, Amélia's true husband was Father Amaro; he was the husband of her soul, for whom she would reserve her best kisses, her inner obedience and her will; the other man would have, at most, her cadaver. Sometimes they even began drawing up the sly plan by which they would correspond secretly and meet in hidden places.

Amélia was, as she had been during the first weeks, afire with passion. Given the certainty that, in a few weeks' time, the marriage would make everything 'white as snow', her moods had vanished, even her fear of Heaven's vengeance had died away. The slap Amaro had given her had been like the flick of a whip that rouses a lazy, idling horse; and her passion, trembling and neighing loudly, was once more carrying her along with all the impetus of a headlong chase.

Amaro was overjoyed. Sometimes, it is true, he still felt bothered by the idea of that other man spending his days and nights with her, but, on the other hand, what compensations! All the dangers would magically disappear and sensation would only be increased. The terrible responsibilities of seduction were over and the woman became even more desirable.

He now urged Dionísia to complete her tedious search. But the good woman, doubtless in the hope of earning more by the multiplicity of her efforts, could not find the typographer, the famous Gustavo who, like one of those dwarves in novels of chivalry, held the secret of the marvellous tower wherein lived the enchanted prince.

'Oh, dear Lord!' said the Canon. 'Things are beginning to look very bad. She's been searching for the rascal for nearly two months now! There's no shortage of clerks. Get her another one!'

Then, one night, when the Canon had dropped in to have a rest at Father Amaro's house, Dionísia appeared and exclaimed from the door of the dining room where the two priests were sitting drinking their coffee:

'Ah, there you are!'

'What's happened, Dionísia?'

She, however, was in no hurry; she even sat down, with the gentlemen's permission, because she was so exhausted. The Canon could not imagine the things she had had to do . . . That wretched typographer reminded her of the story she had been told as a child of a deer that was always within sight, but which the galloping hunters never reached. It had been just like that. But, anyway, she had finally found him . . . and he'd been a bit tipsy too.

'Get to the point, woman!' bawled the Canon.

'Well, here it is,' she said. 'Nothing.'

The two priests looked at her, mystified.

'What do you mean "nothing"!?'

'Nothing. The man has gone to Brazil.'

Gustavo had received two letters from João Eduardo: in the first, in which he gave his address, near Poço do Borratém, he announced his decision to go to Brazil; in the second, he told him that he had moved, but did not give him his new address, declaring that he would be embarking for Rio on the next steamship; he did not say whether he had any money or what he intended to do there. Everything was very vague and mysterious. Since that letter, a month ago, he had not written again, and the typographer had concluded that he must, at that very moment, be on the high seas. 'We must, nevertheless, avenge him!' he had said to Dionísia.

The Canon, dumbstruck, was slowly stirring his coffee.

'What do you think of that, Master?' said Amaro, looking very white.

'Unbelievable.'

'May the Devil take women and throw them all into Hell!' Amaro said darkly.

'Amen to that,' replied the Canon gravely.

XX

How Amélia wept when she heard the news! Her honour, her peace of mind, so many combined joys, all lost and plunged into the mists of the sea, en route to Brazil!

Those were the worst weeks of her life. She went to Father Amaro, bathed in tears, asking him every day what she should do.

Amaro, disheartened and bewildered, went to the Canon, who said sadly:

'We've done all we can. We just have to hold on. You should never have got involved.'

And Amaro would go back to Amélia with feeble consolations:

'We'll sort something out; we have to put our hopes in God.'

It was a fine moment to be counting on God, when He, outraged, was continually heaping miseries upon her! Such indecision in a man and in a priest, who should have had the ability and the strength to save her, made her feel desperate; her tender feelings for him vanished like water into sand, and what remained was a confused feeling in which hatred glimmered beneath her continuing desire.

As the weeks went by, their meetings at the sexton's house became less and less frequent. Amaro did not mind; those lovely mornings in Esguelhas' bedroom were always spoiled now by complaints; every kiss came with a trail of tears; and this so wore him down that he too felt like burying his face in the mattress and weeping out his sorrows.

Basically, he accused her of exaggerating her difficulties and of communicating her quite disproportionate fear to him. Another more sensible woman would not make such a fuss. But what could one expect from an hysterical religious fanatic who was all nerves, all fear, all emotion. There was no doubt about it, the whole business had been 'utter folly'.

Amélia felt the same. Fancy never even having considered that this could happen to her! Honestly! As a woman, she had run foolishly towards love, convinced that she would escape, and only now that she felt the child inside her did the tears and fears and laments begin. Her life was utterly wretched; during the day she had to control herself in front of her mother, apply herself to her sewing, have conversations and pretend to be happy. At night, her overwrought imagination tormented her with an incessant phantasmagoria of punishments, in this world and the next: poverty, neglect, the scorn of honest people and the flames of Purgatory.

Then an unexpected event occurred that provided a diversion from the anxiety that was fast turning into a morbid habit. One night, the Canon's maid appeared, all out of breath, to say that Dona Josefa was at death's door.

The evening before, the excellent lady had felt a pain in her side, but had insisted on going to Our Lady of the Incarnation to say her rosary; she had returned home terrified, in more pain and with a touch of fever, and that afternoon, when Dr Gouveia had called, he had diagnosed acute pneumonia.

São Joaneira immediately rushed over and installed herself there as nurse. For weeks, the Canon's quiet house was abuzz with tearful devotions: her friends, when not visiting churches to make promises and pleas to their favourite saints, were in near permanent residence, tiptoeing like ghosts in and out of the patient's room, lighting lamps beneath images, tormenting Dr Gouveia with silly questions. At night, in the living room, with the oil lamp turned down, there was a constant mournful muttering in corners; and when tea was served, each bite of a biscuit would be followed by sighs and by tears furtively wiped away . . .

The Canon sat in one corner, exhausted and disheartened by the sudden appearance of the illness and by the melancholy scene surrounding him – the bottles of medicine filling the tables, the doctor's solemn visits, the worried faces come to ask if there had been any improvement, the febrile breath that filled the whole house, the funereal tone of the clock on the wall in the absence of all other sound, the dirty towels that lay untouched where they fell, nightfall with its daily threat of eternal darkness . . . Apart from that, he was filled by genuine grief; he had lived with his sister for fifty years and was much spoiled by her; long habit had made her dear to him, and her stubbornness, her black bonnets and the way she fussed around the house had become a part of his own being. Besides, if death did come into his house, it might carry him off too in order to save itself a journey!

Dona Josefa's illness brought Amélia great relief; at least no one was thinking about her or looking at her; given the danger in which her godmother lay, no one was surprised by her sad looks and tear-stained cheeks. Her duties as a nurse took up all her time: since she was the strongest and the youngest, and now that São Joaneira was too tired to watch through the night, she was the one to spend the long nights by Dona Josefa's side, and she spared no effort in her attempts to appease through her charity towards the ill woman both Our Lady and Heaven, so that she might deserve equal pity when it was her turn to be prostrated on a bed . . . Influenced by the funereal atmosphere of the house, she had a repeated presentiment that she would die in childbirth; sometimes, alone, wrapped in her shawl, seated at the foot of the bed, listening to her patient's monotonous moaning, she would feel touched by what seemed to be her own certain death, and her eyes would fill with tears out of a vague sense of nostalgia for herself, her youth and her loves . . . Then she would go and kneel down next to the sideboard on which a lamp flickered before a crucifix and cast a misshapen shadow on the pale wallpaper and ceiling; and there she would sit praying, pleading with Our Lady not to exclude her from Paradise . . . Dona Josefa would shift in bed and groan, and Amélia would rearrange the sheets and blankets and speak to her softly. Then she would go out into the living room to see if it was time for her medicine, and sometimes she would shudder at the sounds coming from the next room – the whistle of a piccolo or the hoarse sound of a trombone – the Canon snoring.

One morning, Dr Gouveia at last declared Dona Josefa to be out of danger. There was great rejoicing among the ladies, each of whom was convinced that this was due to her particular pleas to her particular saint. Two weeks later, there were celebrations in the house when Dona Josefa, leaning on her friends, took her first few tremulous steps about the room. Poor Dona Josefa! The illness had certainly taken its toll! That angry little voice, which spat out words like poisoned darts, was now little more than an exhalation, when, by a great effort of will, she asked for the spittoon or for some cough syrup. Those alert, searching, malignant eyes were now sunk deep in their sockets, afraid of the light, of shadows and shapes. Her body had once been so sturdy, tough as a vine, but now, when she collapsed into an armchair, all bundled up in her clothes, she looked little more than a bundle of rags herself.

Dr Gouveia, though, despite announcing the need for a long and delicate period of convalescence, had joked to the Canon, in front of all her friends (after having seen Dona Josefa express her first desire: to be able to look out of the window) that with great care, a few bottles of tonic and the prayers of all those good ladies, his sister was still in the market for love.

'Oh, Doctor,' exclaimed Dona Maria, 'she won't go short of prayers from us.'

'And I'll make sure she doesn't go short of tonic,' said the doctor. 'So all that remains for us to do now is to congratulate ourselves.'

The doctor's good humour was a guarantee to everyone that good health was at hand.

And some days later, as the end of August approached, the Canon mentioned renting a house in Vieira, as he did on alternate years, to go and take his sea baths. He had not been last year. So this was the year of the beach . . .

'And in the healthy seaside air my sister will gain strength and put on weight.'

Dr Gouveia, however, disapproved of the plan. The sea air would be far too bracing for someone in Dona Josefa's weak state. It would be better to go to his house in Ricoça, in Poiais, a sheltered, temperate place.

This was a great disappointment to the poor Canon, who

complained loudly. What! Go and bury himself in Ricoça for the whole summer, the best part of the year? And what about his sea bathing, for Heaven's sake, what about his sea bathing?

'Just look,' he said to Amaro one night in his office, 'just look how I have suffered. The house has been in uproar throughout the whole of my sister's illness. Tea served at the wrong time, suppers burned. I've even lost weight through sheer worry. And now, just when I was thinking of recuperating by the sea, no, it's off to Ricoça with you, forget about your sea bathing . . . That's what I call suffering! And I wasn't even the one who was ill. But I'm the one who has to put up with missing my sea baths two years in a row.'

Amaro suddenly thumped the table and exclaimed:

'I've just had a good idea!'

The Canon eyed him doubtfully, as if he did not believe it possible for a mere human intelligence to find a solution to his ills.

'When I say a good idea, Father, I should say a sublime idea!'

'Well, out with it!'

'Listen. You go to Vieira, and São Joaneira, of course, goes too. Naturally you will rent houses next to each other, as she tells me you did two years ago.'

'Go on.'

'Right. So São Joaneira is in Vieira. Your sister now departs for Ricoça.'

'What, all alone?'

'No!' exclaimed Amaro triumphantly. 'She'll go with Amélia. Amélia will be her nurse. They will go together. And there in Ricoça, in that dead-and-alive hole where not a soul ever goes, in that vast house where you could live quite happily without anyone knowing you were there, that is where she will have her baby. What do you think?'

The Canon stood up, his eyes round with admiration.

'Brilliant!'

'Then everyone is happy. You get to take your sea baths. São Joaneira will be far enough away not to know what's happening. Your sister can have the benefit of the country air.

Amélia will have a hiding place, because no one will see her in Ricoça . . . Dona Maria will also go off to Vieira, as will the Gansoso sisters. The happy event should take place in early November. No one in our circle should be back from Vieira until the beginning of December, though I'll leave that up to you . . . And when we all meet again, the girl will be good as new.'

'Well, considering that's the only idea you've had in the last two years, it really is an excellent one.'

'Thank you, Master.'

There was one very awkward problem: having to go to Dona Josefa, to the rigorous Dona Josefa, so implacable when it came to any kind of emotional weakness, who believed that the ancient gothic penalties should be imposed on frail women – words branded on foreheads, public whippings, gloomy dungeons – having to go to Dona Josefa and ask her to be an accomplice to a birth!

'My sister will be furious!' said the Canon.

'We'll see, Father,' said Amaro, leaning back in his chair and bouncing one crossed leg, confident in his influence amongst the devout. 'We'll see . . . I'll talk to her. And when I've spun her a lot of nonsense . . . when I've put it to her that it is a matter of conscience for her to cover up for Amélia . . . when I have reminded her that it is precisely on the eve of death that one should perform some good action so as not to arrive empty-handed at the gates of Paradise . . . We'll see.'

'Possibly, possibly,' said the Canon. 'It's a good moment, anyway, because my poor sister is still very weak in judgement and as easily led as a child.'

Amaro stood up, rubbing his hands.

'Let's get to work then!'

'And we mustn't waste any time, because the scandal could break at any moment. This morning, that fool Libaninho started joking with the girl, saying that she was getting a bit thick around the waist . . .'

'The brute!' roared Amaro.

'Oh, he meant no harm. But there's no disguising the fact that she's filled out. What with this business of my sister's illness, no one has had eyes for anything else. But now people might notice. It's serious, my friend, very serious.'

That is why, the following morning, Amaro went, as the Canon put it, to launch a head-on attack on his sister.

First, however, in the Canon's office, he quietly explained his plan: he would start by telling her that the Canon knew nothing about Amélia's predicament, and that he, Amaro, knew about it not from the confessional (in which case he would not be able to reveal it) but from the secret confidences of the two parties involved – Amélia and the married man who had seduced her. It had to be a married man, because Amaro had to prove to the old lady that there was no possibility of a legitimate solution . . .

The Canon was scratching his head and looking unconvinced.

'That won't work,' he said. 'She knows that no married men went to Rua da Misericórdia.'

'What about Artur Couceiro?' cried Amaro, now completely without scruples.

The Canon burst out laughing. Accuse poor toothless Artur, with his horde of children and his sad sheep's eyes, of ruining maidens. That was a good one!

'No, it won't work, my friend, it won't work. Think of someone else.'

Then they both simultaneously came out with the same name – Fernandes the draper! A good-looking man, whom Amélia much admired. She was always going to his shop, and there had even been some indignation in Rua da Misericórdia two years ago at Fernandes' boldness in accompanying Amélia along the Marrazes road to Morenal!

Amaro would not name names, but he would imply that it had been Fernandes.

And Amaro went quickly up to the old lady's room, which was immediately above the office. He was there for half an hour, a long, difficult half hour for the Canon, who only occasionally caught the creak of Amaro's boots or his sister's cavernous cough. And on his habitual walk up and down the office, from the bookshelf to the window, his hands behind his back, he was thinking how much trouble and how much money 'Father Amaro's bit of fun' would yet cost him. The girl would have to be at the house for some five or six months. Then there was the doctor and the midwife, whom, of course, he would have to pay. Then some clothes for the baby. And what would they do with the child? The convent in town no longer took in abandoned babies; in Ourém, because the poorhouse's resources were so limited and because the number of foundlings had reached positively scandalous levels, a man had been posted next to the door bell in order to question the women and generally make matters difficult for them; there were investigations into paternity and children were sometimes handed back; and the wily authorities were combating the growing numbers of foundlings with the threat of humiliation.

The poor Canon could see the future bristling with problems that would disturb his idleness and ruin his digestion. But the excellent Canon was not really angry; he had always felt a schoolmasterly affection for Amaro; he had always had a soft spot for Amélia – half-paternal, half-lewd; and he already felt the stirrings of vague grandfatherly feelings for the 'little one'.

The door opened and Amaro appeared, triumphant.

'It all went perfectly, Father. Didn't I tell you it would?'

'Did she agree?'

'To everything. It wasn't without its difficulties, of course. She started to get angry. I mentioned the married man . . . that the girl was in a terrible state and wanted to kill herself . . . I said that if she wouldn't agree to cover things up she would be responsible for a great misfortune. I reminded her that she herself may not be long for this world, that God could call her at any moment, and that if she had that weight on her conscience, no priest could absolve her. I warned her that she could end up dying like a dog!'

'Ah, you spoke prudently, then' said the Canon approvingly.

'I told her the truth. Now you just have to talk to São

Joaneira about Vieira and whisk her off there as soon as possible.'

'One other thing,' said the Canon. 'Have you thought about what to do with the "fruit of the union"?'

Amaro scratched his head disconsolately.

'Ah, Father, that is another difficulty. It's been worrying me a lot. Obviously it will have to be given to some woman to bring up, somewhere far off, in Alcobaça or Pombal. The best thing, Father, would be for the child to be born dead!'

'Hm, another little angel,' grunted the Canon, taking a pinch of snuff.

That same night the Canon spoke to São Joaneira about going to Vieira. She was downstairs in the parlour sorting out saucers of quince jelly intended for Dona Josefa's convalescence. He began by saying that he had rented Ferreiro's house.

'But it's tiny!' she exclaimed. 'Where will Amélia go?'

'That's just it. Amélia won't be coming to Vieira this year.'

'Not coming?'

The Canon then explained that his sister could not possibly go alone to Ricoça and that he had thought of sending Amélia with her. He had had the idea that very morning.

'I can't go with her, I need my sea bathing, as you know . . . and the poor woman can't be left alone in Ricoça with just a maid . . . Therefore . . .'

There was a sad silence.

'You're right. But to tell you the truth, I don't like to leave Amélia. If I could do without the sea baths, I would go to Ricoça myself.'

'What do you mean? You're coming to Vieira. I can't be left alone either. Don't be so ungrateful!' Then adopting a very grave tone, he said: 'Look, Josefa may not be long for this world. She knows I have enough money for myself and she's fond of the girl; after all, she is her godmother, and if she sees Amélia looking after her and prepared to spend a few months with her, she'll be completely won round. My sister has got a couple of thousand *cruzados*. Amélia could get a nice big dowry. But I'll say no more . . .'

And São Joaneira agreed at once, since that was what the Canon wanted.

Upstairs, Amaro was rapidly outlining to Amélia 'the grand plan' and his conversation with Dona Josefa, saying that the poor woman, brimming with charity, had immediately offered to help; she even wanted to contribute to the baby's layette.

'You can trust her, she's a saint. So everything is all right, my love. It's just a question of spending four or five months in Ricoça.'

That was what made Amélia weep: missing the summer in Vieira and the fun of sea bathing, and having instead to bury herself all summer in that great gloomy house in Ricoça! The only time she had visited the house it had been late afternoon, and she had been rigid with fear. Everything was so dark, the whole place echoed. She was sure that she would die there in exile.

'Nonsense!' said Amaro. 'You should thank the Lord that I came up with this idea. Besides, you'll have Dona Josefa and Gertrudes to talk to and the orchard to walk in. I'll come and see you every day. You'll enjoy it, just you wait.'

'What else can I do? I'll just have to put up with it.' And with her eyes full of tears, she inwardly cursed the passion that had brought her nothing but sorrow and which now, when the whole of Leiria was leaving for Vieira, was forcing her to shut herself up in lonely Ricoça, listening to an old woman coughing and to the farm dogs howling. 'And Mama, what will Mama say?'

'What can she say? Dona Josefa can't go to the farm alone, without a personal nurse. Anyway, don't worry, the Canon is working on her. I'll go down to her now; I've been alone with you too long as it is; we need to be careful during these last few days.'

He went downstairs. The Canon was just coming up and they met on the stairs.

'Well?' asked Amaro in the Canon's ear.

'It's all arranged. What about you?'

'*Idem.*'

And in the darkness of the stairway the two priests silently shook hands.

A few days later, after tearful scenes, Amélia left in a char-à-banc with Dona Josefa bound for the house at Ricoça.

They had piled up pillows in one corner for the convalescent. The Canon went with them, complaining bitterly about the discomfort. And Gertrudes sat up front, in the shadow cast by the mountain formed on top of the carriage by the leather trunks, baskets, tins, bundles of clothes, cotton bags, the cat mewing in its basket, and a package tied up with string containing Dona Josefa's favourite paintings of saints.

At the end of the same week, São Joaneira set off for Vieira, at night because of the heat. Rua da Misericórdia was entirely blocked by the ox cart carrying the china, the straw mattresses and the kitchen equipment; and in the same char-à-banc that had gone to Ricoça, São Joaneira was now setting off with Ruça, who was also carrying a cat basket on her lap.

The Canon had left the previous night, and only Amaro was there to see São Joaneira off. After all the hustle and bustle, after racing up and down the stairs a hundred times for some basket they had forgotten or some package that had disappeared, just when Ruça was finally locking the front door, São Joaneira suddenly burst into tears as she was about to step up into the char-à-banc.

'Now, now, Senhora, now, now!' said Amaro.

'It's having to leave Amélia, Father Amaro. You have no idea how difficult it is. I feel as if I'll never see her again. Will you do me the kindness of going to visit her at Ricoça to see that she's all right?'

'Don't you worry, Senhora.'

'Goodbye, Father, and thank you for everything. I owe you so much . . .'

'Nonsense! Have a good journey and be sure to write to us. Give my best wishes to the Canon. Goodbye, Senhora. Goodbye, Ruça!'

The char-à-banc left. And Amaro walked slowly along

behind it as far as the Figueira road. It was nine o'clock; the moon had already risen on that hot, calm August night. A faint, luminous mist blurred the contours of the silent countryside. Here and there the moonlit façade of a house stood out brightly amongst the shadows of the trees. By the bridge, he stopped to look down sadly into the river that flowed with a monotonous murmur over the sand; beneath the overhanging trees, the water was pitch-black; elsewhere the light on the water trembled like a piece of glittering filigree work. There he stood in that soothing silence, smoking and tossing his cigarette ends into the river, absorbed in a vague sadness. Then, hearing eleven o'clock strike, he walked back into town, feeling a pang of memory as he passed Rua da Misericórdia; the house, with its windows closed and without any curtains, looked as if it had been abandoned for ever; the pots of rosemary had been forgotten on the window ledge. How often he and Amélia had leaned out over that balcony! There used to be a carnation growing there and, as they talked, she used to break off a leaf and bite it. That was all over now. And in the silence, the shrieking of the owls in the poorhouse wall filled him with a sense of ruin, solitude and irrevocability.

He walked slowly home, his eyes full of tears.

The maid came to the stairs at once to say that Esguelhas had come for him twice, around nine o'clock it must have been; he had been in a terrible state. Totó was dying and she would only receive the sacrament from his hand.

Despite Amaro's superstitious repugnance at having to go back there that night, for such a sad end, in the midst of the happy memories of his love, he did so to please Esguelhas; but he felt shocked by Totó's death, coinciding as it did with Amélia's departure and somehow completing the sudden dispersal of everything he cared about or that had been part of his life.

The door to the sexton's house stood ajar, and in the darkness of the hallway, he bumped into two women who were just leaving, sighing heavily. He went straight to Totó's bedroom: two large candles, brought from the church, were burning on a table; a white sheet covered Totó's body, and Father

Silvério, who had doubtless been called because he was on duty that week, was reading the breviary, his handkerchief spread over his knees, his large glasses perched on the end of his nose. He got up as soon as he saw Amaro.

'Ah, Father,' he said very softly, 'they've been looking for you everywhere. The poor girl wanted you. When they came for me, I was just off to the Saturday get-together at Novais' house. What scenes! She died impenitent. When she saw me and realised that you weren't coming, she made such a fuss. I was afraid she might spit on the crucifix.'

Without a word, Amaro lifted one corner of the sheet, but immediately let it fall again on the dead girl's face. Then he went up to the room where the sexton was lying on the bed, sobbing desperately, his face turned to the wall; a woman was with him, but she remained standing in one corner, silent and motionless, her eyes downcast, as if slightly annoyed at the heavy duty that had befallen her as neighbour. Amaro touched the sexton on the shoulder and spoke to him:

'You must resign yourself, Esguelhas. This is what the Lord has decreed. For her it is almost a happy release.'

Esguelhas turned round and, recognising Amaro through the tears veiling his eyes, he took his hand and tried to kiss it. Amaro drew back.

'Come now, Esguelhas! God will be merciful and will remember your sorrow . . .'

Esguelhas was not listening, still shaken by convulsive sobs, while the woman in the corner calmly dabbed at the corners of her eyes.

Amaro went downstairs and relieved good Silvério, taking his place beside the candles, the breviary in his hand.

He stayed there until late into the night. When the neighbour was leaving, she came in to say that Esguelhas had fallen asleep, and she promised to return at dawn with someone else in order to lay the body out.

The whole house was immersed in a silence which the proximity of the vast Cathedral building made still gloomier; occasionally an owl somewhere on the buttressed walls would hoot feebly, or the great bell would echo round the rooms.

And Amaro, seized by an ill-defined terror, but held there by the superior force of an uneasy conscience, kept praying rapidly . . . Sometimes the book would fall onto his knees, and then, feeling behind him the presence of that corpse covered by the sheet, he would remember, in bitter contrast, other times when the courtyard lay bathed in sunlight and the swallows were flying, and he and Amélia would run laughing up to the room where now, on that same bed, Esguelhas was sleeping, his tears barely dry.

XXI

Canon Dias had strongly advised Amaro not to visit Ricoça, at least for the first few weeks, so as not to arouse the suspicions of Dona Josefa or her maid. And Amaro's life grew even sadder and emptier than it had been before when he first moved out of São Joaneira's house and came to Rua das Sousas. Almost everyone he knew had left Leiria: Dona Maria da Assunção was in Vieira, and the Gansoso sisters had gone to stay near Alcobaça with the famous aunt who for the last ten years had been about to die and leave them a large inheritance. After the service at the Cathedral, the hours, indeed the whole long day, dragged by as heavily as lead. He could not have been more cut off from human communication than if, like St Anthony, he had lived in the sands of the Libyan desert. Only the coadjutor who, oddly enough, never appeared in happy times, returned now, like the fateful friend of unhappy hours, to visit him once or twice a week after supper, looking ever gaunter and gloomier, with his eternal umbrella in his hand. Amaro hated him; sometimes, to put him off, he would pretend to be absorbed in his reading or, rushing to the table as soon as he heard his slow steps on the stairs, he would say:

'Oh, I'm sorry, my friend, but I'm in the middle of writing something.'

The man would nevertheless sit down, his hateful umbrella between his knees:

'Oh, take no notice of me, Father.'

And Amaro, tormented by that doleful figure, who did not move from the chair, would angrily throw down his quill, pick up his hat and declare:

'I'm not in the mood for writing tonight, I think I'll go out.'

And he would brusquely get rid of the coadjutor at the first street corner.

Sometimes, weary of solitude, he would visit Silvério, but

the phlegmatic contentment of that obese being, his preoccupation with collecting home remedies and with observing the fantastical perturbations of his own digestive system; his constant praise for Dr Godinho, his little ones and his wife; his ancient jokes which he had been repeating for the past forty years and the innocent hilarity that they caused him, all this irritated Amaro. He would leave feeling exhausted, pondering the hostile fate that had made him so different from Silvério. That, after all, was happiness; why could he not be a good priest, stuck in his ways, with a small tyrannical obsession, the spoiled parasite of a respectable family, possessed of quiet blood that flowed along beneath layers of fat, in no danger of overflowing or provoking misfortunes, like a stream that runs beneath a mountain?

Sometimes he went to see Natário, whose fracture, which had been badly set initially, still kept him in bed with his leg bandaged. But Natário's room made him feel ill, impregnated as it was with the smell of arnica and sweat, with a profusion of rags soaking in various glass bowls and squadrons of bottles lined up on the sideboard amongst the rows of saints. As soon as Natário saw him, he would launch into a litany of complaints: The doctors were all donkeys! It was just his bad luck! The torments they put him through! Medicine in this country was so backward! And he would meanwhile spatter the black floor with expectorations and cigarette ends. Since he had been ill, he took other people's good health, especially that of friends, as a personal affront.

'And you're still fit as a flea, I suppose? Huh!' he would mutter rancorously.

And to think how that animal Brito never had so much as a headache! And that fool Ferrão used to boast that he had never been in bed after seven o'clock in the morning! Idiots all of them!

Amaro would give him the latest news: a letter he had received from the Canon in Vieira, Dona Josefa's improving health . . .

But Natário was not interested in people to whom he was bound by familiarity and friendship; he was only interested in his enemies, with whom he shared bonds of hatred. He wanted to know about the clerk, to find out if he had died of hunger..

'At least I did some good before I got stuck in this wretched bed.'

His two nieces would appear then – two freckle-faced little creatures with dark shadows under their eyes. Their great concern was that their aunt had not sent the faith healer to make his leg better: that was what had cured the owner of the Barrosa estate, not to mention Pimentel in Ourém . . .

In the presence of his 'two little roses', Natário would grow quieter.

'Poor things, it's not for lack of care from them that I haven't yet recovered. But dear God, I've suffered!'

And the 'two little roses' would simultaneously turn aside and dab at their eyes with their handkerchiefs.

Amaro left, feeling even more irritated.

In order to tire himself out, he would go for long walks along the Lisbon road. But as soon as he left behind him the bustle of the town, his sadness only intensified, in keeping with the landscape of sad hills and gnarled trees; and his life seemed to him then just like that long, monotonous road, devoid of any interesting features, stretching out desolately into the evening mists. Sometimes, on the way back, he would go into the cemetery and stroll past the ranks of cypresses, smelling the sweet scent emanating from the clumps of wall-flowers; he would read the epitaphs; leaning on the gilt railings around the Gouveia family tomb, he would study the carved emblems, a helmet and a sword, and read the black letters of the famous ode which adorned the stone:

> Pause, traveller, to contemplate
>   These mortal remains,
> But if with grief your heart o'erflows,
>   Cease your mourning now.
> For João Cabral da Silva Maldonado
>   Mendonça de Gouveia,
> Noble youth and graduate,

Son of illustrious Seia,
Ex-administrator of the municipal council,
And Commander of the Order of Christ,
He, traveller, was a mirror of virtue
And the enemy of vice.

Then came Morais' lavish mausoleum, on which his widow, who, rich and in her forties and now living in concubinage with the handsome Captain Trigueiros, had ordered these pious lines to be carved:

Wait amongst the angels, husband,
For your dear heart's other half,
Left alone on Earth, abandoned,
To weep, to pray, no more to laugh.

Sometimes, at the far end of the cemetery, close to the wall, he would see a man kneeling by a black cross overshadowed by a weeping willow next to the paupers' grave. It was Esguelhas, his crutch laid on the ground, praying over Totó's grave. Amaro would go and speak to him and, on terms of equality justified by the place itself, they would even stroll along familiarly, shoulder to shoulder, talking. Amaro, out of kindness, would try to console the old man: what good had life been to the poor girl if she was to spend it lying on a bed?

'It was still a life, though, Father. And now here I am alone day and night.'

'We all have our solitudes, Esguelhas,' Amaro would say sadly.

The sexton would sigh then and ask after Dona Josefa and about Miss Amélia.

'She's living at the farm.'

'Poor thing, she must be bored there.'

'Well, we all have our cross to bear, Esguelhas.'

And they would walk on in silence amongst the box hedges surrounding plots full of the black of crosses and the white of new gravestones. Sometimes Amaro would recognise a grave that he himself had consecrated and sprinkled with holy water: where would they be now those souls whom he had distractedly commended to God in Latin, hurriedly mumbling his way through the prayers in order to go and meet Amélia? They were the tombs of people from the town; he knew the members of the families by sight; he had seen them with their faces bathed in tears, and now they strolled along together down the Alameda or exchanged jokes over the counters of shops . . .

He would return home feeling even sadder, and then the long, endless night would begin. Sometimes he would write to the Canon. At nine o'clock he had some tea, and then he would pace up and down in his room, smoking cigarette after cigarette, stopping at the window to look out at the black night, occasionally reading an article or an advertisement in the newspaper, only to resume his pacing, yawning so loudly that the maid could hear him in the kitchen.

To pass these melancholy nights, and out of an excess of idle sensitivity, he tried his hand at writing poetry, putting his love and the story of those happy days into the familiar formulae of lyrical nostalgia:

> Do you recall our days' delight,
> Bewitching angel, Amélia mine,
> When everything with love was bright
> And life was tranquil and divine?
>
> Do you recall that poetic night
> When the Moon was shining in the sky,
> And we, Amélia, did our souls unite,
> And offered up prayers to God on high?

But despite all his efforts, he could never get beyond those two stanzas – even though he had produced them with promising facility – as if his being contained only those two isolated drops of poetry, and once they had been squeezed out of him, nothing was left but the dry prose of a carnal temperament.

And that empty existence brought about such a subtle relaxation of the whole mechanism of will and action that any task with which he might have been able to fill the tedious, cavernous, endless hours weighed on him as hatefully as an unfair burden. He far preferred the tedium of idleness to the tedium of occupation. Apart from the strict duties which he could not neglect without provoking scandal and censure, he gradually disencumbered himself of all the practices of inner zeal: mental prayer, regular visits to the Sacrament, spiritual meditations, saying the rosary to the Virgin, the nightly reading of the breviary, the examination of conscience – replacing all these works of devotion, these secret means to progressive sanctification, with his endless pacing from the washbasin to the window, and with the cigarettes that he smoked down to his blackened fingertips. He gabbled his way through morning mass; he carried out his parish duties with mute impatience; he had become the embodiment of the ritualists' *Indignus sacerdos*; and he possessed every one of the thirty-five defects and seven half-defects which the theologians attribute to the 'bad priest'.

All that remained of his sentimental nature was an enormous appetite. And since he had an excellent cook, and since Dona Maria da Assunção, before she left for Vieira, had left him a store of one hundred and fifty masses at one *cruzado* each, he banqueted on chicken and on jelly, washed down with a piquant Bairrada wine that the Canon had chosen for him. And he would spend hours at the table, legs outstretched, smoking a cigarette over coffee, regretting that he did not have his Amélia to hand.

'I wonder what poor little Amélia will be up to now?' he thought, yawning and stretching with boredom and languor.

In Ricoça, poor little Amélia was cursing her life.

During the journey in the char-à-banc, Dona Josefa had tacitly made her feel that she could expect from her neither her former friendship nor her forgiveness. And that is how it was once they were installed in the house. The old woman became utterly unbearable: in the cruel formality with which she ceased to address her as *tu*, addressing her instead as 'Miss Amélia'; in her abrupt refusal to allow Amélia to plump up her pillows or rearrange her shawl; in her reproachful silence whenever Amélia spent the evening in her room, sewing; in her constant weary allusions to the sad burden God had charged her with at the end of her life . . .

Amélia inwardly accused Amaro: he had promised that her godmother would be all charity and complicity; he had ended up abandoning her to the ferocity of a fanatical old virgin.

When she found herself in that great mansion, in a chilly bedroom painted canary yellow and lugubriously furnished with a canopied bed and two leather chairs, she spent all night crying with her head buried in the pillow, further tormented by a dog stationed beneath her window, who kept up his howling until dawn, doubtless bewildered to see lights and movement in the house.

The following day, she went down to the farm to visit the tenants. She thought they might be kindly people with whom she could pass the time. She met a woman, as tall and gloomy as a cypress tree, dressed in heavy mourning; the large black scarf pulled down low over her forehead gave her the look of a penitent in a religious procession, and her whining voice was as sad as a death knell. The man was even worse, rather like an orang-utang, with his two enormous ears sticking out from his skull, a hideously prominent chin, discoloured gums, a gawky, tubercular body and a sunken chest. She hastily left and went to see the orchard; she found it much neglected; the paths between the trees were overgrown with damp grass, and there was something unhealthy about the shade cast by those closely planted trees in that low-lying plot of land surrounded by high walls.

She preferred to spend her days indoors, endless days in which the hours moved by as slowly as a funeral cortège.

Her room was at the front, and from the two windows she had an impression of sad fields stretching out before her, a monotonous undulation of barren plots with, here and there, the occasional scrawny tree, and a suffocating atmosphere in which it seemed there was always a whiff of nearby swamps and steamy shallows whose malarial airs even the September sun failed to dissipate.

First thing in the morning, she would go and help Dona Josefa get up and make her comfortable on the sofa; then she would sit nearby and do her sewing, just as she used to do in Rua da Misericórdia with her mother; but now instead of the chats she and her mother used to enjoy, there was only Dona Josefa's intractable silence and her constant wheezing. She thought about having her piano brought from town, but when she mentioned it, the old woman exclaimed bitterly:

'You must be mad. My health isn't strong enough for music. What a ridiculous idea!'

Gertrudes was no company either; when she was not with Dona Josefa or in the kitchen, she vanished; she had been born in that parish and spent all her free hours talking to her former neighbours.

The worst time was the evening. Having said her rosary, Amélia would sit at the window staring foolishly out at the changing colours of the sunset; gradually all the fields took on the same grey-brown tone; a silence seemed to fall and alight on the earth; then a first small, bright star would twinkle into being; and before her lay only an inert mass of mute shadows as far as the horizon, where a thin strip of pale orange would linger for a moment. Her thoughts, with no gradations of light and shade and no shapes to cling to, would travel far off to Vieira; at that hour, her mother and her friends would be returning from their walk along the beach; all the nets would have been taken in; the lights would be coming on in the fishermen's cottages; it was the time for tea and jolly games of lotto, when the boys from the town would go round in a gang to the houses of friends, with a guitar and a flute, holding improvised parties. Meanwhile there she sat, all alone!

Then she had to put Dona Josefa to bed and to say the rosary with her and with Gertrudes. Afterwards, they would light the brass oil lamp and place an old hat box in front of it to shade the patient's face; and all night, in gloomy silence, the only sound to be heard would be that made by Gertrudes' spindle from where she sat in one corner.

Before they went to bed, they would lock all the doors, in constant fear of thieves; and then the hour of superstitious terrors would begin for Amélia. Surrounded by the black depths of those old uninhabited rooms and by the dark, horrible silence of the fields, she could not sleep. She would hear inexplicable noises: the floor in the corridor creaking beneath footsteps; the flame of the candle suddenly bending as if in response to some invisible breath; or, near the kitchen, the sudden thud of a body falling. Huddled beneath the blankets, she would pile prayer upon prayer, but if she did doze off, the terrors of wakefulness only continued in her nightmare visions. One night, she had been woken suddenly by a mournful voice behind the bedhead saying: Amélia, prepare yourself, your end has come! Terrified, she ran the whole length of the house in her nightdress and took refuge in Gertrudes' bed.

But the following night, the sepulchral voice returned just as she was dropping asleep: 'Amélia, remember your sins! Prepare yourself, Amélia!' She screamed and fainted. Fortunately, Gertrudes, who had not yet gone to bed, heard the scream, which cut through the silence of the house, and ran towards it. She found Amélia sprawled across the bed, her loose hair brushing the floor, her hands as cold as a dead woman's. She went down to wake the tenant's wife and it took them until dawn, after frantic efforts, to bring her back to life. Ever since then Gertrudes had slept near her, and the voice from behind the bedhead had not bothered her again.

But after that, the idea of death and the horror of Hell did not leave her day or night. Around that time, a travelling vendor of religious pictures came by the house, and Dona Josefa bought Amélia two lithographs – *The Death of the Just Man* and *The Death of the Sinner*.

'We should all have a vivid image before us,' she said.

Amélia was sure initially that Dona Josefa – who obviously expected to die with the same pomp and glory with which the Just Man in the picture was dying – wanted to show her, the Sinner, the horrible scene awaiting her. She hated Dona Josefa for that 'cruel joke'. But her terrified imagination soon gave the purchase of the picture another explanation: Our Lady had sent the seller to present her, in that lithograph of *The Death of the Sinner*, with a vivid picture of the spectacle of her own death; and she was sure then that it would be exactly so, point by point: her guardian angel fleeing in tears; God the Father turning away from her in disgust; the skeleton of death roaring with laughter; and brilliantly coloured devils with a whole arsenal of tortures taking hold of her, some grabbing her legs and some her hair, and with howls of joy dragging her off to the flaming cave that shook with the roaring storm of laments that issued forth from the place of Eternal Suffering. And she could even see, in the height of Heaven, the great scales, with one of the pans right up high, in which her prayers weighed no more than the feather of a canary, and with the other pan right down low, the chains pulled taut, containing the sexton's bed and its tons of sin.

She fell into a kind of hysterical melancholy that aged her prematurely; she stopped washing or bothering with her clothes, not wanting to care for her sinful body; she found any movement or effort repugnant; she found even praying too much, as if she believed that prayers were pointless; and she hid away in the bottom of a chest the layette she had been sewing for her baby, because she hated the being that she could now feel moving about inside her and which was the cause of her perdition. She hated it, but not as much as she hated the priest who had made it, the wicked priest who had tempted her, ruined her and hurled her into the flames of Hell! The despair she felt when she thought about him! There he was comfortably ensconced in Leiria, eating well, confessing other women, perhaps even courting them, and there she was all alone, gradually sinking into eternal perdition, with her wretched womb stuffed with the sin that he had placed there!

This permanently overwrought state would surely have killed her if Father Ferrão had not started paying regular visits to the Canon's sister.

Amélia had often heard them talk about him in Rua da Misericórdia; they said that Ferrão had 'odd ideas', but no one could deny his virtue or his priestly knowledge. He had been a priest there for many years; bishops had come and gone in the diocese and he had stayed on, entirely forgotten, in that poor parish, where he was paid little and late and where he lived in a house that let in the rain. The last vicar general, who had never lifted a finger to help him, was, however, generous with words:

'You are one of the good theologians of the kingdom. You are predestined by God for a bishopric. You could get a mitre yet. And you'll go down in the history of the Portuguese Church as a great bishop, Ferrão!'

'A bishop, Vicar General! That would be wonderful! But I would have to have the temerity of an Afonso de Albuquerque or a Dom João de Castro to accept such a responsibility before the eyes of God.'

And so there he had stayed amongst the poor, in a village with little land, surviving on two slices of bread and a cup of milk, wearing a spotlessly clean cassock on which the many darns traced a map, and prepared to march half a league through the wildest storm if a parishioner had a toothache, or to spend an hour consoling an old woman whose goat had died . . . And he was always good-humoured, always had some money in his pocket if his neighbour needed it, and was a great friend to the children, for whom he would make boats out of cork, and if he saw a pretty girl, an unusual occurrence in his parish, he would exclaim: 'God bless you, my dear, don't you look lovely!'

And yet, even as a young man, he had been so famous for the purity of his habits that they had nicknamed him 'the virgin'.

He was also a perfect priest in his zeal for the Church, spending hours in prayer before the Sacrament, carrying out with fervent joy the smallest practices of the devout life; purifying himself for the tasks of the day with a period of profound mental prayer and meditation on the faith, from which his soul emerged more agile, as if from a fortifying bath; preparing himself for sleep with one of those long, pious, invaluable examinations of conscience favoured by St Augustine and St Bernard, as well as by Plutarch and Seneca, and which serve to provide a detailed and subtle correction of minor defects, the meticulous perfecting of active virtue, undertaken with the fervour of a poet revising a cherished poem . . . And any free time he had, he would spend immersed in a chaos of books.

Father Ferrão had only one fault: he loved to hunt! He did his best to restrain himself because hunting is very time-consuming and it is cruel to kill a poor bird going busily about the fields on its domestic business. But on bright winter mornings, when there was still dew on the broom bushes, if he saw a man walking by with sprightly step, his shotgun on his shoulder, his hunting dog at his heel, he would gaze longingly after him. Sometimes, temptation won; he would furtively pick up his shotgun, whistle to his dog Janota and, with his greatcoat flapping in the wind, off he would go, that illustrious theologian, that mirror of piety, across the fields and the valleys . . . And shortly afterwards: bang! bang! A quail or a partridge would fall to the earth. And the saintly man would return, with his shotgun under his arm and the two birds in his pocket; but he always kept close to the walls, repeating his rosary to the Virgin and responding to the greetings of people along the way with downcast eyes and a criminal air.

Despite Father Ferrão's shabby appearance and large nose, Amélia took an immediate liking to him the first time he visited the house; and her sympathy only grew when she saw that Dona Josefa received him unenthusiastically, despite her own brother's respect for Father Ferrão's knowledge.

Indeed, after some hours of talk with him alone, the old woman, in all her authority as an experienced religious devotee, had condemned him with the words:

'The man has no morals!'

They had not really understood each other. Having lived for so many years in that parish of five hundred souls, all of whom, mothers and daughters, fell into the same mould of simple devotion to Our Lord, Our Lady and St Vincent, the patron saint of the parish, good Father Ferrão had had little experience of the confessional, and he suddenly found himself face to face with the complicated soul of a town devotee, with a stubborn, tortured form of religious fanaticism; and when he heard her extraordinary list of mortal sins, he murmured in horrified tones:

'Most odd, most odd . . .'

He realised at once that he had before him an example of that morbid degeneration of religious feeling known in theology as scrupulosity, and by which all Catholic souls are affected nowadays; but after certain of Dona Josefa's revelations, he feared that he really might be in the presence of a dangerous maniac, and, gripped by the singular horror priests have of the mad, he instinctively pushed back his chair. Poor Dona Josefa! The very first night that she had arrived at the house (she told him), just as she was beginning the rosary to Our Lady, she had suddenly remembered that she had left behind the red flannel petticoat that had proved such an efficacious cure for the pains in her legs . . . She began the rosary thirty-eight times and each time that red flannel petticoat came between her and Our Lady. In the end, she had given up out of sheer exhaustion and fatigue. And then she had immediately felt intense pain in her legs and something like a voice inside her telling her that it was Our Lady who was revenging herself by sticking pins in her legs.

Father Ferrão started.

'But Senhora!'

'And that's not all, Father.'

There was another sin that was tormenting her: when she prayed, she sometimes felt an urge to expectorate, and with the name of God or the Virgin Mary still in her mouth, she had to clear her throat; lately, she had taken to swallowing the phlegm, but was worried that the name of God or the Virgin would slide down into her stomach wrapped in phlegm and get mixed up with her faeces! What should she do?

A wild-eyed Father Ferrão wiped the sweat from his brow.

But that was not the worst: the worst thing had happened the night before; she had been sitting quite calmly and virtuously praying to St Francis Xavier when suddenly, how she didn't know, she had started wondering what St Francis Xavier would look like naked!

Father Ferrão was too stunned to move. Then seeing her looking eagerly across at him, waiting for his words and his advice, he said:

'And have you been experiencing these terrors, these doubts, for very long?'

'Always, Father, always!'

'And have you lived with other people who, like you, are subject to these worrying thoughts?'

'Everyone I know, dozens of my friends, everyone . . . The Enemy has not just chosen me. He attacks everyone.'

'And what remedy are you usually given for these anxieties of the soul?'

'Oh, Father, those saintly men in Leiria, Father Amaro, Father Silvério, Father Guedes, they always got us out of any difficulties . . . And they did it so skilfully, so easily . . .'

Father Ferrão said nothing for a moment; he felt sad to think that throughout the land all those hundreds of priests were wilfully leading the flock into these dark realms of the soul, keeping the world of the faithful in abject terror of Heaven, representing God and his saints as a court which was no less corrupt and no better than the court of Caligula and his freed slaves.

He tried then to shed a broader, brighter light on that nocturnal, fanatical mind inhabited by phantasmagoria. He told her that all her anxieties came from an imagination tormented by a fear of offending God. That God was not a fierce, angry master, but an indulgent, caring father. That one must serve him with love not fear. That all these scruples – Our Lady sticking pins in her legs, God's name slipping down into her stomach – were the product of a sick mind. He advised her to trust in God and to eat well in order to recover her strength. And not to wear herself out by praying too much.

'And when I come back,' he said at last, getting up to say goodbye, 'we will talk about all this again and try to calm that soul of yours.'

'Thank you, Father,' she replied coolly.

And when Gertrudes came in shortly afterwards with the hot water bottle for her feet, Dona Josefa burst out indignantly, almost weeping:

'The man's useless, useless! He just didn't understand. He's an impostor, a freemason, Gertrudes! How shameful, and in a man of God too!'

She never again revealed to him the fearsome sins that she continued to commit; and when he dutifully tried to resume the education of her soul, she said bluntly that, since she normally confessed with Father Gusmão, she was not sure that it would be correct to receive moral instruction from another.

Father Ferrão turned very red and said:

'You're quite right, Senhora, quite right; one cannot be too careful in these matters.'

He left, and thenceforth, having gone into her room to enquire after her health, to talk about the weather, the season, the various illnesses doing the rounds, or about some festival at the church, he would hastily say goodbye and go out onto the terrace to talk to Amélia.

Noticing how terribly sad she looked, he had immediately taken an interest in her, and for Amélia, his visits were a distraction from the solitude of the house; and they became such good friends that, on the days that he regularly called, Amélia would put on a shawl and walk along the Poiais road and wait for him by the blacksmith's shop. She found Father Ferrão, who was a tireless talker, very entertaining, his conversation was so different from the gossip of Rua da Misericórdia, just as the sight of a broad valley with trees, planted fields, rivers, orchards and the sound of people working brings rest to eyes accustomed to the four whitewashed walls of a garret room in the city. In fact, these conversations bore a marked resemblance to weekly magazines like *The Family Treasury* or *Evening Readings*, in which there is a little of everything – moral doctrine, travel stories, anecdotes about great men, articles about farming, jokes, the sublime details of a saint's life, the odd poem and even useful tips, like the one he gave Amélia about how to wash flannel without it shrinking. It was only dull when he talked about his parishioners, about their marriages and christenings, about their illnesses and other problems, or when he started on his hunting stories.

'Once, my dear young lady, I was heading for Córrego das Tristes when a flock of partridges . . .'

Amélia knew then that, for at least an hour, she would be regaled with the exploits of his dog Janota and with his own extraordinary feats of shooting, which he would act out, complete with bird noises and the bang bang of the gun. Or else with descriptions of the big game hunting that he read about with such glee – tiger hunts in Nepal, lion hunts in Algeria and elephant hunts, bloodcurdling stories that dragged the girl's imagination far away to exotic lands where the grass grows as tall as pine trees, where the sun burns like a brand, and the eyes of some wild beast glint from behind every branch. And then, apropos of tigers and Malays, he would remember a curious story about St Francis Xavier, and that would set him off, this inveterate talker, on a description of derring-do in Asia, armadas in India and the famous stockades in the siege of Diu!

It was on one such day, in the orchard, when Father Ferrão, having begun by setting out the advantages to Canon Dias of transforming the orchard into arable land, had ended by describing the dangers faced so bravely by missionaries in India and Japan, that Amélia, intensely afflicted by her night-time terrors, had spoken to him of the noises she heard in the house and how they frightened her.

'Why, you should be ashamed of yourself,' he said, laughing, 'a woman of your age being afraid of bogeymen.'

Touched by his kindness, she told him about the voices she heard at night behind the bedhead.

He grew serious.

'Senhora, these are imaginings that you must try at all costs to control. There have doubtless been miracles in the world, but God does not start talking to just anyone from behind the canopies of beds, and he does not allow the Devil to do so either. Those voices, if you really hear them and if your sins are very grave, do not come from behind the bed, but from you yourself, from your conscience. And even with Gertrudes, or indeed a hundred Gertrudes, sleeping near your bed, or even a whole battalion of infantry, you would still hear them. You would hear them even if you were deaf. The important thing is to calm the conscience that is pleading for penance and purification.'

They had gone up onto the terrace as they talked, and Amélia had sat down wearily on one of the stone benches there and was looking out at the farm in the distance, the roofs of the barns, the long avenue of laurel bushes, the threshing floor, and, farther off, the flat fields freshened by that morning's light rain; the evening now was bright, calm and windless, with large, unmoving clouds that the sunset painted with bright, tender pinks ... She was thinking about Father Ferrão's sensible words, about the sense of repose she would feel if each of the sins that weighed like rocks upon her soul were to become light and to be dissipated by an act of penitence. And she was filled by a desire to be at peace and to rest like the quiet fields that lay before her.

A bird sang, then fell silent, and then began again a moment later, such a joyful, vibrant song that Amélia smiled to hear it.

'It's a nightingale.'

'Nightingales don't sing at this time of day,' said Father Ferrão. 'It's a blackbird. Now there's a creature who's not afraid of ghosts and hears no voices. And the rascal sings with such gusto too!'

It was indeed a triumphant sound, the joyous delirium of a happy blackbird, which lent a bright, festive sound to the whole orchard.

And suddenly, for no reason, confronted by the glorious warbling of that happy bird, Amélia, in one of those nervous fits that afflict hysterical women, burst out crying.

'Now, now, what's this?' said Father Ferrão, greatly surprised.

To calm her, he took her hand with the familiarity of an old man and a friend.

'I'm so unhappy,' she sobbed.

And he, very paternally, said:

'You've no reason to be. Whatever your afflictions or worries, a Christian soul always has consolation to hand. There is no sin that God cannot forgive, no pain he cannot soothe, remember that. What you must not do is keep your unhappiness to yourself. That's what troubles you and makes you cry. If I can help to comfort you, then come and see me . . .'

'When?' she asked, already eager to find refuge in that saintly man's protection.

'Whenever you like,' he said, laughing. 'I don't have particular times for consoling people. The church is always open, and God is always there.'

Early the next morning, before Dona Josefa had got up, Amélia went to his house, and for two hours, she knelt before the small pine confessional, which the good priest had, with his own hand, painted dark blue, adorning it with extraordinary little angel heads with wings instead of ears, a work of high art of which he spoke with secret vanity.

XXII

Father Amaro had just finished supper and was sitting smoking a cigarette and staring up at the ceiling in order not to see the long, gaunt face of the coadjutor, a still, spectral presence, who had been there now for half an hour and who, every ten minutes or so, would ask a question that would drop into the silence of the room like the melancholy quarter hours struck by the Cathedral clock throughout the night.

'Do you no longer subscribe to *The Nation*, Father?'

'No, I read *The People* now.'

The coadjutor resumed his silence and began again the laborious process of collating the words for his next question. At last, he said slowly:

'You haven't ever heard any more of that scoundrel who wrote the article in *The District Voice*, have you?'

'No, he went off to Brazil.'

The maid came in at that moment, saying that 'there was a person wishing to speak to him'. It was her way of announcing that Dionísia was in the kitchen.

She had not been to see him for weeks, and Amaro, his curiosity aroused, immediately left the room, closing the door behind him, and called Dionísia out onto the landing.

'I have some extraordinary news, Father! In fact, I ran all the way here. João Eduardo is back!'

'Good heavens!' exclaimed Father Amaro. 'I was just talking about him. What an amazing coincidence!'

'It's true. I saw him today. I was dumbstruck. But I've already found out all about him. He's tutor to the children of the estate owner.'

'Which estate owner?'

'The owner of the Poiais estate. I don't know yet whether he lives there or whether he just goes there in the morning and comes back at night. All I know is that he's back in Leiria. And he looks quite the dandy, new suit and everything. I thought I should warn you because, sooner or later, he's bound to see Amélia up there at the house. It's on the road to the estate. What do you think?'

'The stupid fool!' snorted Amaro angrily. 'When he's not needed, he turns up. So presumably he didn't go to Brazil after all?'

'Apparently not . . . because it certainly wasn't his ghost, it was him in the flesh. Coming out of Fernandes' shop, too, looking very smart. You had better warn the girl, Father, so that he doesn't look up one day and see her at the window.'

Amaro gave her the money she was expecting, and a quarter of an hour later, having rid himself of the coadjutor, he was on his way to Ricoça.

His heart beat faster when he saw the newly-painted yellow mansion, the broad terrace along the side of the house, running parallel to the orchard wall, its parapet adorned at intervals with large stone vases. After many long weeks, he was about to see his Amelia again! And he could already imagine her passionate cries as she fell into his arms.

On the ground floor were the stables, dating from the time when the original owners had lived there, but these were now the domain of rats and mushrooms, and the only light came from narrow, barred windows that were almost entirely covered by thick layers of cobwebs; one entered through a vast, dark courtyard, one corner of which had for years now been home to a mountain of empty barrels; to the right, flanked by two small stone lions, benign and sleepy, was the elegant staircase that led to the rooms above. Amaro went up the stairs to a large salon with a coffered oak ceiling; the room was entirely bare of furniture and half the floor was covered with dried beans.

Not knowing what else to do, he clapped his hands.

A door opened. Amélia appeared for a moment, wearing a white shift and with her hair all dishevelled; she gave a little shriek and slammed the door shut, and Father Amaro heard her running away into the house. He stood glumly in the middle of the room, his umbrella underneath his arm, remembering the easy familiarity with which he used to enter the house in Rua da Misericórdia, where the doors seemed to open of their own accord and the very wallpaper seemed to brighten with joy.

He grew irritated and was about to clap again, when Gertrudes appeared.

'Oh, it's you, Father Amaro! Come in. How good to see you. Senhora, it's Father Amaro!' she called, pleased to see a friendly face at last, a friend from town, in that place of exile.

She led him immediately into Dona Josefa's bedroom at the back of the house, an enormous room, where, on a small sofa tucked away in one corner, the old lady spent her days huddled in her shawl, her feet wrapped in a blanket.

'Dona Josefa! How are you?'

She could not reply, seized by a fit of coughing caused by the excitement of his visit.

'As you see, Father,' she managed to murmur feebly, 'getting older by the day. And how are you? Why haven't you visited before?'

Amaro made some vague excuse about his duties at the Cathedral, and, seeing that pale, hollow-cheeked face beneath the hideous black lace bonnet, he realised what sad hours Amélia must have spent there. He asked after Amélia; he had seen her in the distance, but she had run away.

'That's because she wasn't decently dressed, ' said the old woman. 'It's laundry day today.'

Amaro asked what they got up to, how they passed the time all alone there.

'I spend my days in here and Miss Amélia goes about her own business.'

She seemed to sink under the effort of uttering each word, and her hoarseness grew more marked.

'So the change hasn't done you much good, then?'

She shook her head.

'Don't listen to her, Father,' said Gertrudes, who had remained standing beside the sofa, enjoying Amaro's presence. 'Don't listen to her. She's exaggerating. She gets up every day, walks into the living room, has a bit of chicken to eat. She's a lot better. It's just like Father Ferrão says, good health goes galloping off, but it comes back at a walk.'

The door opened and Amélia appeared, her face scarlet; she was wearing her old purple woollen dressing gown and her hair had been very hastily arranged.

'I'm sorry, Father,' she stammered, 'but today has been rather chaotic.'

He shook her hand gravely, and they stood in silence, as if separated by a vast desert. She fiddled with one corner of the woollen shawl she wore over her shoulders and kept her eyes fixed on the floor. Amaro found her quite changed; her face was plumper, and there was a line at each corner of her mouth that made her look older. In order to break that strange silence, he asked her if she was all right.

'Not too bad. It's a bit of a gloomy house, though. As Father Ferrão says, it's too big for us to really feel at home in it.'

'We didn't come here to enjoy ourselves,' said the old woman, with her eyes closed, although without a trace of fatigue in her cold voice.

Amélia looked down, and the colour drained from her face.

Then, realising in a flash how the old woman must have been tormenting Amélia, Amaro said very sternly:

'No, you didn't come here to enjoy yourselves, but neither did you come here to make yourselves miserable. Being ill-tempered and making other people suffer for it denotes a disgraceful lack of charity, and there is no worse sin in the eyes of the Lord. Anyone who behaves in such a fashion is unworthy of God's grace.'

The old woman burst into hysterical sobs.

'Oh, the things God has reserved for me in my old age . . .'

Gertrudes tried to cheer her up. She would only make matters worse by upsetting herself like that. There was no need to take on so. Everything would sort itself out with God's help. She would get her health back eventually along with her good humour.

Amélia had gone over to the window, doubtless to hide the tears that had started to her eyes too. And saddened by the scene, Amaro began saying that Dona Josefa was not bearing that period of illness with true Christian resignation . . . Nothing so shocked Our Lord as to see his creatures rebelling against the ills and burdens that He had sent them. It was an insult to the justice of His commands.

'You're quite right, Father, quite right,' murmured Dona Josefa contritely. 'I don't know what I'm saying sometimes. It's the illness.'

'All right, all right, but from now on, you must resign yourself to your lot and try to see everything in the best possible light. That is what God wants from you. I know it's hard being shut up here . . .'

'That's what Father Ferrão says,' broke in Amélia, returning from the window. 'Dona Josefa feels disoriented here . . . uprooted from the habits of a lifetime . . .'

Noticing these repeated references to Father Ferrão, Amaro asked if he was a frequent visitor.

'Oh, he's been such good company,' said Amélia. 'He comes nearly every day.'

'He's a real saint,' exclaimed Gertrudes.

'Of course, of course,' muttered Amaro, irked by their enthusiasm. 'He's a man of great virtue.'

'Oh, he is that,' sighed Dona Josefa, 'but . . .' She stopped, not daring to express her devout reservations. Then she said pleadingly: 'But, Father, you're the one who should come to see me and help me bear the cross of this illness.'

'And I will, Senhora, I will. You need distraction, news from outside. In fact, I had a letter from the Canon only yesterday.'

He took the letter from his pocket and read a few extracts. The Canon had already taken fifteen sea baths. The beach was packed with people. Dona Maria had been ill with a boil. The weather was superb. They went for long walks each evening to see the nets being brought in. São Joaneira was well, but never stopped talking about Amélia . . .

'Poor Mama,' whimpered Amélia.

But Dona Josefa was not interested in the news, being too busy wheezing. It was Amélia who asked after friends in Leiria: Father Natário, Father Silvério . . .

It was getting dark and Gertrudes went to prepare the oil lamp. Amaro got up to go.

'Well, Senhora, I'll see you again soon. I'll pop in from time to time, don't worry. And try not to upset yourself. Wrap up warm, eat well, and God's mercy will not abandon you.'

'Oh, come back soon, Father, come back soon!'

Amélia held out her hand to him, intending to say goodbye in the room itself, but Amaro said jokingly:

'If you wouldn't mind, Miss Amélia, could you just show me the way out? I get lost in this big house.'

They left the room and once they were in the vast salon where there was still some light coming in through the three large windows, he stopped and said:

'She's making your life a misery, isn't she?'

'Well, what else do I deserve?' Amélia replied, looking down.

'Shameless creature, I'll make her pay for it. Oh, Amélia, if you knew how hard it's been for me . . .'

And he went to put his arms about her neck.

She drew back in consternation.

'What's wrong?' asked Amaro in amazement.

'What do you mean?'

'Pulling away from me like that. Don't you want to kiss me, Amélia? Are you mad?'

She held up her hands to him in a gesture of supplication, saying tremulously:

'No, Father, just leave me alone. That's all over. We've sinned quite enough. I want to die in God's grace, so please don't ever mention it again. What we did was wrong, but it's over. Now all I want is for my soul to be at peace.'

'Don't be ridiculous! Who put those ideas in your head? Now, listen . . .'

And he went towards her again, his arms open.

'Please, for the love of God, don't touch me,' she said, running back to the door.

He looked at her for a moment, in mute fury.

'All right, if that's what you want,' he said at last. 'Anyway, I came to warn you that João Eduardo has come back; he passes by here every day, so you had better keep away from the windows.'

'What do I care about João Eduardo or about the others or about anything . . .'

He broke in with bitter sarcasm:

'Oh, of course, the man of the moment is Father Ferrão.'

'All I know is that I owe him a lot . . .'

Gertrudes came in just then with the oil lamp lit. And without saying goodbye to Amélia, Amaro rushed off, brandishing his umbrella and grinding his teeth with rage.

However, the long walk back to Leiria calmed him down. He put Amélia's response down to an access of virtue and moral scrupulousness! There she was, far away from him, in that great barn of a house, tormented by Dona Josefa, and impressed by the words of the moralistic Father Ferrão, and that had been her natural reaction, full of fears of the next world and of longings for innocence. What a joke! If he started going to Ricoça regularly, he would have her back under his control within a week. Oh, he knew her well. He would just have to touch her, to wink at her, and she would surrender.

Nevertheless, he spent a restless night, wanting her more than ever. And the next day, he set off to Ricoça, bearing a bunch of roses.

Dona Josefa was thrilled to see him. His very presence did her good! And if it wasn't such a long way to come, she would ask him to do her the favour of visiting every morning. After yesterday's visit, she had even prayed more fervently.

Amaro smiled distractedly, his eyes fixed on the door.

'And where's Miss Amélia?' he asked at last.

'She's gone out. She goes walking every morning,' said Dona Josefa sourly. 'She goes to see Father Ferrão, that's all she ever talks about.'

'Ah,' said Amaro, with a feeble smile. 'A resurgence of devotion, eh? Well, he's an excellent man, Father Ferrão.'

'Oh, he's useless, useless!' exclaimed Dona Josefa. 'He doesn't understand me and he has such strange ideas. He's no help at all . . .'

'He is rather a bookish man . . .' said Amaro.

Dona Josefa lifted herself up on one elbow, her gaunt face aflame with hatred, and in a low voice she said:

'Just between ourselves, Miss Amélia has behaved very badly! I'll never forgive her for it. She has confessed to Father Ferrão. It's so rude, since she's your confessant and has never received anything but kindness from you. The ungrateful girl, the traitor!'

Amaro had turned pale.

'What did you say?'

'It's the truth! Let her deny it if she can. She's even proud of it. She's utterly shameless! Especially after the great favour we're all doing her.'

Amaro disguised the anger churning inside him. He even laughed. One mustn't exaggerate. It wasn't a matter of ingratitude. It was a question of faith. If the girl thought Father Ferrão could provide her with better guidance, then she was quite right to speak to him. What everyone wanted was for her to save her soul, and it really didn't matter under whose direction that happened. And she would be quite safe in Father Ferrão's hands.

Then he drew his chair suddenly closer to Dona Josefa's bed:

'So she goes to see him every morning?'

'Nearly every morning. She'll be back soon. She goes after breakfast and always comes back about now. You've no idea how it's upset me.'

Amaro took a few nervous paces about the room, then, holding out his hand to Dona Josefa, said:

'Well, Senhora, I must be going. It's only a fleeting visit today, I'm afraid, but I'll come and see you again soon.'

And disregarding the old woman, who was urging him to stay to lunch, he hurtled down the steps like a stone and set off furiously for Father Ferrão's house, still clutching his bunch of roses.

He expected to meet Amélia on the road and he spotted her near the blacksmith's shop, crouched down near the wall, sentimentally gathering wild flowers.

'What are you doing here?' he exclaimed, as he drew near.

She stood up with a cry.

'What are you doing here?' he said again.

When she heard that angry, familiar tone, she anxiously placed one finger on her mouth. Father Ferrão was inside with the blacksmith.

'Listen,' said Amaro, his eyes blazing, gripping her by the arm, 'did you confess to him?'

'Why do you want to know? Yes, I did as it happens. It's nothing to be ashamed of.'

'You mean you confessed *everything*?' he asked, his teeth clenched with rage.

She lost control and, still addressing him as '*tu*', said:

'Isn't that what you always told me, over and over, that the worst sin in the world was to keep anything back from your confessor.'

'You fool!' roared Amaro.

His eyes devoured her, and through the choleric mist filling his brain and making the veins in his forehead throb, he found her even prettier than before, with a new roundness to her body that he burned to embrace, with red lips, freshened by the clean country air, which he longed to bite until he drew blood.

'Listen,' he said, giving in to that brutal invasion of desire. 'Listen! All right, I don't care, you can confess to whoever the devil you want . . . but you'll always be mine, you hear!'

'No!' she said forcefully, pulling away, ready to flee into the blacksmith's shop.

'You'll pay for this, you wretch,' snarled Amaro, turning his back and striding desperately away down the road.

And he did not slacken his pace until he reached Leiria, borne along on an angry impulse which, amidst the sweet peace of mid-October, provoked in him plans of cruel revenge. He reached home exhausted, with the flowers still in his hand. But there, in the quiet of his room, he became gradually aware of his utter impotence to act. What could he do, after all? Go around the town telling everyone that she was pregnant? That would be tantamount to denouncing himself.

Spread a rumour that she was Father Ferrão's mistress? That was absurd; he was nearly seventy years old, hideously ugly, and with a totally unblemished past. But to lose her, never to have that snow-white body in his arms again, never to hear those tender words that swept his soul off to some better place than Heaven itself, no, that he could not bear!

And was it possible that in the space of six or seven weeks she could have forgotten everything? During the long nights in Ricoça, alone in bed, did she never think of those mornings in the sexton's room? Of course she did; he knew this from all the female confessants who had revealed to him, in great distress, the silent, stubborn temptation that never leaves the flesh once it has sinned . . .

No, he must pursue her, and use any means he could to communicate to her the desire that burned even higher in him now, even more fiercely.

He spent the night writing her an absurd six-page letter, full of passionate entreaties, mystical subtleties, exclamation marks and threats of suicide.

Dionísia delivered it for him early the next day. The reply came that night, via a small boy who worked on the farm. How eagerly he tore open the envelope. All it contained were these words: 'Please leave me in peace with my sins.'

He did not give up; the following day, he went to Ricoça again to visit Dona Josefa. Amélia was in the room when he arrived. She turned very pale, but her eyes never left her sewing during the half hour that he spent there, while he sat either sunk in the armchair in tormented, sombre silence or responded distractedly to the chatter of Dona Josefa, who was in talkative mood that morning.

And the following week, the same thing happened; as soon as she heard him arrive, she would quickly lock herself in her room and would only come if Dona Josefa sent Gertrudes to tell her that 'Father Amaro wanted to see her'. She would go then and offer him her hand, which always seemed to him scalding hot, only to take up her eternal sewing, next to the window, backstitching away in infuriating silence.

He had written her another letter. She had not replied.

Then he vowed not to go back to Ricoça, to spurn her, but after a night spent tossing and turning in bed, unable to sleep, with the vision of her nakedness fixed unbearably in his mind, he would set off again to Ricoça the following morning, blushing when the timekeeper at the roadworks, who saw him pass by every day, took off his oilskin hat to him.

One rainy afternoon, as he was going into the house, he met Father Ferrão, who was standing at the door, opening his umbrella.

'Fancy meeting you here, Father!' he said.

Father Ferrão responded quite naturally:

'It's rather less of a surprise to see you here, since you visit every day.'

Amaro could not control himself and, trembling with rage, he said:

'And what business is it of yours whether I visit or not? Is this your house?'

This entirely unjustified rudeness offended Father Ferrão.

'Well, it would be better for everyone concerned if you did not visit.'

'And why is that, Father, tell me, why is that?' shouted Amaro, beside himself.

The good man shuddered. He had just committed the gravest fault a Catholic priest can commit: what he knew about Amaro and about his love affair, was a secret of the confessional, and he was betraying the mystery of the sacrament by showing that he disapproved of Amaro's persistent desire to sin. He took off his hat and said humbly:

'You're quite right, Father. Forgive me. I spoke without thinking. Good afternoon, Father.'

'Good afternoon, Father Ferrão.'

Amaro did not go into the house. He returned home in the now pelting rain. As soon as he arrived, he wrote another long letter to Amélia, in which he told her what had happened with Father Ferrão, heaping accusations on him, especially that of having betrayed the secret of the confessional. This, like the other letters, received no reply.

Then Amaro began to believe that such resistance could

not possibly arise so suddenly from mere repentance and a terror of Hell. 'There's some man involved,' he thought. And, eaten away by black jealousy, he began to prowl around the house at Ricoça at night, but he saw nothing; the house remained dark and asleep. On one occasion, however, as he approached the orchard wall, he heard ahead of him on the road from Poiais a voice singing in maudlin tones 'The Waltz of Two Worlds', and saw the bright point of a lit cigar approaching in the darkness. Frightened, Amaro took shelter in a ruined shack on the other side of the road. The singing stopped, and Amaro, peering out, saw someone in a light-coloured cloak stop and gaze up at the windows of the house. A wave of jealousy gripped Amaro and he was just about to leap out and attack the man, when he saw him walk calmly off again, holding his cigar aloft and singing:

> Can you hear ringing in the mountains
> That mighty terrifying roar . . .

The voice, the cloak and the walk he recognised at once as João Eduardo's, but he was sure that if a man was visiting Amélia at night or going into the farm, that man was certainly not João Eduardo. Fearful of being discovered, Amaro ceased his prowlings round the house.

It was indeed João Eduardo, who, whenever he passed Ricoça, by day or by night, would pause for a moment and look sadly up at the walls where *she* lived. Because, despite his many disappointments, Amélia was still the poor lad's beloved and the most precious thing on earth. In Ourém, in Alcobaça, at the various inns where he had stayed, even in Lisbon, where he had arrived like the keel of a wrecked ship washed up on the shore, her presence had not for a moment ceased to inhabit his soul, nor had he ever stopped tenderly thinking of her. During those bitter days in Lisbon, the worst in his entire life, working as a runner for an obscure law firm, lost in that city that seemed to him as vast as a Rome or a Babylon and in which he experienced the harsh egotism of the bustling multitude, he had struggled to keep alive that love which was to him like a sweet companion. He felt less alone as long as he could hold in his mind that image with which he would maintain imaginary conversations on his endless walks along the Cais do Sodré, blaming her for all the grinding sadnesses of his life.

And that passion, which was to him a vague justification for his misery, made him seem more interesting in his own eyes. He was a 'martyr for love' and that idea consoled him, just as, during his first period of despair, it had consoled him to feel that he was 'a victim of religious persecution'. He was not merely another poor devil whom chance, idleness, fate, the lack of friends and the patches on his jacket kept fatally locked in the privations of dependency: he was a man with a great heart who, after a heroic struggle, had been forced by a catastrophe that was part-romantic and part-political, by a domestic and social drama, to traipse from one law office to another with a bag full of legal documents. Fate had made of him a hero like so many of the heroes he had read about in sentimental novels. And he attributed his worn jacket, his frugal suppers, the days when he had no money for cigarettes, to his fateful love for Amélia and to his persecution by a powerful class, and thus, out of a very human instinct, he attributed a very grand origin to his trivial afflictions. When he saw people whom he termed 'happy' – men driving carriages, young men walking along with a pretty woman on their arm, people well wrapped up against the cold on their way to the theatre, he felt less unfortunate thinking that he too possessed a great inner luxury – that unhappy love affair. And when he, by chance, was offered a job in Brazil and the money for his passage, he idealised the banal adventure of emigration, repeating to himself over and over that he was going across the seas, exiled from his own country by the combined tyrannies of the priesthood and of the authorities, and all because he had loved a woman!

Who would have thought then, as he packed his suit away in a metal trunk, that only a few weeks later he would once more be living barely half a league from those same priests and those same authorities, gazing tenderly up at Amélia's window! And all because of that most unusual man, the Morgado de Poiais, that is, the heir to the Poiais estate, who was neither a true heir nor even originally from Poiais, but merely a wealthy eccentric from near Alcobaça, who had bought the property from the noble family of Poiais, and who had received, along with possession of the land, the honorary title of Morgado – it was this saintly man who had saved him from the horrors of seasickness and from the hazards of emigration. He had chanced to meet him in the office where he was still working on the eve of his departure. The Morgado, who was a client of old Nunes, knew his story and knew about the article he had written in *The District Voice* and about the scandal in the Cathedral square, and had conceived for him an ardent sympathy.

The Morgado had a fanatical hatred of priests, so much so that he never read about a crime in a newspaper without deciding (even when the guilty party had already been sentenced) that there must be a priest involved in it somewhere. It was said that this rancour had its origins in his unhappy first marriage to a famously devout woman in Alcobaça. As soon as he met João Eduardo in Lisbon and learned of his imminent departure, he immediately had the idea of bringing him back to Leiria, installing him in Poiais, and handing over to him the primary education of his two small children, as a clear affront to the diocesan clergy. He assumed too that João Eduardo was an unbeliever, and this fitted in with his philosophical plan to bring up his children to be 'out-and-out atheists'. João Eduardo accepted with tears in his eyes, for the post brought with it a magnificent salary, a position, a family, and an ostentatious rehabilitation.

'I will never forget what you have done for me, sir!'

'I'm doing it entirely for my own pleasure. I want to provoke those scoundrels! We leave tomorrow!'

In Chão de Maçãs, as he got down from the train, the Morgado immediately exclaimed to the station master, who did not know João Eduardo or his story:

'I have brought him back with me in triumph! He has

come to beat the whole priesthood to a pulp. And if there are any costs to pay, I will pay them!'

The station master was not in the least surprised, for the Morgado was generally considered to be mad.

It was in Poiais, on the day immediately following his arrival, that João Eduardo learned that Amélia and Dona Josefa were staying at the house in Ricoça. He found this out from Father Ferrão, the only priest to whom the Morgado would speak, and whom he received in his house not as a priest, but as a gentleman.

'I admire you as a gentleman, Senhor Ferrão,' he used to say, 'but as a priest, I loathe you.'

And good Father Ferrão would smile, knowing that the ferocious exterior of this stubborn unbeliever concealed both a saintly heart and a true benefactor of the parish poor.

The Morgado was also a great lover of old books and a tireless debater; sometimes the two of them would have tremendous battles about history, botany, hunting methods . . . When Father Ferrão, in the heat of argument, proposed some contrary opinion, the Morgado would exclaim loftily:

'Are you saying that as a priest or as a gentleman?'

'As a gentleman, Senhor Morgado.'

'Then I accept your objection. It's very sensible. If you were putting the same objection forward as a priest, however, I would break your bones.'

Sometimes, hoping to annoy Father Ferrão, he would show João Eduardo to him, fondly patting the young man on the back, as if he were a favourite horse.

'Look at him! He's already finished off one priest, and he'll kill two or three more yet. And if they arrest him, I myself will save him from the gallows.'

'That wouldn't be very difficult, Senhor Morgado,' said Father Ferrão, calmly taking a pinch of snuff. 'There are no gallows in Portugal any more.'

The Morgado was furious. No gallows? And why was that? Because we had a free government and a constitutional monarchy! If the priests had their way, there would be a gallows on every square and a bonfire on every corner!

'Tell me something, Senhor Ferrão, are you going to defend the Inquisition here in my house?'

'Please, Senhor Morgado, I didn't even mention the Inquisition . . .'

'Ah, that was only because you were afraid to, because you knew perfectly well that I would have plunged a dagger into your heart!'

And he said all this at the top of his voice, cavorting about the room, creating a veritable gale with the prodigious skirts of his yellow dressing gown.

'Deep down he's an angel,' the Father said to João Eduardo. 'He would give his own shirt even to a priest if he knew he needed it. You'll be all right here, João Eduardo. You just have to ignore his little obsessions.'

Father Ferrão had become fond of João Eduardo, and having heard from Amélia all about the famous article in *The District Voice*, he had wanted, to use his favourite expression, 'to get a feel for the man'. He had spent whole afternoons talking with him in the avenue of laurels in the garden of his house, where João Eduardo came to stock up on books; and beneath the 'exterminator of priests' as the Morgado called him, he found a poor, sensitive lad with a rather sentimental view of religion, a longing for domestic peace and a real enjoyment of his work. Father Ferrão had an idea which seemed to him to have come from above, from God's will, because it came to him one day when he had just finished his devotions to the Sacrament; his idea was to marry João Eduardo to Amélia. It would not be difficult to bring that weak and tender heart to forgive her mistake; and now that all passion was spent, the passion that had entered her soul like the Devil's breath, driving her will, her peace of mind and her modesty down into the abyss, the poor girl, who had been through so much, would find in João Eduardo's company a remnant of calm and contentment, a safe and cosy haven, a sweet refuge and a purification from the past. He said nothing to either of them about the idea he was nurturing. It was not the moment now, not while she was carrying in her womb the other man's child. But he was lovingly preparing for that moment, especially when he was with Amélia, telling her all about his conversations with João Eduardo, about some particularly sensible comment he had made, about the excellent skills as a tutor that he was developing in educating the Morgado's children.

'He's a fine young man,' he would say. 'A family man . . . the sort to whom a woman could really entrust her life and her happiness. If I were a man of the world and I had a daughter, I'd happily give her to him.'

Amélia did not respond, she merely blushed.

She could no longer object to these persuasive commendations by bringing up the one great obstacle – the article in *The District Voice*, his lack of belief! Father Ferrão had demolished that one day by saying:

'I read the article, Senhora. The lad was writing not against priests, but against the Pharisees!'

And to attenuate that harsh judgement on the priests mentioned in the article, which was the least charitable thing he had said in years, he added:

'It was a grave fault, for which he has repented. He paid for it with tears and with hunger.'

And that touched Amélia.

It was about this time too that Dr Gouveia began visiting Ricoça because Dona Josefa had grown worse with the coming of the cold autumn days. At first, Amélia used to shut herself up in her room when he came, trembling at the thought of being seen in her present state by old Dr Gouveia, the family doctor, that man of legendary severity. In the end, though, she had had to go to Dona Josefa's room to receive her instructions as nurse, as to when the various medicines were to be taken and what food was to be prepared. And one day, accompanying the doctor to the door, she had stopped in her tracks when she saw him pause and turn, stroking the long white beard that spilled over his velvet jacket.

'I was quite right when I told your mother you should get married!' he said.

Her eyes filled with tears.

'Now, now, child, I meant no harm. You're quite right. Nature demands conception not marriage. Marriage is just an administrative formula.'

Amélia was looking at him, uncomprehending, two round tears running slowly down her cheeks. He patted her paternally under the chin.

'I simply mean that, as a believer in the naturalist philosophy, I am pleased. I think you have made yourself useful to the general order of things. But let's get down to what matters . . .'

And he gave her some advice on questions of health.

'And if, when the time comes, you have any problems, just send for me.'

He started down the stairs. Amélia stopped him and in a tone of frightened supplication, said:

'You won't tell anyone in town . . .'

Dr Gouveia stopped.

'Now you're being silly. But it's all right, I forgive you. It's just your temperament. No, I won't say anything, child. Why the devil didn't you marry poor João Eduardo? He would have made you just as happy as the other man, and there would have been no need for secrecy. But that's a purely secondary matter. I've told you what's important. Be sure to send for me. And don't put too much trust in your saints. I know more about all this than St Brigid or whoever. You're a strong girl and you'll present the State with a fine, sturdy baby.'

She did not understand everything he said, but she sensed in his words both a vague justification for her condition and the kindness of an indulgent grandfather, especially in those knowledgeable assurances as to her good health, to which the doctor's grey beard, the beard of an Eternal Father, lent an air of infallibility, and his words comforted her and increased the serenity she had been enjoying now for some weeks, ever since her first desperate confession in the chapel in Poiais.

It had doubtless been Our Lady, taking pity at last on her tormented state, who had sent down to her from Heaven the idea of going and pouring out her heart to Father Ferrão. It seemed to her that she had left behind in his dark blue confessional all her sorrows and fears, the black ragbag of remorse that was suffocating her soul. With every consoling word he spoke she had felt the blackness covering the sky disappearing; now everything was blue again; and when she prayed, Our Lady did not angrily turn away. His way of confessing was so different. He did not behave like the rigid representative of an ill-tempered God; there was something feminine and maternal about him that passed over her soul like a caress; rather than laying before her eyes the sinister scene of the fires of Hell, he had shown her a vast merciful Heaven with the doors flung wide and with many roads leading to it, so easy and sweet to tread that only the stubborn and the rebellious would refuse to try. According to this gentle interpretation of the after-life, God was like a kindly, smiling great-grandfather, Our Lady was a sister of charity, and the saints were all hospitable comrades! It was a welcoming religion, bathed in grace, in which one pure tear was enough to redeem a life of sin. How different from the gloomy doctrine that had kept her terrified and trembling ever since she was a child – as different as that tiny village chapel was from the Cathedral's vast mass of masonry! There, in the old Cathedral, the cubit-thick walls separated one off from natural, human life; it was all darkness, melancholy, penitence and the stern faces of images; none of the joyful things of the world entered there, no blue sky, no birds, no fresh air from the fields, no smiles from bright lips; the only flowers there were artificial ones; the doorkeeper was stationed at the door to keep out dogs and children; even the sun was exiled, and the only available light came from gloomy candelabra. In the little chapel in Poaias, on the other hand, nature was on familiar terms with the Good Lord! The scent of honeysuckle wafted in on the breeze through the open doors; the whitewashed walls echoed with the cries of little children; the altar was like a combination of garden and orchard; bold sparrows were even to be found perched chirruping on the pedestals of the crucifixes; occasionally a grave-faced ox would poke its snout through the door with all the old familiarity of the stable in Bethlehem, or a lost sheep would come in, overjoyed to see a member of its own race, the Paschal Lamb, sleeping comfortably at the back of the altar with its front legs wrapped around the holy cross.

Besides, Father Ferrão was, as he put it, 'not interested in impossibilities'. He knew that she could not simply extirpate in a moment that guilty love which had rooted itself in the very depths of her being. He asked only that whenever she was overwhelmed by the idea of Amaro, she should immediately seek sanctuary in the idea of Christ. A poor young girl cannot do mortal combat with the colossal force of Satan, who has the strength of a Hercules; when she feels him near, all she can do is to take shelter in prayer and let him wear himself out roaring and frothing beyond the walls of that impenetrable refuge. He himself, with all the solicitude of a nurse, assisted her every day in that repurification of her soul; he was the one who, like a theatre director, had told her what attitude to adopt on Amaro's first visit to Ricoça; he would be there with a few consoling words, as restoring as a cordial, if he saw her falter in that slow reconquest of virtue; if she had spent a restless night remembering the warm pleasures of the past, then he would spend all morning talking to her, not as a teacher, but simply assuring her that Heaven would show her greater joys than any she had known in the sexton's sordid bedroom. He had proven to her, with the subtlety of a theologian, that there was in Amaro's love only brutality and bestial fury; that, however sweet the love of a man might be, the love of a priest could only be a momentary explosion of repressed desire; when Amaro had started sending her letters, Father Ferrão had analysed them sentence by sentence, revealing to her how much hypocrisy, egotism, rhetoric and crude desire they contained.

Thus he gradually weaned her away from Amaro. But he did not wean her away from the idea of a legitimate love, purified by the sacrament; he knew that she was all flesh and desire and that to launch her violently into mysticism might turn her for a moment from her natural instincts, but would never create in her a lasting peace. He did not try to tear her from human life; he did not want her to become a nun; he sensed in her a loving impulse and all he wanted was that it should serve the joy of a husband and the healthy harmony of a family rather than be squandered on casual affairs. Deep down in his priestly soul, Father Ferrão would doubtless have preferred her to leave behind the selfish interests of individual love and to give herself, as a sister of charity or as a nurse in some retreat, to the all-embracing love of humanity. But poor Amélia's flesh was very lovely and very weak; it would not be wise to frighten her with such lofty sacrifices; she was all woman and so she should remain; to limit her activities would be to limit her usefulness. Christ, with his ideal limbs nailed to the cross, was not enough for her; she needed a man like other men, moustachioed and wearing a tall hat. Never mind! Just as long as he was a husband legitimised by the Sacrament.

Thus he gradually cured her of that morbid passion by guiding her through each day, with a missionary persistence born of sincere faith, placing the subtlety of the casuist at the service of the morality of a skilful, fatherly philosopher – a marvellous cure of which the good priest was secretly rather proud.

And great was his joy when it seemed to him that, at last, her passion for Amaro was no longer a living feeling in her soul, but was dead, embalmed, placed in the depths of her memory as in a tomb, hidden now beneath the delicate flowering of a new virtue. That at least is what Ferrão thought, seeing her allude to the past with a serene gaze, without the furious blushes that used to burn her cheeks at the mere mention of Amaro's name.

Indeed, she no longer thought of Amaro with the old excitement: the dread of sin, Father Ferrão's powerful influence, the abrupt separation from the devout environment in which her love had developed and the pleasure she took in a greater serenity, with no nocturnal terrors and without the enmity of Our Lady, all helped to reduce the crackling fire of her feelings to a dully glowing ember. Amaro had initially inhabited her soul as if he were a gold-painted idol, but, since she had become pregnant, in her moments of religious terror or of hysterical repentance, she had so often shaken that idol that all the gilt had come off on her hands, and the dark, trivial shape beneath the gold no longer dazzled her; thus, without weeping or struggling, she watched Father Ferrão tear the idol down. If she still thought of Amaro, it was because she could not help thinking about the sexton's house, but what tempted her now was not Amaro but pleasure itself.

And with her natural good nature, she was genuinely grateful to Father Ferrão. As she had said to Amaro that evening, she owed him everything. That is how she felt now about Dr Gouveia as well, who came to see Dona Josefa every few days. They were her good friends, like two fathers sent to her by Heaven, one promising her health and the other grace.

Sheltered by those two protecting forces, she enjoyed a wonderful sense of peace during the last weeks of October. The days passed by, calm and warm. It was good to sit out on the terrace in the evenings, surrounded by the autumnal calm of the fields. Dr Gouveia would sometimes coincide with Father Ferrão; the two men shared a mutual respect, and once they had paid their visit to Dona Josefa, they would join her on the terrace and launch immediately into one of their endless discussions about Religion and Morality.

With her sewing in her lap, with her two good friends beside her, those two colossi of knowledge and sanctity, Amélia would abandon herself to the charm of that sweet hour, looking out at the orchard where the leaves on the trees were already growing pale. She was thinking about the future; it seemed easy and safe to her now; she was strong and, with the doctor there, the birth would involve only an hour or so of pain; then, free from that complication, she would return to the town and to her mother . . . And then, born of Father Ferrão's constant conversations about João Eduardo, another hope would shine and dance in her imagination. Why not? If the poor man still loved and forgave her . . . She had never found him repugnant as a man, and it would be a splendid marriage now that he enjoyed the friendship of the Morgado. It was said that João Eduardo was to be made administrator. And she could see herself living in Poiais, going out in the Morgado's carriage, being summoned to supper by a bell, being served by a liveried valet . . . For long moments, she would sit very still, immersed in the sweetness of that prospect, while, at the far end of the terrace, Father Ferrão and Dr Gouveia did battle over the doctrine of Grace and of Conscience, accompanied by the monotonous murmur of the water in the irrigation ditches in the orchard. It was at this time that Dona Josefa, concerned that Father Amaro had ceased his visits, sent the tenant to Leiria to ask him expressly to favour her with a visit. The man came back with the astonishing news that Father Amaro had left for Vieira and would not be back for two weeks. The old woman wept with vexation. And that night in her room, Amélia could not sleep out of sheer irritation at the thought of Father Amaro enjoying himself in Vieira, chatting to the ladies on the beach and flitting from party to party, doubtless without a thought for her . . .

With the first week of November came the rains. Ricoça seemed far more depressing during those short days of drenching rain and stormy skies. Father Ferrão, crippled with rheumatism, no longer came to visit. Dr Gouveia would shoot off in his old cabriolet after only half an hour. Amélia's one distraction was to stand at the window: on three occasions she had seen João Eduardo pass by on the road, but he had immediately looked away or taken refuge beneath his umbrella.

Dionísia was another frequent visitor: she was to be the midwife, despite Dr Gouveia's advice that Amélia should use Micaela, a respectable woman with thirty years' experience. But Amélia did not want more people in on the secret, and besides, Dionísia brought her news of Amaro, which she found out from his cook. Amaro was enjoying himself so much in Vieira that he planned to stay until December. This 'infamous behaviour' outraged her: she was sure that he wanted to be well out of the way when the birthpangs began, along with all the perils of childbirth. He had also determined a long time ago that the child would be handed over to a wetnurse near Ourém who would bring it up in the village, but the time was almost upon her, and no wetnurse had been arranged, and there he was gathering seashells on the seashore.

'It's not right, Dionísia!' Amélia would cry.

'Well, no, it doesn't seem right to me either. Of course, I could speak to the wetnurse, but these are serious matters. And Father Amaro said he would take care of everything.'

'It's outrageous!'

Added to that, she had neglected the baby's layette – the child was nearly due and she had no clothes for it and no money with which to buy them. Dionísia had even offered her a few items left in pawn with her by a woman who had been staying at her house. But Amélia could not bear the thought of her child wearing another child's nappies, which might perhaps bring with them illness or misfortune.

And, out of pride, she did not want to write to Amaro.

Added to that, Dona Josefa's rudeness was becoming intolerable. Deprived of the devout aid of a priest, a real priest (not Father Ferrão), poor Dona Josefa felt that her defenceless old soul was left exposed to all Satan's audacities: the strange vision she had had of St Francis Xavier in the nude was repeated now with frightening insistence along with all the other saints: the whole of Heaven's court were throwing off their tunics and their habits and dancing imaginary sarabands stark naked; these spectacles laid on by the Devil were killing her. She called for Father Silvério, but it seemed that a plague of rheumatism was crippling the whole diocesan clergy; Father Silvério had been in bed since the onset of winter. The parish priest from Cortegaça responded to her urgent call, but only to tell her the new recipe he had discovered for making salt cod Vizcaya-style. This lack of a virtuous priest plunged her into the blackest of moods, which fell on Amélia in the form of a rain of insults.

The good lady was seriously thinking of sending for Father Brito in Amor, when one evening, after supper, Amaro unexpectedly appeared.

He looked magnificent, tanned by the sun and the sea breezes, wearing a new overcoat and patent-leather shoes. As he spoke at length about Vieira, about mutual acquaintances he had seen there, about the fishing he had done, the wonderful lotto games they had played, he brought into the sad room of the sick old lady a vivifying breath of jolly seaside life. Dona Josefa's eyes filled with tears to see Father Amaro and to hear him.

'And your mother is well,' he said to Amélia. 'She's taken thirty sea baths already. The other day she won fifteen *tostões* at cards. But what have you two been up to here?'

Dona Josefa unleashed a torrent of bitter complaints. It was so lonely there! And the rain! The lack of friends! She was losing her soul in that ghastly place . . .

'Well,' said Father Amaro, crossing his legs, 'I had such a good time in Vieira that I'm thinking of going back next week.'

Unable to control herself, Amélia burst out:

'Not again!'

'Yes,' he said. 'If the precentor will give me a month's leave, I'm going to spend it there. They'll make up a bed for me in the Canon's dining room, I can take a few sea baths and . . .'

He was sick of sitting bored in Leiria.

Dona Josefa looked bereft. Go back and leave them there to die of sadness!

He laughed.

'You don't need me here. You're in good company . . .'

'I don't know about that,' said the old woman sourly. 'The *others*,' and she placed rancorous emphasis on that word, 'the *others* may not need you, but I am not in "good company", my soul is going to wrack and ruin here. The kind of company we receive here brings neither honour nor advantage.'

Amélia broke in to contradict Dona Josefa:

'To make matters worse, Father Ferrão has been ill. He's got rheumatism. Without him the house is like a prison.'

Dona Josefa gave a scornful laugh. And Father Amaro, getting up to leave, said regretfully:

'Poor thing. And such a saintly man too. I'll go and see him if I have time. Anyway, I'll come by tomorrow, Dona Josefa, and lay that soul of yours to rest. No, don't get up, Miss Amélia, I know the way out.'

But she insisted on accompanying him to the door. They crossed the salon without a word. Amaro drew on his fine, new, black leather gloves. And at the top of the stairs, he ceremoniously doffed his hat:

'Goodnight, Senhora.'

And Amélia stood there frozen, watching him go serenely down the stairs, as if she were of as little importance to him as the two stone lions who were sleeping down below with their chins on their paws.

She went into her room and threw herself down on her bed, weeping with rage and humiliation. The scoundrel! And not a word about the child, about the wetnurse or the baby's layette! He had not even cast an interested glance at her pregnant body, a pregnancy he had caused! Not a single complaint about her scornful response to him! Nothing! He had merely put on his gloves and set his hat at a jaunty angle. It was outrageous!

The next day, Amaro arrived earlier. He spent a long time shut up with Dona Josefa in her room.

Amélia impatiently paced up and down the salon, her eyes like coals. He finally emerged, drawing on his gloves with the same prosperous air as he had on the previous evening.

'You're leaving, then?' she said in a tremulous voice.

'I am, yes, Senhora. I was just having a little chat with Dona Josefa.'

He took off his hat, bowed very low and said:

'Goodnight, Senhora.'

Deathly pale, Amélia muttered:

'You scoundrel!'

He looked at her, as if startled, and said again:

'Goodnight, Senhora.'

And, just as he had the night before, he went slowly down the stone stairs.

Amélia's first thought was to denounce him to the vicar general. Then she spent the night writing him a letter, three pages of accusations and complaints. But the only response from Amaro the next day, sent verbally by little João from the farm, was that 'he might drop in on Thursday'.

She spent another night in tears, while in Rua das Sousas, Father Amaro was rubbing his hands with glee over his 'brilliant stratagem'. He had not thought it up himself; he had got the idea in Vieira, where he had gone to vent his feelings to the Canon and to dissipate his sorrows in the sea air; that is where he had discovered the 'brilliant stratagem' at a party, listening to Pinheiro – a wealthy and witty lawyer who was the glory of Alcobaça – speak about love.

'On this matter, ladies,' Pinheiro was saying to the semicircle of women who sat there hanging on every word that fell from his golden lips, as with one hand he smoothed his poet's hair, 'on this matter, I am of the same opinion as Lamartine' (he alternated between being of the same opinion of Lamartine and of Pelletan). 'Like Lamartine, I say: a woman is like a shadow. If you run after her, she flees you; if you flee from her, she runs after you!'

Someone said 'Oh, very good!' with great conviction, but there was one lady of generous proportions, the mother of four delightful angels all called Maria (as Pinheiro described them), who wanted an explanation, for she had never seen a shadow running away.

Pinheiro set this out for her in scientific terms:

'It's very easy to observe, Dona Catarina. Go and stand on the beach when the sun is beginning to set, with your back to the heavenly object. If you walk forwards, in pursuit of your shadow, it will go ahead of you, fleeing you . . .'

'Hm, recreational physics, most interesting,' muttered the legal scribe in Amaro's ear.

But Amaro was not listening; that 'brilliant stratagem' was already racing around inside his imagination. When he went back to Leiria, he would treat Amélia as if she were a shadow, and run away from her in order to make her follow him. And there was the delicious result: three passionate, tear-stained pages.

He turned up on Thursday, as he had said. Amélia was waiting for him on the terrace, where she had spent the morning watching the road through a pair of opera glasses. She ran to open the green door in the orchard wall.

'Fancy seeing you here!' said Amaro, following her up onto the terrace.

'Yes, I'm alone as it happens . . .'

'Alone?'

'My godmother is asleep and Gertrudes has gone into town. I've been sitting here in the sun all morning.'

Amaro went on into the house, without replying; he stopped by an open door, through which he could see a large canopied bed and next to it a couple of leather convent chairs.

'Is this your room?'

'Yes.'

He walked familiarly in, his hat in his hand.

'It's much better than your room in Rua da Misericórdia. Nice views too. Those must be the Morgado's lands over there.'

Amélia pushed the door to and, going straight over to him, eyes blazing, said:

'Why didn't you reply to my letter?'

He laughed.

'You're a fine one to talk! Why didn't you reply to mine? Who started it? You did. You say you don't want to sin any more. Well, neither do I. It's over.'

'That's not the point!' she cried, pale with anger. 'We have to think about the baby, about a wetnurse and about the baby's clothes. You can't just abandon me here.'

Amaro grew serious and said in wounded tones:

'Forgive me. I pride myself on being a gentleman. I will arrange all that before I go back to Vieira.'

'You're not going back to Vieira.'

'Who says so?'

'I do. I don't want you to.'

She placed her hands firmly on his shoulders, holding him, taking possession of him; and there, without even noticing that the door stood ajar, she once more abandoned herself to him as she used to.

Two days later, Father Ferrão reappeared, having recovered from his attack of rheumatism. He told Amélia of the Morgado's kindness to him, how every evening he had had a heated metal container of chicken and rice sent over to him. But his greatest debt was to João Eduardo, who had spent all his free time at his bedside, reading out loud to him, helping him turn in bed, staying up with him until one o'clock in the morning like a zealous nurse. What an excellent young man!

And then, suddenly, taking both Amélia's hands in his, he exclaimed:

'Will you give me permission to tell him everything, to explain your situation, so that I can bring him to forgive you and to forget, so that we can finally bring about that marriage and make both of you happy?'

Taken aback, she blushed and stammered:

'It's so sudden . . . I don't know . . . I'll have to think about it . . .'

'Think about it, then. And may God enlighten you,' said the old man fervently.

That night Amaro was supposed to slip in through the orchard gate to which Amélia had given him the key. Unfortunately, they had forgotten about the tenant's hunting dogs. As soon as Amaro set foot inside the orchard, the silence of the dark night was shattered by the wild barking of dogs, which sent Amaro racing down the road, his teeth chattering with terror.

XXIII

The following morning, as soon as he had opened his post, Amaro hurriedly sent for Dionísia. The good lady, however, was at the market and did not arrive until later, when he had returned from mass and was finishing his breakfast.

Amaro wanted to know 'at once and for certain' when 'things' would happen.

'The young lady's happy event? In about two or three weeks' time. Why, is something wrong?'

It was. Amaro read to her in confidence a letter he had beside him.

It was from the Canon, who wrote from Vieira saying 'that São Joaneira had had her thirty sea baths and wanted to come back! I (he added) miss three or four baths a week just to eke out the time, because she knows that I won't leave here without my fifty baths. I'm up to forty now, so you can see my problem. Besides, it's starting to get really cold here now. A lot of people have left already. Let me know by return of post how things are with you.' And in a postscript, he said: 'Have you thought yet what to do with the "fruit of the union"?'

'It will be in three weeks' time, more or less,' Dionísia reiterated.

And Amaro wrote a reply to the Canon there and then, which Dionísia was to take to the post: 'Things could be ready in three weeks. Whatever you do, don't let her mother come back. Tell her that her daughter can't write or come and join her because your good sister is still ill.'

Crossing his legs, he said:

'And now, Dionísia, what, as our Canon puts it, are we to do with "the fruit of the union"?'

Dionísia opened her eyes wide in surprise.

'I thought you had arranged all that, Father. I thought you were going to give the child to someone outside Leiria to bring up . . .'

'Of course, of course,' Amaro broke in impatiently. 'If the child is born alive, obviously we'll have it adopted, somewhere outside the region . . . But that's just it. Which wetnurse to choose? That is what I want you to arrange. It's high time we did . . .'

Dionísia looked extremely embarrassed. She had never liked recommending wetnurses. She knew a good, strong woman with plenty of milk, someone you could trust, but unfortunately, she had just been admitted to hospital. She knew another one too, she had even had dealings with her. She was Joana Carreira. But that wouldn't be very convenient because she lived in Poiais itself, right near Ricoça.

'What do you mean, it wouldn't be convenient!' exclaimed Amaro. 'What does it matter if she lives nearby? Once the girl has recovered, they'll all come back to Leiria and no one will ever mention Ricoça again.'

But Dionísia was still pondering, slowly stroking her chin. She knew of another woman too, who lived near Barrosa, a good distance away. She brought up other people's children at home, it was her job . . . but he wouldn't want to use her . . .

'Why? Is she weak or diseased or something?'

Dionísia went over to Amaro and lowering her voice said:

'I don't like to speak ill of anyone, but it's a well-known fact that she's a "weaver of angels".'

'A what?'

'A weaver of angels!'

'What's that? What does that mean?' asked Amaro.

Dionísia stammered out an explanation. It was a woman who took in other people's babies. Without exception, the babies all died. One woman who had been notorious for this had also worked as a weaver, and since all the babies she took in went straight to Heaven, that is where the name came from.

'So the children always die?'

'Always.'

Amaro was walking slowly about the room, rolling a cigarette.

'Tell me, Dionísia. Do the women kill them?'

Dionísia said again that she did not want to accuse anyone.

She had never actually seen anything. She did not know what went on in other people's houses. But the children all died . . .

'Who would hand over a child to a woman like that?'

Dionísia smiled pityingly at the man's innocence.

'Oh, they hand them over in their dozens!'

There was a silence. Amaro continued his pacing between the washbasin and the window, his head down.

'But what does the woman get out of it if the children die?' he asked suddenly. 'She would lose her wages.'

'They pay a year in advance, Father. That's ten *tostões* a month, or less, depending on what they can afford . . .'

Leaning against the window, Amaro was drumming slowly on the glass.

'But what do the authorities do about it, Dionísia?'

Dionísia shrugged and said nothing.

Amaro sat down, yawning and stretching out his legs. Then he said:

'Well, obviously the only thing to do is to talk to that wetnurse who lives near Ricoça, Joana Carreira. I'll make the necessary arrangements . . .'

Dionísia told him about the items for the layette that she had bought on his instructions and about a very cheap, second-hand cradle that she had seen in the carpenter's shop; then, as she was about to take the letter to the post, Amaro stood up, laughing:

'That business about the "weaver of angels" is just a story, isn't it?'

Dionísia was offended. He knew very well that she was not a woman to gossip. She had known the woman for more than four years, both to talk to and from seeing her nearly every week in town. Only last Saturday she had seen her coming out of a tavern. Had Amaro ever been to Barrosa?

She waited for his reply and then continued:

'Well, you know the entrance to the parish. There's the remains of a wall, then a path leading downhill. At the bottom of that narrow path you'll find a blocked-off well. Ahead, set back a bit, is a small house with a porch. That's where she lives.

Her name's Carlota . . . Just to prove to you that I really do know her.'

Amaro spent the whole day at home, pacing about his room, scattering the floor with cigarette ends. He had before him the dreadful task which, up until then, had seemed only a distant worry: getting rid of the child.

It was a serious matter handing it over just like that to an unknown wetnurse in the village. The mother would, naturally, want to go and see the child all the time, the wetnurse might tell the neighbours. The child would come to be known in the parish as 'the priest's child'. Some envious person, who coveted the parish, could denounce him to the vicar general. Scandal, a sermon and an inquiry would follow, and if he were not suspended, he might, like poor Father Brito, be sent off into the mountains with the shepherds again. Ah, if only the child could be born dead! That would be a natural and permanent solution. And a blessing for the child too really. What fate could it expect in this harsh world? It would be an orphan, the 'priest's child'. Both he and the mother were poor. The child would grow up in poverty, an uncultivated, bleary-eyed vagrant, mucking out barns. Living from hand to mouth, it would come to know every aspect of the human inferno: days without bread, freezing cold nights, the brutality of taverns and, finally, prison. A pallet bed in life, a communal grave in death. But if it died, it would at once become a little angel welcomed by God into Paradise.

And he continued pacing sadly up and down his room. It was a very appropriate name really, 'weaver of angels'. For any woman who prepares a child for life with the milk from her breast is also preparing it for travails and for tears. Better to wring its neck and send it straight to blissful eternity. Look at him! What kind of a life had he had these past thirty years! A melancholy childhood with that old bore, the Marquesa de Alegros; then the house in Estrela with his fool of an uncle, the grocer; and then the years shut up in the seminary, the snowy winter in Feirão, and all the problems and sorrows he had experienced since moving to Leiria. If they had smashed his skull when he was born, he would now have two white wings and be singing in the eternal choirs.

But there was no point in philosophising; he had to go to Poiais and talk to the wetnurse, to Joana Carreira.

He went out and walked unhurriedly towards the road. By the bridge, however, he was suddenly seized by an idea, by the desire to go to Barrosa and see this 'weaver of angels'. He would not speak to her; he would merely examine the house, see what the woman looked like and study the sinister aspect of the place. Besides, as a parish priest, as an ecclesiastical authority, he ought to know about this sinful trade that went on, lucrative and unpunished, just off the main road. He could even report it to the vicar general or to the secretary of the district government.

He still had time, it was only four o'clock. On that warm, splendid afternoon, a ride would do him good. He did not hesitate; he went and rented a mare from the Cruz inn, and shortly afterwards, with a spur on his left foot, he was galloping off along the road to Barrosa.

When he reached the narrow lane that Dionísia had described, he dismounted and continued on foot, leading the mare by the halter. It was a beautiful afternoon; high up in the blue sky, a large bird was tracing slow semicircles.

At last, next to two chestnut trees in which the birds were still singing, he found the blocked-off well; ahead, on a flat plot of land, completely isolated, was the house with the porch; the setting sun was shining on the only window on that side of the house, touching it with fiery, golden light; and from the chimney a pale, thin plume of smoke rose up into the still air.

A great sense of peace lay round about; on the hillside, dark with low pinetrees, he could see the gay, whitewashed walls of the little chapel of Barrosa.

Amaro was trying to imagine what the 'weaver of angels' would look like; for some reason, he thought she would be very tall, with a tanned face and glittering, witch-like eyes.

He tethered the mare to the gate and looked through the open door; it gave onto a kitchen with a large fireplace, and there was another door that opened onto the courtyard strewn with grass amongst which two piglets were foraging. White china glinted on the plate-rack above the chimney. Beside it hung large shiny copper pans that would not have looked out of place in a more opulent house. White sheets were piled up in an old cupboard, the door of which stood half-open, and a kind of light seemed to emanate from all that cleanliness, tidiness and good order.

Amaro clapped loudly. A startled pigeon fluttered inside a wicker cage hanging from the wall. Then he called out:

'Senhora Carlota!'

A woman immediately appeared from one side of the courtyard, carrying a sieve in her hand. And to his surprise, Amaro saw a pleasant-looking woman of about forty, wearing a pair of exquisite earrings; she had an ample bosom, broad shoulders, a very white neck, and dark eyes that reminded him of Amélia's eyes, or, rather, of São Joaneira's much calmer gaze.

Taken aback, he stammered:

'Oh, I'm sorry, I think I've made a mistake. Is this Senhora Carlota's house?'

He was not mistaken, it was her; but convinced that the dreadful woman 'who wove angels' must be somewhere, crouched in some gloomy corner of the house, he asked again:

'Do you live here alone?'

The woman looked at him mistrustfully.

'No, sir,' she said at last. 'I live here with my husband.'

At precisely that moment, her husband emerged from the courtyard, and he was indeed a fearful sight: a dwarfish figure whose head, wrapped in a scarf, was sunk between his shoulders, and whose face was a shiny, waxen yellow; he had a sparse, curly black beard and glowering, bloodshot eyes set deep in eyebrowless sockets, eyes that spoke of sleepless nights and drink.

'Can we help you at all, sir?' the man said, staying close to his wife's skirts.

Amaro went into the kitchen with them and told a garbled

story which he hurriedly concocted as he talked. A relative of his was expecting a baby. The husband could not come in person to speak to them because he was ill. They needed a wetnurse to go to the house, and he had been told . . .

'No, we don't work outside the house, only here,' said the dwarf, who still did not leave his wife's skirts, looking warily at Amaro with his ghastly, bloodshot eyes.

Ah, he had been misinformed, then. He was sorry, but what his relative needed was a wetnurse to live in.

He went slowly over to his mare, then stopped and, buttoning up his overcoat, said:

'But you do take in babies?'

'Once we've come to an agreement,' said the dwarf, who was following him.

Amaro put his spur on his foot, gave a tug at the bridle and, still playing for time, walked round the horse.

'The child would have to be brought here, I suppose.'

The dwarf looked back and exchanged a look with the woman, who was still standing at the kitchen door.

'We can come and get it if necessary,' he said.

Amaro patted the mare's neck.

'But if it was at night, with this cold, it would kill the child.'

Then both of them, speaking at once, agreed that it would not do any harm. As long as the child was cared for and well wrapped up.

Amaro got nimbly onto his horse, said goodbye and trotted back up the path.

Amélia was beginning to feel afraid now. Day and night, all she thought of was the approaching time when she would feel the first birth pangs. She suffered more than in the first months; she felt dizzy and had strange cravings, all of which Dr Gouveia observed with some concern. Her nights were particularly bad, full of troubling nightmares. She no longer had religious hallucinations, which had ceased with that sudden appeasement of devout terror; she could not have felt less afraid of God than if she had been a canonised saint. Her fears were different now, she had dreams in which the birth was depicted in monstrous terms: now it was a terrifying creature that leaped from her womb, half-woman, half-goat; now it was an endless cobra that crawled out of her like a league-long tape measure, coiling round and round the room until it reached the ceiling; she would wake from these dreams in a state of nervous prostration.

But she longed to have the child. She trembled at the idea of her mother suddenly appearing in Ricoça. Her mother had written to her, complaining about the Canon, who would not let her leave Vieira, about the storms they were having, about the increasingly solitary beach. Dona Maria da Assunção had returned to Leiria already, but, fortunately, a providentially chilly night had left her with bronchitis and she would, according to Dr Gouveia, be confined to her bed for weeks. Libaninho had visited Ricoça, but had departed regretting that he had been unable to see Amélia 'who had a migraine'.

'If this goes on for another two weeks, everyone will find out,' she would say to Amaro, weeping.

'Be patient, my dear. You can't force nature.'

'The suffering you've put me through,' she would sigh.

He would say nothing, resigned; he was very kind to her now, very tender. He came to see her nearly every morning because he did not want to meet Father Ferrão, who came in the afternoons.

He had reassured her regarding the wetnurse, saying that he had spoken to the woman in Ricoça recommended by Dionísia. Joana Carreira was an excellent choice. She was as strong as an oak tree, with plenty of milk and teeth like ivory.

'It's a long way for me to come and see the baby later on,' she sighed.

For the first time, she was looking forward to motherhood. She was in despair that she would not be able to make the rest of the baby's clothes herself. She wanted the boy – because it was bound to be a boy – to be called Carlos. She imagined him already a man, an officer in the cavalry. She was touched by the thought of seeing the baby crawling . . .

'Oh, if it wasn't for the shame of it, I would like to bring him up myself!'

'It'll be fine where it's going,' said Amaro.

But what tormented her and made her weep every day was the thought of her child being an orphan.

One day, she went to Father Ferrão with an extraordinary plan 'inspired by Our Lady herself': she would marry João Eduardo now, but he would have to sign a document adopting Carlos! She would marry a navvy if it would save her child from being an orphan! And she grasped Father Ferrão's hands, pleading and pleading with him. He must convince João to give Carlos a Papa! She tried to kneel before Father Ferrão, who was her father and her protector.

'Calm down, my dear, calm down. That is what I want too, and we will arrange it all, but later,' said the good old man, troubled by her highly emotional state.

A few days later, she was excited about something else; she had suddenly realised, one morning, that she must not betray Amaro, 'because he, after all, was Carlos' real Papa'. And she said this to Father Ferrão, causing the old priest to blush as she chattered blithely on about her wifely duties to Amaro.

Father Ferrão, who knew nothing of Father Amaro's morning visits, was astonished.

'What are you saying, my dear? What are you saying? Get a grip on yourself. Have you no shame! I thought you had got over that madness.'

'But he is the father of my child,' she insisted, looking at him very seriously.

Then for a whole week, she went on and on at Amaro, with childish sentimentality, reminding him every half hour that he was 'her little Carlos' Papa'.

'I know, my dear, I know,' he would say impatiently. 'Thank you very much, but it's hardly something I want to boast about . . .'

She would sit huddled on the sofa then, weeping, and it would take a whole complicated series of caresses to calm her. She would make him sit on a bench next to her, and she would keep him there like a doll, looking at him, slowly stroking his tonsure; she wanted him to take a photograph of Carlos so that they could both carry it in a medallion around their necks; and if she should die, he was to take Carlos to her grave, have him kneel down, put his two little hands together and make him pray for his Mama. She would hurl herself down on a pillow then, covering her face with her hands.

'Oh, pity me, my dear child, pity me!'

'Be quiet, there are people coming!' Amaro would say angrily.

Ah, those mornings at Ricoça! To him they were like an unfair punishment. When he got there, he would have to go and listen to Dona Josefa's complaints. Then he would spend an hour with Amélia, who lay stretched out on the sofa, as big as a barrel now, her face swollen, her eyes puffy, tormenting him with all kinds of hysterical, sentimental demands.

On one such morning, Amélia, who was complaining of cramp, wanted to take a walk about the room, leaning on Amaro; as she was dragging herself along, huge in her old dressing gown, they heard on the road down below the sound of horses' hooves; they went over to the window, but Amaro immediately drew back, leaving Amélia staring out, her face pressed against the glass. On the road, elegantly mounted on a bay mare, was João Eduardo in a white jacket and a tall hat; beside him trotted the Morgado's two small children, one on a pony, the other strapped onto a donkey; and a short distance behind them, following at a respectful, courtly pace, came a liveried servant, wearing high boots and enormous spurs, a very loose jacket that hung in grotesque folds at his sides and a scarlet rosette on his hat. Amélia stood there, astonished, watching them, until the lackey's back was lost to view around the corner of the house. She said not a word, but went and sat down on the sofa. Amaro, who was still pacing the room, laughed sarcastically and said:

'What an idiot, with a lackey bringing up the rear!'

She blushed scarlet and said nothing. And scandalised, Amaro left, slamming the door, and went into Dona Josefa's room to tell her about the cavalcade and to fulminate against the Morgado.

'An excommunicant with a liveried servant!' exclaimed the

good lady, clutching her head with her hands. 'How shaming, Father, how shaming for this country's aristocracy!'

From that day on, Amélia no longer cried if Father Amaro failed to visit her in the morning. The person she waited impatiently for now was Father Ferrão. She monopolised him, she would have him sit on a chair by the sofa, and then, after circling around like a bird above its prey, she would fall upon the subject that really mattered – had he seen João Eduardo?

She wanted to know what he had said, if he had spoken about her, if he had seen her at the window. She tormented Father Ferrão with her inquisitive questions about the Morgado's house, about how the living room was furnished, about how many servants he had and how many horses, whether the liveried servant also served at table.

And Father Ferrão would patiently respond, glad to see that she had forgotten about Amaro and was interested in João Eduardo; he was convinced now that the marriage would go ahead, she, on the other hand, avoided all mention of Amaro's name, indeed, once, when Father Ferrão asked her if Amaro had returned to Ricoça, she even said:

'Oh, he comes in the morning to see my godmother. But I don't see him, I'm not even decently dressed by then.'

She would spend as long as she could now standing at the window, immaculately dressed from the waist up, which is all that could be seen from the road, and all grubby petticoats from the waist down. She was waiting for João Eduardo, the Morgado's children and the lackey; and every now and then she had the pleasure of seeing them go trotting past, as they were borne along by the easy pace of their expensive mounts; and, as it passed the house, João Eduardo's bay mare would always perform a sidestep, with João Eduardo holding his whip out in front and using his legs according to the Marqués de Marialva's rules for riding, exactly as the Morgado had taught him. But it was the liveried lackey she found most enchanting, and, with her nose pressed against the window pane, she would watch him greedily until, at the turn in the road, she would see the poor old man disappear, with his bent back, his shaky legs, and the collar of his uniform turned up.

And what a delight they were to João Eduardo those rides on the bay mare with the little Morgados. He always made a point of going into town; the sound of the horseshoes on the flagstones made his heart beat faster; he would ride past the pharmacist's wife, Amparo, past the office where Nunes had his desk by the window, past the arcade, past the administrator, who would be there on the balcony with his binoculars still trained on Teles' house, and his one disappointment was that he could not ride with the mare, the Morgado's children and the lackey past Dr Godinho's office, which was, alas, at the rear of the house.

It was on one of these triumphal outings, at about two o'clock, on his way back from Barrosa, just as they were reaching Poço das Bentas and setting off along the cart track, that he suddenly saw Father Amaro come riding towards him mounted on a cob. João Eduardo immediately made his own horse wheel about. The track was so narrow, that even though they both kept close to the hedges, their knees almost brushed, and from the height of his expensive mare, João Eduardo was able then to wield his whip in a threatening manner and stare scornfully down at Father Amaro, who shrank back, looking pale, unshaven and sallow-cheeked, furiously spurring on his sluggish mount. At the top of the road, João Eduardo stopped and turned round in his saddle and saw the priest dismounting at the door of a small isolated house where, only moments before, as they passed, the children had laughed at 'the dwarf'.

'Who lives there?' João Eduardo asked the lackey.

'A woman called Carlota. Bad people, Senhor João Eduardo.'

When they passed Ricoça, João Eduardo, as usual, reined the horse in to a trot. But behind the panes he did not see the usual pale face beneath the scarlet scarf. The shutters were half-closed and, at the door, stood Dr Gouveia's cabriolet with the horses unhitched and the shafts dragging on the ground.

The day had at last arrived! That morning, a boy from the

farm had arrived from Ricoça bearing an almost unintelligible note from Amélia – *Dionísia quick, it's come!* It also contained instructions to send for Dr Gouveia. Amaro himself went to tell Dionísia.

Days before, he had told her that Dona Josefa, Dona Josefa herself, had recommended a wetnurse to him, and that he had been to see her, a big woman, strong as a tree. And now they made rapid arrangements for Amaro to be posted at the orchard door that night, and for Dionísia to come and give him the baby well wrapped up.

'At nine o'clock tonight, Dionísia. And don't keep us waiting!' Amaro said, seeing Dionísia go rushing off, all flustered.

Then he went back home and shut himself in his room, face to face with the problem which seemed to him like a living creature that fixed him with its gaze and asked: What shall we do with the child? He still had time to go to Poiais and arrange things with the other wetnurse, the good wetnurse whom Dionísia knew; or else he could get on his horse and go to Barrosa and talk to Carlota . . . And there he was, before those two roads, in an agony of doubt. He wanted to look at things coolly, to discuss the matter as if it were a point of theology, weighing up the pros and cons, but what hung dangerously before him were not two arguments but two images: the child growing up and living in Poiais, and the child suffocated by Carlota in a house on the Barrosa road. And as he was pacing up and down in his room, sweating with anxiety, he heard the unexpected voice of Libaninho call out to him from the landing:

'Open up, Father, I know you're there!'

He had to open the door to Libaninho, shake his hand and offer him a chair. Fortunately, Libaninho could not stay long. He had just happened to be passing and had come up to see if his friend had any news of the good ladies at Ricoça.

'They're fine, fine,' said Amaro, forcing himself to smile and be pleasant.

'I've been so busy, I haven't been able to get over there myself! I'm on duty at the barracks. Now, don't laugh, Father, because I'm doing excellent work there. I get together with the soldiers and I tell them all about Christ's wounds and . . .'

'So you're converting the whole regiment,' said Amaro, shuffling papers on his desk, then striding about, as restless as a caged animal.

'I couldn't do that even if I wanted to! But, look, I'm just taking these scapulars to a sergeant there. They've been blessed by Father Saldanha and are positively oozing with healing powers. I gave some exactly like this yesterday to a lance-corporal, a lovely lad, so sweet . . . I put them on him myself underneath his vest. A lovely lad!'

'You should let the colonel take care of the regiment,' said Amaro, opening the window, doing his best to hide his impatience.

'That infidel? He'd have the whole regiment un-baptised if they'd let him. Anyway, I'll be off now, Father. You know, you don't look well, my dear. What you need is a good purgative.'

As he was about to leave, he paused at the door:

'By the way, Father, have you heard the latest news?'

'About what?'

'It was Father Saldanha who told me. According to him, the precentor said (and these are Saldanha's very words) that he has evidence of some scandal in the town involving a priest. But he didn't say who or what . . . Saldanha tried to probe further, but the precentor said that the information he had been given was very vague, no names . . . I've been thinking about it. Who could it possibly be?'

'It's just Saldanha showing off.'

'Well, I hope it is. It's precisely the kind of thing that unbelievers pounce on. Anyway, next time you're in Ricoça give my regards to the good ladies.'

And he skipped down the stairs to bear 'virtue' to the battalion.

Amaro was terrified. Obviously secret allegations had brought word of him and his affair with Amélia to the vicar general. And now there would be the child, which would be brought up only half a league from Leiria, as living proof! It seemed to him extraordinary, almost supernatural, that

Libaninho, who, in two years, had hardly ever visited him at home, should have come to him with that terrible news precisely at the moment when he was battling with his conscience. It was as if Providence, in the grotesque form of Libaninho, had come to warn him, whispering: 'Don't allow the very person who can bring you scandal to live! People already have their suspicions!'

It was clearly God taking pity on the child, not wanting one more wretched orphan on the earth, it was clearly God demanding his angel!

Amaro did not hesitate: he went to the Cruz inn and then rode to Carlota's house.

He remained there until four o'clock.

When he got back home, he threw his hat down on the bed and felt a great sense of relief flood through his whole being. It was over. He had spoken to Carlota and the dwarf; he had paid her for a whole year in advance; now he just had to wait for night to come.

But alone in his room, he was assailed by all kinds of morbid imaginings; he saw Carlota suffocating the tiny, red-skinned child; he saw the police disinterring the corpse later, and Domingos in the municipal council offices filling out the declaration of corpus delicti which he rested on his knee, while he, Amaro, still in his cassock, was dragged off to prison in irons, along with the dwarf. He was tempted to ride back to Barrosa and cancel the arrangement. But inertia stopped him. After all, there was no reason why he had to deliver the child to Carlota. He could carry it, instead, well wrapped up, to Joana Carreira, the good wetnurse in Poiais.

To escape from these ideas raging above his head like a storm, he went to see Natário, who was out of bed now, and who called to him from the depths of his armchair:

'Did you see him, Amaro? Did you see that idiot, with a lackey bringing up the rear?'

João Eduardo had passed by in the street below on his bay mare, with the Morgado's children; and Natário had ever since then been roaring with impatience at being stuck in that chair and unable to resume his campaign and get him expelled by cooking up some intrigue at the Morgado's house that would strip him of both mare and lackey.

'But I'll get him, as soon as God gives me back the use of my legs . . .'

'Oh, forget it, Natário,' said Amaro.

'Forget it?'

Forget it? When he had a brilliant idea to provide the Morgado with documentary proof that João Eduardo was, in fact, a devout Catholic! What did his friend Amaro think of that?

It was, of course, an amusing idea. The man doubtless deserved it just for the way he looked down on decent people from atop his mare . . . And Amaro flushed red, still angry at their encounter that morning on the Barrosa road.

'Of course he deserves it!' exclaimed Natário. 'Why else are we priests of Christ? In order to exalt the humble and destroy the proud.'

From there Amaro went to see Dona Maria da Assunção, who was also now out of bed and who regaled him with the story of her bronchitis and listed her latest sins, the worst of which was this: in order to distract herself a little during her convalescence, she had been sitting by the window, and a carpenter who lived opposite had ogled her; under the influence of the Evil One, she had lacked the willpower to withdraw, and bad thoughts had come to her . . .

'You're not listening, Father.'

'Of course I am, Senhora!'

And he hastened to pacify her scruples, because the salvation of that idiotic old soul gave him a much better living than the parish did.

It was getting dark when he got home. Escolástica complained that the food had got burned because he was late. Amaro took only a glass of wine and a forkful of rice, which he ate standing up at the window, watching, horrified, the impassive fall of night.

He was just going into his room to see if the oil lamps were already lit, when the coadjutor arrived. He had come to discuss the baptism of Guedes' son, which was due to take place the following day at nine o'clock.

'Do you need a light?' called the maid on hearing a visitor's voice.

'No!' shouted back Amaro.

He was afraid that the coadjutor might notice his changed face or that he might settle in for the rest of the night.

'Apparently there was a very interesting article in *The Nation* the day before yesterday.'

'Really,' said Amaro.

He was pacing up and down, following his usual track, from the washbasin to the window; he occasionally stopped to drum with his fingers on the glass; the lamps outside had been lit.

Then the coadjutor, shocked by the darkness in the room and by that constant pacing, got to his feet and, with great dignity, said:

'But perhaps I'm bothering you . . .'

'No, no!'

Satisfied, the coadjutor sat down again, his umbrella between his knees.

'The nights are drawing in,' he said.

'They are . . .'

Eventually, in desperation, Amaro told him that he had an appalling migraine and that he was going to bed; the coadjutor departed, reminding him once more about the baptism of his friend Guedes' child.

Amaro left at once for Ricoça. Fortunately, it was a warm, dark night, presaging rain. He was now seized by a hope that made his heart beat faster, that the child would be born dead! And it was quite possible. As a young woman, São Joaneira had had two still births; Amélia's state of anxiety had probably disturbed the child's gestation. And what if she died too? At that idea, which had never before occurred to him, he was suddenly filled with pity and tenderness for the kind girl who loved him so much and who now, because of him, would be screaming out in agony. And yet, if both died, both she and the child, that would mean that his sin and his error would fall for ever into the dark abyss of eternity. He would be, as he had been before he came to Leiria, a tranquil man, concerned only with the Church, and with a life as clean and white as a blank page.

He stopped at the ruined hut by the roadside where he was to meet the person from Barrosa who would come for the child; it had not been decided whether it would be the man or Carlota. Amaro dreaded handing over his son to that dwarf with the evil, bloodshot eyes. He called into the dark interior of the hut.

'Hello!'

It was a relief when Carlota's clear voice said from the blackness.

'Is it here yet?'

'No, we have to wait, Senhora Carlota.'

He felt pleased. It seemed to him that he had nothing to fear if his child was to be cradled against the robust breast of that fecund forty-year-old, so fresh and clean.

He prowled round the house, which was utterly dark and silent, as if, on that black December night, it were just a thickening of the surrounding shadows. Not a chink of light emerged from the windows of Amélia's room. In the heavy air, not a leaf stirred. And no Dionísia appeared.

The waiting was a torment to him. People might come by and see him prowling about outside, but he could not bring himself to go and hide in the ruined hut with Carlota. He walked the length of the orchard wall and back, and then he saw a glow of light appear at the French windows that opened onto the terrace.

He ran to the green door in the orchard wall, which opened almost immediately, and, without a word, Dionísia placed a bundle in his arms.

'Is it dead?' he asked.

'No, it's alive! A big strong boy!'

And she slowly closed the door just as the dogs, alert for any noise, began to bark.

Feeling his son against his chest swept all Amaro's ideas away like a great wind. What? Give him to that woman, to that 'weaver of angels', who would throw him into some ditch along the road or into the latrine at home. No, this was his son!

But what should he do then? He did not have time to run to Poiais and wake up the other wetnurse. Dionísia had no milk. He couldn't take it back into town. How he longed to knock on the front door, to rush up to Amélia's room and place the little one in her bed, all wrapped up, and have the three of them stay there together as if in some cosy, heavenly nest. But how could he? He was a priest. Cursed be that religion that so destroyed him!

A little murmur emerged from inside the bundle. He ran to the ruined shack and almost collided with Carlota who took the child from him.

'Here he is,' he said. 'But listen, I'm serious now. Things have changed. I don't want him to die. I want you to look after him. What we talked about means nothing. I want you to take care of him. I want him to live. You have his fate in your hands. Look after him!'

'Of course, of course,' said the woman hastily.

'Listen . . . The child isn't warm enough. Put my cloak around him.'

'He's fine, sir, fine.'

'No, damn it, he's not! He's my son and he must have the cloak around him. I don't want him to die of cold.'

He threw it around her shoulders and over her chest, covering the child, and the woman, who was beginning to get annoyed, hastened away.

Amaro stood in the middle of the road, watching her disappear into the darkness. Then, after that initial shock, all his nerves succumbed to a womanly weakness, and he burst out crying.

For a long time, he prowled around the house. But it remained sunk in the same terrifying darkness and silence. Then, feeling sad and weary, he walked back into town as the Cathedral clock was striking ten.

At that hour, in the dining room at Ricoça, Dr Gouveia was calmly eating the roast chicken that Gertrudes had prepared for his supper after the toils of the day. Father Ferrão was sitting with him, watching him eat; he had brought the sacraments with him in case of danger. But the doctor was pleased; the girl had been very brave during the eight hours of labour; the birth had gone well and the result was a healthy boy who would do great honour to his father.

In his modesty as a priest, Father Ferrão chastely lowered his eyes when the doctor mentioned these details.

'And now,' said the doctor, biting into a chicken's wing, 'now that I have brought the child into the world, you gentlemen (by which I mean the Church) will get hold of him and won't let go of him until he dies. On the other hand, albeit less enthusiastically, the State will keep its eye on him too . . . And so the poor wretch begins his journey from cradle to grave, flanked by a priest and a police officer!'

Father Ferrão bowed and took a loud pinch of snuff in preparation for the debate.

'The Church,' continued the doctor serenely, 'begins imposing religion on a child when the child barely knows he's alive . . .'

Father Ferrão interrupted, half serious, half joking:

'Doctor, purely out of charitable concern for your soul, I feel I should warn you that Canon 13 of the Holy Council of Trent imposes the punishment of excommunication on anyone who declares baptism to be meaningless, the punishment to be imposed with no right to appeal.'

'Noted, Father. I am accustomed to the kindnesses extended to myself and other colleagues by the Council of Trent.'

'It was a very important assembly!' said Father Ferrão, scandalised.

'Oh, sublime, Father, a sublime assembly. The Council of Trent and the French National Convention were the two most remarkable assemblies of men that the world has seen . . .'

Father Ferrão made a grimace of disgust at this irreverent comparison between the holy authors of doctrine and the murderers of good King Louis XVI.

But the doctor went on:

'Then the Church leaves the child in peace for a time while he does his teething and has his first attack of worms . . .'

'Go on, doctor, go on!' murmured the priest, listening to him patiently, his eyes closed, as if to say: 'Go on, bury your soul deep in the abyss of fire and pitch!'

'But when the first signs of reason appear in the child, when, in order to distinguish him from the animals, it becomes necessary for him to have some understanding of himself and of the universe, in walks the Church and explains everything! Everything! And so completely that a boy of six who doesn't even know his alphabet has a vaster and more certain knowledge than all the royal academies of London, Berlin and Paris combined! The rascal does not hesitate for a moment when it comes to explaining how the universe and its planetary systems were made, how the creation of the earth came about, how the different races arose, how the geological revolutions around the world occurred, how languages developed, how writing was invented . . . He knows everything: he possesses the rules, complete and immutable, for directing all his actions and forming all his opinions; he even has answers to all the great mysteries; he might be as myopic as a mole, but he can nevertheless see what happens in the depths of sky and earth; he knows, as if he had seen it with his own eyes, what will happen to him after death . . . He has a solution to every problem . . . And when the Church has made of this great lad a marvel of knowledge, then they teach him how to read . . . Why? I ask myself.'

Father Ferrão was dumb with indignation.

'Tell me, Father, why do you have them learn to read? The whole of universal knowledge, the *res scibilis*, lies in the Catechism: he only has to memorise it and the boy has immediate knowledge and awareness of everything . . . He knows as much as God. In fact, he is God.'

Father Ferrão started.

'This is not argument,' he exclaimed. 'These comments are mere Voltairean jibes! Such matters should be treated with more respect . . .'

'Jibes, Father? Take just one example: the development of

languages. How did they come about? It was God, who, unhappy with what was going on in the Tower of Babel . . .'

At this point, the door opened and Dionísia appeared. Shortly before, in Amélia's room, he had told her off in no uncertain terms, and now she addressed him in terrified tones.

'Doctor,' she said, in the ensuing silence, 'Miss Amélia has woken up and wants to see the baby.'

'So? The child has been taken away, hasn't it?'

'It has,' replied Dionísia.

'Then there's no more to be said.'

Dionísia was about to close the door, but the doctor called her back.

'Listen, tell her she can see the child tomorrow . . . tell her that they'll bring her the child tomorrow without fail. Lie to her. Lie like a dog. Father Ferrão here gives you permission. Tell her to go to sleep, tell her not to worry.'

Dionísia withdrew. But they did not resume their argument; confronted by the thought of that mother who had awoken after the exhaustion of labour and was demanding to see her son, the son who had been taken far away and for ever, the two men forgot all about the Tower of Babel and the development of languages. Father Ferrão seemed particularly moved. The pitiless doctor, however, was soon reminding him that these were the consequences of the priest's position in society . . .

Father Ferrão looked down, busy with his snuff, and did not reply, as if unaware that a priest was involved in this whole unhappy story.

Taking up his own idea, the doctor discoursed on the preparation and education of clerics.

'There you have an education based on an absurdity: resisting the perfectly fair demands of nature and resisting the most lofty demands of reason. Preparing a priest is like creating a monster who will spend his whole wretched life waging a desperate battle against the two irresistible facts of the universe – the force of Matter and the force of Reason!'

'What are you saying?' exclaimed the priest, astonished.

'The plain truth! What does the education of a priest

involve? *Primo*: preparing him for celibacy and virginity, that is, for the violent suppression of the most natural of feelings. *Secundo*: it trains him to avoid any knowledge and any ideas that might shake the Catholic faith, that is, the forced suppression of the spirit of investigation and examination and, therefore, of all real human knowledge . . .'

Father Ferrão had stood up, filled with pious indignation:

'Do you deny that the Church has knowledge?'

'Jesus, my dear Father,' the doctor continued unperturbed, 'Jesus, his first disciples and the illustrious St Paul all declared in parables and epistles, in that whole extraordinary verbal outpouring, that the products of the human spirit were useless, puerile and, worse, pernicious.'

Father Ferrão was pacing about the room, bumping into the furniture like a goaded ox, clutching his head in despair at such blasphemies. Unable to control himself any longer, he cried:

'You don't know what you're saying! Forgive me, doctor, I humbly beg you to forgive me . . . You are driving me into mortal sin . . . But this is not argument . . . this is the stuff of journalism.'

He then launched into a heated dissertation on the wisdom of the Church, on its lofty studies of Greek and Latin, on an entire philosophy created by the holy fathers . . .

'Read St Basil!' he exclaimed. 'There he says that studying the great secular authors is the best possible preparation for studying the sacred texts! Read *The History of Monasteries in the Middle Ages*! There you had science and philosophy . . .'

'But what philosophy, Father, what science? By philosophy they meant half a dozen concepts of a mythological bent, in which mysticism replaces social instincts . . . And as for science . . . it was the science of commentators and grammarians. Times changed, though, and new sciences were born of which the ancients knew nothing and for which ecclesiastical education offered neither basis nor method, and there was an immediate antagonism between them and Catholic doctrine. Initially, the Church even tried to suppress them by persecution, imprisonment, fire! You can't deny it, Father. Yes, fire and imprisonment. The Church can no longer do that and so it merely fulminates against them in bad Latin. And meanwhile, in seminaries and schools, it continues to teach the old science that predates these new sciences, ignoring them, despising them, taking refuge in scholasticism. There's no use clutching your head . . . The Church is alien to the modern spirit, hostile in its principles and methods to the development of human knowledge . . . You can't deny that! Just look at the *Syllabus* with its third rule excommunicating Reason . . . In Canon 13 . . .'

The door opened timidly; it was Dionísia again.

'Miss Amélia is crying. She says she wants her baby.'

'Oh, dear, that's not good,' said the doctor, adding after a moment: 'How does she look? Is she flushed? Restless?'

'No, sir, she's fine. But she just keeps crying and talking about the baby. She says she has to see him now.'

'Talk to her, distract her . . . See if you can get her to go to sleep.'

Dionísia withdrew, and Father Ferrão asked cautiously:

'Do you think getting upset could harm her?'

'Yes, it could, Father, it could,' said the doctor rummaging around in his bag. 'But I'm going to send her to sleep . . . But it's true, you know, Father, the Church nowadays is an intruder.'

Father Ferrão again clutched his head.

'You don't have to go very far. Just look at the Church in Portugal. It's really most gratifying to see its current state of decay.'

Then still standing, the bottle of medicine in his hand, the doctor painted in broad strokes a picture of this state of decay. The Church had once been the Nation; now it was a minority tolerated and protected by the State. It had dominated the law courts, the royal councils, the Treasury, the Navy, it had waged war and peace; nowadays a member of parliament with a good majority had more power than the whole of the clergy put together. It had been the one great source of knowledge in the country; now all it could do was mumble a bit of dog Latin. It had been rich, it had owned whole districts in the country and whole streets in the city; now it depended for its pathetic daily bread on the Ministry of Justice and had to beg for alms at the doors of chapels. Once it had recruited its members from amongst the nobility, from amongst the best in the land; and now, in order to get enough people, it found itself in the embarrassing position of having to go recruiting in orphanages. It had been the repository of national tradition, of the country's collective ideal, and now, having lost its links with the national consciousness (if there is such a thing) it was a foreigner, a citizen of Rome, receiving both law and spirit from there . . .

'Well, if the Church *is* in such a bad state, all the more reason to love it!' said Father Ferrão, getting to his feet, red-faced.

But Dionísia had once again appeared at the door.

'What is it now?'

'Miss Amélia is complaining of a weight on her head. She says she can see flashing lights in front of her eyes . . .'

Dr Gouveia said nothing and immediately followed Dionísia out of the room. Left alone, Father Ferrão paced up and down, pondering a counter-argument bristling with quotations, with the formidable names of theologians, which he would bring crashing down on the doctor. But half an hour passed, the oil lamp was burning down, and the doctor did not return.

Then he began to feel worried by the silence filling the house, in which the only living sound was that of his own footsteps going back and forth. He opened the door very slowly and listened, but Amélia's room was a long way off, at the far end of the house, near the terrace; neither sound nor light came from there. He resumed his solitary pacing, and a vague sadness began to invade his being. He too wanted to go and see the patient, but his own character and his priestly modesty would not even allow him near a woman in bed, in childbirth, unless she was in danger of dying and in need of the sacraments. Another long, even gloomier hour passed. Then, on tiptoe, blushing in the darkness at his own audacity, he ventured out into the corridor; he listened, terrified, to the sounds coming from Amélia's room, a dull, confused sound as of scampering feet, as if there were a fight going on. But not a sigh or a cry. He went back into the dining room and, opening his breviary, he began to pray. He heard Gertrudes come running by. He heard a door in the distance slam. Then the noise of a brass bowl being dragged across the floor. Finally, the doctor appeared.

Father Ferrão turned pale when he saw him: the doctor had no tie on and his collar was in shreds; the buttons on his waistcoat had come off, and the cuffs of his rolled back shirtsleeves were all stained with blood.

'What's happened, Doctor?'

The doctor did not reply, looking rapidly around the room for his medical bag, his face flushed as if by the heat of battle. He was just about to go out again with his bag when he remembered Father Ferrão's anxious question:

'She's having convulsions,' he said.

Father Ferrão stopped him at the door and very gravely, with great dignity said:

'Doctor, if there is any danger, I ask you to remember that a Christian soul is dying in there, and that I am here.'

'Of course, of course.'

Father Ferrão was once more left alone, waiting. Everything in the house was asleep, Dona Josefa, the tenant farmers, the farm and the fields round about. In the dining room, a huge, sinister-looking grandfather clock that would have looked more at home in an ancient castle, and which had a large sun on its face and the carved figure of a pensive owl on top, struck first midnight, then one o'clock. Father Ferrão kept going out into the corridor from where he could hear either the same sound of scuffling feet or black silence. He returned then to his breviary. He thought about the poor girl who, there in her room, had perhaps reached the moment that would determine her eternity: she had beside her neither her mother nor her women friends; her terrified memory was doubtless filled with visions of sin; the sad face of an offended God would appear before her clouded eyes; her wretched body would be contorted by pain; and in the darkness into which she was plunging, she would feel already the burning breath of Satan as he approached. A dreadful end to both time and flesh! He prayed fervently for her.

He thought of the man who was the other half of her sin, and who was safe in his bed in Leiria, snoring peacefully. And he prayed for him too.

He had a small crucifix on his breviary. And he contemplated it lovingly, thinking tenderly of the certainty of its strength, against which all the doctor's science and all the vanities of reason were as nothing! Philosophies, ideas, profane glories, generations and empires all pass; they are like the ephemeral sighs of human effort; only the cross remains and will remain – the hope of mankind, the comfort of the despairing, the shelter of the fragile, the refuge of the vanquished, the force majeure of humanity: *crux triumphus adversus demonios, crux oppugnatorum murus . . .*

At that point, the doctor returned to the room, his face still scarlet, still shaken by the tremendous battle he was waging against death; he had come for another bottle of medicine, but, without a word, he opened the window and took a deep breath of fresh air.

'How is she?' asked Father Ferrão.

'Bad,' said the doctor, going out again.

Father Ferrão knelt down and mumbled the prayer of St Fulgentius:

'Father, give her first patience and then mercy . . .'

And there he stayed, his face in his hands, resting on the edge of the table.

At the sound of footsteps, he looked up. It was Dionísia, who sighed as she ransacked the sideboard drawers for napkins.

'What's happening, Dionísia?' asked Father Ferrão.

'I think we've lost her, Father. She had the most terrible convulsions and now she's fallen into that sleep which is the sleep of the dead.'

Then looking around her as if to make sure they were alone, she said in agitated tones:

'I didn't want to say anything because the doctor has such a temper, but to bleed the girl in that state is tantamount to killing her. It's true she didn't lose much blood, but you never bleed someone when they're in that state. Never!'

'The doctor is a man of science . . .'

'He may have all the science he likes . . . but I'm no fool either. I've had twenty years' experience and no one ever died in my hands, Father. Bleed someone when they're having convulsions? It's disgusting.'

She was highly indignant. The doctor had tortured the poor creature. He had even wanted to give her chloroform . . .

But the doctor's voice was bellowing for her from the far end of the corridor, and she rushed off with her bundle of napkins.

The fearsome clock, with its pensive owl, struck two, then three. Father Ferrão occasionally gave in now to an old man's weariness and closed his eyes for a moment. But he would quickly open them again and go and breathe in the heavy night air and look out at the darkness covering the village; then he would go back and sit down, head bowed, his hands in prayer, to murmur over his breviary.

'Lord, turn your merciful eyes on that bed of pain . . . .'

It was then that Gertrudes came into the room, looking greatly upset. The doctor had sent her downstairs to wake up the boy and tell him to hitch the mare to the carriage.

'The poor little thing, Father. She was doing so well and suddenly this . . . It was because they took the baby from her. I don't know who the father is, but I know that there's some sin, some crime behind all this.'

Father Ferrão did not reply, praying quietly for Father Amaro.

Then the doctor returned, carrying his bag.

'You can go in if you like, Father,' he said.

But Father Ferrão did not rush off, looking instead at the doctor, with a question hovering on his half-open lips, which he shyly refrained from asking; at last, he could keep it in no longer and he said fearfully:

'Have you done everything you could, Doctor? Is there nothing more to be done?'

'No.'

'Doctor, it's just that only in extreme circumstances are we supposed to go to a woman who has given birth to an illegitimate child . . .'

'These are extreme circumstances, Father,' said the doctor, putting on his overcoat.

Father Ferrão then picked up his breviary and the crucifix, but, before leaving the room, judging it to be his duty to place before the rationalist doctor the certain truth of the mystical eternity implicit in the moment of death, he murmured:

'It is at this moment that one experiences the fear of God and the futility of human pride . . .'

The doctor said nothing, busy buckling up his bag.

The priest went out, but when he was only half-way down the corridor, he turned back and said in rather troubled tones:

'Forgive me, Doctor . . . but sometimes, with the aid of religion, the dying do, by virtue of a special grace, come back to life . . . The presence of a doctor might then be useful.'

'I'm not leaving just yet, don't worry,' said the doctor, smiling involuntarily to see the presence of Medicine invoked to help the efficacy of Grace.

He went downstairs to see if the carriage was ready.

When he went back to Amélia's room, Dionísia and Gertrudes were both kneeling by the bed, praying. The bed and the whole room looked like a battlefield. The two candles had almost burned down. Amélia lay motionless, her arms stiff, her clenched fists a dark purple colour, and her face was the same colour, only darker.

Bent over her, crucifix in hand, Father Ferrão was saying in an urgent voice:

'*Jesu, Jesu, Jesu!* Remember the grace of God! Have faith in divine mercy! Repent in the bosom of our Lord. *Jesu, Jesu, Jesu!*'

At last, realising that she was dead, he knelt down and murmured the *Miserere*. The doctor, who had been standing at the door, withdrew slowly, tiptoed down the corridor and went out into the street where the boy was holding the horse, now harnessed.

'It looks like rain, Doctor,' said the boy, yawning sleepily.

Dr Gouveia turned up his coat collar, placed his bag on the seat beside him and, a moment later, beneath the first heavy drops of rain, the cabriolet was rumbling down the road, the red glow of its two lanterns cutting through the darkness of the night.

XXIV

The following morning, from seven o'clock onwards, Father Amaro sat at home by his open window, waiting for Dionísia to come, his eyes fixed on the street corner, not even noticing the fine rain beating against his face. But Dionísia did not come. Feeling sad and ill, he had to go to the Cathedral to baptise Guedes' son.

It was a real torment to him to see all those happy people filling the sombre atmosphere of the Cathedral, even more sombre on that dark December day, with the barely contained buzz of domestic joy and fatherly celebration; Guedes was resplendent in jacket and white tie; the earnest godfather was wearing a large camellia in his buttonhole; the ladies were all in their Sunday best; and the plump midwife strutted about carrying a bundle of starched lace and blue ribbons amongst which one could just make out two rosy cheeks. Standing at the back of the church, his thoughts far off in Ricoça and Barrosa, Amaro rapidly mumbled his way through the ceremony, breathing on the brow, mouth and breast of the little baby in order to drive out the Devil that already inhabited that tender flesh, placing salt on his mouth so that he would for ever after hate the bitter taste of sin and find nourishment only in the divine truth, putting saliva on his ears and nose so that he would never listen to the solicitations of the flesh and never breathe in earthly perfumes. And around them, bearing tall candles, the godparents and the guests, bored with that jumble of Latin words, were only concerned lest the baby respond with some impudent outburst to the tremendous exhortations of the Mother Church.

Then, lightly touching the white bonnet, Amaro demanded that the baby, there in the Cathedral, should renounce for ever Satan and all his pomp and all his works. The sacristan Matias, who gave the ritual responses in Latin, made the renunciation on the baby's behalf, while the poor little creature opened his mouth in search of his mother's breast. Finally, Amaro went over to the baptismal font followed by all the family, by the devout old ladies who had joined them, and by the boys who were hoping that a few coins might be distributed afterwards. But it was a terrible business trying to do the anointing: the midwife was too overcome to undo the ribbons on the baby's christening robe in order to uncover the child's shoulders and chest; the godmother tried to help, but dropped her candle and poured molten wax over the dress of one of Guedes' neighbours, who fell into an angry sulk.

'*Franciscus, credis*?' asked Amaro.

Matias hurriedly confirmed on behalf of Francisco:

'*Credo*.'

'*Franciscus, vis baptisari*?'

And Matias:

'*Volo*.'

Then the baptismal water fell on the little head, as round as a tender melon; the child was now angrily kicking its legs.

'*Ego te baptiso, Franciscus, in nomine Patris . . . et Filiis . . . et Spiritus Sancti . . .*'

At last, it was over. Amaro ran to the sacristy to divest himself, while, to the pealing of bells, the grave midwife, Guedes, the proud father, the tearful ladies, the devout old ladies and the boys all left the Cathedral and, huddled beneath umbrellas, splashing through the mud, triumphantly bore away with them Francisco, the new Christian.

Amaro raced up the stairs of his house feeling sure that he would find Dionísia there.

Indeed she was, sitting in his room waiting for him, crumpled and begrimed after the previous night's battle and from the mud on the road; and as soon as she saw him, she burst into tears.

'What is it, Dionísia?'

She sobbed loudly, unable to reply.

'Dead?' exclaimed Amaro.

'We did everything we could, Father, everything!' she cried.

Amaro collapsed beside the bed, as if he too had died.

Dionísia called for the maid. They splashed his face with water and vinegar. He recovered slightly, but looked very pale; he silently indicated to them with one hand that they should leave, then threw himself face down on the pillow, weeping desperately, while the two bewildered women withdrew to the kitchen.

'He was obviously very fond of the girl,' said Escolástica, speaking as softly as if someone in the house were dying.

'He often goes to the house. And he was a lodger there for a while . . . They were like brother and sister,' said Dionísia, still tearful.

They then discussed heart conditions, because Dionísia had told Escolástica that the poor girl had died of a burst aneurism. Escolástica had a heart problem too, but in her case it was more fainting fits from the beatings her husband gave her. She too had her misfortunes.

'Would you like a cup of coffee, Senhora Dionísia?'

'To be honest, Senhora Escolástica, what I really need is a drop of brandy.'

Escolástica ran to the inn at the end of the road and brought back the brandy in a pint pot which she concealed beneath her apron; and as they sat at the table, one dipping bread in her coffee, the other gulping down her brandy, they both agreed with a sigh that this world has nothing to offer but calamities and tears.

The clock struck eleven, and Escolástica was thinking of taking a bowl of broth to Father Amaro, when he called for her from his room. He was wearing a tall hat, had his jacket buttoned, and his eyes were red as coals.

'Escolástica, go to the Cruz inn and get them to send me a horse, will you? Quickly!'

Then he summoned Dionísia and, sitting beside her, so that they were almost knee to knee, his face stiff and pale as marble, he listened in silence to her description of the night's events – the sudden convulsions, so strong that she, Gertrudes and the doctor could barely hold Amélia down! The blood, the state of prostration into which she fell! Then the terrible asphyxia that had made her turn as purple as the tunic on a holy image . . .

But the boy from the inn had arrived with the horse. Amaro took a small crucifix out of a drawer, from amongst his linen, and gave it to Dionísia, who was about to go back to Ricoça to assist in the laying out.

'Ask them to place this crucifix on her chest; it was a gift from her to me.'

Then he went downstairs and mounted up, and as soon as he reached the Barrosa road, he set off at a gallop. The rain had stopped now, and from amongst the dark clouds the odd ray of weak December sun glinted on the grass and on the wet stones.

When he reached the blocked well, from where he could see Carlota's house, he had to wait to let a large flock of sheep pass by; and the shepherd, with a goatskin about his shoulders and a wineskin about his neck, suddenly reminded him of Feirão and of his life there, which returned to him in fragments – the landscapes drowned in grey mountain mists; Joana giggling as she pulled the bell rope; the roast kid suppers with the parish priest in Gralheira, sitting by the fireside, where the green wood crackled and spat; the long despairing days spent in his gloomy priest's house, watching the snow falling endlessly outside . . . And he suddenly felt an intense longing for that mountain solitude, for that wolf-like existence, far from men and from cities, buried up there along with his passion.

Carlota's door was closed. He knocked, walked round the house, calling out to the pens and the courtyard where he could hear the cockerels crowing. No one answered. He followed the road into the village, leading his mare by the halter; he stopped at the inn, where a fat woman was seated by the door, knitting. Inside, in the darkness of the inn, two men, their pint pots by their side, were slamming down their cards on the table, watched morosely by a young woman, her skin yellow with fever, and a scarf tied round her head.

The woman had just that minute seen Senhora Carlota,

who had even stopped to buy a pint of oil. She must be at Micaela's house, near the cemetery. She called inside; a squint-eyed little girl appeared from amongst the shadows of the barrels.

'Go to Micaela's house and tell Senhora Carlota that a gentleman from town is here.'

Amaro returned to Carlota's house and waited, sitting on a stone, still holding the horse's reins. But that closed and silent house terrified him. He put his ear to the keyhole, hoping to hear a baby's complaining cry. Inside reigned the silence of an empty cave. But he was consoled by the thought that Carlota must have taken the baby with her to Micaela's. He really should have asked the woman at the inn if Carlota had had a baby with her. And he looked at the brightly whitewashed house, at the window above with its cotton curtains, a luxury unknown in these poor parishes; he remembered how tidy it was inside, remembered the gleaming china in the kitchen . . . The baby's cradle would doubtless be equally spotless.

Ah, he must have been mad the previous evening, when he had placed on the kitchen table four gold *libras*, payment in advance for a year's care, and when he had said coldly to the dwarf: 'I'm relying on you!' Poor babe! But last night in Ricoça, Carlota had seen that he wanted his son to live and to be raised tenderly! No, he would not leave him there now, beneath the dwarf's bloodshot gaze. He would take him that night to Joana Carreira in Poiais . . .

Dionísia's sinister stories about the 'weaver of angels' were surely just ridiculous tales. The child was probably sitting contentedly in Micaela's house, suckling at Carlota's healthy breast. And then he even had the idea of leaving Leiria and going and burying himself in Feirão, taking Escolástica with him and bringing up the child there as his nephew, and through him reliving at leisure all the emotions he had experienced during the extraordinary events of the past two years; and there he would live in melancholy peace, thinking of Amélia, until, like his predecessor, Father Gustavo, who had also brought up a nephew in Feirão, he was laid to rest for ever in the little cemetery, beneath the flowers in summer and beneath the white snow in winter.

Then Carlota appeared; astonished to see Amaro there, she stood with furrowed brow, a look of great seriousness on her handsome face, and did not at first come through the gate.

'Where's the child?' cried Amaro.

After a moment, without a flicker of feeling, she answered.

'You know, I'm that upset, I can hardly bear to talk about it . . . It happened yesterday, just a couple of hours after I got him home. The poor little angel started going purple in the face and he died right before my eyes.'

'You're lying!' yelled Amaro. 'I want to see him.'

'Well, if you want to see him, you'd better come in.'

'But what did I tell you yesterday, woman?'

'What could I do, sir? The child died. See for yourself.'

She had quietly pushed open the door, without a trace of anger or fear. By the fire, Amaro glimpsed a cradle covered in a scarlet petticoat.

Without a word, he turned and hurriedly mounted his horse. But Carlota, suddenly talkative, said that she had just gone into the village to order a decent coffin . . . The child was obviously from a good family, and she hadn't wanted to bury him wrapped only in a cloth. But, since the gentleman was there, it seemed reasonable that he should give her some money for the extra expense. A couple of *mil réis* would do.

Amaro looked at her for a moment, filled with a violent desire to throttle her; in the end, though, he put the money in her hand. And just as he was setting off at a trot down the road, he heard someone running after him, saying: 'Pst! Pst!' Carlota wanted to return the cloak he had lent her the previous night: it had been just the job and had kept the child as warm as toast. Alas . . .

Amaro was no longer listening to her; he dug his spur hard into his horse's flank.

Back in Leiria, having left the horse at the door of the inn, he did not at first go back to his house. He went instead straight to the bishop's palace. He had only one idea now, which was to leave that wretched town, never to see the faces of those fanatical devotees again, nor that hateful Cathedral façade.

It was only as he was going up the broad stone steps of the bishop's palace that he remembered with disquiet what Libaninho had said the previous evening concerning the vicar general's angry remarks about certain dark insinuations. However, his mind was set at rest by the friendly greeting he received from Father Saldanha, the palace confidant, who immediately showed him into the library. The vicar general was kindness itself. He was alarmed by Amaro's pale, troubled face.

'I've had some bad news, Vicar General. My sister in Lisbon is dying, and I've come to ask your permission to go and spend a few days there.'

The vicar general was all compassionate consternation.

'Why, of course. We are all of us unwilling passengers on Charon's bark.

Ipse ratem conto subigit, velisque ministrat
Et ferruginea subvectat corpora cymba.

No one escapes him. But I am truly sorry. I will not forget to commend her in my prayers . . .'

And very methodically, he made a pencilled note.

When Amaro left the palace, he went straight to the Cathedral. He shut himself in the sacristy, which was deserted at that hour, and after thinking for a long time, head in hands, he wrote to Canon Dias:

Dear Master,

My hand trembles to write these lines. The unfortunate girl is dead. As you will understand, I have to go away, because, if I stayed, my heart would break. Your excellent sister will doubtless take care of the funeral arrangements. I, of course, cannot do so myself. Thank you for everything. Perhaps we will meet again, if God so wishes. As for me, I intend to go far away, to some poor parish of shepherds, to end my days in tears, meditation and penitence. Console her mother's grief as best you can. I will never forget the debt I owe you as long as there is breath in my body. Farewell, now. I am almost at my wits' end.

Your devoted friend,

Amaro Vieira.

PS The child is also dead and has been buried.

He closed the letter with a black seal, and having sorted out his papers, he went over and opened the great iron-studded door in order to look out for a moment at the courtyard, the shed and the sexton's house. The mist and the first rains lent that corner of the Cathedral buildings a lugubrious, wintry air. He walked slowly forward beneath the grim silence of the high buttresses and peered through the window into the kitchen: the sexton was there, sitting by the fire, pipe in mouth, occasionally spitting sadly into the ashes. Amaro tapped lightly on the glass, and when the sexton opened the door, that familiar interior, which he took in at a glance – the curtain concealing what had been Totó's bedroom, the stairs up to the sexton's room – filled Amaro with so many troubling memories and with such sudden longing that, for a moment, he could not speak, choked with tears.

'I've come to say goodbye, Esguelhas,' he murmured at last. 'I'm going to Lisbon. My sister's dying.'

And he added, his lips trembling with repressed sobs.

'Misfortunes never come singly. You may not know, but Miss Amélia died suddenly last night.'

The sexton stood in stunned silence.

'Goodbye, Esguelhas. Give me your hand. Goodbye.'

'Goodbye, Father, goodbye,' said the old man, his eyes full of tears.

Amaro fled home along the streets, doing his best not to burst into loud sobbing. He told Escolástica that he was leaving for Lisbon that night. She should have a horse sent over from the Cruz inn so that he could go to Chão de Maçãs to catch the train.

'I only have enough money for the journey, but you can keep all the sheets and towels.'

Weeping at the thought of losing him, Escolástica tried to kiss his hand in gratitude for such generosity and offered to pack his bags for him.

'No, I'll do it, Escolástica, don't you bother.'

He shut himself in his room. Still weeping, Escolástica went immediately to examine the small amount of linen in the cupboards, but, only a moment later, Amaro called to her. Outside in the street, two men, on harp and violin, were tunelessly playing 'The Waltz of Two Worlds'.

'Give the men some money,' said Amaro angrily, 'and tell them to go to Hell. There are people in here who are ill!'

Escolástica did not hear another sound from his room then until five o'clock.

When the lad from the inn arrived with the horse, she assumed Amaro must have fallen asleep and, still weeping over his imminent departure, she knocked lightly on his door. He opened it at once. He had a cloak over his shoulders, and in the middle of the room, packed and buckled, was the canvas bag that was to be stowed behind the saddle. He gave her a bundle of letters to be delivered that night to Dona Maria da Assunção, Father Silvério and Father Natário, and he was just about to leave, accompanied by Escolástica's sobbing, when he heard a familiar sound on the stairs, and the sexton appeared, looking terribly upset:

'Come in, Esguelhas, come in.'

The sexton closed the door and after a moment's hesitation, said:

'You must forgive me, Father, but I've been so forgetful lately, what with all my troubles . . . I found this in the room some time ago and I thought . . .'

He placed a gold earring in Amaro's hand. Amaro recognised it at once. It was Amélia's. She had spent ages vainly searching for it; it had doubtless come off during one of those mornings of love on the sexton's mattress. Overcome, Amaro embraced Esguelhas.

'Goodbye! Goodbye, Escolástica! Remember me. And give my regards to Matías, Esguelhas.'

The boy buckled the bag onto the saddle and Amaro set

off, leaving Escolástica and Esguelhas both weeping at the door.

But once he was past the weir, at the corner of the street, he had to stop to adjust his stirrups, and just as he was about to remount, around the corner came Dr Godinho, the secretary-general and the administrator of the municipal council, who were all firm friends now and were returning to town after a walk. They stopped to speak to Amaro, surprised to see him there, with his bag on the saddle, as if set for a journey.

'Yes,' he said, 'I'm off to Lisbon!'

The erstwhile Bibi and the administrator both sighed, envying him his luck. But when Amaro mentioned his dying sister, they were politely distressed on his behalf, and the administrator said:

'How very upsetting for you . . . And then there's that other misfortune at your friend's house. Poor little Amélia, dying so suddenly . . .'

Bibi exclaimed:

'What? Amélia, that pretty girl who lived in Rua da Misericórdia? Dead?'

Dr Godinho had not heard the news either and appeared shocked.

The administrator had learned about it from his maid, who had heard it from Dionísia. Apparently, she had died of an aneurism.

'Well, forgive me, Father, if I offend your honoured beliefs, which, naturally, I share, but God has committed a real crime . . . carrying off the prettiest girl in the town! What eyes, gentlemen! Eyes made all the more piquant, of course, by her evident virtue!'

Then, in mournful tones, each added his regrets at what must have been a devastating blow to Amaro.

He said very quietly:

'Yes, it has upset me greatly. I knew her well, and with her excellent qualities, she would, I feel sure, have made a model wife. Yes, indeed, it has upset me greatly.'

He silently clasped everyone's hands, and while the gentlemen returned to the town, Amaro continued along the road in the growing darkness to the station at Chão de Maçãs.

The next day, at eleven o'clock, Amélia's funeral procession left Ricoça. It was a raw morning: the sky and the fields were drowned in a greyish mist, and a very fine, icy rain was falling. It was a long way from the house to the chapel in Poiais. The choirboy bearing the cross strode on ahead, splashing through the mud; Father Ferrão, wearing a black stole, murmured the *Exultabant Domino* as he huddled beneath the umbrella held by the sacristan who was walking beside him, bearing the aspergillum; four of the farmworkers, heads lowered against the slanting rain, were carrying the box containing the lead coffin on a kind of stretcher; and beneath the tenant farmer's vast umbrella, Gertrudes, a veil over her head, was telling her beads. Dropping away from the road on either side lay the sad valley of Poiais, all grey in the mist and immersed in a great silence; and the vicar general's booming voice braying out the *Miserere* rolled over the damp, undulating fields through which ran swollen, gurgling streams.

But when they reached the first house in the village, the lads carrying the coffin stopped, exhausted; and a man who had been waiting beneath the trees with his umbrella silently joined the procession. It was João Eduardo in black gloves and heavy mourning, with dark circles under his eyes and great tears running down his cheeks. Two liveried servants, bearing candles, and with their trouser bottoms carefully rolled, immediately fell in behind him – two lackeys sent by the Morgado to honour one of the ladies of Ricoça, friends of Father Ferrão.

When he saw these two servants, who had come to lend nobility to the procession, the choirboy raised his cross still higher and set off again; the four young men, feeling rested now, took up the poles of the stretcher, and the sacristan roared out the *Requiem*. The funeral proceeded through the mud up the steep road to the village, while the women stood at their doors making the sign of the cross, watching as the white surplices and the coffin decorated with golden rosettes moved off, followed by the cluster of umbrellas open beneath the sad rain.

The chapel was on a hill, on a square surrounded by oak trees; the bell was tolling, and the funeral procession disappeared into the dark interior of the church to the strains of *Subvenite sancti*, which the sacristan growled out. But the two liveried servants did not go in because the Morgado had forbidden them to do so.

They stood in the doorway, beneath their umbrella, listening and stamping their frozen feet. Inside, the plainsong continued, then there was a whisper of prayers that gradually died away, followed by a burst of lugubrious Latin spoken in the vicar general's low, grave voice.

Bored, the two men left the square and wandered into Serafim's tavern. Two herdsmen from the Morgado's farm, who were sitting silently drinking their beer, got up as soon as the two liveried servants appeared.

'At ease, lads, sit down and finish your drinks,' said the shorter, older man, who normally accompanied João Eduardo on his rides. 'We're up at the chapel for that wretched funeral. Good afternoon to you, Senhor Serafim.'

They shook hands with Serafim, who poured out two measures of brandy for them and asked if the dead girl had been Senhor João's fiancée. He had been told that it was a burst artery that had done for her. The older man laughed.

'Burst artery indeed! What did for her was the baby boy she was carrying . . .'

'Senhor João's doing?' asked Serafim, opening wide, mischievous eyes.

'I don't believe so,' said the other authoritatively. 'Senhor João was in Lisbon at the time. It was some other gentleman from town. Do you know who I suspect, Senhor Serafim?'

But at that point, a breathless Gertrudes burst into the tavern announcing loudly that the cortège was nearly at the cemetery and that 'those gentlemen' were the only people missing. The two lackeys rushed off and caught up with the cortège as it was passing through the little cemetery gate and as the last verse of the *Miserere* was being sung.

João Eduardo was now carrying a candle and following so closely behind Amélia's coffin that he was almost touching it, his tear-filled eyes fixed on the black velvet cloth. The chapel bell tolled desolately on and on. The rain was falling harder. No one broke the sad, grey, cemetery silence, their footsteps muffled by the wet ground, all heading towards the corner of the wall where Amélia's grave had been freshly dug, deep and dark amongst the damp grass. The choirboy thrust the staff of the silver cross into the earth, and Father Ferrão, going over to the edge of the black hole, murmured the *Deus cujus miseratione* . . . Then João Eduardo, deathly pale, suddenly swayed on his feet, and the umbrella fell from his hands; the two liveried servants rushed forward and grasped him round the waist; they tried to lead him away, to remove him from the graveside, but he resisted and stood there, teeth clenched, clinging desperately to one of the servant's sleeves, watching the gravedigger and the two farmhands tying the ropes around the coffin and lowering it slowly down into the crumbling earth with a creak of hastily nailed together planks.

'*Requiem aeternam dona ei, Domine*!'

'*Et lux perpetua luceat ei*,' said the sacristan mournfully.

The coffin hit the bottom of the grave with a dull thud; Father Ferrão scattered a little of the earth on top in the form of a cross and, slowly shaking the aspergillum over the velvet cloth, the earth and the surrounding grass, he said:

'*Requiescat in pace*.'

'*Amen*,' came the deep voice of the sacristan and the shrill voice of the choirboy.

'*Amen*,' said the others in a sighing murmur that was lost amongst the cypresses, the grass, the graves and the cold mists of that sad December day.

XXV

Towards the end of May 1871, there was a tremendous uproar in the Casa Havanesa in the Chiado in Lisbon. People arrived, breathless, and fought their way through the crowd blocking the doorway, then stood on tiptoe and craned their necks in order to see the noticeboard hung on the grille above the counter on which were pinned the telegrams from the Havas Agency; men walked away with looks of horror and despair on their faces, exclaiming to some more placid friend who had waited for them outside:

'Lost. Gone up in flames.'

Inside, amongst the multitude of prattlers squeezed against the counter, heated discussions ensued; and on that already hot day in early summer, everywhere – the pavements outside, the Largo do Loreto opposite, the Chiado all the way up to Magalhães – was filled by a gabble of shocked voices in which the vehemently uttered words: Communists! Versailles! Terrorists! Thiers! Crime! The International! constantly came and went amidst the rumble of passing carriages and the cries of newspaper boys advertising the latest bulletins.

Indeed telegrams kept arriving which described the unfolding events in the battle being waged in the streets of Paris: terrified telegrams sent from Versailles listing the burning palaces and the streets reduced to rubble; the mass shootings in barrack squares and amongst mausoleums in cemeteries; the revenge that would seek satisfaction even in the dark depths of sewers; the fatal madness that was gripping both government troops and insurgents; and the resistance that combined the frenzy of a death agony with scientific method, shaking up the old society by means of petrol, dynamite and nitroglycerine. A convulsion, an end of the world, which twenty or thirty words suddenly lit up as if in the glow of a bonfire.

The whole Chiado spoke with angry regret of the

ruination of Paris. They named out loud the buildings that had been burned, the Hôtel de Ville, 'so lovely', the Rue Royale, 'exquisite'. Some were as enraged by the burning down of the Tuileries Palace as if it had belonged to them; those who had spent a few months in Paris expressed their outrage, taking a Parisian pride in the beauty of the city, scandalised by an insurrection that showed so little respect for buildings on which they themselves had gazed.

'Honestly,' exclaimed one obese gentleman, 'they've destroyed the Palace of the Legion of Honour! Why, I was there with my wife only a month ago! It's absolutely disgraceful! Pure vandalism!'

The rumour spread that the Ministry had received another even more depressing telegram saying that the whole boulevard from Bastille to the Madeleine was in flames, and even the Place de la Concorde and the Champs Elysées as far as the Arc de Triomphe. That insane rebellion had thus laid waste to a whole network of restaurants, cafés, dance halls, gambling dens and houses of prostitution. An angry shudder ran from Largo do Loreto to Magalhães. The flames had destroyed that cosy centre of revelry. It was outrageous! What was the world coming to? Where were all the best restaurants? Where could one find the most experienced women? Where would one ever see the like of that prodigious procession around the Bois on crisp, dry winter days, when ladies of easy virtue ensconced in splendid victorias vied with stockbrokers in their phaetons? It was an abomination. They forgot about the libraries and the museums, but felt sincere regret at the destruction of the cafés and the burning of the brothels. It was the end of Paris and the end of France!

In a group near the Casa Havanesa the talk had turned to politics; amongst the names mentioned was that of Proudhon, who, around that time in Lisbon, was beginning to be talked of as a bloodthirsty monster; insults were consequently heaped on Proudhon. Most thought him personally responsible for the fires. But the esteemed poet of *Flowers and Sighs* said that 'if one disregarded the nonsense Proudhon spouted, he was, nevertheless, a rather fine stylist'. The gambler França burst out:

'Style, my eye! If I bumped into him in the Chiado now, I'd break every bone in his body!'

And he would have too. After a couple of glasses of cognac, França was like a wild beast.

However, some young men, their romantic instincts stirred by the dramatic accounts of the catastrophe, applauded the heroism of the Commune – Vermorel, his arms outstretched like the crucified Christ, crying out as the bullets pierced him: 'Vive l'humanité!' Old Delécluse, with the fanaticism of a saint, calling on his deathbed for violent resistance.

'Such great men!' exclaimed one over-excited lad.

Serious-minded people around them roared their disapproval. Others moved away, pale-faced, imagining their Lisbon homes doused in petrol and the Casa Havanesa itself consumed by socialist flames. Then the angry watchwords in all the different groups were 'authority' and 'repression'; it was important that society, under attack by the International, should take refuge in the strength of its conservative, religious principles and surround them with bayonets! The bourgois owner of a chain of novelty shops spoke of 'the rabble' with the imposing scorn of a La Trémoille or an Osuna. Men, wielding toothpicks, urged vengeance. Professional idlers seemed incensed by 'these workers who want to live like princes!' They spoke devoutly of property and wealth.

On the other hand, there were the loquacious youths, the excitable journalists, who railed against the old world order and against old ideas, uttering loud threats, proposing to demolish them with thunderous newspaper articles.

Thus a torpid bourgeoisie hoped to halt social change with a few policemen, and youths with a veneer of literature were convinced that a single pamphlet could bring down a society that had been in existence for eighteen hundred years. But no one was more excited than a hotel bookkeeper who, from the top of the steps to the Casa Havanesa, was advising France to bring back the Bourbons.

Just then a man in black, who was leaving the Casa

Havanesa and threading his way past the various groups, stopped when he heard a startled voice beside him exclaim:

'Father Amaro, you rascal!'

He turned; it was Canon Dias. They embraced warmly and, in order to talk more quietly, they walked across to the middle of the Largo do Loreto and stood there by the statue.

'When did you arrive, Master?'

The Canon had arrived the evening before. He was in litigation with the Pimentos in Pojeira over a right of way through his land; he had lodged an appeal and had come to Lisbon to follow the case more closely.

'And what about you, Amaro? In your last letter, you said you wanted to leave Santo Tirso.'

Indeed he did. The parish had its advantages, but the post at Vila Franca had fallen vacant and, wanting to be closer to Lisbon, he had come to talk to 'his' Count, the Conde de Ribamar, who was sorting out the transfer now. He owed him, and more especially the Countess, everything.

'How are things in Leiria? Is São Joaneira any better?'

'No, poor thing. She gave us all a terrible fright at first . . . we thought she was going to go the same way as Amélia, but it turned out to be dropsy . . . oedema . . .'

'Poor dear lady. And how's Natário?'

'Oh, he's aged a lot. And he's had a few misfortunes too. But then he's his own worst enemy.'

'And what's happened to Libaninho?'

'I wrote to you about him, didn't I?' said the Canon, laughing.

Father Amaro laughed too, and, for a moment, the two priests said nothing, both holding their sides in mirth.

'Oh, dear,' said the Canon. 'It caused a huge scandal. Because they caught him with a sergeant in circumstances that left no possible room for doubt. At ten o'clock at night in the park too! Most imprudent. But it all died down eventually, and when Matías died, we gave Libaninho the job of sacristan, which is a really good post, much better than his office job . . . And he'll carry out his duties zealously I'm sure!'

'Oh, he will,' agreed Father Amaro gravely. 'And what about Dona Maria da Assunção?'

'Well, a few rumours have been flying around about her new servant, a carpenter who used to live opposite . . . He's unusually well turned out apparently . . .'

'Really?'

'Oh, yes. Cigar, watch, gloves . . . Funny, don't you think?'

'Hilarious!'

'The Gansoso sisters are just as they always were,' the Canon went on. 'Your maid Escolástica works for them now.'

'And what about that fool João Eduardo?'

'I thought I told you. He's still in Poiais. The Morgado is suffering from some kind of liver disease. And they say João Eduardo's consumptive. I don't know for sure because I haven't seen him. It was Ferrão who told me.'

'And how's Ferrão?'

'Fine. And do you know who I saw a few days ago? Dionísia.'

'And what's she up to?'

The Canon whispered something in Father Amaro's ear.

'Really?'

'In Rua das Sousas, a few doors down from your old house. Dom Luís da Barrosa gave her the money to set up the establishment. Anyway, that's the latest news. But you're looking very well, man! The move did you good.'

Guffawing, he planted himself in front of Amaro and said:

'And to think you wrote to me saying that you wanted to retreat to the mountains or to a monastery and live the life of a penitent.'

Father Amaro shrugged.

'Well, what do you expect, Master? Those first few hours were really hard for me . . . But everything passes.'

'Oh, yes, everything passes,' said the Canon, adding after a pause: 'Ah, but Leiria isn't what it was.'

They walked for a moment in silence, immersed in memories of the past, of the fun they used to have playing lotto at São Joaneira's, the chats over tea, the walks to Morenal, Artur Couceiro singing, accompanied on the piano by poor Amélia, who was sleeping now in the cemetery in Poiais, beneath the wild flowers . . .

'And what do you think about these goings-on in France, Amaro?' exclaimed the Canon suddenly.

'Oh, dreadful. The archbishop and any number of priests were shot. It's no laughing matter!'

'No, indeed!' growled the Canon.

And Father Amaro said:

'And it looks like the same ideas are beginning to take hold here as well.'

The Canon had heard as much. Then they both spoke angrily about the rabble made up of freemasons, republicans and socialists, people who wanted to destroy everything that was decent – the clergy, religious education, the family, the army and even wealth . . . Society was under threat from these unchained monsters! They should bring back the old repressive methods, the dungeon and the gallows. And above all, people should be taught to have faith and to respect the priesthood . . .

'That's the problem,' said Amaro, 'they don't respect us! They do nothing but insult us. They are destroying the common people's veneration for the priesthood.'

'Yes, they say the most terrible things about us . . .' said the Canon in cavernous tones.

At that moment, two women passed by, one, whitehaired, had a very noble bearing; the other was a skinny, pale, listless creature with dark circles under her eyes; she kept her bony elbows close in to her sterile waist and was wearing an enormous bustle, a large chignon of false hair and very high heels.

'I say!' said the Canon quietly, nudging his colleague. 'What to do you think of that, Father Amaro? That's the kind of woman you want to confess.'

'Not any more, Master,' said Amaro, laughing. 'Now I only confess married ladies.'

For a moment, the Canon shook with laughter, but resumed the plump, ponderous air of a priest as soon he saw Amaro respectfully doffing his hat to a gentleman with a greying moustache and gold-rimmed spectacles who was crossing the square from the Loreto side, a cigar clamped between his teeth and a parasol under his arm.

It was the Conde de Ribamar. He walked amiably over to the two priests, and Amaro, standing to attention, his hat still off, introduced 'my friend, Canon Dias, from Leiria Cathedral'. They talked for a while about the unseasonably warm weather. Then Father Amaro mentioned the latest news.

'What do you think of events in France, Excellency?'

The Count held up his hands in a gesture of desolation, a feeling reflected in his face.

'Don't even talk to me about it, Father, don't even talk to me about it. To see half a dozen thugs destroying Paris. *My* Paris! Do you know, gentlemen, it has made me quite ill.'

The two priests both looked suitably concerned and added their feelings of sorrow to the Count's.

Then the Canon said:

'And how do you think it will all end?'

The Conde de Ribamar spoke very deliberately and his words emerged slowly as if burdened by the sheer weight of ideas:

'The result? Oh, it's not hard to predict. When one has had some experience of history and politics, one can see how it will all turn out as clearly as I can see you two gentlemen now.'

The priests hung on the statesman's prophetic words.

'Once the insurrection has been crushed,' continued the Count, looking straight ahead of him, one finger raised, as if following and pointing out historic futures discernible only to his eyes, with the aid of his gold-rimmed spectacles. 'Within three months of the insurrection being crushed, we will have the empire back. If, as I have, you had been to a reception at the Tuileries or at the Hôtel de Ville in the days of empire, you, like me, would say that France is a profoundly and purely imperialist nation . . . That means we will be left with Napoleon III, unless he abdicates and the Empress takes on the regency until the imperial prince is old enough. I would advise this as the most prudent solution and I have already said as much. One immediate consequence will be that the Pope in Rome will once more be the lord of temporal power. To tell the truth, and, again, I have already said as much, I do not approve of a papal restoration. But I am not going to tell you what I approve or disapprove of. Fortunately, I am not lord of all Europe. That would be a burden too great for a man of my age and my infirmities. I am merely saying what my experience of politics and history tells me to be true . . . Now what was I talking about? Ah, yes, with the Empress on the throne of France, Pius IX on the throne of Rome, democracy will be crushed between those two sublime forces, and you can believe me, as a man who knows his Europe and the elements that make up modern society, when I say that after the example of the Commune, we will hear no more talk of a republic, the social question or the people for a good one hundred years.'

'May God hear your words, Excellency,' said the Canon unctuously.

Amaro, enchanted to find himself in a Lisbon square in intimate conversation with an illustrious statesman, then asked with all the anxiety of a startled conservative:

'Do you think these ideas about a republic and about materialism will spread here?'

The Count laughed and, strolling along between the two priests, almost as far as the railings surrounding the statue of the great poet Luís de Camões, he said:

'Don't you worry your heads about that, gentlemen. There may be one or two radicals who complain and spout all kinds of nonsense about the decadence of Portugal, who say that we're stagnating and becoming brutish and stupid, and that they give the current regime ten more years at most, etc. etc. Utter rubbish!'

He was almost leaning against the railings now and, adopting a confiding tone, he said:

'The truth, gentlemen, is that foreigners envy us . . . And I'm not saying what I'm about to say merely to flatter, but, as long as we have priests like you worthy of respect, Portugal will maintain, with dignity, its place in Europe. Because faith, gentlemen, is the very basis of order.'

'Absolutely, Count, absolutely,' agreed the two priests warmly.

'Well, just look around you! What peace, what vigour, what prosperity!'

And he made a sweeping gesture that took in the whole of the Largo do Loreto, which, at that hour, at the close of a serene afternoon, contained the essence of city life. Empty carriages rode slowly by; women in twos tottered past, wearing false hair and high heels and displaying the anaemic pallor of a degenerate race; trotting by on a scrawny nag came a young man, the bearer of a famous name, still green about the gills from the previous night's drinking spree; on the benches in the square people lay sprawled in a state of idle torpor; an ox cart lurching along on its high wheels was like the symbol of an antiquated agricultural system dating back centuries; pimps swayed past, a cigarette clenched between their teeth; the odd bored bourgeois gentleman stood perusing advertisements for outmoded operettas; the haggard faces of workers seemed the very personification of moribund industries . . . And beneath the warm, splendid sky, this whole decrepit world moved sluggishly along past urchins selling tickets for the lottery or for a raffle and boys with plangent voices offering the latest issue of some almanac; they meandered indolently back and forth between two gloomy church façades and the long ranks of houses round the square where three pawnshop signs glinted in the sun and the entrances to four taverns beckoned blackly, and flowing out into the square were alleyways, squalid and dirty as open sewers, issuing from a neighbourhood steeped in prostitution and crime.

'Just look around you,' said the Count. 'Just look at all this peace, prosperity and contentment. It's hardly surprising that we're the envy of Europe!'

And the man of state and the two men of religion stood in a row by the monument railings, heads held high, savouring the glorious certainty of their country's greatness, there, beside that statue, beneath the cold, bronze gaze of the old poet, erect and noble, with the broad shoulders of a mighty paladin, his epic poem in his heart, his sword grasped firmly in his hand, and surrounded by the chroniclers and heroic poets of the old country – a country for ever past, a memory almost forgotten!

October 1878-October 1879

Dedalus European Classics

Dedalus European Classics began in 1984 with D.H. Lawrence's translation of Verga's *Mastro Don Gesualdo*. In addition to rescuing major works of literature from being out of print, the editors' other major aim was to redefine what constituted a "classic".

Titles available include:

Little Angel – Andreyev £4.95
The Red Laugh – Andreyev £4.95
Seraphita (and other tales) – Balzac £6.99
The Quest of the Absolute – Balzac £6.99
The Episodes of Vathek – Beckford £6.99
The Devil in Love – Cazotte £5.99
La Madre (The Woman and the Priest) – Deledda £5.99
Undine – Fouqué £6.99
Misericordia – Galdos £8.99
Spirite – Gautier £6.99
The Dark Domain – Grabinski £6.99
The Life of Courage – Grimmelshausen £6.99
Simplicissimus – Grimmelshausen £10.99
En Route – Huysmans £7.99
The Cathedral – Huysmans £7.99
The Oblate – Huysmans £7.99
The Other Side – Kubin £9.99
The Mystery of the Yellow Room – Leroux £7.99
The Perfume of the Lady in Black – Leroux £8.99
The Woman and the Puppet – Loüys £6.99
Blanquerna – Lull £7.95
The Angel of the West Window – Meyrink £9.99
The Golem – Meyrink £6.99
The Opal (and other stories) – Meyrink £7.99
The White Dominican – Meyrink £6.99

Walpurgisnacht – Meyrink £6.99
Ideal Commonwealths – More/Bacon et al £7.95
Smarra & Trilby – Nodier £6.99
The Late Mattia Pascal – Pirandello £6.99
The Notebooks of Serafino Gubbio – Pirandello £7.99
Tales from the Saragossa Manuscript – Potocki £5.99
Manon Lescaut – Prévost £7.99
The Crime of Father Amaro – Queiroz £11.99
The Mandarin – Queiroz £6.99
The Relic – Queiroz £8.99
The Tragedy of the Street of Flowers – Queiroz £9.99
Baron Munchausen – Raspe £6.99
The Wandering Jew – Sue £10.99
I Malavoglia (The House by the Medlar Tree) – Verga £7.99
Mastro Don Gesualdo – Verga £7.99
Short Sicilian Novels – Verga £6.99
Micromegas – Voltaire £4.95